What others are saying about *I Know Why the Angels Dance*

This book should be on every physician's desk. It would help them gain a better understanding of emotional suffering and how they can go beyond merely performing the physical aspects of their job.

—**Scott VanLue, MD**

You have struck the delicate balance between the assault on our physical senses when a beloved child dies and the promise we believe through our faith in Jesus Christ. Not only is it written with the grace of a poet, it poignantly strikes the chord that brings the heart to tears even while the spirit within us sings.

—**Rosemary Upton,** author of
The Court and the Kingdom and Glimpses of Grace

This novel is a masterful tale of sorrow and hope, sure to leave readers searching for love and healing that can only be fulfilled in Jesus. It is interwoven with genuine portrayals of Christians and non-Christians, their respective questions in life, and their bond as human beings living in a world paradoxically full of suffering and beauty. After reading this stirring book my heart knows why the angels dance, and I yearn to make them dance again and again.

—**Nicole Cragin**

I Know Why the Angels Dance is WONDERFUL—what a beautiful story. It is truly one of the best books I have ever read—it may even be the best. It's amazing how you told the story of salvation through the eyes of a child. Tabitha was responsible for leading so many to Christ. I can't wait to read it again and encourage others to read it.

—**Fran Harris**

Incredible! I was immediately drawn into this book from the first page. The characters were so real that they became friends whom I fussed at or cheered. Tears freely flowed as I read the final pages! It encouraged and challenged me to remember that each believer's life has a profound effect on the people around us. That God calls us to obedience even when we don't understand what He is asking us to do, and in that obedience we can draw others to His throne of grace.

—**Ruth Vath**

I Know Why the Angels Dance is a p   evotion,
faith, and learning to understand eare it was
over. Spiritually the strongest book   that not
only tugs at the heart strings but y   ntion to
the message of faith. This is a tale   ıntil the
words become too blurry to read. I absolutely loved it, and it will find a special place on your bookshelf and in your heart.

—**C.J. Giacomini**

A heart-warming story about God's grace and provision in one of the most difficult times a parent can face—the death of a child. The tremendous impact of a single, though brief, life lived for Christ by one with His care and compassion for others, is presented in an inspiring drama that emotes joy and hope in the reader in the midst of the turmoil, pain, and grief of sickness and death. As a central character surrenders his notions of how a Christian parent should grieve, the Lord ministers in a special way, making real the truth that Christians need not grieve as do those who have no hope in Christ and turning mourning into joy.

—JM Hawks

I Know Why the Angels Dance was one of the most thought-provoking books I have ever read. Mr. Davis' emergence into the adult literature scene is certainly to take every reader on a thrilling search as they explore the significance and reality of what a loss of an unsaved friend or family member truly means in comparison with the glorious reunion of a falling asleep of a saved loved one. The simple elegance of telling most of the story through the eyes of the child and bringing it down to the simplicity of comprehension reveals a jewel of a talent in Mr. Davis. This page turner had me guessing every moment. As I read through blurry eyes, the message of what it truly means to have a non-Christian die was driven home by the desolate and horrific images surrounding the death of an unsaved person. This was in contrast to the joyful reunion of loved ones that had been saved and the celestial glory of finally coming home. I would definitely recommend this read to anyone who is looking to deepen their Christian walk.

—Katrina Ford

The story contained within these pages will not fail to move you. As Bryan Davis brings this touching narrative to a close, you will be hard put to keep your eyes from brimming with tears of sadness and joy. Curl up with this powerful book and discover why the angels dance … and come away with a desire to make them dance again.

—Jordan Smith, Incredibooks.com

This is without a doubt the best book I have read in many years. Many of the characters are relatable, and the ones who are not are revealed to us through understanding and grace. It tugs at your heart while also satisfying the intellectual side, through sure facts and biblical truths. I believe this book will easily become a classic, so I have already recommended this book to everyone I know and a few that I don't. This is now my favourite book.

—Jessica Hill

I Know Why the Angel's Dance is a novel unlike any I have ever read. Memorable characters fill every page and glorify our God with every selfless act. I cried with them during their hardships and celebrated alongside their triumphs. Altogether an amazing book that truly touched me with its spiritual truths. Mr. Davis' best yet.

—Ariel Hicks

I Know Why the Angel's Dance is filled with tales of faith, sorrow, heartache, and love. Through the life and example of one precious little girl, these emotions overflow out of the pages and into the hearts of its reader, showing them the truth of God's love. Tabitha's harvest will bear fruit, even beyond the limits of this story. While reading this book, you will truly weep with those who weep, and you will rejoice with those who rejoice.

—Connie Wolters

Bryan Davis, probably best known for his young adult fantasy novels, once again proves himself a master storyteller in I Know Why the Angels Dance. It is a tale of sorrow and joy, of death and eternal life, at once applying a healing balm and encouraging catharsis. Readers will laugh and weep with the characters in this breathtaking novel that will thaw even the coldest of hearts.

—Luke Gledhill

Bryan's new book takes the reader on a roller coaster of tears, joy, and rejoicing in God's faithfulness. I found myself crying with the characters late into the night when I should have been sleeping. Out of this book has come deeper faith in God, and I pray that this book will touch others as much as it has touched me.

—Jennifer Pettigrew

Mr. Davis always surprises me with the simple profoundness of the messages in his books. I Know Why the Angels Dance is certainly no exception. It gives an incredible look at the hope in the Christian faith through the eyes and heart of a very special little girl. Clear an afternoon, because you might not be able set this book aside once you start reading.

—Victor Vath

"Now they were all weeping and lamenting for her;..." Luke: 8:52 (NASB). From the very beginning, these words captured my attention. Should Christians grieve when another Christian dies? This book left me wondering until the very end and I now Know Why the Angels Dance.

—Cathy Hicks

Truly remarkable. Never before have I been so convicted, overjoyed, and emotionally moved while reading a book. Through the point of view of a preteen brimming with love for God, Mr. Davis reveals the trials that come with hardship. This book raises the deep topics of how to express grief and joy in times of loss and how to share the Good News with others despite one's greatest fears. I Know Why the Angels Dance not only displays the sorrow that comes with loss but also shows the profound joy and abiding love that stretches far beyond this mortal world.

—Jessica Sly

The emotional story of a heartbreaking loss takes the reader on a journey of love, hope, and healing. The characters are well-written and suit the style of the story ... very enjoyable and sure to be read again and again.

—Curt Harrison

I love this book! It will reach out to you emotionally as well as spiritually. It will make you strive to walk closer with the Lord.

—Selena Sunderland

A girl teaches, her friend learns and finds the ultimate redemption. This novel sends you on a roller coaster ride of emotions. It is bittersweet, and full of beauty. A must read!

—Nick Battaglia

I Know Why the Angel's Dance is a remarkable story of faith, hope, and love. Covering many topics about life and death, Bryan Davis answers such questions as: How should a Christian react to a brother's death? The death of one lost? How do we comfort those in need? This book is a beautiful tale of the extraordinary faith of a child, faith in a God that is able to do anything.

—Nathan Petrie

A painful, heart-wrenching journey that is well worth every minute spent and every tear shed. This book is a story of childhood friendship, family love, tragedy, grief, and triumph. I felt emotionally exhausted at the end; exhausted yet encouraged, inspired, and oddly enough, content. Settle in for the evening because you will NOT put this book down!

—Michael Ann Rentz, Thetford, England

I know why the

ANGELS
DANCE

Bryan Davis

I know why the ANGELS DANCE

Bryan Davis

Living Ink Books
An Imprint of AMG Publishers, Inc.
Chattanooga, Tennessee

Chapter 1

Now they were all weeping and lamenting for her; but He said, "Stop weeping, for she has not died, but is asleep." Taking the child by the hand, He said to her, "Talitha kum!" (which translated means, "Little girl, I say to you, get up!").

—*Luke 8:52; Mark 5:41* NASB

Tears are salt. When shaken out with miserly fingers, life is sweet. All is candy. Sweetness and smiles decorate life, though shallow rivers impersonate still waters. When salt is spared, meat is bland, and little is consumed. Candy makes few men strong.

Tears are seeds. They die in fallow ground, already watered, mixed with fertile earth. Only pain brings strength. Only death begets life. Only grief fosters the hardiest growth.

Tears are signs. Wet drops of torment tell a story, one that need not be uttered. A father's joy, a mother's love, lost in a moment. Who knows such pain but one who has suffered its oppression? When one grieving soul finds another, it does not find consolation; there is no joy found in the pain of another soul. Yet both discover an aching heart that finds comfort in reading the signs.

Sprinkle salt with liberal hands. Sow seeds with vigor. Look to heaven and read the signs. A father, a son, death swallowed up in victory. We will find solace when we learn to see beyond the veil.

Chapter 1

TABITHA LAID her hands on the coffin and peered inside. Her arms trembled. Waiting until everyone else viewed the deceased had done nothing to soothe her troubled nerves. She had never seen a dead body before. Sure, she had watched actors playing dead in movies and viewed photos of corpses in books. But this was different. The face in front of her was a three-dimensional fact. She could touch the dead woman's cheek if she were so bold, but she didn't dare. It was too . . . too unreal.

Yes. That was it—unreal. The rag doll nestled between the woman's folded hands seemed out of place, a symbol of youth in the grasp of wrinkled fingers. And the head propped on the satin pillow looked more like a mannequin than Tabitha's great-grandmother. The face seemed stretched, smoothing out most of the deep creases Nanna had earned during her ninety-plus years of life. And besides, everyone knew Nanna wouldn't think of wearing the rouge and lipstick the mortician had painted on her face. She preferred "the way God decorates me—with spiritual war paint, not cosmetic fluff."

As she gazed at the dead woman's eyelids, forever closed to this world, Tabitha sighed. The family's aged prophetess now lay silent, and not everyone would weep at the loss of her counsel, advice that was always straightforward, sometimes uninvited, but never dispensed without love.

In so many ways, Nanna was like her grandson, who drank in her every word and restated them all in the same plain-spoken manner, the man Tabitha knew as—

A familiar hand clasped her shoulder, interrupting her thoughts.

"Daddy?" she said, swiveling to see him. "Was I standing here too long?"

"Not at all." Tabitha's father reached into the casket and slipped the doll from Nanna's fingers. "Nanna's original instructions said to bury her doll with her, but her attorney found a handwritten note that was dated later." The love-worn doll lay across his palm. "Deborah is yours now."

Tabitha tried to hide a grimace. Although she always slept with that doll whenever she visited Nanna's house, now it had been wrenched away from the clutches of a dead body.

Her father pulled the doll back. "Too morbid?"

Tabitha nodded.

"If we wash it?" he asked, leaning closer.

His warm, cinnamon breath tickled her nose. She nodded again, this time adding a smile. His bent posture and firm chin warned of another one of his practiced speeches, but she didn't mind. As an author and former pastor, writing eloquent prose had become a habit. Although the speeches sometimes sounded too rehearsed, he always meant well.

"A dead body isn't to be feared, Tabitha. Nanna's inner being simply outgrew the decaying package that held captive her ever-strengthening, immortal soul. At last the old cocoon was left behind, and

Nanna has flown to her new life above, finally to worship her Lord face-to-face. This body is merely a cast-off shell."

"Is that from your funeral speech?" Tabitha asked.

He straightened his tie and cleared his throat. "Too obvious?"

"Uh-huh." She reached for the doll. "You're right, though. I'll take Deborah now."

After handing it to her, he gave her shoulder another comforting clasp before marching toward another room. The breeze from his departure swept his familiar scent away, and his clicking footsteps joined the low hum of mingling friends and relatives.

Tabitha gripped the doll loosely in her fingers. How should she hold it? What would people think of a twelve-year-old carrying a rag doll around? Combing back Deborah's hair—faded orange yarn, yet clean and unknotted—Tabitha smiled. It really didn't matter what people thought. She would love this doll in honor of Nanna.

She laid a hand on the coffin and studied the corpse again, pondering her father's words. *A cocoon. A cast-off shell.* The shadowy figure lying on the satin bed could no longer produce its familiar noble smile. The artificially blushed lips remained frozen in ghastly pretense.

Tabitha closed her eyes and clutched the doll close to her chest, trying to imprint on her mind Nanna's real face, the one that could smile and laugh and sing. The real image—the joyful, animated one—must never fade away.

While she meditated, a vision resurfaced in her mind, a dream from about a month before Nanna died. Tabitha had awakened from it in a fright, rising in an unfamiliar bed at Nanna's house while visiting her for the last time.

Although Nanna had lost her ability to walk almost a year earlier, in the dream the elderly lady and an unfamiliar companion paced swiftly through hazy darkness, both wearing long white robes. Eventually they reached a garden and stopped at a narrow, primitive gate. The surroundings blurred, and the companion's features stayed in shadows, but one image remained clear—Nanna's face, adorned with a glorious smile and beaming with delight.

With her eyes still tightly shut, Tabitha turned away and faced the door she had entered only a few minutes earlier. One more time Nanna's joyful face flashed into her memory. Tabitha nodded confidently and opened her eyes, knowing now that an old friend's smile would comfort her in her dreams rather than the gloomy specter of a sad, empty shell.

As she padded away from the coffin, her vision readjusted to the bright fluorescent lights. After viewing the specter of death, everything seemed out of place. Blazing spring flowers decorated the doors and windows. Music played from hidden speakers, a bouncy tune with happy voices singing of a glorious new world in the heavens.

She slowed her gait and brushed her fingers across the petals of a beautiful lily. Where were the muted colors, the grays and blacks? Where was the sound of gloomy violins playing the dirge of the brokenhearted? The mourners, if they could be called that, wore genuine smiles on their faces, and hearty handshakes coupled with vigorous embraces passed around the room like good news after a season of trouble.

Tabitha's brother Andrew looped his arm around her elbow. "C'mon, Sister Golden Hair. Grandma and Grandpa are here now, and so's Aunt Betty and Uncle Frank. You know what that means."

"A family photo?" Tabitha asked, shivering.

"You got it!" He pulled gently. "This way."

As they weaved through the mingling crowd, Tabitha hurried to keep up with her escort's lively pace. When they reached an adjacent room, she stopped at the door and peered inside, while Andrew bustled in and disappeared in a sea of people—dark-suited men and boys intermixed with a group of ladies and girls wearing equally dark dresses.

Tabitha smoothed out the front of her own black dress and slipped quietly into the room, hoping the shades of sadness would subdue the company and keep her fawning relatives at bay. As a dozen pairs of eyes flashed in her direction, she gave them a polite nod and a trembling smile, ready to endure the coming ordeal—a series of slack-jawed matrons welcoming her with squeals of delight and annoying, cheek-pinching fingers.

Aunt Betty began the routine, petting Tabitha's head. "Oh, John, just look at her! She's beautiful! Just like Melody and Sarah. But where did she get that hair? It's blonde to the roots!"

Tabitha's father pushed his hands into his pockets. "You won't get any argument from me, Sis. I'm kind of biased about how beautiful my kids are." Stroking his chin, he glanced toward the viewing room. "But come to think of it, wasn't Nanna blonde, I mean, years ago?"

Aunt Betty grabbed her brother's forearm, as if trying to strangle it. "Yes, of course! Remember that picture that used to hang in the hallway by the bathroom? It showed Nanna with Granddad at Mom and Dad's wedding. She was every bit as blonde as Tabitha."

Lowering her head, Tabitha slinked away, only to run into another gushing relative, a bent, wispy-haired great-aunt who laid a sloppy kiss on her cheek. Tabitha waited a few seconds for the kind old lady to turn around, then stealthily used her thumb to wipe the moisture away.

With her doll still in her grip, she folded her hands over her waist and sighed. The discomfort was tolerable. This was Aunt Cornelia, who had recently been widowed, had long since swept her empty nest clean, and now longed for the simple pleasure of a youthful touch. Tabitha vowed that she wouldn't disappoint her with a stony face or a grimace.

A tall man waved a camera over his head and called out from the opposite side of the room, "Everyone gather over here!"

Tabitha rushed forward and took Aunt Cornelia's hand. "Will you stand next to me?" she asked.

"Why, yes!" Aunt Cornelia said, her eyes sparkling. "Of course!"

As the chattering group huddled alongside a wall, the cameraman gestured with his lanky arms. "All Hansons to the left; everyone else to the right. Tall in the back; short in the front."

Aunt Cornelia pulled Tabitha closer. "We short people will stick together up front, right?"

Tabitha laughed and intertwined her fingers with her aunt's. "Just let them try and separate us!"

While the younger subjects shifted uneasily in their stiff collars and patent leather shoes, the men straightened their ties, and the ladies fussed with their hair. Tabitha leaned her head against Aunt Cornelia's shoulder. Her first funeral wasn't like what she had seen in the movies. Wasn't anyone sad about Nanna dying? Where were the gloomy faces? Where were the crying women with white hankies pressed against their noses?

When the photographer called out, "Smile!" Tabitha straightened and flashed a plastic grin, hoping it didn't look too fake or cheesy. A genuine smile seemed impossible, at least now, a day when she was supposed to weep. Someone had to grieve for Nanna. It might as well be her.

Just as the camera flashed, a familiar face peeked in the door—Tabitha's best friend, Rose. When Rose's lips wrinkled into her patented smirk, Tabitha had to restrain a laugh—both to keep from offending Rose and to maintain her grieving demeanor.

"Just one more," the photographer called, holding up his hand. "Keep smiling!"

With her gaze trained on Rose, Tabitha relaxed her face into a stoic mask. As soon as the flash dissipated, she squeezed her aunt's hand and whispered, "Thank you for posing with me."

New tears glistened in Aunt Cornelia's eyes. "My pleasure, sweet angel."

Tabitha kissed her on the cheek, then leaped toward the door. Rose had already entered with her father in tow, a man with an athletic build that belied his forty years of life. She hugged Rose warmly and led her back into the viewing room. "You came! I'm really glad you could!"

"Where'd you get that?" Rose asked, pointing at the doll.

"My great-grandmother's. She left her to me."

Rose straightened the doll's pinafore. "She must be a hundred years old! What's her name?"

"Deborah. And she might be that old. Nanna was over ninety, and she got her from her grandmother."

A deeper voice interrupted their conversation. "Good afternoon, Dr. Grayson."

Tabitha swung her head around. That was Daddy's voice.

"I'm John," her father said, extending his hand. "Tabitha's father."

Dr. Grayson accepted the handshake. "Call me Phil." His salted hair shook as his arm pumped up and down.

Tabitha's father withdrew his hand and clenched it as though his fingers hurt. "I'm glad to finally meet you."

"The feeling's mutual. Tabitha bubbles about you every time she comes to our house."

"Well, I should have visited earlier, but since my wife knows your wife, I decided . . . uh . . ." Her father shifted his weight, unsure of what to add.

"That we passed inspection?" Dr. Grayson offered.

Her father laughed nervously. "I guess you could say that. I didn't want to put it that way."

"Don't worry. I understand. It's a crazy world we live in."

"In any case," her father said, nodding at Rose, "you and your daughter coming to pay your respects to my grandmother is a pleasant surprise."

"A surprise?" Dr. Grayson's eyebrow twitched, but he maintained his smile. "Oh . . . I see. Well, this isn't really a church service. We all have to be laid to rest somehow." He let out a short laugh, then cleared his throat. "It's a morbid lesson, but Rose could learn something here about the end of life."

Tabitha's father patted Dr. Grayson's arm. "Excuse me. The pastor's waving for me at the coffin." As he strode away, he called back, "I hope we can talk more later."

Tabitha let her gaze follow her father's progress. Grandpa Hanson joined him and the pastor, and the three exchanged hearty handshakes and laughter. She squinted at the strange sight. Why would Grandpa be so happy? After all, that was his mother's body in the casket just an arm's length away.

She pictured her own mother lying dead in a coffin and imagined herself standing in front of it. Would she be laughing? What a horrible thought! Tears came to her eyes, and she wagged her head to shake the image away. Clutching Deborah more tightly, she searched the room and found her mother standing next to Aunt Betty, still smiling and talking, still alive.

Tabitha scolded herself. Her silly fears had almost made her cry. Still, all these happy faces didn't make sense. No wonder her mind was in a whirl.

Rose prodded Tabitha's shoulder. "Earth to Tabitha. Are you still here?"

Turning toward her, Tabitha laughed. "Maybe not. I think my brain might have hitched a ride on a spaceship. I feel—"

"Ladies and gentlemen." Her father's amplified voice sliced through the room. "We will now line up our cars on the street out front. The memorial service will be at the gravesite in thirty minutes."

He stepped away from the casket and marched straight to the exit. The crowd responded with low, buzzing conversation and a milling about that eventually funneled through the door.

Tabitha waved at Rose. "I'll see you there!" Tabitha joined her family as they exited, and after a short ride, they arrived at the cemetery. A stranger wearing a carnation boutonniere ushered her and her four siblings—Joshua, Sarah, Andrew, and Jonathan—to the first of several rows of chairs lined up under a large canopy. Although they were among the first to arrive, Tabitha's father, who had ridden with his parents, was already there, setting the closed casket in place along with the other pallbearers.

Tabitha sat between her mother and her older sister, Sarah, trying not to fidget. She pulled the hem of her dress down to cover more of her legs. Although the black, warm-weather material extended past her knees modestly, she still felt unsure of herself, crossing and uncrossing her legs a few times. What was the right posture for a funeral? Casual and laid-back? Drooping shoulders? She finally decided to stand and look for the Graysons, who had followed about a dozen cars back in the procession.

The freshly watered landscape between the cemetery plot and the parking area sparkled with dazzling greenery—lush, neatly trimmed grass and magnificent oaks with huge arching limbs, a perfect portrait of central Florida's beauty. The trees looked like guardians as they stretched their arms to shade the little tombstones in their care. The silky lawns begged for Tabitha to come and run barefoot down the slopes, and the trees waved their branches, beckoning her to climb up and ride the wind.

It seemed a mockery. None of the cemetery's residents could possibly enjoy the delightful fruits of the gardener's labor. They could never wiggle their toes in the soft grass or perch high in an oak to feel the limbs sway to and fro in the breeze. Her father had been right, she concluded, when earlier that morning he said, "The people left behind are the ones who define the last rites of the departed. Our dance with the dead is choreographed by the living."

Rose finally arrived. The rest of the front row had been reserved for family members, so she and her father chose seats in the second row. Tabitha quietly chattered with Rose until the rest of the mourners arrived and Pastor Jenkins addressed the crowd, his thick gray eyebrows arching high as he spoke.

"The Hanson family would like to thank everyone for coming. Today we lay to rest the body of Natalie Elizabeth Hanson, an aged saint who brought blessings to all who knew her. As she requested before her death, her grandson, John Hanson, will deliver her eulogy."

Tabitha's father stood in front of the coffin, facing his family and friends. Tall, slender, and freshly shaved, he reminded Tabitha of a young Gregory Peck, like Atticus Finch in *To Kill a Mockingbird*, both in looks and demeanor. Very few people knew the fun-loving Daddy hiding behind that dark suit and gloomy mask.

He began his speech in a clear monotone, reading from a single sheet of paper. "Natalie Elizabeth Holmes was born on September sixteenth, in the year of our Lord eighteen hundred and ninety-seven. She married Thomas Aaron Hanson at the age of nineteen. She bore four children, Thomas Junior, Rachel, Joseph, and Matthew. Her husband died ten years ago at the age of eighty-six, and she passed away October thirtieth, in the year of our Lord nineteen hundred and ninety. She is survived by three of her children, eleven grandchildren, and twenty-seven great-grandchildren." At this point, he paused and put the fact sheet down on a chair. He had been formal and straight-laced, and the onlookers mirrored his sobriety, but now his face blossomed into a radiant smile. "Family and friends, now that I've told you the facts about Natalie Elizabeth Hanson, I want to talk to you about our dear Nanna."

The sober expressions broke into smiles. The mere mention of the departed's nickname felt like a fresh breeze on a sultry afternoon.

As the mood shifted, Tabitha clutched her doll and looked back at Rose. Her grin reflected in the face of her friend. Dr. Grayson, however, sat stone-faced, neither smiling nor frowning.

Tabitha's father went on to tell about Nanna's life, how she became a Christian during her twenties and witnessed to her husband, who followed suit soon after. He related a few short tales about how Nanna raised her children, helping each of them to know the Lord Jesus at an early age and encouraging them in their faith, even as adults. He laughed as he recounted stories that proved this woman to be the originator of a spiritual lineage, and he called on his listeners to follow the Lord whom Nanna had so faithfully served.

As he finished, he walked solemnly to Grandpa Hanson and took his hand firmly. He spoke more softly, but still loud enough for all to hear. "A wise man once said, 'A true Christian rejoices when a loved one goes to heaven to be with the Lord. Grief is an indulgence for ourselves.'" He released Grandpa's hand and nodded toward the canopy ceiling. "Dad, when you picture Nanna in heaven, I'm sure you feel the joy of knowing that your mother is in a better place. Maybe she's sitting in her favorite rocker, ready to tell one of her amazing stories, and a dozen children are sitting around listening and laughing."

As her father continued, Tabitha glanced at the casket. Something caught her eye, something moving. A ghostly image appeared in front of a flower arrangement, Nanna sitting in her chair exactly as Daddy had described, only she was younger somehow, not a fragile old granny, but a vibrant, angelic woman. Yet, she was still Nanna, rocking back and forth and beckoning with a wave of her hand as if asking Tabitha to come.

Still clutching her doll, Tabitha rose to her feet, staring at the vision. Taking one quiet step after another, she drew closer to Nanna's glorious, shining face. Her father's voice fell silent. A few whispers reached her ears, but they seemed cast toward her from another world. As the sunlight faded and all other sounds drained away, Nanna's gentle whisper became clear. "I'm glad to see you, my dear. Would you like to sit with the others and hear a story?"

Tabitha looked around. No one sat nearby. She opened her mouth to answer, but a sharp voice shattered her reverie. "Tabitha! What are you doing?" It was her father. She tried to reply, but her words stuck in her throat.

Sunlight returned. As the buzz of her fellow funeral goers sprang back to life, Tabitha's voice returned. "I see her! I see Nanna sitting in the chair, just like you said."

Her father's strong hands gripped her shoulders. "There's no one there, sweetheart. You're imagining things."

"I'm not imagining! I really see her!" She pointed again. "See? She's looking right at you!" She felt his hands pull her back, but the image's draw seemed stronger. She broke free and reached for Nanna, but the vision evaporated. Waving her arm back and forth where Nanna had been, she cried out, "She was here! I saw her!"

Her father turned her around and, stooping low, gazed into her eyes, his own blue eyes glistening with tears. "I didn't realize how upset you were about Nanna's death," he said, stroking her hair. "We'll make sure you get plenty of rest tonight."

"Rest is a good idea, John, but it won't cure her."

Tabitha swung toward the voice—Dr. Grayson. He stood at his seat, one hand in his pocket.

"Hallucinations often arise from a deep-seated problem that requires therapy," Dr. Grayson said, eyeing Tabitha from under a furrowed brow. "I'll be glad to be of assistance."

"I don't need therapy," Tabitha insisted. "I really saw her." She tapped her father on his chest. "Just like I'm seeing you right now."

Her father straightened and laid a hand on Tabitha's head. "I can't say what we'll do, Phil, but thank you for your offer."

Dr. Grayson nodded. "Feel free to call me anytime."

Tabitha lowered her head and shuffled back to her seat, feeling the weight of dozens of gazes resting on her body. Of course everyone was staring. She had just made a fool of herself. Did it matter that the image was real? Not to them. Since no one else saw it, she was the weird one, the distraught great-grandchild overwhelmed by grief. A few "tsk, tsk" sounds made their way into her ears, like the sweeping brooms of old biddies who couldn't mind their own business.

She sat heavily in her chair, folded her arms, and drooped her head. The rest of the funeral seemed a blur of speeches and hymns. She clutched Deborah as tightly as she could. This funeral day had now become the saddest day of her life.

Sarah slipped her hand into Tabitha's and intertwined their fingers. Her wordless touch felt good and affirming. Her one and only sister always knew how to make her feel better.

Tabitha took in a deep breath. She could get through this. As long as Sarah believed in her, not much else mattered.

Chapter 2

THAT EVENING after dinner, Tabitha tried to listen to the whispered conversations of the adults in her house. Some of her relatives were planning to stay the night, and the grown-ups had gathered in the family room, taking up all the available seats. Tabitha sat quietly on the floor in their home's schoolroom, mentally stretching her sense of hearing. Her father's voice came through, clearly the moderator, while tones of courteous disagreement bounced around.

An agitated female voice barged in, and the volume made for good listening. "John, I believe in visions from God just as much as the next Christian, but there is such a thing as mental illness, you know. Having faith doesn't mean throwing out science."

Tabitha crossed her arms and frowned. Aunt Betty had never been one to mince words.

"Yes, Sis, I know. I'm taking everything into consideration. But Tabitha has so much faith, I can't deny the possibility that she really saw something, so I'm not ready to throw all my faith into a scientific hat, especially a secular one."

Tabitha smiled. That was Daddy, her knight in shining armor. He would believe her. Of course he would. She tried to picture his facial expression as he spoke, his stern jaw in contrast to his compassionate blue eyes. He was probably leaning forward in his chair, his long torso unintentionally intimidating those who might disagree, and his distinguished, graying locks shaking slightly as he spoke his perfectly reasoned points.

"I think we should just leave her alone," another female piped up.

It was Aunt Cornelia. Tabitha smiled again. Having a new ally gave her a warm feeling all over.

"Leave her alone!" Aunt Betty's shriek rattled Tabitha's eardrums. "She needs help!"

"*Shhhh!*" Tabitha's father scolded. "The children might hear you."

His warning ruined Tabitha's listening post. From that time on, the conversation dropped off to a low hum, too low to distinguish any intelligible words.

Tabitha sighed. Maybe it was just as well. Although she ached to sit in her father's lap and take in every word, she wasn't sure she should be listening at all. She had already been told to find something to do or go play with the other children. But wasn't listening to their conversation something to do? She had already bathed and brushed her teeth, so just sitting around seemed best for the moment.

"Time for bed, sweetheart," came a tired but tender voice.

Tabitha looked up at her mother. "Can't I sit and listen just a little bit longer?"

Her mother shook her head, the bags under her eyes showing her exhaustion. Still, she was as pretty as ever, her shoulder-length hair probably more ragged than she would have liked, and her hazel eyes less than sparkling, but her lovely spirit shone through all the same. "It's been a long, hard day, and we'll be going back to our studies tomorrow." She extended her hand. "Come with me now."

Tabitha took her hand and walked down the hall, quietly at first as she listened to her mother's gentle humming, but when they arrived at her bedroom door, she pulled her hand away. "Mama, do you believe that I really saw something, I mean, something real that wasn't just in my head?"

Her mother's hummed tune faded away. "Daddy and I will talk with you about it tomorrow." She brushed Tabitha's hair back and kissed her forehead. "Try to go to sleep now. Since Sarah's already asleep, I'll stay with you for a few minutes, if you want."

Tabitha watched Sarah for a few seconds, comfortably cuddled on her pillow. With the same brown hair and hazel eyes as their mother, and only an inch shorter, she could have passed for their mother's younger sister, yet far more carefree. Most eighteen-year-olds had all sorts of growing-up problems, but not Sarah—no school headaches, no boy troubles, nothing more than a couple of pimples to battle. No wonder she could snooze without a care.

Finally, Tabitha nodded and took her hand again. "I'd like it if you stayed."

While her mother closed the door and pulled up a rocking chair, Tabitha picked up Deborah and pushed under the sheets and comforter. Even after such a trying day, however, with the image of Nanna still burning in her mind, she was sure she would never get to sleep. Closing her eyes and burying them in her pillow couldn't shut out the millions of pressing questions.

"Mama?" she whispered into the darkness.

"Yes?"

"I can't sleep."

"How do you know? You've only been in bed two minutes."

"I'm thinking about something I heard Daddy say, something about me having so much faith. Do you think he believes me?"

She stroked Tabitha's blanketed thigh. "Of course he does. But I can ask him to come and talk to you if you want."

Tabitha nodded. "I'd like that."

Click. The noisy door latch interrupted their quiet conversation, and a bright stream of light made a path into the bedroom, framing the silhouette of Tabitha's father with a royal, back-lit glow.

"You're just in time," her mother whispered. "Tabitha needs to talk to you."

Daddy tiptoed in and extended an open palm toward the bed. Tabitha took his hand and pulled herself up to her feet, leaving her doll behind. With catlike steps, they made their way out the door and closed it carefully after Mama passed through behind them. Then down the hall and into the family room they walked hand in hand until they reached a rocking chair.

Her father sat first, and Tabitha curled up in his lap, one arm around his neck and her feet pulled up behind her thighs. Although she was twelve, she didn't feel too big for Daddy's lap. She had always said there was a Tabitha-sized hole wherever her daddy sat, and it was her job to fill it. Tonight, the hole felt especially cozy. The days of autumn were still quite warm, but the nights cooled into crispy snuggle weather. Her fuzzy nightgown's long sleeves and skirt helped warm both bodies as they nestled into their comfortable poses.

Her father closed his eyes and began to rock slowly, sighing gently. She rested her head against his cheek, now a bit scratchy. Still, it felt good, like a stiff brush rubbing an itchy spot. Soon, the fresh toothpaste smell on her breath, the sweet scent of clean hair, and her softly whistled respiration lulled both of them into a sleepy, dreamlike bliss.

"I love sitting in your lap," Tabitha crooned.

"And why is that?" he asked without opening his eyes.

She pondered the question for a moment. Did it have to be explained? It just felt right, that's all. "Well . . . don't you like it?"

He held her closer and slowly rubbed his hand across her upper arm. "Oh, of course I do. It's the magic of two bodies melting into one heart."

She looked up at him. "That's poetic, isn't it, Daddy?"

Opening his eyes a slit, he shrugged his shoulders. "I suppose so."

Tabitha sat up straight and patted his chest. "Then let's write a poem about it!"

"Together?"

She snuggled up again, curling her legs even more tightly and nuzzling his neck. The vibrations of his gentle humming, the tune of a lullaby she remembered from long ago, buzzed into her ears. "Yes, together, like when we wrote that poem about Jonathan when he was born."

"Oh, yeah," he said, interrupting his melody. "I remember that." He rocked a little harder, getting into Tabitha's playful mood. "Okay, you start."

"Umm . . . 'My Daddy's lap is warm and snug.'" She stopped and waited.

"My turn?"

She giggled. "Yes. Your turn."

"Okay, how about, 'My favorite place to sit'?"

Tabitha looked at him expectantly, but he just stared back at her.

"Your line was shorter than mine," she said.

He winked at her. "It'll work. Trust me."

She sat still and cuddled again, taking in the feelings she wanted to convey. "His arms abound with tender love."

Her father laughed. "That was good. Where'd you learn to keep to the meter like that?"

"Meter?" she asked.

"You know. How the sentence bounces."

"I learned it from you."

"From me? I don't remember teaching you about meter."

"You didn't teach me. I just listen to your poems. It's not too hard to figure out."

"Oh, poetry is that easy, huh?" He shook her teasingly and then wrapped her up again. "Okay, from the top now," he continued, rocking to the beat of the poem. "My Daddy's lap is warm and snug, my favorite place to sit. His arms abound with tender love . . ." He paused, stopping the chair for a moment.

Tabitha pulled in her bottom lip. Had Daddy run out of creative juices? Usually he could come up with a perfect line in just a few seconds.

Finally, he raised a finger. "It's there I truly fit."

"Fit?" she asked, raising her head to see her father's expression.

"Yes. You know, fit like a hand in a glove."

Tabitha smiled and rested her head again. "Okay, that works. Next stanza?"

"Oh, I think that's enough poetry for now," he said, sitting up in the chair. He grasped Tabitha's shoulders and moved her to a comfortable, face-to-face position. "Why don't we talk about what's on your mind first?"

Tabitha leaned back, trying to avoid her father's piercing gaze. How should she begin? Sometimes it was so hard to talk to Daddy, because he wanted so badly to fix her problems, he would blurt out his answer before she was ready to hear it. He meant well, but quick and tidy answers made her feel so young, like a child who had shallow questions with easy answers.

Pressing her lips together, she furrowed her brow. Maybe it would be best to try to sound grown-up and tell it like it is. If she wanted to be treated like the young lady she knew she was, it was time to act like one.

She cleared her throat and lowered her voice. "Even though I sit in your lap, I'm not really a little girl anymore."

He lifted his eyebrows. "I know that."

Tabitha interlocked her fingers and wrung them nervously. His answer had popped out, short and quick . . . not a good sign, but she

had to press on. "And I know the difference between seeing something real and seeing it in my head."

"Of course you do. You're practically a teenager."

"So how do I get people to believe that I really saw Nanna? I
mean, for real, like a vision from heaven."

"Hmm . . ." He pushed her head against his shoulder again and
restarted the rocking, this time thrusting back a little farther and not
letting the chair come as far forward. This created a more comfortable angle, but it also made the old wooden chair complain in a low,
moaning creak, and, worst of all, it made her feel like a baby.

This time she hoped his answer would come quickly, but the
soothing rhythm of sound and motion continued uninterrupted, calling her to the edge of slumber. She resisted, blinking rapidly and
twisting her fingers until they hurt.

After almost a minute, he stopped rocking. "Dr. Grayson suggested that you draw a picture of what you saw."

Tabitha raised her head. "Why?"

"He thinks it will help us understand what's going on in your
mind."

"But he doesn't believe me," she said, spreading out her hands.
"Why should I do what he thinks?"

Her father tapped himself on the chest. "But *I* believe you, and
I would like to see what you draw."

"I don't get it. If you believe me, what difference does it make if
I draw a picture?"

"Please don't misunderstand. I believe that you saw Nanna. What
I don't know is whether or not it was a vision of what's really going
on in heaven, or just a memory vision that God provided to bring
you comfort."

Tabitha raised her finger to her lips and bit her knuckle. "A memory vision?" she repeated, talking through her finger. "What's that?"

"I just made up the term, but I'm wondering if God gave you an image of your memories of Nanna—a real vision, not a hallucination—that would help you know that she's okay."

Tabitha shook her head. "I don't think so."

"Why not?" His eyebrows scrunched, the way they always did when he was truly perplexed.

"Because she didn't look the way I remembered her. She was . . . well . . . kind of angelic."

"I see." He stroked his chin, making a slight scritching noise.

Tabitha knew that pause. The "I see" pause meant that he really didn't see at all. In fact, he probably wanted to challenge what she said but didn't want to upset her, so now he hoped "I see" would hang in the air long enough for him to think of something better to say.

Finally he lifted her away from his shoulder and looked her in the eye. His gentle smile was pleasant, and the minty aroma of dessert that evening rode on his warm breath. "Tabitha, only you really know what you saw. You have to agree with that, right?"

"Sure," she said, shrugging her shoulders. "I guess so."

"And even you admit that you're a good artist, right?"

"I'm okay." She shrugged again. "With some things."

"Then show me what you saw, and maybe God will help me understand."

Tabitha bit her knuckle again. Daddy's logic was overpowering, as usual. What would it hurt? Just draw the picture and hope something would come of it. "Okay," she said. "But I think I already know what it's all about."

He smiled. "What might that be?"

"God wants us to be happy and not grieve. He showed me Nanna in heaven, and she's happy, so we should be happy, too."

One eye closed halfway as he pondered her comment. "Well, being happy is a lot easier when the person who has died was old and had been suffering. That's why we made Nanna's funeral kind of festive."

"Yeah, I was wondering about that." Tabitha paused for a moment, tapping her chin. "But shouldn't we be happy for anyone who goes to heaven?"

Her father's brow wrinkled further, and he gazed toward the fireplace, though no fire burned there.

Tabitha smiled. Now he was really thinking, not just trying to appease her with a standard, got-it-from-a-book response. It was time to drive the point home. "If I believe God," she continued, "then I shouldn't feel pain about Nanna dying. It wouldn't be right to grieve."

He shook his head. "I can't argue with your reasoning."

Tabitha breathed a deep, relaxing sigh and nestled into her father's lap again. She had finally won a debate with him, one that seemed really important. Now she was sure she could go to sleep.

"I guess I'll draw the picture, if you think it might help." She yawned and smacked her lips. "Can we finish our poem now?"

"Okay. One more stanza and then to bed you go."

"It won't take long. I already thought of the next line: I'll never get too old or big . . ."

"To take my special place," her father added.

Tabitha beamed. "That was quick, too."

"Well, you got my creative energy revved up."

"Okay, Mr. Daddy Poet," she said, poking her finger in his chest. "You write the rest."

"You asked for it." He cleared his throat and spoke in a mock, little girl's voice. "I'll never get too old or big to take my special place. So Daddy, dear, when I grow up, reserve my parking space!"

They both laughed out loud and traded tickles and hugs. Then her father stood, sweeping her up in his arms, and carried her back to her bedroom, where he deposited her gently on her mattress.

Now content, and with her questions vanquished, Tabitha listened to the clicking of the door latch and the gentle tapping of her father's shoes in the hallway. Daddy was out there and on duty. All was well.

As she cuddled Deborah, the thoughts of the day danced around in her head, swirling in a mental kaleidoscope, each one tumbling over the other as contorted faces took turns closing in on her mind's eye. Their garbled voices rang loudly in her ears, taunting her, challenging her to decipher their meaning. After a few minutes, the sounds transformed into music, a sad funeral march, and the clutter of images molded into one—Nanna's coffin with its pallbearers. The ornate box was closed, and the men carrying it marched solemnly away into a gray mist. Only darkness remained, a hazy but familiar scene.

Where had she seen this place before? Oh, yes! She had dreamed of Nanna walking in this gloomy twilight with a mysterious companion. It was only a few days later that her mother informed her of the dear lady's terminal illness. But this time the darkness was empty and silent.

No. Not so silent. Grunts and the rasping of labored respiration rose from somewhere in the distance, and they were growing louder, getting closer. The sound was like a runner, troubled and perhaps in fear. Now footsteps sounded, tired and falling heavily on an invisible surface, making a hollow echo through the dim expanse of nothingness. Finally, a shadowy figure appeared. Too tired to run, it slowed to a frantic walk, and fitful sobs poured forth, apparently from fright and exhaustion.

Soon, the terrified traveler's gender became clear, a girl about Tabitha's age. The dark hair of this poor waif shook back and forth as she jerked her head in every direction, constantly wary of a pursuer lurking in the mist.

What was wrong? When Nanna was in this place, she was at peace and accompanied by a strong but gentle friend. This girl walked alone, terrified.

Tabitha strained to see her face, but shadows veiled her features. As the girl continued living a nightmare, she drew closer. The image became strikingly clear, and the face unmistakable. Horror filled her deep brown eyes, but Tabitha recognized their distinctive shade. Tears stained her cheeks, but the tracks could never hide the familiar contours. Her hair flew around, stringy and dripping, and every other part of her body revealed the strain of her ordeal, but it was not enough to mask her identity.

Suddenly the girl stopped and looked behind her. A monstrous shadow, even darker than the surrounding gray, loomed over the shrinking figure. The girl's face rushed forward, her mouth opening in a horrible scream. The blood-curdling shriek pushed into Tabitha's own throat. She sat bolt upright in bed, the scream startling her sister awake. The desperate cry spent her breath. She coughed and sputtered, able to squeeze out only three words to describe the night terror.

"It was Rose!"

Chapter 3

TABITHA HUGGED a thick tree limb and dangled underneath, her fingers intertwined on top. She pressed her feet against the trunk, making her body a suspension bridge of sorts as she swayed back and forth a few feet above the ground.

Sitting on the limb a few inches from Tabitha's hands, Rose pried up loose chunks of bark while blowing breathy whistles through her dry lips. She flipped a flat piece into the air with a snapping backhand and watched it sail away on the breeze.

"I love this tree," Tabitha said dreamily.

Rose stopped whistling. "Why?"

"I dunno."

Still gripping the limb, Tabitha pushed her feet away from the trunk. She let her feet dangle, pretending to be miles from the ground. Her once-white tennis shoes kicked beneath her slender legs and dirty knees, and her green T-shirt rode up higher than the belt on her shorts, exposing her midriff.

For a moment she was a daring heroine, clinging frantically to the side of a large boat as she kicked at the hungry, snapping alligators below. But when her fingers screamed for relief, she changed her fantasy, opting for a safer adventure. Now she was sliding down an enormous redwood after saving a magic kitten from a branch at the very top.

"Oof!" she grunted when she finally let go and slammed her feet to the ground. She clapped her dirty, grass-stained palms together. "Yep. This is one fine tree."

"But you don't know why?" Rose asked. "That's not very logical."

"You need an explanation for everything, don't you?" Tabitha looked up into the oak's thick foliage. "I guess it helps me think about nice things when I'm climbing it."

Rose scrambled down the tree. Not quite as agile as Tabitha, her thicker limbs and torso made her swings and jumps clumsier and more precarious as she tried to shinny down the trunk. She made up for her lack of grace with brute force.

"Nice things?" Rose asked when she reached the bottom. "Have you been thinking about not-so-nice things?"

Tabitha grinned at the serious expression on Rose's usually playful face. "Now don't go playing psychology again. You're not your father."

"But I like psychoanalysis. I was hoping you'd show me the picture you drew, you know, the one of Nanna at the funeral."

Tabitha lowered her head. "I haven't drawn it yet. Daddy said I could wait until I'm ready."

"That's cool as far as I'm concerned." Rose raised her right hand to signal an oath. "A doctor always keeps his patients' secrets private. You can tell me what's bugging you, even without showing me a drawing."

The two girls strolled toward a small, round pond that lay nestled in a corner of Tabitha's spacious backyard, one of their favorite

getaways. They sat at its grassy edge and watched a swarm of min-
nows darting around in pursuit of invisible prey. The miniature
ecosystem provided a tapestry of wildlife to identify and scrutinize.
From frogs leaping into the water whenever humans approached, to
a heron that flew by for his evening stalk in the shallows, there was
always some creature prowling or playing.

Tabitha breathed in the varied odors—sweet, freshly mown grass,
musty muck near her toes, and Rose's familiar cologne that smelled
like the women's restroom at Macy's department store. Rose thought
wearing it made her more mature, somehow, though it really didn't.
It was all just part of her idea of growing up.

Smiling, Tabitha turned her nose back to the pond—reality, the
unpretentiousness of life's ebb and flow, acted out before her daily in
her own little biosphere. New smells brought new delights, the delicate scent of the flowering lily pads and the stronger odor of the
damp fennel trading back and forth in the shifting breeze, creating
an ever-changing smellscape of sorts. This was a haven, indeed. With
her troubling dreams of late, this refuge of newness and restoration
proved to be a refreshing escape from the nighttime tremors.

"So," Rose said as she blew dandelion fluff into the air, "are you
going to keep ignoring my question, or what?"

Tabitha blinked and turned toward her. "Question?"

Rose's voice sharpened. "What's bugging you?"

"Oh . . . that." Tabitha hugged her knees and pulled them close
to her chest. "I guess with Nanna dying, I've been thinking a lot
about death. My father agrees I should be happy that she's gone on
to a better place, but that seems strange somehow. Shouldn't I be sad
that she's gone? I mean, I loved her. I wanted her to stick around a
while longer."

She paused to snatch a grasshopper that landed in her lap. As she
lifted it closer to scrutinize its features, she wrinkled her nose at its
bugged-out eyes. "And I had these weird dreams last night." She

paused, concentrating on the wiggling insect pinched gently between her thumb and finger.

Rose drummed her fingers on her thigh. "Go on, Miss Drama. I'm waiting."

"Well, the dreams were pretty much the same, except one time you were in it, and the second time there was a girl I've never seen before."

Rose's eyes brightened, and she assumed the posture of a psychoanalyst, her pen a long strand of Bahia grass. "You've been dreaming about me? So, what happens?"

Tabitha ignored Rose's clownish pose and shrugged her shoulders. "I can't really describe it. Just scary stuff."

"Scary stuff?" As Rose scribbled on her invisible pad, the seeds at the end of the blade bobbed near her cheek. "Go on. This is very interesting."

Tabitha held the grasshopper closer to Rose. "It's a bird grasshopper. It didn't hop. It actually flew into my lap." With an upward toss, she thrust the insect into the air, and it flittered to a resting place a dozen or so yards away.

Rose sighed, her pen still scribbling. "You really shouldn't be thinking about scary stuff. You have everything going for you, you know. You have a great mom and dad, nice sister and brothers, a big house, and good looks."

Tabitha let out a low groan. "Why do you always bring up my looks?"

"Because it's true. You're the prettiest girl around."

Tabitha dug out a pebble, flung it into the pond, and watched the rippled circles grow. She let a scowl wrinkle her face. "I don't care much about how I look. Besides, Sarah's a lot prettier than I am."

"That's different." Rose pointed the blade of grass at her. "Your sister's a grown woman. She's just more developed than you, that's all. And you have something she doesn't."

This time Rose paused, apparently waiting for the obvious question. Tabitha rolled her eyes. "So who's being dramatic now?"

"Humor me."

"Okay, so what do I have that Sarah doesn't?"

Rose reached out and combed her fingers through Tabitha's hair. "Your hair is so blonde, it shines. Look at how the sun makes it glow. It's almost like gold!"

Tabitha took a handful of her long tresses and held it out in front. "I guess when you've had it all your life, it's nothing special."

"I think it's special. I'd give anything to have hair like yours." With a hiss of disgust, Rose pulled on the ends of her own hair. "Just look at this mess! Plain, ordinary brown, dry and stringy. It's ugly."

"It is not!" Tabitha slapped the ground. "Why are you trying to tell me to be positive when you're always so negative?"

Rose's chin dropped, and her bottom lip swelled. With a hard swallow, she managed to erase her frown. "Because you have so much. I know your family. They're all so happy and friendly."

"Your mom and dad are both nice," Tabitha offered, reaching out to touch Rose's hand.

"You're right; they're nice." Rose drew her hand away, avoiding Tabitha's touch, then pushed a strand of hair from her eyes. "But Dad's always so gloomy, like he's always waiting for something bad to happen. He never seems to be really happy about anything."

Tabitha stared at her friend. Rose avoided eye contact, the same way she always did when she was trying not to cry. She hated showing her emotions.

Turning toward the pond again, Tabitha watched a dragonfly alight on the tip of a bulrush. What could she say to help? Almost anything could set Rose off now. After several seconds, she spoke softly, keeping her gaze fixed on the dragonfly.

"Your dad's gloomy, but that's just when he comes home from work. All that stuffy psychology all day is enough to make anyone drag a brick home. But when he sees you, he brightens up like a kid with an ice cream cone." She turned back to Rose and grasped her hand. "I've seen him! And he'd always be happy if only he would just—" Tabitha swallowed the rest of her sentence. Rose would jump on it like a crazed rottweiler.

"I know, I know," Rose said with a wag of her head. "Jesus makes you happy." She raised her blade of grass and imaginary pad again and lowered a pair of invisible eyeglasses to peer smugly at Tabitha. "But my father explained to me why there can't possibly be a God. It's just not logical."

Tabitha bit her lip. Raising her voice wouldn't help. Her father always said that the one who first resorts to anger is the loser in any debate. After taking a deep breath, she replied in an even tone. "My dad is the most logical man I know, and he says there *is* a God."

Rose tossed her "pen" behind her. "Here we go again."

Tabitha read the irritation in Rose's voice. She was already riding the border of an out-and-out rant. Tabitha had to choose her words wisely if she wanted this conversation about God to continue. "I talked to my father about it just this morning. I said, 'Daddy, if Dr. Grayson is so smart, then why doesn't he believe in God?'"

Rose lifted her brow. "And what did he say?"

"He used some words that were about this long," Tabitha replied, holding her hands as far apart as she could, "but I don't remember them exactly. Something about presuppositions, or some other word like that."

"Presuppositions? I've heard that word, but I'm not sure what it means."

Tabitha's eyes rolled slightly upward as she tried to remember what her father had so recently taught. "The way I understood it," she explained, now closing her eyes to concentrate, "it means that some people use their smarts real well, but they don't start at the right place. They start out thinking something is true without proving it, like there's no such thing as miracles and stuff, and they go on from there."

Rose shook her head. "I don't think I get it."

"I didn't either until my father told me a story. It was pretty funny."

Rose leaned over on her elbow. "Okay. Tell it to me, then."

Tabitha tucked one knuckle under her chin, thinking about how to start. Then, with a grin and hand gestures, she began. "There was a man who believed he was dead, even though he was actually alive. No one could convince him otherwise. One day, a smart friend of his had an idea. The friend showed him in books that dead men don't bleed. They even visited a mortician, and the mortician agreed that dead men don't bleed. Finally, the friend convinced him. Then, without warning, his friend stuck him in the hand with a needle, and blood started oozing out. The first man cried out, 'Dead men do bleed after all!'" Tabitha rocked back and forth, laughing.

Scowling, Rose leaned back on her hands. "What? He must be nuts!"

Tabitha stifled her giggles. "Don't you get it? He was convinced that he was dead, and nothing could change that. Since he bled, he had to conclude that dead men really do bleed! It was a logical conclusion, but he started out with a wrong idea. Being dead was his wrong presupposition."

Rose shook her head. "I still don't get it."

Tabitha exhaled a long, frustrated sigh. "I guess my father told it a lot better than I did." She found another pebble and slung it into the water. "The story made sense to me then, but now I can't explain it very well." After a few seconds, a new idea popped into her mind. "There is one thing I do understand, though."

"What's that?"

Tabitha watched the dying ripples lap against the sides of the pond while she constructed her thoughts. "Well, you said you don't get it, but a lot of other people don't get it either. My father said that only a few people ever find the way to God. The entrance into heaven is a narrow gate, and those who are wise in their own eyes miss it."

Rose pointed at Tabitha. "You see? Already it doesn't make sense. If God is loving, the entrance wouldn't be narrow; he would want everyone to find it." She waved her arms dramatically. "There would be billboards and neon lights, advertisements on television, personal interviews on the talk shows. Surely God could afford a full-page ad in every major newspaper in the country. He obviously needs an ad agent on Madison Avenue to help him with his promo campaign."

"Madison Avenue? Promo campaign?" Tabitha narrowed her eyes. "What are you talking about?"

"You know, the place in New York where the big shots run the ad campaigns. I know about that stuff, because my dad wrote a paper on the effect of ads on people's minds." Rose finished with a snobby smirk.

Tabitha stared. Her best friend was mocking her! A sharp pain stabbed her stomach, tying it into a knot. As she tried to keep her lips from trembling, a Bible verse eased into her thoughts. *Do not be overcome by evil, but overcome evil with good.*

The words acted like a salve, soothing the verbal wound. After a few seconds of awkward silence, Tabitha reclined on the grass with her hands behind her head. She spoke softly, her gaze locked on the blue sky. "Rose, God has an advertising campaign bigger than anything even the best Madison Avenue big shot could ever dream of."

Apparently unaware of the pain her antics inflicted, Rose joined Tabitha in a reclining position. "How can that be? I would have heard of something that big."

Tabitha gazed into the deep blue canopy. "Have you ever heard of the sky, Rose?" She pulled a tuft of Bahia at her side and held it up. "How about the grass? And who made that cute little hopper we looked at, and who taught him how to hunt through the grass to look for food? If we can't see a designer in those advertisements, we must be either blind or stupid." Tabitha sneaked a glance at Rose, who seemed engrossed in the narration, watching the sky with a gaping mouth.

Tabitha went on. "The creation trumpets God's existence! What's more logical, to believe in a creator, or to believe like your father that all this got here by chance? How could the world have so much dumb luck for billions of years?"

Rose remained quiet, so Tabitha ended her short sermon and maintained her upward stare. Pushing her friend too hard at this point would be a mistake. After all, the argument wasn't even a fair one. Tabitha had borrowed her eloquence from her father's many dinnertime discussions on this very issue. She could even hear his tone and cadence in her head, which she had also copied without shame.

After a minute or so of silence, Rose spoke up. "You sure know how to talk about this stuff. Where did you learn it all?"

Tabitha turned toward her. With her friend deciding to be so vulnerable, it wouldn't hurt to confess. "I've listened to my father for as long as I can remember. I didn't use his exact words, because some of them are from his theology books. But I do understand this much. It's much wiser to believe in a creator I can't figure out than it is to trust in something that's totally impossible. I don't pretend to understand God, but I know the beauty around me didn't get here by itself."

Rose sat up and slapped at an annoying mosquito. "It's not all beautiful," she said. "Did God make mosquitoes, too?"

"I guess so." Tabitha sat up, as well, trying to hide her disappointment. This was the furthest they had come in their many God conversations, and now a stupid mosquito had to interrupt. "They're not the most wonderful part of God's creation, but he must have some reason for letting them bite us."

The buzzing pests accompanied the approaching evening in growing swarms. Tabitha swatted the air. "I guess we'd better go in."

She jumped to her feet and helped Rose to hers. As the two girls strolled toward Tabitha's house, the reddening sun approached the horizon. Rose walked deliberately, her head angled downward in thought. Tabitha followed, her gaze on Rose's old play shoes shuffling through the grass.

As a chorus of frogs began an evening song, Rose spoke above the din. "You said there was another girl in your dreams."

Tabitha hesitated. Should she relive the nightmare by telling all the gory details? Or would Rose be satisfied with just another morsel of knowledge? It was worth a try. "There was just one girl in each dream, either you or an older girl, a black girl. I'd say she was fifteen or sixteen."

After a few seconds of silence, save for the peeping choir, Rose spoke up again. "Aren't you going to tell me what happens?"

Tabitha winced. Her plan didn't work. Rose wasn't going to give up until she heard the whole story. "I'd rather not talk about it," she finally replied, with enough shortness to keep Rose from any further prying.

"All right then; have it your way." Rose tossed her head back and jumped on her bicycle in a huff, pausing to look back at Tabitha.

Crossing her arms, Tabitha smiled and shook her head. She knew Rose too well to be fooled by her mini tantrum. "So we're archenemies now, huh? Want to start a feud?"

"Okay, smarty-pants. You win." Rose pumped her bicycle pedals and waved as she rode away, calling back, "I'll see you tomorrow, okay?"

Tabitha waved, barely able to keep from jumping up and down. Although she had tried to talk to Rose about God before, this was the first time she had made progress, real progress. Of course, she had a long way to go, but it was a great start.

As she watched Rose shrink in the distance, Tabitha's thoughts turned to her visit at her friend's school. Rose was so different there! She played petty games among her peers, the manipulative one-upmanship that included cutting remarks and backbiting gossip. Even if she wasn't the instigator, Rose frequently allowed herself to be caught up in the rude habits. After all, that's how all the other kids acted, and to survive in school she felt she had to be accepted in the right cliques—to dress like everyone else, speak the lingo, and protect her territory. If someone got out of line, it was up to the others to bring her back, cut her down a peg or two. They couldn't let anyone get the upper hand.

Tabitha was different in so many ways. She knew it. Rose knew it. And those differences drove Rose to distraction, even angering her at times.

Sighing, Tabitha turned and shuffled toward the house. What could she do? She couldn't put on an act for Rose. That wouldn't be right. She had to be straightforward about her faith, unashamed, just like her father had always taught. She had tried to be the sower Jesus talked about, casting out seeds, hoping they would land in fertile soil. And now, finally, a seed might have taken root.

She stuffed her grass-stained hands into her pockets. Another thought streamed in, Rose's questions about the dreams. Tabitha had managed to dodge them, at least for now. Her nightmares would stay hidden, concealed in their own dark mists. Still, she, too, wondered about the dreams, their purposes, their meanings. Who was the mysterious black girl who shared Rose's terror in the night shadows? What were they so afraid of?

As real shadows grew all around, signaling the last stretch of the sun's dying rays, a tingle began creeping up Tabitha's back, making the hair on her neck rise. Somehow she knew the answers would soon be revealed.

Chapter 4

TABITHA SOFT-STEPPED into her father's office and paused just inside the door. Near the wall on the far side, her father sat in a wheeled swivel chair. With his reading glasses sliding low and his torso leaning over his desk, he seemed entranced by the contents of a book, thick and ancient looking. A bright desk lamp illuminated his study, casting his shadow across the bare carpet between her and him.

She tiptoed over the shadow and slid a sheet of paper next to the book.

Removing his glasses, he picked up the page. "What's this?"

"The drawing." She folded her hands behind her. "I just finished."

He glanced at his watch. "So late? I thought you'd be in bed."

"Couldn't sleep. Knowing I had to do this was like the sword of Damocles hanging over my head. Besides, tomorrow's Saturday. No homeschool."

"I understand." His thick eyebrows arched toward his nose as he studied the drawing.

Tabitha curled her arm around his and looked on. Somehow, the multicolored pencil sketch seemed different now—more detailed, vibrant, alive—almost as if her father's gaze had transformed it into something richer and lovelier.

In the drawing, in various shades of peach, gray, and light brown, Nanna sat in an old rocker with her hands folded on a patchwork quilt, patterned in triangles of blue and green. With old-fashioned spectacles perched near the end of her nose, and a friendly smile stretching her smooth cheeks, she seemed ready to tell one of her famous folktales.

Tabitha's father turned toward her, his eyes wide. "This is really remarkable. Your artwork is truly beautiful."

Warmth surged into her cheeks. "Thank you. I wanted to do the best job I could."

He ran a finger across Nanna's face. "She looks younger, like she's maybe forty or so."

"I know. I thought it was strange that she looked so young, but I still knew right away that it was her. Maybe it's because she's in heaven now, so God restored her youth."

"Could be, but why would she need her glasses?"

Tabitha shrugged. "I just drew what I saw."

"Interesting." He slid the page back to his desk and looked her in the eye. He took on his professorial pose, a hand on his lap and another stroking his chin. "Tabitha, is it possible that you just imagined this as a way to overcome your grief? If this were a vision of heaven, wouldn't it be consistent? I mean, the youthfulness in her face makes sense, but the eyeglasses don't. I purchased those for her myself when she was about eighty."

Again warmth coursed through her face, this time so hot and fast, it rushed into her ears. "I . . . I don't know." As she lowered her head, a tremor shook her voice. "I just drew what I saw, like you asked."

He laid a hand on her shoulder. "I'm sorry, sweetheart. I didn't mean to hurt your feelings. I'm just trying to get to the bottom of this."

"It's okay. I understand." As she looked up at him, a tear tickled her cheek. "You do believe me, don't you?"

He pulled her into his lap and wrapped her in his arms. "Of course I believe you. I'm absolutely certain you saw a vision of Nanna. What I'm trying to figure out is where it came from." He tapped her on the head with a finger. "Did it come from this amazingly creative mind of yours, or was it really a picture of Nanna in heaven?"

She kept her gaze on his deep blue eyes. "You don't believe it was from heaven, do you?"

"You're a sharp girl, Tabitha." He ran a hand through her hair. "I won't hide from you that I'm leaning that way, but I promise I'll think about it."

She let a smile break through. "I guess it's not really important. I mean, what difference does it make, right?"

He pushed a wayward hair from her face, then averted his eyes. His hesitation seemed too long, much too long.

"I'll pray about it, Tabitha. Just go to bed, and we'll talk more later."

After they exchanged pecks on the cheek, she slid off his lap. She reached for the drawing but quickly drew back her hand. Maybe it would be better to let him keep it. If he looked at it long enough, maybe he'd eventually see it her way.

As she again tiptoed over his shadow, she called back, "Good night, Daddy."

"Good night. Sweet dreams."

She hurried out of the office, down the hallway, and into her bedroom. Again, Sarah had already fallen asleep, but this time she had left the floor lamp on. A handwritten note lay on Tabitha's bed.

She picked it up, glancing at her sleeping sister as she read. "Please wake me if you need me. I love you. Sarah."

After turning off the lamp, Tabitha folded the note and laid it on her night table. As she sat on her bed, she looked across the carpet separating her from her big sister. It would take only three steps to walk across and slide into Sarah's bed, two, if she took giant steps.

She laughed to herself. *One, if a monster's chasing me.*

After finding Deborah next to her pillow, she wrapped her up tight and nestled under the covers. She breathed in her doll's scent— old cloth and yarn mixed with laundry detergent. The smell of death and loss had faded away with the rinse cycle, but Deborah's reminders of many years with her mistress remained. She would be enough to help Tabitha fall asleep in peace.

Yet, peace seemed elusive. Her father's doubts echoed. *I'll pray about it, Tabitha.*

What did that mean? Would he pray for wisdom to find out if the vision came from heaven? Or would he just pray for a way to tell her that he didn't believe it?

She closed her eyes and imagined her surroundings, counting all the comforts of familiarity—Sarah, strong and confident; the floor, solid and supporting; the dim light from the hallway, an illuminated path that would bring her parents running should she cry out for help.

A shiver ran up and down her spine. Soon, new dreams would filter into her mind, possibly more dark and scary dreams of people being stalked by unseen predators. What did they mean? Whom would she dream about next? The shiver spread to her skin, raising goose bumps, yet it wasn't terror, not really. Another chance to peer into eternity carried a thrill. It was a daring glimpse over a cliff, a wild ride on a swaying bridge, an unbuckled plunge down a roller coaster, yet with a safety rope tied to her waist during each dramatic adventure. She would always wake up and escape the fall.

The images of her room warped and grew vague, a sure sign that the world of dreams was drawing near. As darkness folded her in, doubts arose. Why would God send her prophecies, predictions of blessings for some and doom for others? Was she some kind of prophetess? Or was she just a gullible little girl who couldn't separate reality from fantasy? Maybe it would be better if the whole thing just went away. Maybe if she ignored the dreams long enough, they would dry up and never come back.

Rose's face drifted into her thoughts. It had been a few days since she had talked to Rose about God, and no real opportunities had arisen since. Did seeing her now mean that she should try to carry the conversation further? She didn't want to be pushy, but letting the issue die didn't make sense, either.

A multitude of faces and scenes flowed like a river through her mind, but none stopped to form a true dream. After what seemed like hours, the river shrank to a stream, then to a creek, as if someone had dammed the flow somewhere upstream. A dark sky took over the landscape of her mind, a million stars sparkling against the black canopy. They drifted back and forth, as if dancing to music, though all was silent.

Tabitha fluttered her eyelids open and stared into the darkness. The light from the hallway had dimmed further, and the door had been pulled nearly closed. She sat up in bed and set her feet on the carpet. Now wide awake, her turmoil still churning, she knew sleep wouldn't return anytime soon.

She looked at her window. The thick drapes, bright and pink during daylight hours, had been drawn together. Would the stars outside be as glorious as they were in her most recent dream?

What time was it, anyway? She turned to her night table and read the digital clock. Two thirty. Everyone would be asleep by now.

With a blanket draped over one shoulder, she slipped on her house shoes and sneaked out of her bedroom. Then, cautiously opening the front door, begging the latch to be courteous enough to muffle its click, she glided out to the porch and down the steps. The moonless, early morning sky was stark and cold, displaying a clear, star-filled blackness all around.

Tabitha strolled out onto the driveway, wrapping the blanket around her shoulders as she walked on the balls of her feet. When she found a good sitting spot near the street, she plopped down, crossed her legs, and stared at the heavens.

As in her night vision, stars speckled the black ceiling, bright and twinkling, though, of course, they didn't dance. Still, it seemed as though the dream acted as a beckoning call, as if someone had invited her to step into this unguarded sea of glory.

The awesome endlessness of infinity flooded her senses. With no rope tethering her to the security of home and family, her mind raced into the deep distances, flying by galaxies and nebulae at hyper speed. Stars zipped by, some white and blazing, others red and pulsing like dying embers. Icy comets, dark asteroids, and gaseous planets of blue, red, and silver drifted past at various speeds. This interstellar roller coaster was better than anything Disney could ever build.

Shivers again tickled her skin and raised bumps from head to toe. Wrapping herself tightly, Tabitha drew her mind back to reality. With cold and darkness again holding sway, her troubling dreams and their haunting turmoil returned. She looked into the sky and, focusing on an empty spot in the midst of the stars, spoke into the cold air, using a candid but respectful tone. "God, I need to ask you about my dreams. You already know all about them, so I guess I don't need to describe them to you, but I do need to know what you want me to do about them."

After a deep sigh, she went on. "Are you trying to teach me something? Is there something you want me to do? I'm already talking to Rose about you, but I don't know who the other people are that I see in the dreams." She paused a few seconds, dropped her gaze, and moaned, "I don't know what else to say, so please help me."

A cool breeze found a gap in her cocoon, forcing her to wrap the blanket even more tightly. Her shivering body begged to go back inside where it was warm, but it could wait. Mornings like this were always Daddy's favorite time to go stargazing, sometimes providing a few streaking meteors showing off their flaming tails like proud peacocks of the night. At least that's what he called them. They never seemed to want to strut for her, yet he had promised that if she waited long enough, someday one would spread its beautiful tail for her. Maybe she would be lucky enough to see one this morning.

After a minute or two, a long streak of pale yellow light, bright but fleeting, sizzled across the sky and disappeared in a flickering instant.

"Oooh!" she sang out. "That must have been one!"

She stared even harder, examining each pinpoint of light, hoping to see the majestic spectacle once again. Maybe God was trying to encourage her by showing off this tiny miracle, mere seconds after she had hoped to see one.

"Oh, one more would really be a sign." She clutched the blanket with tight fists. "Just one more."

As if trying to rip apart the fabric dividing this world and the next, she drilled her stare into the backdrop. Ten seconds passed, then twenty. A full minute. Finally, something changed, so strange, she blinked twice before resuming her stare. Tiny lights in the distant sky shifted, as if trading places or playing musical chairs. How many were there? Maybe ten or twelve? They couldn't be stars; they were shifting too quickly, and they seemed to be moving around each other in some sort of pattern.

She blinked once more. Yes, it was definitely a pattern, like they were dancing in a choreographed play. The points formed a circle, then drew together in the center and exploded out again, spinning around the focus at blinding speed. Once the spinning stopped, they tumbled over and around one another in a rollicking celebration of togetherness, as if congratulating themselves for being such good dancers. The show lasted for twenty, maybe thirty seconds; then, as abruptly as it had begun, it ended, and the lights disappeared.

Tabitha stood and clapped her hands. "Wow!" she cried. "Stars dancing in the sky!" She spun in a circle with her hands in the air, still gripping her blanket and letting it float like a cape in the wind. "Wheee! God told the angels to dance for me!"

After several more spins, she stopped and gasped for air, her hot breaths condensing into white puffs all around. For a moment, the stars continued to orbit her head, her dizziness making the dance continue. She lowered herself to her knees and bowed her head. Closing her eyes this time, she prayed in a whisper, "Thank you, God. Now I know you're giving me visions of heaven, no matter what anyone else thinks."

* * *

John Hanson jerked his head up and looked around. With the desk lamp illuminating the office, he quickly drew in the missing pieces of the puzzle. Obviously he had fallen asleep studying, kind of unusual, but with the events of recent days plaguing his mind, his exhaustion seemed reasonable. Only a few hours of sleep for a week would drain anyone.

Something weighed down his shoulders. He shrugged, letting a blanket slide down his back. The warm covering proved that Melody had come to give a silent goodnight, not wanting to awaken him.

After a long yawn and stretch, John picked up Tabitha's drawing and stared at it, blankly at first, but as the details of her colorful sketch took hold, its simple beauty mesmerized him again. There was something odd about it, something he couldn't quite put his finger on.

Letting his eyes drift slowly over the picture from top to bottom, he studied each detail. Everything seemed logical. Nanna's hair was styled the way Tabitha had often seen it, and her glasses were the same ones she had used the last few years of her life. She wore her burial dress, a simple flower print, certainly an appropriate choice for a young girl who hoped for a vision of heaven.

His gaze halted at the quilt on Nanna's lap. The blue and green diamond-shaped patches seemed familiar, but not from a recent memory. From what source had Tabitha conjured this? Maybe a photo?

After standing slowly and arching his back to uncoil from his awkward sleeping position, he snatched up the drawing, strode into the hallway, and flipped on the light. Dozens of portraits covered the walls on either side. Walking at a snail's pace, he stared at each one. Fewer than a third featured Nanna, and the quilt appeared in none.

Picking up his pace, he marched to the opposite end of the house, guided by a series of night-lights plugged in at strategic locations. He stopped at the kitchen, opened a cupboard door, and plucked a key from a hook inside before continuing.

Near the doorway to the garage, he pulled down a collapsible stairway from its ceiling hideout. After scaling the fifteen wooden steps, he pulled a string, lighting a bare bulb attached to the attic wall.

Dust caked nearly everything—from old bicycles, to Christmas decorations, to piles of books that he would someday read when he found the time. As he shuffled across the bare wood floor, his sneakers raised tiny clouds into the air. He coughed and waved his hands to clear his breathing space. His target, an old trunk near the far corner, should provide a quick answer. Then he could get out of this dust trap and go to bed.

He knelt in front of a weathered trunk and inserted the long key into a hole. For a moment, the key wouldn't budge. Gripping it tightly in his palm, he turned with all his might, hoping the old metal wouldn't break. If it didn't open soon, he would shoot in some WD-40, but he would have to go back downstairs for that.

Finally, the lock emitted a grinding sound and gave way. He flipped up a pair of brass latches, raising a dull clank. As he lifted the heavy wooden lid, the hinges in the back creaked. Holding the lid open with one hand, he rummaged through the contents with the other—Grandpa's shirts and pants, old *Reader's Digest* and *National Geographic* magazines, and a stack of framed photos.

Sliding his fingers behind the top frame, he picked it up. Dressed in a blue and white pinafore from days gone by, the towheaded girl in the photo clutched a rag doll and sat on a high-back upholstered chair. Cracks etched the plaster background, drawing jagged lines through the angled shadow of a taller person, perhaps an adult who had helped the girl pose and then stepped out of the way in time for the photographer's flash.

John drew the frame close. The girl looked remarkably like Tabitha—same hair, same eyes, and even the same age. If not for the newness of the doll, this could have passed for a portrait of Tabitha and Deborah, though the subtle differences were plain enough to a parent's eyes—a slightly larger nose than Tabitha's, a more rounded chin, and shallower dimples.

He set the frame down. This girl had to be Nanna—Nattie, as family members called her in her younger years. In her later diaries she had described herself as shy to a fault, so getting her to smile so convincingly for this photo was probably quite a feat.

Reaching deep into the treasures, John pulled a handful of soft material from underneath the pile of photos, a patchwork quilt of blue and green diamonds Nanna had made. Broken stitches and worn edges gave evidence of hundreds of nestling nights, children cuddling on Grandpa's lap for songs or bedtime stories, or a tall tale that even the youngest listeners knew was nothing more than an impossible yarn spun by the imagination of a man born long before the age of television.

"I *thought* I had seen this before," he whispered. In his later years, Grandpa had often used the quilt to cover his aging legs, too feeble then for bouncing children, though he would still spin a yarn or two when the great-grandchildren visited. When he died, Nanna couldn't bear to look at it and asked that it be stowed away someplace safe. And here it had rested ever since.

John stuffed the quilt back in place. As he lowered the lid of the trunk, concealing Grandpa's possessions once more, he caught another glimpse of a magazine. Grandpa used to love sitting and reading out loud, especially the humor section in *Reader's Digest*, trying to get a laugh out of Nanna. Of course, she had always obliged, even if the jokes weren't very funny.

John drummed his fingers on the trunk. Ten years had passed since he packed the quilt away and slid the trunk into this corner, long before Tabitha was old enough to understand what was inside. But could she have come up here more recently? If so, how could she have turned the key?

He left the key in the lock and soft-stepped back to the stairwell, not wanting to startle any sleepers who might wonder about an intruder stalking the attic. As he paused with his fingers around the lightbulb's string, he looked back at the trunk. Maybe Tabitha had seen the quilt as a two-year-old and remembered it in her subconscious mind. But was that the most logical option? Not really. The chances of her seeing it at all were low enough, and her remembering it ten years later and attaching it to Nanna seemed even more unlikely, especially considering that she was able to reproduce it with such precision.

He pulled the string, darkening the room. Maybe it would be better to wait a while longer before drawing conclusions. If Tabitha really was hallucinating, therapy might be in order, as Phil had suggested, but that wasn't an option to jump into without complete certainty. And even if he and Melody decided to go in that direction, Phil wouldn't be their chosen doctor. After all, he was an atheist. He didn't believe in anything beyond the physical. How could he possibly discern the spiritual aspects that could be involved?

After tiptoeing down, John slowly raised the access stairs. Once they settled in place, he walked through the dim blue glow of the night-lights, each one plugged in near a closed door. He stopped at Tabitha's and Sarah's room, pushed the door ajar, and peeked in. Tabitha sat upright, her blanket draped over her shoulders.

"Daddy?" she whispered.

He grasped the knob and pushed the door open a few more inches. "Yes, Tabitha. I'm here."

"Can't you sleep, either?"

"I was asleep." He chuckled softly. "In my office with my head over a book, like some overzealous workaholic. I'm going to bed now."

"Oh." A moment of silence ensued. Even in the dim light, her eyes seemed to sparkle. "I saw something strange tonight, Daddy."

"In your dreams?"

"I don't think so. I wasn't in bed."

He paused. Should he trust her perception, show more confidence in her version of reality than his own? He quietly cleared his throat. "Another vision of heaven?"

"Maybe." Silent seconds passed by again, counted by John's ticking watch. "It seemed just as real as Nanna at the funeral."

John tightened his grip on the knob. What now? Dreams often seemed so real, even to the point of convincing us that we're awake. Sometimes only the light of full day stripped off their hypnotizing shell. But he couldn't show any hint of skepticism, especially since he had no good reason to doubt her word.

As his watch measured his own silent pause, he gazed into Tabitha's eyes, shadowed yet fully sincere. "Do you want to talk about it now or in the morning?"

She yawned before resting again on her pillow. "I think morning would be better. I'm sure I'll remember it."

"Very well. Just let me know when you're ready." He kept his hand on the knob. Was another bedtime kiss in order now? One part of his brain said, yes, of course; she needed his reassurance. She had gone through so much emotional turmoil. Yet, another part said no; bedtime had long passed, and a kiss now would send a message of condescension: Daddy didn't really trust his little girl's words. She was too young and inexperienced to understand the heights of heaven's gateways or the depths of spiritual discernment. No, treating her like a baby would definitely give the wrong impression.

His watch ticked. As he kept his gaze locked on her snuggled form, the lyrics of his recent rocking-chair poem echoed in his mind.

I'll never get too old or big to take my special place. So Daddy, dear, when I grow up, reserve my parking space!

Easing the door open farther, he stepped in and walked to her bedside. As he knelt, the sounds of heavy, rhythmic breathing rose to his ears. He bit his lip. It was too late. His stupid self-debate had spoiled a potentially precious moment. Once again his logic and emotions had been unable to compromise. Tabitha could be tuned in on heaven's frequency, a little girl so in love with God that she could see through the veil clouding the ultimate reality for most mere mortals. And at the same time, she could remain his little girl, a doll-clutching preteen who would still sit in his lap and sing songs in time with the squeaks of an old rocking chair.

He leaned close and kissed her cheek. Whispering softly, he said, "I believe in you, Tabitha. Don't let my doubts close the curtains of heaven. I'm ready to have my eyes opened and see through yours."

* * *

"Tabitha!" Her mother sang out. "Telephone for you!"

Tabitha popped out of her bedroom and hurried to the kitchen. She glanced at the clock on the wall. It was only eight twenty in the morning. Who would be calling so early?

She grabbed the phone. "Hello?"

"Tabitha, it's me, Rose."

"Hi. You comin' over today?"

"Can't. Gotta go to another funeral. There's a girl in my class that has a sister who got killed in a wreck a couple of days ago. Her name's Kashema Williams."

Tabitha glanced up at her mother, who was looking for something in the bakery cupboard, but obviously listening in. "Oh, that's too bad," Tabitha said. "Did you know her?"

"I saw her once in a while. But since I know her sister, Tonya, Dad wants us to go. Another one of those lessons in life. Ya know what I mean?"

"Too well." Tabitha sat down at one of the breakfast-table chairs. "I guess I won't see you today then."

"I was hoping you'd come with us."

"To the funeral?"

"Yeah, it's at one o'clock. Can't you come? It's Saturday. You don't have lessons, do you? I can never figure out the schedule you home-schoolers keep."

"Let me ask my mom." Tabitha covered the mouthpiece and turned toward her mother. "Rose wants me to go with her and her father to a funeral. That's kind of a strange request, isn't it?"

Her mother pulled a bottle of olive oil from the cabinet and set it on the counter. "Not really. You asked her to come to Nanna's funeral, didn't you? It's probably something she really doesn't want to do, so she wants some company to make it a little easier."

"Oh." Tabitha glanced at the phone. "You probably don't want me to go with her, right? I mean, since you're going grocery shopping this afternoon, you probably need me to stay home to babysit, right?"

Her mother smiled. "I think you should go. Just get your morning chores done, and you'll be free for the day. I think Sarah's around to watch Jonathan."

"She is." She lowered her head until her chin almost touched her chest. Of course she should help Rose. Who would want to be alone at a time like this? But attending another funeral wasn't exactly the best idea for a fun Saturday. Besides, it was sure to bring back memories of her troubling dreams.

After washing dishes and vacuuming, Tabitha changed clothes and moped around the house, watching the clock. When the hours finally ticked by, she shuffled outside and stood in the driveway, her hands folded behind her. She smoothed out her dark gray dress, probably the best choice. This would be only her second funeral, so she wasn't sure, but black would likely be the color of the day. The fabric was warm, perfect for this breezy, late autumn afternoon.

As she shuffled her feet, the hem flapped against her calves. What would Dr. Grayson say? Would he ask about the vision of Nanna and her drawing? He meant well, but he couldn't possibly understand. He seemed like a color-blind man trying to describe a rainbow, insisting that the bands had to be shades of gray. How could he fathom the mysteries of realities he couldn't even see?

Tabitha glanced at her watch. Rose was ten minutes late, very unusual for her, especially considering her father was driving. She had once said, "Dad has an internal atomic clock, and I inherited it. We're Mr. and Miss Punctual."

When Dr. Grayson's tea-colored Honda pulled up to the curve, Rose rolled down the window. Her face pale, and her eyelids half closed, she leaned back on the headrest in the front passenger's seat. "Sorry, Tabitha. I got a headache, so I had to lie down. Before I knew it, Dad said it was time to go. I wasn't even dressed."

"That's okay. I hope you're feeling better." Tabitha opened the back door and slid in. "You do look kind of pale."

"I'm just tired. I took some Advil, so my head isn't splitting now."

"And how are you doing today, Tabitha?" Dr. Grayson asked.

"Fine, thank you."

He put the car into gear and accelerated. "Any more . . . uh . . . visions?"

"Well . . ." Tabitha caught sight of Dr. Grayson's eyes in the rearview mirror. He was looking directly at her. "Didn't my father talk to you yet? I drew the picture."

He shook his head. "I understand your reticence. Your parents certainly aren't obligated to acquire my services, and family matters such as this are deeply personal, so I won't pry any further."

Tabitha scooted closer to the door and looked down at her folded hands on her lap. "Thank you for understanding."

"To change the subject," Dr. Grayson continued, "I should tell you that this service will likely be quite different from your great-grand-mother's. The violent death of such a young person will be seen as far more tragic than the gentle passing of a long-suffering, aged lady."

"Yeah," Rose said, turning toward Tabitha. "And Kashema was into drugs and alcohol, and she had two abortions. She was driving drunk at the time of the accident, so she was probably the cause of her own death."

Her father frowned. "That's enough, Rose. There's no need to speak ill of the departed."

Tabitha scrunched lower. Maybe going to this funeral wasn't such a good idea.

Soon, they pulled into a gravel-topped parking lot, jammed with dozens of cars, trucks, and SUVs. When Dr. Grayson found a spot for his compact car, everyone squeezed out and quickly marched to the adjacent church. With pristine white boards wrapping its two-story frame and tall steeple, it looked like a throwback to an earlier century, something from a Mark Twain novel or a Civil War movie.

Tabitha searched the grounds. No one milled around outside, so they had to be pretty late. A tall, withered black man opened the front door and bade them a friendly "Good afternoon" as they entered. Tabitha returned his smile and followed Dr. Grayson and Rose to a half-empty pew in the very back.

A choir had already assembled behind the pulpit, about thirty black men and women, mostly women, adorned in bright green robes with white collars. The organ crooned a rhythmic, soulful piece. Tabitha hummed along quietly. It was sad but pretty, a melody that begged for words. It must have held power, because as the chords wafted across the sanctuary, they seemed to create an invisible current. First came ripples of nodding heads and whispers of "Thank you, Jesus" and then shifting and swaying robes in the choir loft. As the organ played on, the waves of passion moved upward into the throats of the choristers and began flowing out as they softly hummed.

Another robed man, a middle-aged gentleman who had been sitting in a chair on the stage, smiled, like a cook who recognized the aroma of readiness. He stood, and with a wave of his hand, a cascade of emotion poured forth from the choir in a sweet, poetic melody. It told a story, a tale of pain and bondage, of crying and prayer, and of final release and rest in paradise. In very few words it moved from sympathy and grief to happiness and celebration, from sadness and tears to joy and clapping hands.

A young girl in the choir's front row began to sing, her face glowing as she lifted her head and presented an offering in musical solo. With her angelic company humming around her, the voice of the bright cherub resonated, casting the brilliant tones of a warbling songbird throughout the building. This was not simply the rote presentation of a well-practiced hymn. No, it echoed with passion as the young nightingale sang a requiem to her lost friend, her eyes glistening with tears, her face contorting during the soulful refrain.

The assembly stirred with the swirling passion. A strange mixture of smiles and weeping broke out on the faces of young and old alike. Some stood and waved their hands; others sat and buried their eyes in handkerchiefs. One lady sitting in front of Tabitha began shouting "Praise the Lord!" and her cry repeated with every beat of the penetrating melody.

Shouts of joy, sobs of mourning, and even dancing swirled into a confusing brew in Tabitha's mind. The familiar doubts and questions arose again. Was this a happy time? A sad time? How can it be both at once?

Rose's earlier gossip filtered back into Tabitha's mind. With drug abuse, drunkenness, and sexual promiscuity proving her rebellion, Kashema couldn't have been a real Christian. That could only mean one thing. Her death would be followed by eternal punishment. There should be only sadness at a time like this.

Tabitha's thoughts drifted to a recent history lesson her mother had taught. This funeral service was reflecting a heritage of viewing death as an escape from bondage, the only true release from the slavery that held the black race in chains in this life. The wicked torment of that people during the previous centuries was buried in the past, but the present culture carried some of its memories, in traditions and customs if not in attitude.

As new lyrics sprang forth, telling of a grand reunion day in the sky, Tabitha slumped her shoulders. Kashema was traveling from what she thought was freedom to a bondage that would last forever. The singers had it all backwards. This service was a lie! A sham! Tabitha let her tears flow. From deep inside, a wail begged to escape, but she swallowed it down. It would be too much. The poor girl couldn't be helped now. It was too late, much too late.

Tabitha peeked at Rose. A tear trickled down her cheek as well. But why? Not for Kashema's soul. Rose didn't even believe in an eternal soul. Yet, if something horrible like this ever happened to Rose, she, too, would come face-to-face with the everlasting Judge and be cast into eternal darkness, forever to run from her tormentors, year after year, century after century, millennia after millennia.

As everyone stood up and started sidestepping toward the aisles, Tabitha shook herself back to reality. She shot to her feet and wiped her eyes with a knuckle. The parade of people shuffled toward the front, pushing her along at barely more than a snail's pace. Soon, between two huge collections of flowers, a coffin came into view near the pulpit.

Tabitha shivered. Every step brought her closer and closer to the dead body. But why the anxiety? After all, she had never met this girl before. Tabitha was only here because her friend had asked her to come. There was no sense of loss, no need to say good-bye, no worry about whether or not she should grieve.

She kept her gaze trained on the flowers, then the pulpit, then the high-heeled shoes of the stately lady now viewing the body. Then Dr. Grayson looked into the casket and nodded respectfully. Rose copied his motions to a tee. In just a few seconds, it would be Tabitha's turn. She would just get a quick glance and leave right away. No use causing a scene by letting that wail rise to her lips, a lament that would surely raise questions about this white stranger who seemed to love Kashema so much.

But when she finally reached the side of the casket, Tabitha froze in place, staring at the dainty head so delicately pressing the white satin beneath it. She gulped. She had seen Kashema before, in her nightmare, the black girl who ran from the terrors of the darkness!

The wail pushed up again, and again Tabitha swallowed it down. This time it hurt. She cried inside. Tears streamed. She had to get out before she lost control.

She slowly backed away from the coffin, then hurried to catch up with Rose as the line of mourners filed toward the exit. She let the dreams replay in her mind. Kashema and Nanna had both traveled through the darkness of the night visions before they died. Nanna was a Christian; Kashema apparently was not. Nanna was accompanied by a loving guide; this girl was hunted by an evil predator.

Tabitha took a quick peek back at the coffin. A tall somber man made ready to close the lid. What could it all mean? Did this girl go to hell, captured by some haunting wraith and dragged away to everlasting torment? Were the expressions of grief she had just witnessed so terribly insufficient? How could anyone properly bewail the loss of an eternal soul?

As she plodded back to the Graysons' car, she kept her head low. Rose and her father would want to talk about the funeral. After all, that was Dr. Grayson's reason for taking Rose in the first place, to teach her about life and the finality of the end of life—a conversation Tabitha wanted to avoid.

She slid into the backseat, and this time, Rose joined her. As soon as they made their way out of the crowded parking lot, Dr. Grayson piped up. "I'm sure you noticed, Rose, that the expressions of grief at this funeral were much more obvious than they were at the previous one. Kashema was younger, her accident was tragic, and familial relations were likely never healed before she passed away."

"They sang a lot about heaven." Rose smiled, frequently glancing at Tabitha as if looking for a reaction. "I guess that helped them feel better."

"In the midst of tragedy, humans need something they can grasp," Dr. Grayson said. "Hope is the ultimate soother of sorrows. Hope keeps people going. If not for hope, no one could survive for long, even if they're hanging on to the false hope of an afterlife." Tabitha saw his eyes appear in the rearview mirror again. "I apologize, Tabitha," he said. "I shouldn't cast aspersions on your family's beliefs."

"It's okay." Tabitha shifted her gaze to the passing houses outside. "I'm not offended."

As Rose and her father chattered on, now turning to planning the rest of their day, Tabitha looked at every person they passed by—a hunched-over man walking a lively schnauzer, a young woman jogging with headphones attached to a hip-mounted radio, a man and a woman in dirty jeans and T-shirts walking hand in hand. What hopes were these people living for? Love? Significance? A good time? But what good were any of those hopes in the long run? When these people died, every hope they ever had on earth would become a vapor that faded away when they stood before the Judge of all souls.

Without moving her head, she shifted her eyes toward Rose and her father. How could they understand? How could she ever explain the spiritual world to them? Yes, Rose was smiling now, but was she in peril, teetering on the edge of destruction? Like Kashema, Rose had also been hunted in the dark dream, stalked by the mysterious, relentless shadow. What would become of her? Was she also assigned to hell, destined for destruction? Were the shadow dreams really prophetic? And what about last night's display in the sky? Were those lights really dancing angels?

Dizziness swirled Tabitha's thoughts, and a familiar shiver gripped her spine. She could not get home soon enough.

Chapter 5

THE DREAM had become all too familiar, the dimness of late dusk and a hazy nightscape, foglike but with a supernatural aspect. Lurking shadows signaled the presence of a light source, but the light remained hidden, allowing the darkness to reign and the shadows to strike fear with impunity.

Rose was there again, still haunted, still hunted. Her screams continued, frightening shrieks that seemed to pour from every orifice. Her eyes told most of the story, wide open orbs, wild and white with horror. The dream ended in the usual fashion, with Rose's final terror screaming through Tabitha's throat.

"Tabitha!" Sarah called out from her bed. "What's wrong?"

Tabitha sat upright, her face in her hands.

Sarah jumped to her feet, crossed the gap between the beds in a bound, and sat next to Tabitha. As she cradled Tabitha's head against her shoulder, she crooned softly. "That's the third time this week. When are you going to tell me about it?"

Tabitha shook her head, her eyes buried in Sarah's nightgown. "It's too scary, and you probably wouldn't believe me if I told you what I think it means."

Sarah gently stroked her sister's temples with her fingertips. "I can't know for sure what I'll believe, but I know you wouldn't lie. You'll tell me the truth the best you can."

Tabitha looked up. Sarah's kind eyes twinkled in the dim light. Older and wiser, she seemed to pour out sympathy.

"Let me help you bear the burden," Sarah whispered, wiping away Tabitha's tears with her thumb.

"Give me a minute." Tabitha swallowed a lump. Even thinking about describing the nightmare made her sick to the stomach. Could she do it without crying again?

Sarah began humming. It started out as something sweet but nondescript and then transformed into a familiar hymn. Tabitha added the lyrics, singing it in her mind.

> *Be still, my soul; the Lord is on thy side;*
> *Bear patiently the cross of grief or pain;*
> *Leave to thy God to order and provide;*
> *In every change he faithful will remain.*
> *Be still, my soul; thy best, thy heavenly friend*
> *Through thorny ways leads to a joyful end.*

Tabitha sniffed and rubbed the remaining tears from her eyes. As Sarah's hum continued, quieter now, Tabitha related her dreams, beginning with those about Nanna and finishing with the recurring nightmares of Rose.

"I think I'm seeing people who are going to die," Tabitha explained. "Nanna was a Christian, so someone was with her; Jesus, I think. That girl who died in the car crash wasn't a Christian, so she didn't have a guide. I saw them both before they died, and now I'm seeing Rose almost every night."

Sarah nodded, her eyes now aimed toward the ceiling. "That's very interesting."

"Do you think . . ." Tabitha's voice elevated to a higher pitch. "Do you think Rose is going to die?"

"I don't know," Sarah murmured as she continued her gentle massage. "I just don't know."

Her sister's tender fingers eased Tabitha's shakes but not her shattered emotions. She couldn't help the hint of a whine in her voice. "I think it means she's going to die and go to hell."

"I see." Sarah paused for several seconds, still humming. "Have you told Daddy about these dreams?"

"Not in detail."

"Well, Rose and her parents admit they're atheists. And we also know what the Bible says about the final destiny of unbelievers."

"So she *is* going to hell," Tabitha concluded.

"But she can repent and believe."

Tabitha half closed one eye. "But what if she's pre . . . predestinated."

"Predestined?"

Tabitha nodded. "Right. If my dreams predict it, doesn't that mean it's already decided?"

Sarah laughed softly. "You know we don't believe in the kind of predestination that would keep us from having hope. You've heard Daddy. God predestined that all believers will be saved, and anyone can become a believer."

Tabitha shook her head. "I never did understand that."

Sarah pushed Tabitha back. "This is all you need to understand. If Rose repents and believes in Jesus, she will be saved. And if her time to go is soon, then you have to be diligent to help her come to Christ soon."

Tabitha shivered. The night terrors still chilled her soul. "Do you think it's all true? I mean, do my dreams see into the future? Do they see who's going to die and what's going to happen to them?"

Sarah rubbed Tabitha's back, pushing warmth into her skin. "There's a Bible verse Daddy taught me once. I had some dreams that were bothering me, so I made sure I memorized it. It's Job thirty-three, verses fifteen and sixteen, and it goes like this: 'In a dream, a vision of the night, when sound sleep falls on men, while they slumber in their beds, then he opens the ears of men, and seals their instruction.'"

"I don't think I've heard that one."

"With all you're going through, maybe it would be a good one to memorize. Since your dreams have proven themselves true twice, and one of them was a person you didn't even know existed, I would guess there's some message from God."

"Or the Devil trying to scare me, maybe?"

Sarah took both of Tabitha's hands into hers and gazed into her eyes. "As long as you do what's right, you don't have to worry about that."

"Do what's right? You mean tell Rose about Jesus?"

"That's what I would guess, wouldn't you?"

"But her father won't like it," Tabitha said. "Rose might tell him, and maybe he won't let us be together anymore."

Sarah nodded. "I'm afraid that's a real problem, but you can't afford to worry about it."

"Easy for you to say."

Sarah winked. "Oh, yeah?"

"Yeah." Tabitha pointed at her. "You're not the one who has to speak up."

Laying her palms on her chest, Sarah gasped in mock pain. "You got me, Sister! Right in the heart!"

"Then will you help me?"

"You mean, talk to Rose?"

"Sure." Tabitha shrugged. "I mean, you're the one with all the Bible verses memorized."

Sarah grinned. "Don't con me, kid. You know more than I did at your age." She kissed Tabitha on the forehead. "I'll help you. How about if I take you both out to lunch after church tomorrow? If you promise to start the conversation, I'll pitch in if you get in trouble."

Tabitha extended her hand. "It's a deal."

* * *

As soon as Tabitha and her family arrived home from church, Tabitha rushed to the answering machine. No messages. She hurried to the kitchen, picked up the mobile phone, and punched the speed dial for the Graysons. Maybe if she was home, they could still set up their lunch date.

A male voice answered. "Grayson residence."

"Oh, hi, Dr. Grayson. It's Tabitha. Is Rose home?"

"Yes, but she came down with some kind of bug."

"Really? Is it bad?"

"The usual symptoms—headache, fever, body aches, loss of appetite—so she's sleeping. Can I give her a message?"

"Um . . ." Tabitha glanced at Sarah as she trailed the rest of their siblings into the house. "Do you mind telling her that I'll pray for her? I mean, I know you don't believe in—"

"Don't worry about that, Tabitha. I'll tell her, and I'll have her call you when she's able."

"Okay. Thank you."

"You're welcome. Good-bye."

"Good-bye." Tabitha bit her lip. This was not good, not good at all.

Sarah walked into the kitchen. With dark brown hair draped over the shoulders of her navy dress, her bright blue eyes seemed to shine. "What's wrong, munchkin?"

"Rose is sick today, so she can't go to lunch with us. She mentioned a headache yesterday, but we both thought she was just tired."

"What does she have?"

"Sounds like the flu."

Sarah nodded. "That's really going around with the cooler weather."

"So," Tabitha said as she untied a ribbon bow on the back of her dress, "what's our next step?"

"Don't want to give up, huh?"

"Nope. This is a matter of life and death."

Sarah looked up at the ceiling, her eyes nearly closed. "How about if we take lunch *to* her?"

"I don't think so. Her father said she lost her appetite."

Kicking off her shoes as she marched toward their bedroom, Sarah called back, "Then we'll just pay her a social call."

Tabitha trotted to catch up. "And skip lunch?"

Sarah turned around and flashed a grin. "Trust me. I won't let you go hungry."

When Sarah disappeared into the bedroom, Tabitha halted at the door. "I trust you. I'm just not sure my stomach does."

* * *

About a half hour later, Tabitha and Sarah, both now dressed in jeans and T-shirts, walked along a concrete path that led through the Graysons' front lawn. Carrying a wicker picnic basket and leading the way, Tabitha kept the pace slow, hoping to come up with a good opening line.

A soft breeze blew across the neatly manicured grass, still green in spite of the cooling weather. The front porch at the end of the walkway boasted a dangling wooden swing and dozens of clusters of surrounding bushes, some with bright yellow flowers.

Tabitha soft-stepped up the stairs and halted at the top. She stared at the front door, a dark oak entrance that seemed more formidable than it ever had before, more like the opening to a lions' den than an inviting door to her friend's house.

Sarah nudged her from behind. "Go on. You can do this."

Letting her sneakers slide across the planks, Tabitha shuffled forward and pressed the doorbell. Seconds later, the door opened, and Dr. Grayson appeared. "Greetings, ladies. What can I do for you?"

As promised, Tabitha spoke up first. "Hi, Dr. Grayson. We came over to see Rose." She nodded toward Sarah. "You know my sister, Sarah, don't you?"

"We met at your great-grandmother's funeral." He smiled amiably, one hand still on the knob. "How are you, Sarah?"

Sarah returned the smile. "Fine, Dr. Grayson, but I hear Rose is under the weather. How is she feeling?"

"Not too good. This flu bug hit her pretty hard."

"May we see her?" Tabitha lifted the basket. "This might cheer her up."

Dr. Grayson shook his head, his lips tight and gray. "I don't want you to catch it."

"I had it last month," Sarah offered.

"And I never catch anything," Tabitha chimed in.

He chuckled. "Okay, but not for too long. She's tired and has to rest for her doctor's appointment."

"On a Sunday?" Tabitha asked.

"The doctor on call has agreed to see her." He glanced at his watch. "In about two hours."

"Oh, we'll be gone long before that." Tabitha nodded toward the basket. "Is it okay to offer her some food?"

"Sure. I've been trying to get her to eat something." He extended his arm toward the inside. "You know the way."

Tabitha ducked past Dr. Grayson and marched to Rose's bedroom, glancing back to make sure Sarah followed. She paused at the open bedroom door and peeked inside. Rose was sitting up in bed, her knees high and a book propped in front.

"Hey, girl," Tabitha said, holding up the basket. "We brought lunch."

Sarah joined her. "And dessert."

Rose's face, pale and gaunt, brightened. "Hi, Tabitha, Sarah." She laid the book on her stomach, pages down. "Come on in."

The girls walked by Rose's craft gallery, a wall filled with hanging baskets, hooked rugs, canvas artwork, and an assortment of decoupage mosaics. Sarah paused, gazing at Rose's labors. "These are amazing! Did you make them all?"

Rose's eyes sparkled. "Most. My mother helped me with the older ones. I can do them all myself now."

"You have a great eye for detail." Sarah touched the side of a watercolor painting. "You blend hues so well. I would have guessed this was college-level work."

A hint of redness colored Rose's cheeks. "Thank you."

Sarah walked to the bedside and took Rose's hand in a tender grip. "How are you feeling?"

Rose glanced at the touching hands, then made eye contact. "Okay, I guess. It seems to come in waves. I tried to work on my cross-stitch, but that made my head hurt too much. I can read for a few minutes at a time, though, and Dad's taking good care of me. Mom's out at Grandma's, 'cause she promised yesterday she would visit for lunch. Dad told her to go ahead."

Tabitha set the basket down and nodded toward the book. "What're you reading?"

Rose slipped her hand away from Sarah and snatched the book up again. She flipped quickly through the pages, then closed and lifted it. "It's called *When Bad Things Happen to Good People*. Dad gave it to me just after Kashema's funeral. It's supposed to help me understand pain and suffering."

Sarah took it and scanned the text on the back cover. "I've heard of this book. Doesn't it talk a lot about God?"

"Dad said it would, but he said it had a lot of good things to say. I told him I'd read it, but it's really kind of depressing."

"Oh? Depressing?" Sarah gave Tabitha a gentle nudge.

Tabitha slid her hands into her pockets and shifted from side to side. "Why is it depressing?"

Rose gave them a little shrug. "Dad's always said there's no God, but the author believes in God, and he says God isn't able to stop the suffering in the world."

Tabitha frowned. "Just because someone wrote a book about God, that doesn't make him right." She grimaced at her tone—too combative.

Sarah laid her hand on Tabitha's shoulder and gave her a reassuring squeeze. "What do you think, Rose? If God exists, would he be able to stop the suffering?"

Rose rolled her eyes upward, pausing for several seconds. "I've always thought it would be nice for God to really exist, someone to believe in, to protect me, to make me better when I'm sick. But it doesn't make sense. No one could be that powerful, and to really be God, he would have to be powerful enough to do anything."

"Well," Sarah said, "you're right about the last part . . ."

The three girls talked for the next hour about deep spiritual issues, certainly not stereotypical girl talk. With Sarah leading the way, the topics moved from the suffering of the innocent to the will of man and finally to God's purpose for mankind. Tabitha helped as much as she could, but Rose looked to Sarah for answers to tough questions. Sarah had to pause at times, but she was never completely stumped.

At the end of the hour, Rose, now paler, laid a hand over her stomach. "I'm starting to feel real sick again. I think you should go now."

"Will you at least think about what we said?" Tabitha begged. "You really need to believe before you—" She stopped short and bit her bottom lip.

Rose squinted at her. "Before I what?"

Tabitha let her head droop. "Well . . ."

Sarah stepped between Tabitha and the bed. "Tabitha thinks you should believe in Jesus before you pass another day. You never know what the next day will bring."

The furrows in Rose's brow deepened. "Is there something wrong with me that nobody's telling me?"

"Not that I know of," Sarah said. "It looks to me like you just have a bad flu."

Rose nodded, apparently satisfied. "I guess I worry too much. Every time I get sick, I think about dying. I've always been scared of dying . . . you know, no more thinking, crumbling to dust in nothingness . . ."

Sarah picked up Rose's book again and fanned through the pages. "I'd be scared of that, too, but when a person dies, there's a judgment that's much scarier for the person who doesn't believe, and most people end up in that position. It's the wide path. Believers enter in through—"

"I know," Rose said, her voice sharpening. "Tabitha told me once before. Through the narrow gate. God must not want very many people in heaven."

"No, that's not it at all," Tabitha said. "It's not narrow because God doesn't want people to come in; it's narrow because there's only one way to get in—Jesus! There are lots of ways to go to hell. God's gate is narrow, but I'm sure there's a welcome mat at the front."

Sarah and Rose stared at Tabitha, their eyes unblinking.

"Tabitha," Sarah said. "A welcome mat! That's so profound!"

"It's not like you to be so . . . so passionate," Rose added, her cheeks reddening again.

"I know." Tabitha stepped back. Warmth surged through her own cheeks. "I . . . I guess it's just so important. Will you at least think about it?"

Rose yawned, her eyes beginning to close. "Okay, I'll think about it. Thanks for coming." With that, she fell asleep.

Wrinkling her forehead, Tabitha looked at Sarah. "Is she all right?"

Sarah laid her palm on Rose's cheek. "She's real warm. We'll tell her father."

Tabitha hooked her arm into her sister's as they departed the room, leaving her ghostly looking friend all alone.

After telling Dr. Grayson about Rose's condition, the two girls left the house and strode along the sidewalk. "Do you think she'll be all right?" Tabitha asked.

Sarah paused and turned around. "She looked real bad there at the end."

Tabitha followed her sister's gaze. Rose's house, visible through a stand of tall oaks, seemed to change, taking on a morbid aspect. Somehow it looked like a mausoleum or a funeral home. It carried the feel of death.

She shuddered. "Can we go home now?"

"I know what you mean. Your dreams have me worried now, too."

They walked together in silence for another moment before Sarah continued. "I think it's time we told Daddy more about your dreams."

"Do I have to?"

"Yes, you have to. It's no use keeping it all bottled up."

Tabitha grimaced. That meant she would have to tell him every gory detail. In a way, though, it was a relief. She could finally release the pressure and give the problem to someone else. But would it do any good if he didn't believe her?

* * *

Sarah marched down the hallway, pulling Tabitha along by the hand. When they reached their father's office, Tabitha slipped free and waited just outside the door while Sarah stepped inside.

Tabitha listened. The usual tapping of fingers on a keyboard made their way into the hall, then her father's voice. "Hello, Princess."

"Dad," Sarah said, "Tabitha and I . . ." A hand reached into the hall, grabbed Tabitha's wrist, and pulled her through the doorway. "Tabitha and I have something to talk to you about."

Their father nodded toward the love seat that backed up to an adjacent wall. "Sure. Sit down."

The two sat, and Sarah looked at her sister. "Go ahead, Tabitha."

Tabitha stared at Sarah, her jaw hanging open.

Sarah nudged her with an elbow. "Daddy won't bite you."

Their father leaned forward in his swivel chair and showed his canine teeth. "Not hard, anyway."

"I, uh . . . ," Tabitha began, now staring at the ceiling.

"She's been having dreams," Sarah said.

"Yes, I've heard." He smiled, apparently enjoying the girls' interchange. "Is there something new?"

"I've been dreaming about . . ." Tabitha tightened her fingers into a fist. This was a lot harder than she had imagined.

"She's been dreaming about people who are going to die," Sarah blurted.

He made a low shushing sound. "Let Tabitha tell it," he said as he leaned back in his chair.

Tabitha closed her eyes, trying to escape Sarah's drilling stares. "I dreamed about Nanna a couple of weeks before she died. She was in this dark place, but someone, I think it was Jesus, was walking next to her." With her eyes still closed she broke into a smile. "She looked so happy and strong, stronger than I ever saw her in real life."

"Yes," her father said. "I remember you telling me about that."

"There's more." She felt her smile melting away. "On another night I started dreaming about Rose in the same place and also about another girl." She opened her eyes. "But only one at a time. They were alone there, and something was trying to get them. They were really scared. It always ended with them screaming, like they were caught, but I could never tell what was chasing them."

She stopped and looked at her father and Sarah in turn. Both had faraway stares. "I finally found out who the other girl was," Tabitha continued. "It was Kashema Williams, the girl who died in the car accident. But I never saw her before until I saw her body in the coffin, only in my dream."

Her father leaned forward, his elbows on his knees. "You mean you saw her as a stranger in your dream, never having seen her before, but you recognized her when you looked into the coffin?"

Tabitha felt a tickle on the back of her neck. "Yes."

He raised a hand to his chin. "Now that's interesting."

"And now Rose is sick." Tabitha spoke quickly. If she paused at all, she would cry for sure. "Kashema wasn't a Christian, and neither is Rose. Kashema is dead, and I'm afraid Rose is going to die, too. Does this all mean that Rose is going to die and go to hell?"

He took in a deep breath and let it out in a long sigh. "If it weren't for the dream about Kashema, I probably wouldn't think much about it. We knew that Nanna was terminally ill and that she was bound for heaven, so your dreams about her could be expected. We also know that Rose isn't a Christian, and you're concerned about her eternal destiny. But seeing a girl you've never heard of is quite remarkable. There's no natural explanation."

Apparently in thought, he closed his eyes. Tabitha looked at Sarah. She raised a shushing finger to her lips, a signal that their father needed silence to mull things over.

Finally, he blinked and leaned forward again. "Have you seen anyone else in your dreams?"

Tabitha shook her head, then stopped. "Wait a minute," she said slowly. "There *was* another one, but since it was just once, I didn't think much about it. It was on a Sunday night, I think, a couple of weeks ago. It was a man, but I haven't seen him since."

"Was Jesus with him?" Sarah asked.

"Yes. Just like with Nanna."

"What did he look like?"

"He was an old man." Tabitha set her hands against her temples. "Bald, except for on the sides."

"Tall?" her father asked. "Short? Black? White?"

Tabitha clenched her eyelids shut. "Pretty tall, I think. It's hard to tell. He was definitely a white man." She looked at her father and touched her scalp. "I remember he had a funny looking brown patch on the top of his forehead, like that Russian leader."

"Gorbachev?" her father guessed.

Tabitha made an oval with her thumbs and index fingers. "Yes, except the spot was bigger, and egg shaped."

Her father's face turned pale. "Dr. Wilkins!"

"Who?" Sarah asked.

He pulled open a desk drawer and thumbed through the files. "A seminary professor I had. He had a birth mark just like Tabitha described. He's also over six feet tall. I thought I had a picture around here somewhere."

Sarah got up and tried to look over his shoulder. "Is he still alive?"

"As far as I know. Let me make a quick phone call." He grabbed the phone and flipped through an address book. After punching the dial pad, he picked up a pencil and doodled on a calendar page. "This is John Hanson calling. Is Dr. Wilkins available?" His brow furrowed. "I see. I'm terribly sorry to hear that, Mrs. Wilkins. . . . Yes, I was a student of his almost twenty years ago. Your husband was a great man." Sweat beaded on his forehead. "I understand. No flowers. I'll be glad to make a contribution. . . . You're welcome, Mrs. Wilkins. Good-bye."

As he hung up the phone, he gazed at Tabitha and whispered, "He died yesterday morning after a long illness."

Sarah's mouth dropped open, and she stared in silence.

"Is Rose going to die?" Tabitha asked, her voice frail.

Her father put a hand on her shoulder. "Even if your dream is a prophecy of her death, we don't know how long she has. She might have years."

"She's real sick, Daddy," Sarah explained, her eyes glistening, "and she's already worried about dying."

"You talked to her?" he asked.

Tabitha buried her face in her hands and listened as Sarah continued. "Yes, we just got back from her house. Tabitha and I decided to try to witness to her, but she got too sick to listen before we could finish. She seems to have a bad case of the flu, and her father's probably taking her to the doctor right now. She's weak, but she doesn't look like she's near death or anything."

"I know she's going to die," Tabitha said, looking up at her father, "I just know it!"

Sarah patted her on the back. "Daddy, Tabitha's always been very discerning, you know."

"You're right, and it's not just her discernment I'm thinking about." He turned his chair to one side and looked at the books on the surrounding shelves.

"Any ideas, then?"

He nodded toward his shelf of Old Testament studies. "The dreams are a message we don't understand yet. God has been known to deliver puzzling dreams that reveal the future. Joseph, even as a boy, saw his family bowing down to him long before it happened. Pharaoh saw fourteen years of harvest in advance. Nebuchadnezzar saw the rise and fall of future kingdoms. Paul saw a Macedonian calling him to preach in his country. The Bible is filled with examples."

He moved his chair directly in front of Tabitha and put his hands on her shoulders. "Tabitha," he said softly, "this is nothing to worry about. If you're right, and she *is* going to die, then you've been given a wonderful gift."

Tabitha sniffed hard and spoke with a squeaking voice. "A gift? These nightmares are a gift?"

"I know you feel like you're being oppressed," he replied with a reassuring tone, "but in fact you've been blessed. How often are we informed of future possibilities? How often are we given an opportunity to act in response to a vision, to be prompted to action to prevent a tragedy? If you had never had these dreams, how long would it have taken you to start telling Rose about the Lord?"

"I . . . I don't know."

"And if she does die," he continued, "and you hadn't received this prophecy, if that's what it is, then you might have delayed too long. This teaches us to always live as though it's our last day on earth."

Tabitha wiped the flowing tears. She then firmed her lips, but her voice still squeaked. "Then we have to talk to her again, and soon."

Sarah stroked Tabitha's hair. "Let's call Rose's house again in a couple of hours. That'll give them a chance to get home from the doctor."

Tabitha shook her down-turned head. "We have to wait two hours? That'll be like waiting for a cat to fetch a stick."

* * *

Standing in the kitchen, Tabitha stared at the oven's digital clock. Only one more minute until she could call. Sure, she could cheat by a minute, but the thought of possible bad news kept her waiting. She had promised two hours, so no use changing it now. Sarah was keeping her own promise to stay away while Tabitha made the call, so it was best to stick with the plan.

She took in a long draw of the aroma hanging in the air, pot roast simmering in the oven. With her stomach growling, supper couldn't come soon enough, but her mother had planned a late evening meal. She hadn't even started the vegetables.

When the final minute ticked away, Tabitha picked up the phone, her hand shaking. Pressing the speed dial, she raised the phone to her ear and waited through two rings.

"Grayson residence."

Tabitha licked her lips. "Hi, Dr. Grayson. It's Tabitha again."

"Hello, Tabitha." His voice sounded cold and worried.

"I was . . . I was wondering how Rose is doing. I mean, you know, I was praying for her and everything. Since you said you were going to the doctor, I thought you might know something."

"Is your father home?" Now his voice sounded abrupt and commanding.

She swallowed hard. "Sure. I'll get him." Holding the phone loosely, she exited the kitchen and found her father reading a book at the family room love seat.

"Dr. Grayson wants to talk to you." Tabitha extended the phone. "Could you repeat everything he says out loud?"

"We'll see." He raised the phone to his ear. "This is John. . . . Yes, Phil. . . . Listen, do you mind if I turn on the speakerphone? Tabitha's really worried and . . . Yes, I'm sure. She's very mature for her age."

He pushed the speakerphone button on the phone and laid it on a coffee table at the center of the room. "Phil, can you hear me all right?"

Static rattled the voice coming from the speaker. "Yes, John. I can hear you."

"Go ahead." He returned to his seat. "You were telling me about Rose."

Dr. Grayson's voice trembled. "She's very sick, John. She has some brain swelling, but there's no sign of meningitis. Since there's an encephalitis alert in our area, the doctor's worried about that. We're getting some tests done at the hospital. Her mother's there with her now."

Tabitha's father reached for Tabitha and took her into his lap. "I've heard of encephalitis," he said. "How serious is it?"

"We really don't know yet. It varies greatly, but it can be fatal."

Tabitha stiffened her body. *Fatal.* That was the word she feared, the awful, hated word. Every passing second proved her fears to be true.

"Phil," her father said, "come have dinner with us. Since your wife is with Rose, she'll be fine for a while. You shouldn't be alone right now."

"Thanks, John, but I have to stay here until Myrtle's mother arrives. I was hoping to be gone already, but she just called, and it'll probably be about an hour. She lives up in Eustis and doesn't know how to get to the hospital, so I told her to stop by here and I'd give her a ride. Rose is likely to be there pretty late, so we'll both still get to be with her."

Tabitha's father whispered into her ear. "Any idea if your mother has anything planned for dinner?"

"Pot roast," she replied. "It'll take a while, but Sarah and I can whip up something else."

"Perfect." He turned back to the phone. "Phil, we'll bring some dinner over to you as soon as possible. Would that be all right?"

"Yes." His voice seemed to take on a hint of cheer. "Yes, I would like that very much."

"Then I'll send a couple of couriers over there in a little while."

"Tabitha and Sarah, I assume?"

"Yes, it's becoming a well-worn path from here to there."

"I'll be looking for them," Dr. Grayson said. "Thank you."

Tabitha scurried to find Sarah in their bedroom, told her about the plan, and the two rushed into the kitchen. They found lasagna in the refrigerator, canned green beans in the pantry, and a home-made loaf of bread in the bread drawer.

As they worked to warm up and pack everything, the busyness helped Tabitha take her mind off the death prophecy. Yet, every few minutes, Dr. Grayson's words invaded her thoughts—*Fatal. It can be fatal.* They sounded like a death knell, a low gong that called her to yet another funeral march.

She poured a steaming pot of beans into a casserole dish. "Sarah, if Daddy doesn't know what's going on, how am *I* supposed to figure it all out?"

"You don't have to." Using oven mitts, Sarah reached in and pulled the bubbling lasagna off the rack, one level above the pot roast. "Just keep doing what you're doing. Be a servant to Rose and her family. Be a witness for the truth. Let God do the rest."

While Sarah packed the dinner in a box, Tabitha looked on. "That's easier said than done."

"What?" Sarah winked. "Packing dinner?"

"No, silly. Letting God do the rest."

Sarah leaned back against the counter and pulled off her mitts. "Listen, Sister Golden Hair, letting God do his thing is really the easy part. You have plenty to do, so don't worry yourself about God's business. You can't reach into a heart to convict, you can't cleanse anyone from sin, and you can't die to save anyone, not even your best friend."

Tabitha pressed her lips together. Her sister's words stung. "Sorry. I didn't mean—"

"And I didn't mean to hurt your feelings." Sarah laid an arm around Tabitha's shoulder. "Come on. It's time to do our part."

Chapter 6

TABITHA PULLED her blanket up and turned to her side. This had to be the twentieth time she had changed positions. Sleep just wouldn't come. After delivering supper, they had heard nothing from Dr. Grayson the rest of the evening, nothing to allay Tabitha's tortured thoughts. Was Rose okay? Did the doctor figure out what was wrong? And that awful word kept echoing in her mind—*fatal, fatal, fatal.*

As she closed her eyes, Tabitha prayed once again. Was this the fourth or fifth time she had prayed since going to bed? No matter. Surely God didn't mind listening, even if it was the hundredth time.

After glancing once at Sarah, now sound asleep, she whispered, "God, please heal Rose. She's not ready to face you. If she came before your judgment seat, she'd be so scared she might just faint dead away. And even if the angels revived her, it would be too late for her to repent then, wouldn't it?"

She let out a quiet sigh. "Sarah said I can't die to save anyone, but I'd be glad to go in Rose's place. I mean, I'm looking forward to seeing you, and I'm ready to go. Maybe Rose could see that I'm not afraid to die, and that would help her have faith somehow."

She looked out her window. With the drapes open, a scattering of stars shone through the glass, yet they sat still in the purple sky. No hint of a celestial dance tonight. "Anyway," she continued, staring at the twinkling lights, "please show me what to do to help Rose. I'll do anything . . . anything at all."

Closing her eyes, she nestled into her pillow and concentrated on pleasant thoughts. Like fleeting shadows, the haunting words flew away. Sarah came to mind, then her brothers—Joshua, Andrew, and Jonathan. Was she dreaming now?

They were leaving church, everyone smiling and laughing as they strolled across the parking lot toward the family's car. It must have been an evening service, maybe in the summertime, for the setting reddish sun beat hot on Tabitha's brow. Suddenly, she halted. "I forgot my Bible!" she called as she hurried back to the sanctuary.

When she pulled open the glass door, she stepped into an empty sanctuary, dark except for the failing sunshine peering through the windows. At the front of the church, just below the speaking platform, there was an altar, an altar she knew well. On many Sundays she had seen mourners come forth to kneel and confess their sins, giving their lives to the Lord through prayers and tears.

She squinted through the dimness. Someone, a man, it seemed, sat quietly on the speaker's platform just in front of the altar, watching—waiting. She tiptoed his way. Who could this stranger be? Did he know she had entered? Would it be safe to find out, though the two of them were alone?

As she neared, she could tell that he was looking straight at her. A shiver crawled along her skin, and her heart raced. The man's eyes became visible, but the rest of his face stayed hidden in the shadows. He greeted her with a still, quiet voice. "Hello, Tabitha."

"Hi," she replied, her hands folded behind her back.

"Do you know who I am?"

Tabitha glanced around, taking note of the exits in the room before looking again at the stranger. "No."

He placed his palm on the top of the altar. "We met right here about two years ago. You were wearing a pink dress with white lace, and you had a white ribbon in your hair."

The man's easy manner felt like a balm as it washed away Tabitha's shivers. She nodded. "The day I became a Christian."

"Yes, you were kneeling in prayer."

She swallowed a lump. "I . . . I was a sinner."

"And I cleansed your heart."

Her voice began breaking. "I was crying."

"And I wiped all your tears away."

She let her gaze run along the empty altar. "So why are you here now?"

"I'm waiting for a friend of yours."

Tabitha felt herself waking up. The voices began to echo, and the images faded. Questions still burned in her mind, so she had to hurry. "Will she come? My friend, I mean."

"It's up to her."

Tabitha looked back again at the door, this time seeing it as an entrance, a way of salvation for her dearest friend. "How long will you wait?"

The man rubbed the wooden top of the kneeling bench with strong, roughened fingers. "As long as love demands."

"Does Rose have to come right here?" she asked, placing her hand on the altar next to his.

"I will meet her wherever she wishes, wherever she kneels at the altar of her heart." He took her hand in his. It felt warm, both tender and strong at the same time. "You must go now, Tabitha."

His hand slipped away. As if pulled from another world, Tabitha drifted toward the door. The man's face shrank, but his resonant voice remained strong. "Be brave, my love. Help Rose find me. I will talk to you again soon."

Tabitha opened her eyes. The light of dawn gave the room a purplish tint, a warm, soothing hue that promised to scatter the shadows. Turning, she looked at Sarah's bed—empty and neatly made.

She jumped up, dressed quickly, choosing the same jeans she had worn yesterday and a University of Florida T-shirt, and hurried to the family room. Her mother sat on the love seat, her Bible on her lap. She lowered her reading glasses and smiled. "Good morning, sweetheart. Did you sleep okay?"

"Not really." Tabitha slid into the empty spot next to her. "Did we get any phone calls last night, after I went to bed, I mean?"

"No, none at all." She pulled Tabitha close. "You're up early, aren't you?"

"More dreams." She swiveled her head from side to side. "Where's Daddy?"

"Still in bed. He was up very late praying for the Graysons."

Tabitha looked toward the kitchen, but the phone was out of sight. "May I call their house?"

Her mother shook her head. "It's too early. If they're home, they're probably still sleeping."

"Can I ride my bike over there, then? I'll wait outside until I see a light come on."

"It's too dark, honey. If you want to go later, you can ask your father when he gets up."

"Did someone mention me?" came a yawning voice. Wearing sweatpants and a loose T-shirt, Tabitha's father walked into the room, scratching through his mussed hair.

"Daddy!" Tabitha jumped to her feet. "Can I call and see if Rose is all right, or should I go over there and wait for someone to get up?"

"Neither one." He raised a finger. "But, if you'll make my breakfast, I'll call the hospital and see if she was admitted last night."

"The hospital!" Tabitha smacked her forehead. "Why didn't I think of that?"

Grinning, he touched the top of her head. "Do you really want me to answer that, little Miss Wound-So-Tight-She-Can't-Think-Straight?"

"No." She darted into the kitchen and threw open the pantry door. "What do you want for breakfast?"

Her father shuffled in and picked up the phone book. "Surprise me."

"Anything?" Tabitha asked, grinning.

He set his finger on the listing and picked up the phone. "Anything."

Tabitha's mother called from the family room, "You'll be sorry!"

While Tabitha prepared breakfast, her father sat at the table, staying on the phone for several minutes while being transferred from department to department. Finally, he finished with, "Thank you, Ms. Donald. You've been a great help."

Tabitha plopped a cereal bowl at the table space in front of him and handed him a spoon. "What did you find out?" she asked.

"Rose is home. They did tests until almost midnight, and since she was feeling better and didn't have meningitis, they let her go. Depending on the results of the tests, they may bring her back in." He looked down at the bowl, his spoon poised over the concoction. "What in the world is this?"

Tabitha began counting on her fingers. "Instant grits with brown sugar, sliced grapes, and one crushed up moon pie."

As her father lifted a spoonful of the brown mass closer, his face contorted. "Where did you learn this recipe?"

"From Andrew. It's his new favorite."

"Your brother eats this stuff?"

"Not exactly, but we were out of garlic powder."

* * *

Later that morning, Tabitha sped to the Grayson home on her bicycle, her backpack filled with snacks to share with Rose. She had placed her Bible in the outside pocket, hoping it would come in handy. Last night's church-altar dream had infused her with new confidence. As she pumped the pedals to ascend the final hill, she firmed her chin. She could do this, even without Sarah.

After leaning her bike against the porch, she leaped up the stairs and punched the doorbell. Bouncing on her toes as she waited, she slid off her backpack and let it dangle near the planks.

The door swung open, revealing Dr. Grayson. A warm smile graced his lips, and his voice seemed just as friendly. "Well, well, Tabitha. It's good to see you again. Come on in."

Tabitha strode in and spun back toward him. "How's Rose?"

Still smiling, he pointed toward the bedroom. "See for yourself."

She hurried down the hall, slowing as she walked into the room. Rose sat up in bed, her eyes brighter and her skin less pale.

Tabitha grinned. "You're looking better."

"I feel better." She offered a weak smile. "Not great, but better."

"My father prayed for you most of the night."

"I guess it must've worked." Rose's smile grew. "But don't tell anyone I said so."

Tabitha stretched out her toes. She could barely keep from jumping up and down. "You believe the prayer worked? Then you do believe in God?"

Rose set a finger to her lips. "Shhh!"

She gestured for Tabitha to come closer. "I'm ready to listen," she whispered, "but I don't think Dad's ready to let me."

"Okay," Tabitha whispered back. "I understand."

Rose nodded toward the door. "Let's talk about it in private."

After dropping her backpack on the bed, Tabitha scooted to the door. Setting a hand on the knob, she peeked out. The sounds of talking echoed from another room, but no one was in sight. She pushed the door closed, turning the knob to silence the click.

"I've been thinking about what you said," Rose continued as Tabitha approached again.

"What I said? Which time?"

"By the pond, remember? God's big advertisement. When we got home last night, I went to bed, and there was this grasshopper on my covers. It must have hitchhiked on my jacket between the car and the front door, but it reminded me of what you said. 'Who taught him how to jump through the grass to look for food?'"

"And how did you answer it?"

"Well, my radio was playing, and when I heard the forecast for rain the next day, it reminded me of all the stuff in the world and how it all has to work together perfectly, from the clouds all the way down to this little bug. There has to be a God."

"You believe now?" Tabitha grabbed Rose's hand and kissed it. "Oh, I'm so happy for you!"

Rose pulled her hand back. "Okay, okay. I understand. But just because I admit God's there doesn't mean I'm happy about it."

Tabitha wrinkled her nose. "What do you mean?"

"Well, obviously God gives some people more and better things than others. It just isn't fair sometimes." Rose waved her hands around. "Look at all I have, a nice room, a big house, plenty of food, all because my father has a good job. But most people in the world are poor, and some only have dirt huts to live in, or worse. Some people have diseases that make them ugly, while some are healthy and beautiful." She looked at Tabitha with a longing stare.

"You're not going to talk about my hair again, are you?"

Rose glanced away. "Well, there *is* that, but like I said, there's so much suffering going on, it's hard to believe in a loving God."

Tabitha chewed on her lip. Rose's comment deserved an answer, and a good one. But what? That problem had raised questions in her own mind. "Well," Tabitha said, giving a casual shrug. "He gave us all Jesus, and he's all we really need." She held back a cringe. That sounded too trite, too canned, even to her own ears.

"Oh, yeah." Rose squinted at her. "I forgot about Jesus. How does he fit into it all?"

Tabitha stared at Rose's curiosity-filled expression, so open, so honest. This was exactly the opportunity she had hoped for, but no answer came to mind. "Well, it's like this—"

"Wait a minute." Rose readjusted her position in bed, kicking the backpack.

As Tabitha moved it out of the way, she felt the Bible in the pocket. She pulled it out and flipped through the pages. "Mind if I read something to you?"

A furrow dug into Rose's brow. "Go ahead . . . I guess."

Tabitha looked at her friend's face. Was the pain from her sickness, or did she really not want to hear the Bible?

She took in a deep breath. It didn't matter. She had to be brave and shoot straight from the heart. This was no time to be timid. "For God so loved the world, that he gave his only begotten Son, that whoever believes in him should not perish, but have eternal life."

"Eternal life?" Rose asked. "You mean, like, going to heaven?"

"Right. If you believe in him, you'll go to heaven when you die."

Rose crossed her arms, her eyes narrowing. "Just by believing in Jesus?"

"Yes, but believing in him is more than just believing he exists. It means giving your life to him, to serve him, because he died to take away your sins."

"Sins. That sounds like a loaded word. I've heard some TV preachers banging people on the head about it."

"Yeah, I know what you mean. I guess they mean well, but I don't want to bang anyone over the head. Sins are really just the things you've done wrong in your life, you know, things God doesn't want you to do."

Rose closed her eyes. "Okay, I can deal with that. I haven't always been good." A little smile bent her lips. "Actually, sometimes I've been pretty bad."

"Me, too, back before I gave my life to him."

"How did you do that . . . give your life, I mean?"

"Well, you don't have to do it exactly like I did. You can do it anytime, anyplace. God listens no matter where you are." Tabitha put the Bible down on the bed. "At our church we have an altar," she explained, trying to create the scene by drawing invisible lines on the bedspread. "It's a place up front where you kneel to pray, and it really helped me concentrate and feel close to God when it happened."

Rose stared at the bedspread, gently touching Tabitha's "altar" with her finger. "So, you were in church, huh?"

"Uh-huh. I always went to church growing up, but I didn't really give my life to Jesus until one Sunday when Daddy was the guest preacher. He used to be a pastor, and he still preaches sometimes. Anyway, his words really made the difference. And we sang a hymn that said what was on my heart. Its chorus starts, 'Hallelujah! I have found him.'"

Rose's ears perked up. "I don't get to hear hymns very often. Can you sing it for me?"

"Sing it for you?" A knot formed in Tabitha's throat. Her cheeks burned. That was unexpected, but what could she do? She had to go for it.

Taking a deep breath, she began singing in a soft, sweet voice,

All my life long I had panted for a drink from some cool spring
That I hoped would quench the burning of the thirst I felt within.
Hallelujah! I have found him whom my soul so long has craved!
Jesus satisfies my longings; through his blood I now am saved.

She ended with a shrug. "That's all I know."

"That was pretty. I like it. Can you sing it again?"

Now a little more at ease, Tabitha obliged, this time adding more emotion, trying to communicate the meaning of each word in her expression.

When she finished, Rose stared at the ceiling with a yearning look in her eyes. "I think I can relate to that. Once after soccer practice, I was so thirsty, I could've knelt at a mud puddle and lapped it up, but I couldn't find anything. Finally, someone offered me a Gatorade, and it was the best drink I ever had in my life. I guess it was something like that."

"Sure. That sounds pretty close."

Rose let out a deep sigh. "Singing in church," she said with a breathy whisper. "That's where I want to be. And I want to hear your father preach. Maybe it will make the difference for me, too."

"Maybe. You never know. I listened to him at home all my life, but he sounded so different at church, like his words burned with fire. You'd have to have been there to understand."

"I think I understand." Rose looked out the window toward the street. "Where is your church?"

Tabitha glanced that way, but the church wasn't close enough to be in sight. "It's the one with the tall steeple by the 7-Eleven."

Rose nodded. "I know the one. I'll go there sometime to look for my faith."

"That would be great, but you can have faith anytime, anywhere."

"That's easy for you to say. I grew up hearing my parents laugh at people who believe in God."

Tabitha shifted back and forth. Rose had a point. Her life was so different from Tabitha's own background, where she was primed and ready for faith from her parents' years of teaching. Somehow it didn't seem fair. "I'm sorry," Tabitha said. "I can't explain it very well."

Rose slid her hand into Tabitha's. "Yes, you did. It's just not sinking into my stubborn head. I have a lot of my father in me, you know. I've always had to see something to believe it."

Tabitha squeezed Rose's hand. "I'll ask Daddy to come over if you'd like. He'll answer all your questions."

"I'd like that." Rose closed her eyes. A new furrow wrinkled her forehead. "Ask him to come later this afternoon if he can. I'm going to sleep for a while."

Tabitha reached to the floor and lifted her backpack to the bed again. Giving Rose a sly grin, she pulled a package halfway out of the bag. "I brought some cookies. Your favorite kind."

Rose opened one eye. "Double Stuf Oreos," she said, laughing weakly.

Tabitha wagged a finger. "But don't you dare eat all the cream in the middle first."

"Can you leave them here for me?" Rose murmured, barely lifting her hand to point at her night table.

Tabitha broke the package open. The lovely smell of chocolate wafted up to her nose, mixing with the sickeningly sweet odor coming from a tiny spill near a bottle of Pepto-Bismol sitting on the table. After moving a glass and pitcher to make room, she set the cookies next to the bottle, close enough for Rose to reach. "There you go. Now you can—"

She looked at Rose. With her eyes shut and her face taut and pale, she breathed with a rasp, heavy and even. She gently stroked Rose's hair, sweeping a dark strand out of her eyes. "God's gift to you is greater than golden hair," she whispered. "He will give you the crown of life and a robe of white."

She jerked back. Where did those words come from? They hadn't come to mind at all. It was like someone else had spoken through her. But why?

Now shivering, she hurried from the room, nearly running into Dr. Grayson in the hall.

"Whoa!" He grabbed her shoulders. "Slow down, Tabitha. What's wrong?"

She pointed toward the bedroom. "I think Rose is feeling worse. She just kind of dozed off."

"Yes, she's been doing that, but I'll check on her."

"Okay. I'm going home now." Tabitha pulled away. "Thank you for letting me visit."

"Anytime."

When Dr. Grayson turned, Tabitha bolted for the front door. As she retrieved her bike and mounted, she looked toward home. Daddy would have to come, and soon.

Chapter 7

AS JOHN AND TABITHA walked to the Grayson home, a dark band of clouds hustled across the skies, masking the sun and mopping the blue ceiling with its murky wash. The breeze picked up, and a thickening mist swirled all around.

"Looks like rain," he said.

"No big deal." Grinning, Tabitha took his hand. "You won't melt."

"Hey! That's my line!" He reached down to tickle her, but she pulled away, a shadow of anxiety darkening her face.

"Can we hurry?" she asked. "It's been almost two hours. She should be awake by now."

He gazed at her lovely face—narrow cheeks, strong chin, button nose, the image of Nanna as a little girl. So much percolated behind those blue eyes, something mysterious, something heavenly. "Sure. Let's jog the rest of the way."

Hand in hand, they stepped into a lively trot, bringing them to the Grayson's porch just in time to avoid a heavy shower. As they wiped their wet shoes on the mat, Phil jerked open the front door.

"Phil," John said, smiling. "You didn't even give me a chance to ring the doorbell."

"I was on my way out." Wearing a gray, hooded rain slicker, Phil dangled his keys, making them jingle in his shaking hand. "Rose took a turn for the worse, and she's back at the hospital. They're admitting her, so I came home to get her things. Her mother's with her now."

"That's terrible!" Tabitha's face turned pale. "Is she going to be all right?"

"I hope so," Phil said, averting his eyes. "I mean, I think so."

John laid a hand on Phil's shoulder. "I'd like to help. What can I do?"

Phil glanced at John's hand. "Nothing, really. I'll probably just stay at the hospital, unless I have to run some errands or come back here for something."

"If you'll give me a key to your house," John said, extending his other hand, "I'll be your courier. I work from home, so I make my own schedule."

Phil shook his head and managed a weak smile. "I don't think that will be necessary."

"Please. Let me take some of the burden for you." John nodded toward his daughter. "Besides, it will help Tabitha, too."

Phil looked at Tabitha. Two large teardrops streamed down her pale cheeks. "All right," he said, pulling a key from its chain. "I really appreciate it."

"Which hospital?" John took the key and stuffed it into his pocket.

"Arnold Palmer. Do you know where it is?"

"Sure. South Orlando."

Phil patted his front and back pockets. "But I don't have your phone number. My address book is inside somewhere."

John moved his hand to Phil's back and eased him toward the porch steps. "Don't worry about that. Just go and be with your daughter. I'll call the hospital and leave our number with your wife. Don't hesitate to ask for anything."

After pulling up the hood on his slicker, Phil ducked through the porch's drip line and walked toward his Honda. When he reached the door, he stopped and looked back. "Thanks. I really do appreciate it."

"You bet." Taking Tabitha's hand, John edged closer to the steps and gazed into the misty yard. As Phil backed out onto the rain-slicked street, John took note of the worried father's tight expression. Poor guy. How terrible it must be to feel so helpless—no power to fight the disease, no idea what the outcome will be, and no heavenly father to ask for help.

As soon as the car chugged out of sight, John tugged on Tabitha's hand. "Come on. We have a lot to do."

They jogged along the sidewalk through the persistent drizzle, but Tabitha lagged behind. John slowed his pace and turned her way. As she set one foot haphazardly in front of the other, her eyes seemed to lack focus.

He stopped and knelt in front of her. "Tabitha, what's wrong?"

With her face whiter than ever, she closed her eyes. Her legs collapsed, and her body crumbled to the sidewalk.

John scooped her into his arms and ran, trying not to bounce her limp body. Soon, he burst into the house and ran past Melody and Sarah toward Tabitha's bedroom.

"John!" Melody shouted after him. "What's wrong?"

"Tabitha fainted!" He turned the corner and rushed into her room. After sliding her damp body onto her bed, he laid a hand on her forehead. Warm, but not overly so. Rainwater dripped from his chin to her clothes, but that couldn't be helped.

Melody rushed in, followed by Sarah. "Is she all right?" Melody asked. "Is she breathing?"

"She's breathing fine." He looked up at them. Both his wife and Sarah looked back with wide eyes. "Get a cool, damp cloth."

Sarah ran out while Melody laid her palm on Tabitha's cheek. "Is she feverish?"

John wiped his sleeve across his cheeks and forehead. "I don't think so. She just fainted. Rose is very sick and in the hospital again. It must be from stress and lack of sleep."

Sarah flew back into the room, cloth in hand. John took it and gently washed Tabitha's tear-stained cheeks and mopped her rain-dampened brow. Within seconds her eyelids fluttered, and she stared, a confused look on her face. "What happened? How did I get here?"

"You fainted, sweetheart," Melody explained.

"What? Why?"

John handed the cloth back to Sarah. "We were just at Rose's house, remember?"

Tabitha grabbed her father's wrist and jerked herself up to a sitting position. "Rose is dying," she cried out, "and she isn't a Christian yet! You have to talk to her!"

"I will." John patted her shaking arm. "I'll go to the hospital first thing in the morning."

She heaved in gulps of air. "That may be too late. She could die tonight."

"Okay, okay. As soon as you calm down, I'll call to check on her condition. If it's real bad, I'll go as soon as I can."

Tabitha lowered herself back to the bed and let out a relieved sigh. "Okay, then, if you go, I want to go with you."

"Of course you can. That is, if you're feeling better."

Tabitha sat up again. "I'm fine. It's just a headache."

"I can see why," John replied, gently pushing her back down. "You've been under a lot of pressure. What's been happening to you is quite stressful for a girl your age."

"For my age?" She narrowed her eyes. "Do girls older than me have visions of people dying that come true?"

John shook his head. "Not that I know of."

As he caressed Tabitha's cheek, her eyes fluttered sleepily. "Then I'd better go," she mumbled, "no matter how I feel. God's got something special cooking, and it ain't grits and moon pies."

John chuckled. "I guess I can't argue with that."

* * *

As the cold November rain fell outside the open garage, John opened the front passenger door and helped Tabitha in. She looked better today. Maybe a good night's sleep was all she needed.

After sliding behind the wheel, he backed out to the street and stared past the beating wipers. "Do you still have a headache?"

"Not really." Her voice sounded stoic, detached from reality. "I think I was just tired. I'm fine now."

"Any dreams last night?"

"Yes."

"Do you want to tell me about it?"

"Later."

With every answer, Tabitha kept her gaze straight ahead, her head leaning back, almost trancelike.

John glanced at her at every opportunity. Her tone carried no disrespect. She just seemed faraway, in another world. Not even hitting big potholes could liven her up. The bumps and huge splashes used to make her laugh, and she would ask him to find the biggest puddle in the road and drive through it as fast as he could. She loved watching the huge wave arc over the sidewalk and soak everything in sight.

Not today. The little blonde head hardly bounced, and only the slightest twitching in her eyes gave any clue that she even noticed the bumps or splashes or cared to answer his questions at all.

As traffic increased, he kept his stare straight ahead. With Tabitha so out of it, it was better not to push her, just concentrate on the task at hand—how to talk to Rose. If Tabitha had read her correctly, she would be open to the idea of God and salvation, but how do you answer the questions of someone reared by atheists? Try to be eloquent? Down to earth? Funny? Since her father was a scholar, she would probably respond better to serious and eloquent, but not too eloquent. That would be as fake as plastic apples.

As he drove on, he wrote a short essay in his mind entitled, "What Is Faith?" That would probably work. Faith is really the main thing an atheist lacks, right? Once she grasped that, filling in the details would be a lot easier.

Soon, the hospital came into view. Tabitha perked up, lifting her head and looking all around, but she said nothing. The moment John eased the car into a space in the parking garage and turned off the engine, she flung the door open and jumped out, not waiting for her father to help her, as was his custom.

She ran around the car and took his hand, looking up at him, as if searching for a sign. He squeezed her hand in return and smiled, but apparently that wasn't enough to assuage her fears. She just looked away and slumped her shoulders.

"What's wrong?" he asked as he led her along the sidewalk leading to the entrance.

"I prayed for something, and it didn't happen."

The drizzle continued, prompting John to pick up the pace. He had chosen the shorter path, an uncovered sidewalk, instead of the longer covered one, but they would be under the hospital's portico in a few seconds. "What did you pray for?"

"I guess it was like Gideon's fleece. Just before we parked, I asked God to make you say, 'Rose is going to be all right,' but you didn't. So I think that means she's *not* going to be all right."

When they stepped under the portico, John stooped and looked her in the eye. "Tabitha, Rose is going to be all right."

She pushed her finger against his lips. "It doesn't count. I already told you."

With a puff, he blew her finger back. "Ah! I see! You're a girl of mystery and drama. You don't want God to make me say it unless it's a miracle."

"I guess I wanted a miracle of some kind. It would make me feel better."

He enveloped her hands in his. "You've already seen miracle after miracle in your dreams and visions. Isn't that enough to know that God is using you to bring Rose into his kingdom? No matter what happens, this sickness of hers will work out for God's glory."

She nodded. "I guess you're right."

As they rode the elevator, Tabitha's hand began to shake within his, and the closer they got to Rose's room, the more it trembled. He quietly prayed for her. Now wasn't the time for more stress.

When they arrived at Rose's room, John tapped on the door three times.

"Come in," a quiet voice replied.

He pushed the door open, and the two entered slowly. A woman sat on an otherwise empty bed, looking at them as she hung up a phone on a side table.

Tabitha spoke up first. "Mrs. Grayson. Where's Rose?"

"She's in the ICU." Her voice trembling, she dabbed her eyes with a tissue. "It got real bad last night. She's been convulsing and may be going into a coma."

John sat next to her. "Mrs. Grayson, I'm John Hanson."

She kept her stare on her lap. "Myrtle Grayson," she murmured.

"May I see Rose?"

She shook her head. "Only immediate family or clergy."

Tabitha sniffed and squeaked, obviously trying to hold back a sob.

"I have a clergy card," John said. "Is Phil with her?"

Myrtle lowered her head and wept. "Yes. He's with her."

John grabbed a clean tissue from a box next to the phone and handed it to Myrtle. "I'm so sorry. Is there anything I can do for you before I see Rose?"

She shook her head, still weeping.

He pulled another tissue and dabbed Tabitha's eyes. "You've been a strong young lady," he whispered. "You have to be strong again now. Stay here with Mrs. Grayson while I visit Rose."

Tabitha took the tissue and nodded while wiping her reddened eyes. As soon as John rose from the bed, she took his place and gently rubbed Myrtle's back.

When John showed his clergy card to gain access to the ICU, the nurse on duty, a petite Hispanic lady, gave him a broad smile. "I'm glad to see you," she said. "I tried to talk to him about God, but he wouldn't hear of it."

John pressed his hands together. "Pray for me."

"I will. I promise."

He entered the unit and found Phil standing by a bed. Monitors surrounded the curtain-partitioned area, one of them sounding a rhythmic beep. Other devices guided silent needles across long strips of paper. The jagged lines told an indecipherable story.

Phil looked up, and then down at Rose again. His hands clenched the metal bed rail, his knuckles white. "The doctor says it's eastern equine encephalitis. There's no real cure. They can only treat the symptoms. It's touch and go."

John walked up and stopped at the opposite side of the bed. "What are her chances?"

"Not too good. She's deteriorated rapidly—convulsing, hallucinating. It's been a nightmare. This is the quietest she's been all morning."

John took Rose's hand and gently caressed it while looking at Phil. "Hallucinating?"

Phil's gaze seemed locked on John's fingers. "She opens her eyes real wide and starts talking, even yelling, but she's unresponsive."

"What does she say?"

His brow protruded, darkening his eyes in its shadow. "What does it matter?" he sputtered. "She's incoherent."

John flinched. Phil's nerves had obviously reached a breaking point. "I'm just grasping for something that might help. She and Tabitha were close. Maybe I could ask Tabitha what her yelling means."

Closing his eyes, Phil pinched the bridge of his nose. "She . . ." After taking a long, deep breath, he continued, his voice pitching higher. "She cries out, 'I have to find it' and 'I have to get there.'"

John looked down at Rose and repeated the words in a whisper. What could it mean? Maybe Tabitha would know where Rose wanted to go. He looked back at Phil. "Any idea what she's after?"

"The only other word I could make out was 'church.' She's only been to church at weddings and funerals, so I have no idea why that's on her mind. Maybe it's because of the last funeral we went to. She seemed impressed by the service."

"I see . . ."

"The worst part," Phil continued, "is that she keeps trying to get up. The doctor wants to strap her down because of the central line in her neck, but I told him I'd make sure she stays put."

John touched a loose strap on the bed frame, just inches from Rose's arm. The sight had to be torture for Phil—his only child desperately sick, incoherent and hallucinating, and add to that leather straps? Terrible!

Pulling back, he looked at Phil again. "You must be exhausted. How long can you keep watch?"

Phil's teeth clenched. "As long as it takes."

John stroked Rose's forearm. How could he use this opportunity, this mention of church, to open a spiritual door? "Is it possible she's searching for something in her subconscious mind, maybe something she wants to find at church?"

"Of course it's possible, but what would she want to find at church? The funeral was really kind of depressing."

John cleared his throat. "Faith, maybe?"

A knowing smile crept across Phil's lips. "John, I realize what you're trying to do, and I don't mean to be offensive in any way, but we don't believe in God. Rose is very comfortable with that."

"No offense taken. I just assumed you were trying to understand Rose's hallucinations. I'm sure Tabitha has told her about God, so she might be thinking about it. There's no reason to be skeptical about that possibility."

"I'm not really a skeptic, more of a pragmatist." Phil looked him in the eye. "I know you're trying to combine your concern with an attempt to evangelize, and I understand your motivations. They're altruistic. But you're wasting your time, especially now." He clenched the bed rail again. "I'm not about to believe in a God that allows this kind of suffering in the world. Maybe if an angel came into this room and healed her, then I'd have something concrete to believe in."

"A miracle is concrete?"

"In a way." Phil held out his hands as if holding an invisible ball. "I need to see something, feel it, smell it. It has to be tangible. As they say, 'Seeing is believing.'"

"But doesn't seeing eliminate the possibility of faith?"

Phil stared at him for a moment before lowering his head. "I see your point." Phil took Rose's hand, mimicking John's caressing movements while avoiding the pulse oximeter on her finger. "I guess I'm not even sure what faith is."

John blew out a quiet sigh. Phil's tone was sad but not combative. It could have been a lot worse. "Do you mind if I try to explain what faith is?"

"You might as well." Phil's gaze seemed drawn to a jagged line on one of the machines. "I'm not going anywhere."

John took a deep breath and began speaking slowly and methodically, trying to remember his rehearsed speech. "Okay. Faith is believing that God will work according to his promises, his purposes, and his character. Faith neither presumes that God will act according to our understanding, nor is it surprised when he performs a marvelous work. The miracle that we desire, like healing, for example, may seem appropriate in our limited vision, but if God does not so deem, then we let God be God and don't question his wisdom or our faith. If, however, his grace covers our request, then we humbly give him thanks and give him the glory for what he has done."

As he finished, John glanced at Rose. One of her eyelids fluttered but quickly closed again.

Phil's cheeks reddened. His fingers wrung out the bed rail. Finally, like an erupting volcano, he shouted, "Let God be God? Even if he lets an innocent girl die for no reason?" Trembling, he extended his hand toward Rose, a vein throbbing on his forehead. "If there is a God, then he would be more loving than this."

John met his stare. Obviously the words had plunged deeply, but for good or for harm? Was it time to back off or go for broke? The next part of his speech might sound cruel and callous, but it was the truth.

As they faced each other from across the bed in a nervous standoff, John changed his tone, trying to sound more sympathetic. "Phil, all people will die, whether it's from a disease during youth or from the decay of old age. Don't despair if God allows an innocent daughter to follow the path we all must travel eventually. A miraculous healing does give a person more time to serve the Master, but it also makes the sojourner tarry until the next grave assault on the mortal frame."

Straightening, Phil wagged his finger, the vein bulging even more. "Oh, that's a pretty sermon, John. How long did you practice it before you got here?"

"Well . . . I . . ."

"Just as I thought. I'm a project for you, the poor misguided atheist who just needs to hear the right words, and then he'll drop to his
knees, crying like a baby, 'Oh, Jesus, forgive me! I have faith now! I
really do! I must be saved!'" His voice quaked. "It's easy for you to
pretend there's a God. Your God concept has never let you down. If
there is a God, he's let me down plenty of times. If Rose dies, it will
just prove me right. If anything like this ever happens to you, *then*
come and talk to me about faith."

John stuffed his hands into his pockets and turned away. He felt
naked, exposed. Although his motivations had been pure, his sermon
was practiced, just as Phil had said. His words must have carried the
air of academic aloofness, a tidy apologetic that served as nothing
more than a burning antiseptic.

He bit his lip hard. Why couldn't he be a healing salve for Phil's
open wounds? Why couldn't his sympathy pour forth like living water?
Instead, his words were a bitter tonic that Phil spat out in disgust.

He turned back and kept his gaze trained on Rose. Her eyelids
were closed but not resting; they twitched and wrinkled sporadically.
Keeping his head low, he looked at Phil again. He was also watching
Rose. His cheeks had regained their normal color, and a tear tracked
down each one.

John cleared his throat. "I'm sorry, Phil. You're right, and I'm very
sorry. It was a practiced sermon, but it wasn't my intent to offend
you."

Phil bowed his head and breathed a deep sigh. "I know you're
just trying to help."

"Yes. I'm trying to help. Is there anything I can do?"

Phil shuffled around the bed and stopped in front of John, but
he kept his eyes averted. "She's my only child," he whispered. He
opened his mouth to speak again but then drooped his head. Spinning around, he lifted a clenched fist to his mouth and bit it.

John reached toward him, but hesitated. His words had been thrown back at him; would an embrace also be misunderstood? Would it be interpreted as another heartless and empty attempt at evangelism?

As he pondered, the image of Tabitha lying in bed returned to his mind, the night he had wrestled with whether to give her another kiss. He had opted for distance, the easier choice . . . the stupid choice. But not this time.

Just as he reached again, a new voice spoke up from the curtain. "How is Rose?" A doctor dressed in scrubs walked in.

John pulled back. Phil spun toward the doctor, apparently unaware of John's aborted gesture. "She's been quiet for a while. The sedative must have worked."

John's voice trimmed to a hoarse whisper. "I'd better go now."

Phil nodded but said nothing.

As he strode down the hall, John rolled his hands into fists. When would he figure out how to say the right thing . . . do the right thing? It seemed that words, at least from his lips, had become a sledgehammer. What good was all the seminary training, all the sermon writing, if he couldn't communicate love? It was worthless!

Nearing the room where he had left Tabitha, he slowed. A verse came to mind, a very appropriate verse. *If I speak with the tongues of men and of angels, but do not have love, I have become a noisy gong or a clanging cymbal.*

And that's what he must have sounded like to Phil, a noisy gong . . . a self-righteous idiot.

* * *

John pushed open the hospital door and held it for Tabitha. With his hands in his coat pockets, he shuffled alongside her under the covered walkway to the parking garage. The rain had grown heavier, and wet air breezed through the passageway. Somehow the weather felt right—dreary, gray, cold—the same way his heart felt . . . miserable.

Pulling his jacket closer, he reached for Tabitha's hand. "Come on. Let's hurry."

They hustled to the car. During the trip home, John tried to talk to Tabitha, but she politely asked to stay quiet, leaving him to his thoughts. He had blown a golden opportunity to give spiritual help to a suffering father, stupidly focusing on filling his deepest need, a need he didn't even acknowledge, rather than addressing his pain. How could he do better next time? . . . If there ever would be a next time.

As he pulled into the driveway, he looked at the front deck. Melody and Sarah stood under the roof's overhang, both fidgeting. Sarah ran to the driveway, ignoring the driving rain, while Melody hustled back inside.

Sarah met the car before it came to a stop, waving frantically.

John rolled down the window. "What's wrong?"

"It's Rose. She's missing."

"Missing!" Tabitha cried. "How could she be missing?"

Sarah brushed back her dampening hair. "Her father fell asleep, and when he woke up, she was gone. Nobody in the hospital knows where she is."

Melody ran out to the car, blinking away the raindrops. "I just talked to hospital security and told them you're here. They want to know if you have any ideas about Rose."

"Not yet." He shifted the car into reverse. "But I'm going back. The more people searching for her the better."

"What about Tabitha? Shouldn't she stay home now?"

John turned toward his daughter. One look at her pleading eyes provided the answer. "No. She's gone this far. We'll see it through together." He wheeled the car around and sped out of the driveway, splashing through the growing puddles.

Tabitha remained quiet again while John went over the possibilities out loud, sometimes pausing for minutes at a time.

"She couldn't have gone far, as sick as she is. Some closet somewhere, maybe, that they're overlooking. . . . How could she have passed by the nurses unseen? I suppose patients walk by all the time. . . . I guess she must have pulled the central line out. I wonder how dangerous that is. . . . Her parents must be beside themselves. I can't imagine it."

He looked at Tabitha. She focused straight ahead, a death grip on the inside door handle. She seemed to be peering right through the sheets of rain.

"Tabitha, what are you staring at?"

She shrugged. "Nothing in particular. I was just thinking."

"Thinking what? Do you have any ideas?"

"I was just thinking that you're right. She couldn't have gone that far."

When they arrived at the hospital, John and Tabitha rushed through the passageways, rode the elevator to the seventh floor, and quick-marched to the nurses' station.

"I'm John Hanson." He paused and took a few deep breaths as he read the nurse's name tag—Brenda, the head nurse. "Is there any news about Rose?"

"Her father's trench coat is gone," Brenda explained, "and someone saw a person with a trench coat and long hair getting into a taxi down at the street. We're still sweeping the hospital. Some of the search crew are on the fifth floor now, and a few others are calling all the cab companies. If she got in a taxi, she could be anywhere. Her father's wallet was in the coat."

Tabitha stepped up to the nurse and tilted her head upward. "But she must have gotten better to be able to do that, right?"

Brenda laid a gentle hand on the side of Tabitha's head. "That's the way with this illness, honey. The brain swells, and she has convulsions and hallucinations. Then sometimes her vitals are strong and she rests." She pointed toward the floor. "She must have sneaked away during one of the good times. There was blood on the floor where she pulled out the line, and the drips stopped halfway down the hall. Obviously, she's able to walk now, but she's very sick, she's barefoot as far as we know, and she may be out in that dreadful cold rain."

"C'mon," John said. "Let's see if we can find the search party." He pulled on Tabitha's sleeve, but his grasp slipped. She stood still, trancelike, staring at the nurse with wide eyes.

"Tabitha, what's wrong?"

Her monotone reply came in a whisper. "I know where she is."

"What?"

She turned to her father, her face red as her voice spiked. "I know where she is!"

"Where?"

"At the church!"

"Her hallucinations?"

"Right! You asked me if I had any dreams last night. I said I did, but it seemed silly. We both said she couldn't have gone far. But in my dream, I saw Rose at church, kneeling at the altar!"

John turned to the nurse. "Call for her parents and an ambulance. Call the police, too."

Brenda jerked up a telephone and reached for the dial pad. "What should I tell them?"

"I have a card." After fumbling through his wallet, John threw a business card down on the desk. "Here's the address where we think she went. If you believe in visions from God, then let everyone know."

She punched a series of numbers into the phone. "I'm on it!"

John grabbed Tabitha's hand. "Let's roll!"

They sprinted past the elevator, then flew down the stairs and through the emergency exit. Ignoring the blaring alarms, they burst through the frigid wall of rain, up one flight of stairs to their parking level and into the car, slamming doors and squealing tires on the way out.

When they arrived at the church, he parked in the empty lot and ran with Tabitha to the front entry. Sirens sounded in the distance, closing in. He jerked on the door handle, rattling it in place. "She couldn't have gone in this way."

Tabitha cupped her hands on the glass and looked inside. "I can't see a thing."

"Right. It's too dark."

"Once when I had nursery duty, Mama and I got here early. The door to the social hall was unlocked."

"It's worth a try."

They raced around the building, Tabitha puffing and clutching her side. The sirens grew deafening, and the motors of approaching vehicles roared.

John jerked on the door, flinging it open. He waited for Tabitha to catch up. Still holding her side, she stepped in.

"Are you all right?" he asked.

She nodded but said nothing.

"Careful, the floor's wet. Someone's been through here recently." As they made their way toward the sanctuary, someone banged at the front door beyond the sanctuary.

"Rescue! Open up!"

With Tabitha in tow, John hustled to the sanctuary through an inside entryway. To the left, uniformed men shook the door. In the shadows to the right, a huddled, shaking trench coat lay draped over the altar. A single ray of light shone from one window and cast its beam on the trembling mass, though the sun had been obscured by rainclouds.

"Tabitha," John said, pointing. "Run and let them in."

Tabitha bolted for the door while John dashed to the altar. He dropped to his knees beside the shaking coat and pulled back the collar.

Yes, it was Rose. Her cheek lay flat on top of the altar, but she maintained her bent knees. The trench coat was dappled with patches of blood, some dry, some fresh.

John scooped her up. She trembled in his arms, cold and wet.

Two paramedics rushed to his side, Phil following closely behind.

"Put her down," one of them ordered. "We have to stabilize her."

While John laid her on the floor, the other paramedic ran for the exit, calling back. "I'll get the stretcher."

Phil dropped to his knees at Rose's side. "Is she okay?"

"She's alive." The paramedic pulled Rose's arm back through the coat sleeve and searched her skin for a vein. "We'll get her vitals in a minute."

As the paramedic worked to establish an IV, John and Phil looked on while Tabitha peered over Phil's shoulder.

Rose's lips, blue against her white skin, moved, emitting a faint whisper.

"What's she saying?" Tabitha asked.

Phil leaned down and set his ear near her lips. At first his eyes clenched shut and then opened wide. He raised his head again, his mouth agape, his face turning gray. His own lips quivered. Finally he rasped, "She's singing."

Sniffing, Tabitha wiped tears from her cheeks. "Is she singing, 'Hallelujah, I have found him'?"

Phil stared at Tabitha. "How did you know?"

"I sang it to her. She really liked it, so I just guessed."

He cocked his head to the side. "How did you know she'd be here?"

"Well, it's kind of hard to explain. You see—"

"Okay, let's go!" The two medics hoisted Rose onto the stretcher, wrapping her in blankets, and wheeled her toward the waiting ambulance. Phil stayed one step behind the stretcher, listening as one of the paramedics recited her vitals.

Tabitha tried to follow, but John grabbed her. "Stay here."

She looked up at him with pleading eyes. "Why can't we go?"

"I don't think we can help anymore." He pointed at a puddle of water and smears of mud on the carpet. "Besides, we have some cleaning up to do."

"We can be with her. We can comfort her parents."

"They'll all be in the ICU. We'll just pace around, twiddling our thumbs, and we can pray from here as well as there."

Tabitha sighed. "I guess you're right."

John looked out the glass door and watched the paramedics load the stretcher into the ambulance. Tabitha joined him, taking his hand as she whispered, "Rose is going to die, isn't she?"

He waited for the ambulance doors to slam shut before replying. "That's what your dreams have said, and they've been pretty accurate so far. But they also said she wandered alone, without Christ, and that's not true anymore."

Tabitha squeezed his hand. "You're right. Everything's changed now."

"If her heart matched her song, then she's now a child of God."

Tabitha sat on a pew and looked at him, new tears forming. "But will she be more likely to die now because she pulled out her IV thing and came out in the cold rain?"

John picked up the abandoned trench coat, soaked with water and stained with blood. "I don't think cold and wetness will cause the infection to get worse." He draped the coat over the top of a pew. "But she's probably weaker now, less able to fight it."

She nodded, her head more down than up. "If she does die, she won't be alone in the valley of shadows. If I stop dreaming about her being chased there, it'll be a good sign."

"The place in your nightmares?"

She nodded again, her gaze on her father. "But how can we know for sure?"

The ambulance siren blared. John paused until it grew weak enough to talk without shouting. "Rose went against her father's wishes and risked her life to answer God's call. She ripped out the tubes that might have saved her life. She gave up everything to find salvation. If these aren't acts of true faith, then surely no one can be saved."

Tabitha touched the trench coat, rubbing her finger across a bloodstain. "She could have been saved in the hospital, too, couldn't she?"

"Maybe, maybe not." John took off his own coat and laid it next to Phil's. "Sometimes we have to go on a journey to find our faith."

"So what do we do now?"

John helped Tabitha peel off her wet coat and draped it over the others. "We clean up. We go home. We pray."

Sighing again, Tabitha took his hand but said no more.

As the siren faded to a background whine, John echoed Tabitha's sigh. "Her family needs us now more than ever," he said. "I may be wrong, but what just happened could make her father even more bitter."

Chapter 8

JOHN PUSHED his daughters' bedroom door open a few inches and peeked through the crack. Taking a deep breath, he stepped inside and closed the door quietly. The glow of early dawn shone through the window, allowing him to survey the room. It seemed different somehow, almost like he had never really considered all the lovely details.

Even in the murky shadows, one fact was obvious. This was a room for girls. A tumbled pile of barrettes rested on one dresser, the remains of a little girl's failed attempt at sorting them out, along with a brush with strands of blonde hair tangled in its bristles. A long navy blue dress hung from the top of the closet door, ready to be worn by the young lady who had ironed it the night before.

In her bed against one wall, Sarah dozed, snuggling a large stuffed bear—Boris, she had named it years ago, a gift from Grandpa Hanson when she was only four.

On the opposite side of the room, Tabitha sat up in her bed, leaning back on the headboard, clutching her legs with both hands and bringing her knees close to her chest. Her soft cries broke the silence.

John crept closer and whispered, "Tabitha? Are you okay?"

"No." She looked up. Even in the dimness, her glistening eyes gave away her tears.

John sat on the bed and draped his arm around his little girl. He had another rehearsed speech ready for this moment but decided to scrap it. It just didn't seem right.

"Tabitha, Rose died last night."

Tabitha sniffed hard. "I know."

"Another dream?"

She buried her face between her arms and nodded.

With a soft touch, he rubbed his hand up and down the flannel on her back. "Was Jesus with her this time?" he asked.

Again, she nodded but said nothing.

"You brought your friend to salvation. That should make you feel a little better." He bit his tongue. Was he about to make another stupid gaffe?

Tabitha looked up again, this time straight at him. Two plump tears dangled from her cheeks, and two more waited to follow their course. "I know," she whimpered, "but I can't help it. I know she's in a better place, but I feel like I'm being torn apart."

"Tell me about it," John said as he wiped the dangling tears away. "How are you being torn?"

She took a deep breath and waited for the pulsing spasms to subside. Her voice was fragile, weak. "It's like at the funerals I've been to. Some people are happy and some are sad. Some are both at the same time. Nanna went to heaven, and you say we're supposed to be happy. Kashema went to hell, and some people at her funeral celebrated, but they should've been sad. I feel both. I'm sure Rose is with Jesus now. I saw it myself in my dreams. But I'm still sad."

"Sad for her or sad for yourself?"

She choked out a pitiful, "I don't know."

John pulled his hands to his lap. "There's good reason to be happy for Rose. She's in heaven, far away from this wicked world. If you're sad, then . . ." He paused. Even though he wanted to cheer her up, with every word he felt like he was pounding her with a verbal club.

"I know, I know," she said, bitterness creeping into her tone. "It's selfish."

John massaged her shoulders. "I'm sorry, Tabitha. I shouldn't have mentioned that. I know she was your friend. I was hoping to cheer you up by reminding you of how happy Rose must be right now."

"But didn't you say once that it's selfish to grieve for yourself?"

He gave her a nod. "When Nanna died, I did say that grief is an indulgence for ourselves, and there is some truth to it, but . . ."

"But what?" She looked up at him, her eyes as wet as ever. "You mean it's only partially true?"

John stared at her. What could he say? Logically, it had to be true. Grieving for someone celebrating the wonders of heaven was selfish, and she had pushed him into a corner. "I guess I have to say it's all true, but I don't want you thinking that I consider you selfish just because you're crying."

"But you don't have any choice." Tabitha pulled the hem of her nightgown to her face and wiped her eyes and cheeks. She turned her face upward and gave him a weak smile. "I'll try to be happy."

John rubbed her back again. "You're a brave girl. I'm sorry if I made you feel worse." He rose to his feet and headed for the door, then turned around at the hall. "By the way, I talked to the floor nurse. Just before she died, Rose woke up and started talking."

"What did she say?"

"She stared at the ceiling and said, 'I see him. I see my Savior.' Then she looked at her parents and said, 'I love you, but I have to go now.' Then, strangely enough, she pulled her father down to the bed and whispered something to him that the nurse couldn't hear. She died just a few seconds later."

"That was around midnight," Tabitha said in a matter-of-fact tone.

"That's right. How did you guess?"

"It wasn't a guess." Tabitha got up and pulled the sheet tight on her bed. "I woke up right after I dreamed about Rose. It was twelve fifteen."

John stepped back into the room and glanced at Sarah, still sleeping peacefully. Would Tabitha now be able to rest in such comfort? Were the troubling dreams finally over? Had God completed his purpose?

Tabitha tucked the bedspread under her pillow and placed her rag doll on top. "There, Debbie. You'll be comfortable on the pillow. I'm sorry I knocked you off during the night."

John watched his daughter as she fussed with the doll's clothes and hair. She was still such a little girl in so many ways. How could she possibly bear these weighty visions from above? What was God trying to do? For now, he could only guess.

A Bible verse came to his mind, shedding some light, but somehow also adding to the mystery.

I will pour forth of my Spirit upon all mankind; and your sons and your daughters shall prophesy, and your young men shall see visions, and your old men shall dream dreams.

Of course the prophets of old received visions from God, but a little girl?

Tabitha turned from her bed and smiled sheepishly. "I know Nanna called her Deborah," she explained, turning to pick up the doll. "I shortened it to Debbie."

"That's nice. I like it." He stared at Tabitha and the doll. What an image of innocence! How can one so young have such an amazing gift? It's as though she's a prophetic portal from God. Again the words of the verse entered his mind, and they blew through his own lips in a whisper. "Your daughters shall prophesy . . ."

"What did you say, Daddy?"

He jerked himself out of his trance. "Uh . . . I was just thinking about a Bible verse."

"Which one?"

"I . . . I don't remember the reference." He hurried to the door and turned back. "If you want to talk more, I'll be in the kitchen." With a twirl and quick steps, he left the room.

* * *

Tabitha pulled a sock up past her calf, then reached for the other sock on the floor. The phone rang in the distance. She glanced at her clock radio—7:02 a.m. Maybe the call was about Rose.

She yanked the other sock over her foot, dashed out of the bedroom, and rushed to the kitchen just in time to hear her father close the conversation.

"Yes, of course, Phil. I'll be glad to. I'll see you on Saturday."

As he hung up the phone, Tabitha bounced on her toes. "What's up?"

"That was Rose's father. He wants me to speak at the funeral on Saturday."

She drew her head back. "He wants *you*? I thought he was mad at you."

"He was . . . or is, I guess." Her father eased down in one of the breakfast-table chairs. "Remember I told you that Rose whispered something to him? She asked to have me speak at her funeral. Since it was her last request, Phil felt obligated to grant it."

Tabitha jumped into his lap and hugged his neck. "Rose wants you to bring her parents to the Lord!"

Her father returned the hug and looked away. "I hope so. Phil was very short with me on the phone. I'm not sure if it was anger or grief."

"Do you think he blames me?" Tabitha asked, pointing at herself. "Does he think Rose wouldn't have died if I hadn't told her about Jesus? Does he think if she stayed at the hospital she would have survived?"

"I wish I knew." He gently pushed her down from his lap, walked to the kitchen cupboard, and retrieved a cereal bowl, a faraway look in his eyes. "I can't say I'd blame him for thinking it was our fault."

"My fault, you mean. I was the one who told her about coming to our church."

"Well, he might blame me for teaching you." He opened the pantry door and searched the shelves. "Do we have any cereal left?"

Tabitha folded her hands behind her back. "Do you want me to make breakfast for you, Daddy?"

He turned around. "No," he replied with a playful grin. "I'll save the moon pie for later."

"Seriously, Daddy. I'll make some oatmeal."

"No grapes?"

"No grapes."

"No moon pies?"

"No moon pies."

"Okay, go ahead. And thank you."

Tabitha pulled a tin canister of oatmeal from the pantry and pried the lid off, making a metallic-sounding pop. After turning on the hot water tap and sticking her finger into the stream, she watched her father seat himself at the dining table and pick up the newspaper. On these cool mornings it seemed to take forever for the hot water to start flowing. As she filled a pot, she called out, "We do have garlic powder now, though."

Her father stared at the paper, the corners of his mouth turning upward. "Save it for Andrew," he grunted in a mock sour tone.

Tabitha left the pot on the stove and pulled up a chair next to him. "Do you know what you'll say at the funeral?"

He folded the paper and set it down. "Not yet, but I'm already working on it in my head."

She gazed into his eyes, smiling. Joking around with him was always fun. Although most people thought of him as Mr. Serious, everyone at home knew how funny and tender he could be. If only they could see the side of him she knew so well.

As his recent words tumbled through her mind, the news about an upcoming funeral crushed her mood. Soon she would again be faced with battling emotions, as the casket lid closed over Rose's lifeless body.

Tabitha's lips trembled. She sniffed and wiped a tear from her eye. She couldn't cry . . . not now. Not after her father had confirmed that it would be selfish.

He put the paper down. "What's wrong, sweetheart?"

"I . . . I think I'd better go." Tears now flowing, she got up to run away, but he caught her wrist and pulled her into his lap. He wrapped both arms around her and hugged her, allowing her to bury her face in his chest. As she cried pitifully, he caressed her head and whispered, "Take all the time you need, little angel. Take all the time you need."

* * *

The days of waiting until the funeral passed by with little to no excitement. Tabitha enjoyed dreamless sleep each night, and the family talked about Rose's death sparingly that first morning. Her father had placed two calls to the Grayson home, leaving messages on the answering machine, but they went unreturned. He had to search for the name of the funeral home in the newspaper's death announcements and called to learn the time and place of the service. It was becoming clear that Dr. Grayson's bitterness was worse than her father had thought.

When the day came, Tabitha arose early and put on the same dress she had worn to Nanna's funeral. She carefully tied the bow in the back and straightened out the front, rubbing the velvety material with both hands. She stood close to her mirror, the dim light in the room making it hard to see, and she shook a finger at her reflection.

Now remember, no crying. Rose is in heaven. You don't want to be selfish about this.

She practiced a big smile, fake at first, but then she broke into a real one, amused at her phony grin.

With her leather shoes clacking on the tile floor, she walked down the hall toward the kitchen. Nobody was around. She made her own breakfast, ate quickly, and then hustled down the hall to sneak a look into her father's office. Yes, he was there, staring at his computer.

"Are you working on your speech for today?" she asked quietly.

Her father turned and smiled. "I was working on it, but I'm not sure about it anymore."

Tabitha entered and stood at his side, studying the glowing characters on the monitor. "Not sure? Why's that?"

"I'm having a hard time putting my feelings into words. It's just not coming out right. I kind of know what I want to say, so I'm thinking about winging it when the time comes instead of writing it all out."

Tabitha pointed at the screen. "You spelled *their* wrong. It's t-h-e-i-r, not t-h-e-r-e."

He clicked a few keys and corrected his mistake. "Thanks, but I don't think I'm going to use this."

Tabitha reached over her father's lap and gripped the mouse, trying to scroll down to read more. "Why not? This looks good."

Together, they watched the text crawl up the screen, little by little. "It's pretty," he said, "but it's too canned. I think that was my problem when I talked to Phil at the hospital. I practiced so much in my mind, it was plastic, kind of phony."

"But wasn't it true?"

"I thought so." He leaned back in his chair and sighed. "I just need to have a basic idea of what I should say. My job will be to bring comfort to mourners and conviction to unbelievers, all in the same speech. I'll just pray for the Holy Spirit to speak through me."

"I like the conviction part," Tabitha said, pointing at the screen again. "Like this here. This is good. 'If Rose were alive, she would implore you to believe in God and repent of your sins.'"

"But is her family ready to hear it in such a blunt way?"

"Isn't that why Rose asked for you? You might not get another chance."

Her father tapped her on the nose with a finger. "We both assume that's why she asked. She wants her parents to find the same peace she found, but bluntness isn't the only way to bring conviction. I think giving the proper balance is the best way to shine the light that will show them the path to freedom."

"There," she said, pointing a finger back at him. "You see? You can be eloquent without writing it first."

"Actually, I wrote something like that in the last paragraph."

"Oh . . . you did?"

"I did. I guess I'm like Moses. I'm a lot better writer than I am a speaker."

Tabitha hugged her father and kissed him on the cheek with a dramatic smack. "Well, if anyone can do it, I know you can."

He set an elbow on his desk and rested his head on his palm. "Thank you, sweetheart. I'll do my best."

* * *

John sat motionless, staring at his computer screen. After reading yet another paragraph of overstuffed, plastic words, he shook his head and flipped the desk lamp and monitor switch off, darkening his office. Sighing heavily, he leaned back in his chair and looked toward the ceiling. While his eyes adjusted to the lack of light, the silence allowed his thoughts to drift.

The blank ceiling provided a natural screen for his imagination as he pictured the funeral scene and the many faces in attendance. Would the extended Grayson family be attentive, or had Phil already poisoned their attitudes, warning them of the fanatical Christian preacher and his false hopes of heaven? How could he possibly prepare himself to speak to stone walls? No amount of eloquence can break a barrier whose builder is hopelessness. They needed truth, but how could he present it without watering it down? He had told Phil the truth at the hospital, but it came whipping back like a boomerang, a crack in the head that maybe knocked a little sense into him.

He pulled his speech from the printer and stared at it. These words flowed beautifully, but they were fake—dressed-up mannequins. When he turned to the second page, he read the first sentence, another lousy attempt at eloquence. He slung the pages toward his desk, scattering them across the surface. *Yeah, I got the truth right! I'm great with the truth!*

He spun his chair around and glared at the wall, crossing his arms and rocking. As he stared, one of the pictures caught his eye, a photo of himself with Joshua, his firstborn, the two of them cuddling before his son could even walk. He remembered how this child of his own flesh melted his frozen exterior, the unflappable and straight-faced stoic that he had always been. To this day he habitually reserved his warmth and gentle ways for his family, leaving his cold, academic manner for others.

He frowned again. Cold and academic? Where was Jesus in that? How could he show the love of Christ without truly weeping with those who weep? He looked again at the photo and whispered, "Lord, help me weep with Phil and his family."

After a few seconds, the words of a Bible verse flowed gently through his mind. *He who did not spare his own Son, but delivered him over for us all, how will he not also with him freely give us all things?* John allowed the words to soak into his troubled thoughts. *His own*

Son . . . His only Son? How valuable was an only son? More valuable than if God had begotten more sons? Did Joshua become less valuable when Andrew was born? Or Sarah when Tabitha was born? Or was value appraised on the consequence of loss? An only son is supremely valuable because his loss would leave a father with . . .

He looked up at the photo again, then at his scattered speech. He whispered, "With nothing."

Grabbing a page from the desk, he wadded it into a ball. *Rose was Phil's only child!*

Suddenly the images of his five children flashed through his mind, his most precious treasures on earth. How could a person as spiritually dead as Phil ever withstand losing everything dear to him in one devastating blow? How could he find any glimmer of light when his soul is filled with darkness? How could he understand that Rose is happy in the glory of paradise? He didn't believe in paradise at all!

Like one metal melting into another to create an alloy, Phil's pain seeped into John's soul. A tear came to his eye. Then, like a rushing stream, his emotions burst forth. He laid his hands over his face and wept. *That poor man! That poor, poor man!*

Leaning back, he wailed out loud. "Oh, dear God, have mercy! Oh, have mercy, please have mercy!"

He cried on and on, growing quieter as the minutes passed. Finally, he sniffed, wiped his eyes, and turned his face toward heaven.

I know what to say now. I know how to show compassion, and I can still tell the truth. I will honor Phil's precious daughter. Thank you for guiding me down this confusing path.

Then, pointing upward, he whispered, "I'm still going to need your help when the time comes."

* * *

John walked hand in hand with Melody, following the grassy path toward the gravesite. Sarah and Tabitha followed, also hand in hand.

He looked at a sheet of paper, the order of events the funeral director had given him earlier. There would be no church service and no
reception in the funeral home chapel, no chance for a spiritual aura to
mask the dark face of death. Only grim reminders would be suitable
for this occasion, no stained glass or altars of prayer, just names
etched in tombstones lined up and down the neatly trimmed grass
telling stories of lost loves and aching grief. This was Phil's story, and
that's how he wanted it told.

A crowd began gathering at the gravesite, the mob of dark clothing and gray faces huddling in the brisk wind. The tent draped over
the area helped but not quite enough to make the site comfortable.
November was not usually this cold in central Florida, but the weather
reflected the mood of many in attendance that day, lacking the
warmth of loving comfort and feeling the dimness of obscured light.

As they approached, John saw Phil and waved, but Phil turned
his head and spoke to a man in a dark suit standing next to him. The
man waded through the crowd and stopped in front of John, extending a program in his outstretched hand.

"I already have one," John said, waving the sheet. "It looks like
I'm supposed to talk after someone else greets everyone."

"That is correct." The man spoke in brisk monotone. "I will start
the program with the usual pleasantries; then you will come up and
speak. How long will your sermon be?"

"Very short. Only a few minutes."

"Good. Short and sweet. With the death of a child, a long sermon on a cold day would not work very well."

John nodded. "My thoughts exactly."

The man pointed toward the tent. "The casket will be at the front.
It will be open, and a viewing will follow the service." He turned
toward John, an apologetic tone now flavoring his voice. "It's a little
unusual, but I'm following the father's wishes, you understand."

"Of course."

The man reverted to his businesslike countenance. "You will sit next to me facing the mourners. Your daughter, Tabitha, I believe, has a seat reserved for her at the front. Your wife and other daughter will find seats elsewhere."

"That will be fine," John said, nodding.

The funeral attendant gestured with his head. "Follow me."

As mourners continued to stream in, John and company followed the stoic gentleman to the tent. Heeding their instructions, John sat at the front next to the coffin, Melody and Sarah chose two seats near the back, and Tabitha found her place on the front row. Myrtle Grayson greeted her with a smile, weak, but warm enough, considering the circumstances. Phil sat on the other side of Myrtle, quiet and expressionless.

The funeral attendant stood up. His black, perfectly pressed suit and ramrod straight body made him look like a wrought iron fence post, immovable and stiff. With a wave of his hand, he signaled for the crowd to sit. Most did, but with a lack of chairs, some had to stand, huddled together in groups of three or four.

As the crowd grew quieter, he began. With an unconvincing, humdrum tone, he greeted the audience, speaking a few consoling words such as "tragic illness" and "beautiful child." He recognized the family members in attendance, Phil and Myrtle, along with the maternal grandparents and two sets of aunts and uncles. He then briefly introduced John and sat back down, keeping the same robotic expression as before.

As John stepped up to a small lectern, the breeze strengthened, and mourners wrapped their coats tighter against themselves. Other than a few shivers, the crowd sat stone still and deathly silent.

John scanned the family members. Most carried frowns that reflected more than sadness. They seemed to harbor scorn. In contrast, Tabitha, sitting in the same row, flashed a bright smile. With her blonde hair and blue eyes, she seemed to glow.

He turned toward the casket. Its dark wood grain and contrasting inner white lining stood out brilliantly against the backdrop of colorful flowers. He stepped up to the coffin and set his hands on the rim, taking several seconds to gaze at the still, quiet face before him.

He looked back at Tabitha once more, returning her smile, then, grabbing his folding chair, he walked around to the opposite side of the coffin. After rearranging the flowers to make room, he set the chair behind the casket.

As he stepped up on the chair, a low murmur buzzed in the audience. Now that he had elevated himself to where he could see the audience and Rose's body at the same time, some of the scowls transformed into attentive stares, and the mourners seemed more prepared to listen than before.

John pulled a pocket Bible from his jacket, opened it to a marked page, and, after whispering a quick prayer, began reading. "O daughter of my people, put on sackcloth and roll in ashes; mourn as for an only son, a lamentation most bitter."

He then looked down at Rose, raised a hand as if giving a benediction, and spoke with a loud, trembling voice. "Do not fear, little Rose, for although your body has been dashed by the ravages of disease and now lies still before us, you will not be abandoned. Yes, the shell that failed you in this life will waste away into the dust of the ground, but what blows with the wind to the four corners of the earth will not be lost among the waves of sea or sand. The one who weaved you together with the strands of human purpose and breathed his image into your precious soul, even as you slept in your mother's womb, will gather together the fibers of eternal life and knit for you a resurrected body.

"As you doze again in your final slumber, the one who holds the keys of heaven will fashion your kingdom clothes, and he himself will adorn you with a robe of holy white, wake you with a kiss of the new dawning, and lead you from the valley of the shadow of death through the narrow gates of everlasting salvation. Frail child of dust, who once harbored the fear of the great unknown, go now to the holy city that brightened your eyes during your final hours, for its streets of gold are lined with angelic majesties who eagerly await your march into Zion.

"We, however, are left with only memories of your life, images in our minds of your smile, voices in our ears that mimic your laughing presence, and the lasting impression of your loving embraces. But we will not dwell on these, for they are the past; they are Rose dust, dying embers of bittersweet recollections that make us smile and then break our hearts. These broken petals are laid at our feet, and looking down on their faded glory will not bring back the fragrant blessings of your short visit. No, we will set our eyes on what is not yet seen, on that joyful reunion day, when you, in the fullness of bloom of an unveiled face, welcome us into the New Jerusalem and teach us the songs of praise that we will sing together to our Lord and Christ for all eternity.

"We now commit your body to the bowels of the earth, but may he who first took your hand only a few days ago now reach out to take the hearts of those you love, so that your joy may be full when you gaze upon an unbroken family circle in the glory of heaven."

Without further comment, he stepped down from the chair, returned to his place, and sat down, his head bowed. He wanted to cry. He wanted to find the tears that flowed earlier that day, but they wouldn't come.

He looked up and scanned the audience again, this time finding a different aspect. The faces of the family members melted into weeping. Only one set of eyes stayed dry, Tabitha's. She beamed at her father, and he smiled in return, but as the weeping continued, the sadness drew him back to his mourning posture, his head downturned and hands folded in prayer.

The funeral director stood again and announced the procedure for viewing, this time with a voice that trembled with emotion. He finished with, "Please allow those in the front row to go first."

Without hesitation, Tabitha jumped up and rushed toward the casket as quickly as a hurried walk could carry her. All eyes fixed on her sweeping form. She gazed at Rose's body and, with a loving tilt of her head, smiled. Reaching into her pocket, she pulled out a pair of scissors and glanced briefly at those still seated.

Before anyone could rise to stop her, she raised the scissors and cut an inch-wide lock from her silky blonde tresses, creating a noticeable gap. Carefully folding the several inches of hair, she placed the lock under Rose's hand. "I know that you come into the world empty-handed and leave it the same way, but I'm hoping God will let you take this with you. Maybe you can have whatever hair you want in heaven."

The crowd's silent stupor allowed her words to carry, as if amplified, throughout the tent. John rose from his seat and took her by the hand. She offered no resistance and followed her father. They found Melody and Sarah, who were now standing near the back while the rest of the mourners lined up to file past the coffin.

John took Melody by the hand. "Do you want to view the body?"

She shook her head. "Let's just go home."

The two walked toward their car, followed by Tabitha and Sarah, but a strange feeling made John stop and turn around. Phil stood at the edge of the tented area. He offered a smile and a weak wave before turning back and disappearing into the viewing line.

John looked at Melody. "What do you think that meant?"

Melody kept her gaze trained on the crowd under the canopy. "He left the door open. I think it means, 'I'll talk to you, but not too soon.'" Her dark hair blew in the wind, and her cheeks had chafed red. Teardrops streamed back toward her temples, following thin lines etched by years of sacrificial love and concern.

"I hope you're right," he said. "I pray to God you're right."

Chapter 9

TEARS ARE CONTAGIOUS. *A grieving sigh is passed to a neighbor and becomes planted in his heart. Taking root in sympathy and fed by scars not yet healed, the seed of anguish grows in its new host and overwhelms the mind. Grief is a cleansing blight, expelling the poisons of loss and sorrow in tearful secretions of woe, unmistakable proof that the friendly infection has taken hold. A soft heart can muster no defense. Trained to respond to emotional triggers, it flutters and heaves, perhaps even becoming reckless in its mourning. But the tears bring relief—loss and emptiness released in streams of sorrow. After a season, they finally dry, marking the paths of pain. But can grief place its tracks on a heart of gold, the one who has died completely to selfish desires, or on a child of innocent faith? The mystery is great, and stifled sobs of brave hearts choke out the disease as it travels to its next victim. The contagion spreads; it leaves weeping in its wake, a heart attack of sorts, but is it a malady or a remedy?*

As he drove along the narrow country road, John absorbed the sights, filling page after page of prose in his mind, but nothing he would ever want to submit for publishing. His mental manuscript was too flowery, too pretentious. Still, the words soothed his troubled thoughts.

The bleakness of late autumn is enough to make even the most cheerful soul melancholy. Gray blankets in the sky cover the yawning trees, already undressing for the months of slumber ahead. Even the cold rain with its lazy drizzle holds none of its summer anger nor the gleeful announcements of its springtime wake-up calls. It seems that rainbows hide from the coming chill, knowing their happy messages are really a deception until they can truly forecast a final thaw. A drive through the country on such a day pushes the dreariness through our senses as the dying scenes rush past, hypnotizing us, the hum of tires on pavement singing the dirge of sunny days gone by.

"Daddy, why are you so quiet?"

Tabitha's voice shook him from his reverie. "Quiet? Was I being quiet?"

"Everyone is. No one's said a word since we left the cemetery."

John ascended a ramp and accelerated onto an interstate highway. After safely merging into traffic, he replied. "I've just been meditating, thinking about life and death and how the weather reminds me of death's darkness."

"You've been writing poetry in your head again, haven't you?"

He laughed. "I guess so, something like that. But I was also thinking about Phil, wondering how to approach him in the future."

Tabitha leaned forward and propped her chin on the front seat. Her belt stretched out to oblige. "And Mom? Why are you so quiet?"

Melody looked at her, frowning. "Sit properly."

Tabitha plopped back to her seat.

"I'm just sad, honey. The Graysons are hurting very much, and I feel for them."

"Same here," Sarah added from Tabitha's right. "Did you see how ashen Rose's parents looked? I couldn't hold back the tears."

"Well, I don't feel that way," Tabitha chirped. "Rose is in heaven. She's happy, so I'm as happy as can be."

John turned and gave Tabitha a wink. Now that she had bought into the truth, he could speak it more freely. "I understand how you feel. I'm happy for her, too."

"Honey," Melody said. "The Bible tells us to weep with those who weep, like Jesus did at Lazarus' tomb."

"Good point." John took her hand in his. "I've often wondered if Jesus wept because he was about to bring Lazarus back from heaven, but I agree that we should weep with those who weep."

"But they shouldn't be weeping," Tabitha countered. "They just don't understand. If we weep, too, then we'll be acting like it's a tragedy, when it isn't."

John peered at his side mirror while easing into the left lane, trying to pass a sluggish dump truck as it labored up the hill. Gaps punctuated his reply. "We don't weep . . . because we've lost Rose. . . . We weep because our friends are suffering, . . . whether they're suffering for the right reasons or not."

Melody touched his shoulder. "If we were ever to lose a daughter, I hope you would weep for her."

He remained quiet for nearly a full minute, biting his lip in thought. "If I were certain of her faith," he said, "I think I wouldn't weep, or at least I shouldn't. She would be in a better place, and any grief on my part would be selfish, focusing on my own loss. It wouldn't be like it is for Phil. He doesn't have any hope."

Melody shook her head. "We're just going to have to disagree on this one. There's nothing wrong with grieving."

John tapped the steering wheel with a closed hand but kept his voice soft. "If it's selfish, it has to be wrong."

"I'm with Daddy," Tabitha chimed in. "It's simple. Rose is happy, so I'm happy. I can't see her for a while, but if I worried about that, then I'd be selfish."

"Okay, you two. I give up. But I still have reservations."

"That's okay, Mama. Jesus will teach us what we need to know."

John took an exit off the interstate and drove along the familiar road toward home. "Now there's a philosophy I can live with."

* * *

Melody hung up the phone and drummed her fingers on the kitchen table. "Their answering machine seems to be working."

John peeked over the top of the morning newspaper. "How many times have you called?"

"That was the fourth." She lifted a pair of fingers. "The ladies at church planned the meal schedule two days ago, but we can't get started without making contact first."

"We can't force our sympathies on people. They probably just want to be left alone for a while."

Melody drummed her fingers again. "I think I'll walk over there later today and leave a dinner, something she can put in the fridge."

He set the paper down on the table. "What are you planning to make?"

"Not sure. Tetrazzini?"

"Mmmm. Perfect."

She patted him on the shoulder. "Want to help?"

"You bet." Flashing a grin, he slid his chair back. "I'll be the slicer and dicer . . . and the taste tester."

After an hour of preparation and thirty minutes of summoning her courage, Melody left the house and drove to the Graysons. As she approached their door, the autumn breeze lifted the edge of the foil covering of the casserole she carried, giving her a whiff of the steaming chunks of chicken that lay in their bed of pasta and bubbling white sauce. The hint of nutmeg was a delight, and the warmth of the rising vapor soothed her chilled skin. This would be a welcome treat, indeed.

She balanced the dish in one hand and pushed the doorbell, craning her neck to listen. No footsteps. No calls of "Come in."

She pushed it again, this time straining to hear a buzz, a ring, or a *ding-dong*, but no sound came. She pulled open the screen door and knocked on the dark wood. While walking up the sidewalk, she had noticed movement in the front room, so someone had to be home.

Finally, the door opened, revealing a tired-looking woman, her face careworn and pale.

"Oh, Myrtle. You look so tired. Have you been able to sleep?"

Myrtle shook her head. "Not much." With sloped shoulders, she gestured toward the inner hall. "Come on in."

Melody followed her to the kitchen, glancing to and fro at her surroundings. The house looked clean and tidy, everything in its place. Yet even the neatness likely caused Myrtle pain—no sign of an active preteen at home.

After placing the dish on the counter, Melody wrapped her arms around the grieving mother. "I've been praying for you. I'm so sorry for your loss."

Myrtle's weak hands barely touched her sides in return. Melody resisted the urge to cringe. It was like hugging a statue. Pulling back, she cleared her throat. "I brought you some chicken tetrazzini. I hope you like it."

"Thank you. Rose told me about your tetrazzini. She said it was—" Myrtle gulped and raised a hand to her mouth. "I . . . I think you should go now. I'm not really ready for company."

Melody patted her on the shoulder. "I understand." She then turned to walk out but swiveled back. "Please call me when you're ready, or have Phil call John. We can get together."

"I'll call," Myrtle said, "but I don't know about Phil."

"Is he home?"

Myrtle shook her head. "He comes. He goes. Sometimes he tells me where; sometimes he doesn't."

"My friends at church have set up a schedule for bringing meals for your family. Is it all right if they—"

"No." As if struggling to breathe, Myrtle laid a hand on her chest. "No, please don't. It was all I could do to answer the door this time. I don't want visitors right now."

Melody dipped her head. "I understand. I'll let them know."

"Thank you. I . . . I appreciate the thought." Her face twisting in anguish, Myrtle covered her mouth. "Please, I need to be alone now." She rushed from the room. Quick footsteps sounded from a nearby stairway.

Tears welling in her eyes, Melody walked out the door and closed it behind her. Poor Myrtle was suffering so terribly! But how could anyone ease her pain? A few meals would only fill her stomach, not the aching void in her heart.

As she drove home, questions filled Melody's mind. How was Phil handling Rose's death? What was going on with his relationship with John? Or lack thereof. So far, that situation seemed darker than ever—scowling family members at the funeral, unreturned phone calls, and now Myrtle's confirmation that Phil might not be open to friendship at all. Was Phil really so angry at John's apparent lack of sympathy? Was he pulling farther and farther away? How could they possibly reach him now?

* * *

While bustling around the kitchen, Melody hummed a tune, an old song, something from her childhood. A few words popped in now and then, something about a river and a mountain, but most of the lyrics stayed lost in the annals of days gone by.

She looked at a glass bowl on the counter, filled halfway with the Wheaties Tabitha had requested an hour ago, now wilted by the milk.

John had finished his breakfast long ago, and the other four kids had opted for Pop-Tarts and made their way to the schoolroom to get started on lessons.

"Tabitha!" Melody called. "In one minute, your cereal is going to the cat."

"Coming."

A few seconds later, Tabitha shuffled down the hall, dressed in a calf-length skirt and polo top. Yawning, she sat at the table and set down a sheet of cream-colored paper.

"Are you sick?" Melody asked.

"Just a headache."

"Do you still want your cereal?"

Tabitha shook her head. "I was hungry when I woke up, but not anymore."

"Did you go back to sleep?"

"No." She set a finger on the sheet of paper and slid it back and forth. "I was working on something."

"May I see it?"

Tabitha slouched in her chair. "If you want."

"I'll be over there in a minute." Melody poured the cereal into the cat's dish, rinsed out the bowl, and put it in the dishwasher.

"I'm going to visit the Graysons." Pushing up to her feet, Tabitha gazed toward the front door. "They should be up by now."

Melody locked the dishwasher and turned it on. "You said you have a headache."

"It's not too bad. It'll go away soon."

"Then let's wait for soon to come. Besides, the Graysons might not be up to having company." Melody wiped her hands on a towel and joined her at the table. "Let's have a look at your drawing."

Tabitha held it up. "It's Rose in heaven."

Melody stared at the drawing. The multicolored pencil sketch seemed far more complex than she expected from a twelve-year-old. A little girl, who looked remarkably like Rose, sat at the far left side of the page, not in the center where Melody thought Tabitha might place her best friend. She rested at the outer edge of a garden, facing the foreground and sitting on a flat rock beneath a large shade tree, the boughs of which arched over a tiny brook. The splashes of water pelting the carefully drawn stones gave the image of a rapid, shallow flow.

In the drawing, Rose seemed oblivious to the peaceful scene. With her long white robe spilling onto the grass surrounding her seat, her eyes focused downward. Her hands were occupied with some kind of craft on her lap, her face carrying a smile neatly outlined in bright red pencil. Close by and to her right stood a narrow, ivy-covered gate, slightly ajar as if ready to allow a wandering sojourner to find the peace of the garden within. It seemed to be the only entrance, or the only exit, in Rose's view. Here, dark vertical bars on the gate's facade interrupted the gay colors. Its foreboding appearance stood in stark contrast to the peace and beauty it guarded. The rest of the garden's border was an endless wall of ivy—lush, dark green, and impenetrable.

On the right half of the picture, and to Rose's left on the other side of the brook, a festival took place, a revelry of glistening shapes. They seemed human in form, but the swirling beings masked their details with blurring gyrations. Each dancer spun within bright colors, yellows and golds highlighting their featureless faces. They had no feet, just wavy golden robes, giving them the appearance of a unit, their individuality apparent only from the waist up. Raised high in worship, their arms ended in flickering tongues of fire.

The circle of celebrants seemed to move in time to an imperceptible beat, their exuberance building to an immeasurable crescendo, but still controlled, in pace with an eternal jubilee.

Nearly breathless, Melody spread out the picture neatly on the table. "Tabitha, it's extraordinary!" She pointed at the page. "Who are these people on the right?"

"Angels, I guess. Or maybe Christians in heaven."

"What's Rose working on? I can't tell what's in her lap."

Tabitha shrugged. "I couldn't tell either, so I kinda had to hide it in the picture, you know, make it blurry."

"You couldn't tell? What do you mean? You did the drawing."

"I didn't make this up," Tabitha explained. "I saw it in a dream. That's why Rose still has dark hair. I thought God would have given her blonde hair by now. That's what she always wanted."

Melody picked up a corner and let her gaze cross the entire drawing one more time. "So you think this is a real picture of heaven?"

Tabitha sat down and shrugged again. "Maybe. All my other dreams came true. But I couldn't really draw what I saw last night; it was so much more beautiful than this. I drew it as soon as I got up this morning. You know how dreams fade away so fast."

"Yes, I know," Melody agreed blankly, continuing to stare at the picture. "Why do you think Rose is off by herself?"

"I dunno. That's just the way it was. Those people were dancing, and she just sat there making something. It only lasted about a minute, but the dancers seemed to come and go from the group as they pleased."

Tabitha paused and closed her eyes, as if trying to recreate the scene in her mind. After a few seconds, she shook her head. "It's already fading away, but I know Rose didn't dance while I was looking. She's happy; that's all I care about. I want to show it to her parents. Maybe seeing that she's happy will help them feel better."

Melody handed the drawing back to Tabitha. "I . . . don't know . . ."

"Do you think Dr. Grayson is still mad at Daddy?"

Melody raised a hand to her chin and gazed at Tabitha's longing eyes, filled with sincerity that seemed to melt away every misgiving. *Maybe this is just what we need to break the ice with the Graysons, and I think Myrtle's usually home in the mornings.*

Finally, she reached for the drawing again. "Let's show it to your father and see what he thinks."

Tabitha jumped up with a smile but stopped suddenly, laying a hand on the back of her head.

"Tabitha, what's wrong?"

"I guess I *am* getting sick. The headache came back." She gulped and looked up at her mother, her eyes pleading again. "But I'm not too sick to visit the Graysons."

Melody felt Tabitha's forehead. Warm. Quite warm, in fact. "I'd better take your temperature."

"Can we show Daddy the picture first?"

Melody sighed. "Okay. Let's go." She walked toward John's office with Tabitha following close behind, soft-stepping as they drew near. This was John's office time, a period of the morning he reserved for uninterrupted work. Oftentimes, he would finish shortly after noon, leaving the rest of the day for the family, so she and the children usually honored the sanctity of his morning hours.

Melody cracked open the door. Inside, John sat staring at a computer monitor, his eyes darting back and forth as his fingers pecked rapidly, raising sharp clicks. With large books open on each side and a dozen or so Post-it Notes hanging in "can't miss" places in his field of vision, he was obviously in the midst of a productive writing time.

She smiled at the handsome profile of her dedicated husband, so focused, so determined to change the world. But he always trusted her to know when an interruption was appropriate. "John?" she called, knocking on the doorjamb. "Do you have a minute?"

He turned, his face lighting up. "What's up, good-lookin'?" he sang out, his fingers still pecking.

Melody walked in and motioned for her daughter to follow. "Tabitha has something to show you. I think it's important."

John reached out a hand. "Whatcha got, Babe?"

"Just a picture." She shuffled closer, extending the drawing.

John took it, looking first at Melody, and held the sheet with both hands. As he studied it, Melody and Tabitha glanced at each other several times. Melody read the nervousness in Tabitha's eyes. She desperately wanted everyone to believe in her dreams, and Daddy was the most important convert she could hope for.

After a full minute, John laid the drawing on his lap and looked at Tabitha. "Another dream?"

Intertwining her fingers nervously, Tabitha nodded.

"Tabitha wants to show it to the Graysons," Melody explained. "She thinks it will make them feel better."

John looked again at the drawing and bobbed his head. "Could be. At least it might open up the lines of communication, give us an idea of where Phil stands."

"She wants to take it over there today," Melody added, "but I think she's coming down with something. She's got a headache, and she might have a fever."

John laid his palm on Tabitha's forehead. "Not real warm, but could be something." He lowered his hand down to feel her cheek, then playfully poked her nose. "If she feels up to it, I don't see what's wrong with her making a quick visit. Phil might still be on leave from his job, and Myrtle's bound to be there."

"I'll go right away," Tabitha said, reaching for the drawing.

Her father held it back. "Mind if I scan it into the computer first? This is a Tabitha Hanson original, and I want to save a copy."

Tabitha grinned. "I'll get my shoes on while you're doing it." With a prancing skip, she hurried out of the office, leaving her mother and father alone.

John laid the drawing on his scanner bed and started the copying process on his computer. As the motor hummed, he extended his arm toward his wife. "What do you think?"

Melody sat in his lap and snuggled close. "About what? Whether she's seeing visions from God or whether she should visit the Graysons?"

"I'm already sure about the visions. I have no doubt God is speaking to her."

"I know what you mean. Too many coincidences."

John raised a finger for each point. "The quilt, the girl in the coffin, Dr. Wilkins. There isn't any other explanation."

"So now God wants her to be a bridge for the Graysons?" Melody asked. "Are we sending our little girl to do something we should be doing ourselves?"

"A bridge has to be welcome on both sides of a rift." He kissed her tenderly on the cheek and let his touch linger. "Maybe she's the only one who can reach them."

* * *

Tap, tap, tap. The fourth series of knocks finally prodded Myrtle to her feet. She had ignored many other knocks in the past few days, no matter how persistent, but these light taps called so gently, like a lost little bird, somehow communicating the same loneliness she felt inside.

She shuffled to the door, each lumbering step reminding her of her exhaustion. *No visitors, please. I'm just too tired. I never thought I'd be happy to have a broken doorbell.*

Discreetly pushing the curtain to one side, Myrtle peered through the living room window. On the front porch, a little blonde head swiveled back and forth—Tabitha, apparently trying to figure out if anyone was home.

Myrtle looked at the empty driveway. Tabitha knew. She had to know. If Myrtle had gone somewhere with Phil, her car would be parked outside to make people think someone was home. Rose had revealed that family habit long ago.

She shook her head. Why would she want to hide from such a

sweet little girl? It didn't make sense. Still, hours and hours of crying had taken their toll. She was just too tired to have company, too exhausted to entertain the bubbly cherub who had called Rose her best friend.

Her inner debate ended when Tabitha spied her in the window and waved, her smile so broad, it seemed impossible. Myrtle managed a smile in return. Tabitha's charms were simply irresistible.

When she released the curtain, the room fell dark, plunging her again into a deep emotional hole. Even walking to the front door felt like an uphill climb. As she reached for the knob, it seemed to withdraw and shrink. She had to stumble forward to catch it before it dropped out of sight.

Now leaning against the door frame, she turned the knob and pulled. As the light of midmorning poured in, the darkness within the house scattered like demons of sorrow fleeing the presence of the little yellow-haired angel.

Still smiling, Tabitha displayed a cream-colored sheet of paper with both hands. "Look, Mrs. Grayson! I drew this picture for you!"

Tabitha's enthusiasm seemed to leap across the gap between them. Myrtle felt a glimmer of joy squeeze into her tightly closed emotions. She took the paper from the eagerly outstretched hand and held it at her side. "Thank you. I appreciate it."

Tabitha's eyes dimmed. "Aren't you going to look at it?" she asked politely.

Myrtle shook her head as if throwing off cobwebs. "Oh. . . . oh, yes, of course." Still standing in the doorway, a full step above her visitor, she stared at the drawing.

At first the marks seemed only scribbles, undecipherable. She closed her eyes and then opened them and looked again. The image of a girl caught her attention, and the small face slowly clarified, colored pencil scratches transforming into a living, beloved face in her mind. Her emotional drought eagerly absorbed the colors, like a parched field soaking up drops of rain. Her eyes danced across the page to find more of the precious water she hadn't even realized she longed for.

Myrtle had no need for an interpreter. This was an image of happiness. Her daughter was in a place of joy. Finally, the living water burst through, flooding her soul and washing into her eyes in tears, fresh soothing tears, not the stinging acid that had poured forth the last few days.

She raised a hand to her face, covering her nose and mouth. She let out a short laugh and then a sob. Finally, she put the drawing on the floor, leaned over, and embraced Tabitha, enveloping her in tender, motherly arms. "Oh, you precious, precious girl!"

Tabitha tensed. No adult had ever done something like this before. Usually *she* was the one needing a hug from Mama or Daddy. What should she do?

She glanced heavenward for an answer. As she felt the growing wetness on her shoulder and the peaceful swaying from the gentle rhythm of Mrs. Grayson's sobs, she tried to fathom the depths of her friend's sorrow.

Her father's words returned to her mind—*Weep with those who weep*. Reaching up, Tabitha wrapped her arms tightly around Mrs. Grayson and let the grieving mother's horrible pain seep in. Second by second, a sense of anguish grew in Tabitha's mind—a lost child, an empty bed, a third place at the table, also empty. Scene after scene flooded her thoughts, each one lamenting the travails of loneliness and loss.

Tabitha's tears began to flow. She patted Myrtle on the back, and sang, whispering the words of a hymn into her ear. "Love lifted me; Love lifted me; When nothing else could help, love lifted me . . ."

A burst of maturity filled the little servant of God. Tabitha became a mirror image of the sadness represented in the crying woman in her arms, whom she clutched ever more tightly. Instead of releasing pain, Tabitha absorbed it. Instead of begging for relief from her burdens, she begged to take them on. Her tears were not from the wringing out of a weary and desperate heart; they were the purified tears of another, washed in love and released in a liberating cleansing of the soul.

Tabitha sighed and sang on. This love would be her song, the love that lifts the brokenhearted.

Chapter 10

MYRTLE WALKED past the front window and looked outside. With the curtains drawn back, daylight poured in, illuminating the living room for the first time since Rose's death. Now each glance into the yard brought hope rather than despair. Maybe Phil would be home soon. Maybe she could help him feel what she felt. The ten-ton weight of despair had been taken away.

Why? Who could tell? Ever since Tabitha left an hour earlier, she just felt lighter. Nothing had changed. Rose was still gone. Her husband was out again on one of his long drives in the country. "I need to be alone for a while," he always announced as he walked out the door, leaving her to her tortured thoughts.

She leaned her head against the glass. It wasn't too bad. She always occupied herself with housecleaning. That was easy. No one would ask how she felt, and she didn't have to smile bravely for well-meaning visitors. With Rose gone, the house stayed pretty clean anyway. So when a few minutes of vacuuming sapped all of her energy, it didn't really matter. She could sit and rest, cry a little, and then get up to do the dishes or sweep the floor . . . again. She just wanted to be alone. . . . No, she didn't really want to be alone; it just seemed easier that way somehow.

Now, those hours of pointless grief were finally over. The visit from the little angel had brought strength and purpose. Myrtle still felt tired and sad, just not quite as sad as before. The hopelessness was fading away, and now she wanted companionship, the gentle touch of someone she loved.

Sighing, Myrtle turned from the window and strode to the kitchen. Phil would surely be home soon, and if he could return to a house of hope, maybe his mood would change.

For the next half hour, she bustled from the refrigerator to the pantry to the stove. Probably nothing would help more than a nice lunch; a hearty bowl of hot beef stew would surely warm Phil up on this cool, late autumn day. But it was still hard. Microwave meals had been all she could muster lately, and even now she could barely poke at the chunks of meat and vegetables simmering in the pot. The last home-cooked meal they had enjoyed had been brought by Melody, a much greater comfort than the many cards and flowers delivered by anonymous van drivers.

She turned the stove down to simmer and set a lid over the pot. After glancing toward the front room again, she sat at the table and repositioned Tabitha's drawing near Phil's place. Maybe it would help him deal with his sorrows. Yes, that and a hot meal should do wonders.

Myrtle stared at Tabitha's picture again. Could Rose really be living somewhere wonderful, happy and busy with a fun craft? She had always enjoyed making things with her hands. Might she also be in the company of magnificent beings?

As her trembling finger touched one of the angels, Myrtle shook her head. Her professors had told her no, again and again. Rose's life was over, and nothing lay ahead. The cemetery plot was her final home; nothingness filled her dead mind. But Myrtle's heart told another story. A life so vibrant could never end. How could a soul spring forth fountains of love and joy even for a few short years, only to spill its treasures at the mere stopping of a heart?

Myrtle moved her finger to the image of Rose's face. Who summoned her to the altar on the last day of her life, and who sang the song that called her to the grave? Did Tabitha know something that others could not? Was she some kind of prophetess, a mistress of heavenly secrets?

A rattling sound shook her away from the drawing. White vapor lifted the pot's lid. She turned off the burner and began wandering around the house again, looking for something left undone. After another pass by the window, a rumbling sound reached her ear. She spun back. A car motor?

She rushed to the glass and looked out. Yes, it was Phil's car. His returns home had become routine, at least the times she had watched him—parking in front of the garage door, shutting off the engine, and then, after sitting for another moment with his chin drooping near his chest, huffing a tired sigh.

As he shuffled up the walk, Myrtle opened the front door and tried to infuse her voice with a hint of cheer. "Welcome home, dear."

Phil lifted his head. "Oh. . . . . Hi."

Myrtle held the door as he passed. "Lunch is ready."

"Huh? Oh, good."

She hooked her arm around his and led him into the kitchen, taking in a deep draw through her nose. "Now, doesn't that smell delicious?"

Phil shed his lightweight jacket and aimlessly tossed it on the back of his chair at the table. "Sure. I guess so."

"Sit down," she said, pulling out his chair. "I'll bring you some stew. It's homemade. I had a little taste, and it's real good, but I'm sure it'll be even better tomorrow; it hasn't had much time to simmer. The potatoes might not be very soft yet, but you like them that way, right?"

"Potatoes? Yeah, sure. Potatoes are fine." Phil sat in his chair, staring out the window at the backyard. His eyes seemed glazed over—faraway, lost, alone.

Myrtle set a steaming bowl in front of him and also at her own place. She again drank in the hot, aromatic vapors, drenched with the flavor of tomatoes and basil. "Ah!" she crooned. "If that doesn't wake up your . . ." She looked at him again, still staring out the window. He apparently hadn't even noticed his lunch. "What are you looking at?"

"Just the grass. It needs cutting."

"Don't worry about that right now." She pointed at his bowl. "Eat the stew. It'll make you feel better, warm you up all over."

Phil turned and took a sniff. "It does look good, honey."

Honey? Myrtle smiled. That was the first term of endearment she had heard from him since before Rose died. She reached over and rubbed his back. "I knew it would make you feel better."

Phil blew across his spoonful. "*You* seem to have perked up." After slurping the hot liquid, he leaned his head back and closed his eyes. "Oh, that *is* good."

Giving his back a final rub, she drew away. "Good for what ails you?"

After swallowing, he looked down at the bowl and poked at the stew with his spoon. "I'm not sick or anything. Just tired. I'm not sleeping very well. Bad dreams, you know."

"I know." She touched his arm. "I've heard you."

He dropped the spoon into the bowl. "You have?"

"Sure. I'm not exactly far away."

Phil grabbed a napkin and swiped it across his lips. "Sorry. I didn't know I was talking."

"You weren't talking, really. Just moaning now and then." She tried to make eye contact, but he didn't oblige. "What have you been dreaming about?"

"Rose." He retrieved his spoon and stirred, his tone quiet and melancholy. "It's always Rose. Even though I know she's dead and gone, I still see her. She's happy and seems to be with people she loves, like the Christian idea of heaven—singing, dancing, the whole nine yards."

"But that's not really a bad dream, is it?"

"No, but it's not reality. How can I get through the grief process if I'm bombarded nightly with false hopes?" He lifted a spoonful of broth and let it drip slowly over the side of the spoon. "They make me feel worse, not better."

Myrtle patted the back of his hand. "Been thinking a lot about it, huh?"

Phil nodded. "Every day. Especially on the long drives. The dreams haunt me, and I can't shake them."

Myrtle raised her brow. "Well, maybe you shouldn't."

"Shouldn't? What do you mean?"

"I have something to show you." Myrtle glanced around the table. "Where did I put it?"

"Put what?"

"Tabitha's picture. She drew it to cheer us up. I thought I put it here by your place mat." She scooted the chair back and caught a glimpse of the paper underneath the table. "Here it is. Something must have blown it." While Phil slurped another mouthful, his eyes averted once again, she set the page in front of him, just beyond his bowl.

Myrtle tapped it with a fingertip. "Do you mind taking a look?"

Phil turned and stopped chewing. His jaw dropped open, and his eyes widened.

"Phil, what on earth is wrong?"

"It—it's the same! It's exactly the same!"

"What's the same?"

Phil coughed and stood, trying to catch his breath. He shook a finger at the drawing. "It can't be! It's exactly the same as my dreams. How could she know?"

Myrtle stared at him. "I . . . I don't understand. What are you—"

"Look," he explained, pointing. "Here's the brook. This is the same tree, with that low-hanging branch. These odd creatures are over here dancing that strange dance. And over here is the gate. It's the only thing that's different."

"Different? How?"

Still standing, he stared again at the picture. He closed his eyes. His fingers tapped the table, apparently in time to the rhythm of a familiar but inaudible tune. After a tense moment, he pressed his palms to his temples and shouted. "I can't remember!"

"Remember what? Phil, what are you talking about?"

He picked up a corner of the page. "Myrtle, this picture is a snapshot of the dreams I've been having about Rose. The similarity in detail is astounding!"

"Tabitha drew a picture of your dreams? How could she do that?"

Phil paced between the table and the stove, hands in his pockets. "I don't know . . . I just don't know."

"Okay, so you don't know. But why are you so upset?"

He grabbed the picture and held it close to her. "This is my nightmare! This is the ghost that haunts me everywhere I go."

"It's not a ghost. It's Rose!"

"Rose is dead!" Phil shouted, snapping the paper down. "She's dead!"

"Then how did Tabitha—"

Phil slammed the picture flat on the table. Myrtle blinked and stared. Bowing his head, he whispered a slow count to ten.

Myrtle swallowed. Now wasn't a good time to say anything. Just wait.

Finally, he looked up again, the redness in his cheeks fading with his tone. "How should I know how Tabitha did it? We must have both seen the same image somewhere, maybe in a movie or a picture in the newspaper. There's always a logical explanation."

"Logical?" she repeated.

Phil caught his breath and stood next to his chair as if ready to sit again, but he pushed the picture to the side and glared at Myrtle. "Yes, logical. The evidence for extrasensory perception is relatively poor, and of course the spiritual theories aren't scientifically based. We're only left with the probability of a coincident experience."

Myrtle stared at him. As usual, his explanation had the solid ring of scholarship, not the tinkling of a thin hope. Had she fallen back into the foundationless faith of her mother? Not even the tragedy of a dead son could convince *that* woman of the cruel void in the heavens. No, Myrtle's brother would never return, and the stories her mother had told her of amazing events in their childhood, demonstrating God's love and care for them, really were coincident experiences. Those two words brought back the voice of a long-forgotten lecture, and with it the comfort of academic camaraderie. The confidence and scholarship of her professors had always been impressive, and a wave of intellectual satisfaction returned to her mind.

"Maybe you're right," she finally conceded.

"Of course I'm right. What else could it be?"

"What about the craft Rose is making?" she asked, trying not to make her doubt obvious in her voice. "Was that in your dream?"

"Yes."

"Why would you both think of that?"

"Simple." Phil lifted a finger. "We both want to remember Rose as being happy. When was she always the happiest?"

"When she was making something?"

"Right. It stands to reason that we would imagine the same thing."

Myrtle shifted her gaze, looking toward the floor as she tried to stifle a sob. "I thought it meant something. I thought maybe it was some kind of message." She began to cry but tried to finish through the spasms. "If only you could have seen Tabitha. She was so sweet, thinking about us, trying to make us feel better. She was just . . ." Myrtle lost her battle and wept.

Phil took her into a clumsy embrace. "Myrtle, you know I like Tabitha. I know she was trying to help. It's just that she's influenced by her father. His ideas are confusing a lot of people."

She pulled away from him, barely able to speak. "All I know is that I was feeling better, but now I can't even stand to live." She turned and walked to the other side of the room, crossing her arms over her chest as she glared out the window, though she glanced at him every few seconds.

Phil paced a short path, back and forth, hands on hips. After a few circuits, he shook his head and sighed, shoving his hands into his pockets. Just as he turned to walk away, Myrtle spun toward him. "Phil," she cried. "Wait!"

He froze in place, his gaze falling once again on Tabitha's picture. For a moment he seemed unable to catch his breath. In a flash of hands, he flipped the page over and turned to her. "Either get rid of it or put it away where I'll never see it." With that, he stalked out of the dining area.

Still weeping, Myrtle followed. She wanted to call to him, but his name caught in her tight throat.

Phil stormed out the front door and slammed it behind him. Myrtle hurried to the window and stared out. He jerked open his car door, started the engine, and drove away.

* * *

Melody looked at the thermometer. "You're going to the doctor," she announced with the authority of a military officer.

"I'm okay," Tabitha moaned softly. "Just need some sleep."

Sitting on the bed, her father took the thermometer and squinted at it. "103.4?"

Tabitha lay on the sheet, the covers pulled down past her socks. Except for her missing shoes, she was still dressed for the day, but her glazed eyes said she was less than ready to face the rest of it.

Melody looked at John. "What do you think?"

"She could have picked up a virus," he said. "Being so stressed over Rose and her family took its toll on her immune system."

"Maybe, but I'm not taking any chances." She reached into a medicine pouch and pulled out a bottle. "Please give her some Tylenol. I'm going to call the doctor."

John nodded and stayed with Tabitha while Melody left the room. After reading the label, he poured out the tablets and held them in his palm. She sat up and dutifully took them with a gulp of water.

He knelt beside the bed and brushed a strand of silky gold from Tabitha's eye. "Down for the count, huh, little lady?"

She smiled weakly. "It's just a bad headache. I'll be all right after I get a nap."

John held the thermometer up to her eyes. "That's not what this says."

Tabitha crossed her arms over her chest. "So, what does a little piece of glass know, anyway?"

"It knows you have a fever. That means you're worse than tired. But if I know your mother, she'll have an appointment set up for you in no time."

"John?" came a call from the other side of the house. "Please get her ready to go."

"There, see?" He patted her on the shoulder. "You'll have to find the energy to get up."

"I can't," Tabitha moaned. "My head hurts."

"I'll help you."

She held her hands up toward her father, and he gracefully lifted her out of bed. With her arms clutching his neck and his arms around her back and under her legs, he walked into the hall. The pulsating warmth of her hot face against his cooler skin rang an alarm in his mind. He could even feel the heat through her clothes.

He hurried his pace toward the kitchen. Melody met him at the door to the garage. "I got a three o'clock," she said, "so we need to leave right away. You help her into the car, and I'll get her some more water. Sarah knows she's in charge now, so we can scoot."

John detected a hint of apprehension in Melody's tone, causing his own concern to grow. He dared not think about Rose nor breathe the word *encephalitis*, but surely Melody had pondered the unmentionable.

As he carried Tabitha toward the car, his mind raced. *It's probably just a virus. There's an encephalitis alert in our county, but it's so late in the season for mosquitoes, the possibilities are too low to worry about. Rose was only the second person in all of central Florida to get the eastern equine variety, the deadlier strain. It's just too rare for such a coincidence to occur, two girls in the same neighborhood.*

Relieved by his own rationale, he lifted Tabitha into the backseat and tried to help her get as comfortable as possible. Seconds later, Melody arrived, carrying a pillow for Tabitha's head and a Thermos of water.

During the ride to the doctor's office, John stayed quiet at first. Melody kept glancing back and forth between the windshield and Tabitha, whispering to her at times, asking if she needed anything.

Soon, Tabitha fell into a peaceful sleep, undisturbed by the bumps. John accelerated more quickly than usual after stops at traffic signals, gripping the wheel tightly with his left hand and tapping it on the side with his right. He kept his eyes locked straight ahead, as if he could will the other cars out of the way.

Melody touched his arm. "Don't worry. We'll get there all right."

"I'm not speeding," he replied.

"Maybe not, but your mind is in a stock-car race."

John relaxed his grip, allowing blood to flow back into his knuckles. "It's just that there've been so many strange things going on lately, with young girls dying, dreams coming true in great detail, haunting drawings . . ."

Melody sighed. "It's enough to make your head spin."

While both remained silent for another minute, John tried to read Melody's mind. With her brow knit and her lips tight, she was obviously in turmoil. Finally, she took a deep breath and spewed out her words. "John, do you think Tabitha might have encephalitis?"

Although he had asked himself the same question a dozen times during the last several minutes, he had no ready answer. "I . . . I can't say for sure. I mean, I don't think so. The coincidence would be incredible."

"I know what you mean."

"But still . . ."

"Right," Melody agreed. "Stranger things have already happened." She turned toward Tabitha and reached back. "Her skin's still blazing hot. The Tylenol should have helped by now."

John looked at his watch. "Maybe."

Melody turned again toward the front. "Be anxious for nothing," she whispered.

John reached an open palm toward her. She took it, and they prayed together for the remainder of the drive.

Chapter 11

I T'S ALL RIGHT," Tabitha said sleepily as her father lifted
her out of the car. "I can walk." He set her down gently on
the parking lot pavement, testing her balance before letting
her go.

Tabitha dared not quiver. She stood straight up and turned
toward the medical building with confidence. Yes, she knew the way.
With five children in the brood, the path from the family home to
the doctor's office was well worn. Some of the children would tag
along with their siblings for their well checkups, but Tabitha had
never visited the doctor as a sick patient, at least not that she could
remember.

"What's Dr. Van Dorn going to do?" she asked while taking
deliberate, clumping steps.

"Oh, probably look at your ears and throat," her father replied.
He teasingly poked her head with his finger. "And see if there's an
infection lurking around in there anywhere. He'll probably listen to
your lungs and your heart. The usual stuff."

Her mother, who had been walking a few steps ahead of the two, stopped. "John, this is a first for her."

"A first?" He caught his wife's hand. "Hasn't she ever been sick before?"

Melody shook her head. "Never."

"Never? They all had ear infections or something, didn't they?"

Her eyes rolled upward. "No, at least nothing of consequence, and not at an age that she would remember. She's had well-child checkups, but it's easy to be brave when you're feeling good."

John held open the front door of the medical building. "Come to think of it, I can't remember her being sick, either." He took Tabitha by the hand again and looked down at her as they walked. "Are you scared?"

Tabitha shook her head, still trudging forward, staring at the large tiles beneath her. Better to stay quiet, just listen, and keep her head from pounding. They were right. She couldn't remember feeling anything like this. Surely it would go away soon. But the dizzying headache continued to throb. As the dull brown ceramic squares passed slowly beneath and around her, they seemed to draw closer and then farther away in rapid pulses. Was she falling? No. Her feet were still moving.

She clutched her father's strong hand and let out a silent sigh. Heaven and earth would fall before her father would let her slip away.

Finally, they stopped walking. Tabitha looked up. The elevator. That meant she had only a minute to try to feel better before they reached the doctor's office. Time to steel herself, gather her wits, and look up at her parents with a smile. After all, why make them worry?

When the doors slid open, her parents stepped inside without looking down. They never saw her smile. Now inside the elevator car, she let her countenance wilt. It hurt too much. Maybe it was better just to keep from looking completely miserable—stay calm and rely on her mother and father. They had never failed her before.

* * *

After breezing through the check-in routine, signing in and affirming the insurance information, the trio sat in the waiting area. Melody intertwined her fingers, nervous, restless. Every few seconds, she looked at Tabitha, then at John. Both sat with their eyes closed. Were they praying? Just trying to escape the dark cloud of mystery?

She scanned the room, reading each patient's face. Here were strangers, not quite willing to share their pain openly, but they seemed like kinfolk. Those who were well of body waited here for the sake of another, a love gift of time and comfort.

She smiled at a woman across the way holding a sniffling, red-eyed toddler. *Sore throat with a cold and fever*, Melody guessed. *With those droopy eyes, he looks just like Andrew did when he had the same ailment at that age.*

An elderly couple sat in the next two seats, the man with both hands clasped over the hook of a cane he straddled, and the woman with her right leg extended, her foot completely bandaged except for her five toes.

Melody stared for a moment at the big toe, somewhat gnarled and discolored. It might have been from an older injury, or maybe she had recently stumbled, stubbing her big toe first and then falling to break a bone in her foot.

As the elderly couple whispered sweetly to one another, smiling and gesturing with loving facial expressions, Melody lowered her head, unable to keep from smiling herself. What a wonderful display of enduring love! They had probably been married for fifty years or more, growing ever closer year by year, finding fresh reservoirs of love in themselves and virtue in one another.

She spied a metal band on the lady's wrist, a soldier's missing-in-action bracelet. Obviously, they had been through trials. Was it a son? A nephew? A loved one, to be sure, for the war was long over, but the dear lady's longing continued. What torture! They likely still had no idea where he was. At times, the agony probably threatened to rip them apart.

Melody read a hint of tired sadness in the lady's eyes, sad but somehow comforted and consoled. She then noticed a shiny, but dainty, gold cross hanging from the woman's neck. That explained a lot, a symbol of the strength they needed to pass through their dark valley.

Melody looked at Tabitha, who was now staring at the same couple. The lady smiled, and it looked like Tabitha was trying to smile in return, but a new grimace dug furrows into her brow.

The lady's expression bent to reflect Tabitha's agony. "Oh, you poor girl. What's your name?"

"Tabitha Hanson?" a nurse called from the door leading out of the waiting room.

The three rose as one, and Tabitha waved a quick good-bye to the lady as they left the waiting area of the office. Melody offered the lady a nod and whispered, "If you are so inclined, please pray for us."

The nurse, a big-boned woman with bright red hair, weighed Tabitha and led them to a typical exam room, serviceable and sterile, but a bit cramped for the nurse, two parents, and a miserable little girl.

"Sit up here, honey," the nurse chirped, motioning toward the paper-draped bed.

Tabitha set her hand on the bed and tried to raise herself, but she paused, holding the top of her head.

John boosted her the rest of the way. "There you go."

Tabitha braced herself with one hand, crinkling the paper. "I don't think I could sleep on this. It's too noisy."

"Open your mouth, please," the nurse said.

Tabitha obeyed.

The nurse pushed a thermometer under Tabitha's tongue. "Now close it."

Again, she obeyed.

"Now you just don't worry about a thing," the nurse said. "I'll take your temperature and we'll fix you up in no time." After waiting for the meter to beep, she read the digits and jotted the number down on a chart. "What are her symptoms? Anything besides the fever?"

"A severe headache," Melody replied.

"Other body aches?"

"Just her neck."

"Diarrhea? Vomiting?"

"No."

The nurse finished her notes and stepped toward the door. "The doctor will be in shortly." She pulled the door but didn't quite close it.

John stroked Tabitha's hair. "Is your headache real bad again?"

Tabitha's forehead wrinkled. "It hurts, but it's been worse."

He looked at her, almost nose to nose. "Can you describe the pain to me?"

Tabitha raised her hands to the sides of her head. "It feels like there's a big balloon in there, and someone's blowing it up, and it's pushing from the inside out."

"I heard that," came a friendly voice from the hall. Dr. Stephen Van Dorn stepped in, carrying a clipboard. Melody felt a wave of relief. Here was someone who might be able to uncover the mystery.

"Hi, Steve," John said, extending his hand.

"John, how are you?" The two shook hands warmly. "Hi, Melody," Steve added, nodding in her direction.

He then turned toward his patient. "Well, it's Tabitha, my little blonde poster child of perfect health." He tried to contort his face into a droopy frown to match her gloom. "I don't think I've ever seen you looking so sad."

Tabitha gave him a weak smile, but it quickly disappeared as a grimace bent her brow, and tears formed in her eyes.

John drew closer and touched her cheek. "Don't be afraid," he whispered. "I know it hurts, but the doctor is going to examine you and find out what's going on." After planting a soft kiss, he stepped back.

"So someone's blowing up a balloon in there, huh?" Steve laid the clipboard on the bed and set his fingers above Tabitha's eyelids, raising them slightly past their normal range. He studied her glazed orbs for a few seconds. "What was her temperature?" he asked himself, looking over at the clipboard. "A hundred and three?" He glanced at Melody. "Did she take anything for fever?"

"Tylenol, about forty-five minutes ago."

Steve pulled an otoscope from his lab coat pocket and flicked a switch on the side. A beam of light danced on Tabitha's shirt, the white dot darting from one sleeve to the other. "Well, let's see if we can find where that balloon came from."

The doctor checked the usual attack points of infection, gently probing and listening. After several minutes, he sighed. "With such a high fever, I usually find a pretty clear indication in the ears, throat, or sinuses, but not this time."

"Then what do you suggest?" John asked.

"Well, there are a couple of important things I haven't checked, so—" Steve stopped, eyeing Tabitha carefully. Her head had drooped slightly, and her bottom lip quivered.

"Okay . . ." Melody prompted.

Steve held up a hand. "Tabitha, do you feel like you have to throw up?"

She managed a nod, then covered her mouth. Steve lunged for a cabinet door, jerked out an emesis basin, and rushed it to Tabitha just in time. After a small heave, she was finished.

Melody jumped to her feet, but by the time she could get to Tabitha's side, Steve already had a towel and was dabbing her lips. "Don't worry. That happens quite often."

"Can I have some water?" Tabitha's cheeks blazed red. "It burns."

Steve pointed at a supply cabinet hanging on the wall. "There are paper cups right under there."

John filled one with water from the sink, careful not to spill it with his shaking hands.

"How many times has this happened?" Steve asked.

"That's the first time," Melody replied.

After taking a drink, Tabitha shook her head and spoke with a soft, weak voice. "Twice last night."

Melody stroked her hair. "Why didn't you tell us?"

"I didn't want to worry you. Anyway, I felt better after I threw up, so why bother you?"

Steve threw the towel into the bin. "Well, we certainly have a sick little girl here. I think we should get back to figuring out what's bugging her."

John slid his hands into his pockets. "I didn't really want to say this before, but since you haven't found anything yet, I was wondering . . ."

Steve looked at him, a curious expression on his face. "Go ahead, John."

Shifting his weight from side to side, John glanced at Melody. He motioned for her and Steve to come closer. As soon as they had huddled, John whispered, "We were wondering if she might have encephalitis."

Steve kept his voice low as well. "Encephalitis?"

"Did you read about Rose Grayson?" Melody asked.

Steve looked at Tabitha. "The girl who died from it just a few days ago?"

"She was Tabitha's best friend."

Steve kept his gaze on Tabitha. "And you think she might have been exposed to it?"

"Yes," John replied, "something like that."

Melody glanced at Tabitha to see if she was trying to listen. She sat quietly, her head turned away.

"Did you know that it's not spread through human contact?" Steve asked.

"Yes," John said, "but they often played together, sometimes near the pond. There are a lot of mosquitoes out there. Who knows? Maybe they walked through the same swarm."

Steve raised his brow. "I suppose it's possible, but it would be an amazing coincidence. I don't think you should be worrying about it, at least not yet."

Melody grasped Steve's wrist. "Could you check for it anyway?"

"Of course. Because of her severe headache, I was about to check for a symptom of meningitis, a symptom that also occurs with encephalitis."

"And what's that?" John asked.

"Watch." Steve turned back to Tabitha and infused a cheery tone into his voice. "Tabitha, would you please touch your chin to your chest?"

Tabitha strained her neck muscles and forced her chin down. As her chin inched its way, her body twitched, and tears began to flow. After a few seconds, she had lowered her chin only an inch or so.

"That's enough." Steve raised her chin up and rubbed her neck with his other hand. "Do these muscles feel stiff?"

Tabitha gave a barely perceptible nod.

Steve continued the neck rub. "Well, folks, I think we'd better check her into the hospital. Considering her fever after Tylenol, her possible dehydration, and this symptom, we should test her for the conditions we discussed."

"What kinds of tests would you do?" Melody asked.

"Well, when I heard about the Grayson girl, I was surprised by the speed at which the disease killed her. Since the area is under an encephalitis alert, I decided to read up on it more thoroughly."

Melody noticed Tabitha's ears perk up. Steve was too loud this time.

"What did you find out?" Melody asked, lowering her voice and hoping Steve would take the hint.

"Rose had eastern equine encephalitis, a dangerous variety. It mimics flu symptoms and meningitis in its early stages, so it's sometimes hard to diagnose. Since meningitis is contagious, we have to rule that out first. That would involve blood cultures and a spinal tap."

She motioned with her eyes toward Tabitha and whispered. "Isn't that a needle in the back?"

Steve finally lowered his voice. "I'm afraid so, but I think Tabitha will be brave about it, and I advise that you let her know what's going on."

As Melody imagined the procedure in her mind, she could feel the color draining from her face.

"You really should go right away," Steve continued. "I don't suppose you brought anything for an overnight stay, did you?"

Melody shook her head. "I didn't really expect—"

"I can call Joshua or Sarah," John said. "One of them can bring whatever we need."

"Good." Steve resumed his normal tone as he turned back to Tabitha. "Let's all go to the hospital and figure out how to deflate that nasty balloon."

Tabitha lifted her head, her expression now serene. "Did I hear you say if I got bit by the same mosquito that bit Rose, that I could have encephalitis, too?"

Taking a step back, Steve glanced at her parents. "Well . . . yes, it *is* possible, but not probable."

"I don't mind the tests," she said, staring straight into the doctor's eyes, "but I already know what you're going to find out."

Chapter 12

HOLDING THE PHONE to her ear, Myrtle paced back and forth in front of the kitchen counter, waiting for someone to answer. Finally, a strong "Hanson residence, Andrew speaking," sounded from the earpiece.

"Oh, hello, Andrew. This is Myrtle Grayson."

"Hello, Mrs. Grayson. What can I do for you?"

"I heard Tabitha's sick. How is she doing?"

"I'm not sure. My parents are checking her into the hospital."

"The hospital? What does she have?"

"We don't know. They'll be running some tests, I'm sure."

"Which hospital?"

"Arnold Palmer."

Myrtle bit her lip. The hospital's name brought a sudden rush of sadness. As her mouth dried out, she managed, "Thank you, Andrew," and pressed the button that disconnected the call.

Still holding the phone, she paced in front of the kitchen table. What could she do? Go to the hospital and see her?

She looked at her watch. Still visiting hours. She could make it. With a determined nod, she scooped up Tabitha's drawing from the table, dashed out of the kitchen, and hurried to a closet near the front door. After jerking a coat from its hanger, she flung it over her shoulders and bolted out the door leading to the garage, punching the opener on the way.

She jumped into her car and started the engine. *That poor darling. She doesn't deserve to be sick, not her.*

Myrtle zipped out of the driveway. With Phil's car gone once again, there were no obstacles to slow her down.

Screee! With a sudden spin of squealing tires, the car vaulted into gear. She stopped and smelled the oily stench of singed rubber.

"Oh, dear! Calm yourself, Myrtle. There's no use killing yourself just because . . ." She moved from verbal browbeating to silent meditation as she drove on.

She was there for me at the hospital. It really helped. But what can I do for her? She needs faith and hope, and I can't help her with either one.

The signs on the road became symbols as she passed each one— Stop, Yield, Slow— making her waver as they shouted her own misgivings. With her doubts weighing heavily, she slowed the car and pulled off to the side of the road. She contorted her face, trying to stifle the tears that struggled to pour forth once again, then, with a heavy thud, she let her arms fall to the steering wheel as she burst out in sobs.

"I can't give her anything!" she wailed. "She has more hope than I could ever give, and I have no faith at all." Myrtle sat and cried for a few more minutes, each pause between sobs growing longer and longer. Finally, with a long sniff, she raised her head and slammed the gearshift back into drive. *But I can be with her. Just sit, tell a story, anything to get her mind off her illness. That should count for something.*

She pulled the car back onto the street and sped toward the hospital, passing under a bright green traffic light.

* * *

Dr. Van Dorn studied the report, his jaw muscles tight. After taking a few notes, he slid his pen into his front pocket and stepped into the hall, closing the door behind him. With a sigh, he turned and marched across the ivory white tile floor, keeping his eyes downward as he walked. Reaching a room with a closed door, he knocked and then entered while pulling a sterile mask over his mouth and nose.

Inside, John shot up from his seat, while Melody stayed bowed over Tabitha's bed, half seated on a stool. Tabitha nestled on a pillow, asleep, her long tresses splayed over the white linens.

Sarah stood near her father, shuffling her feet nervously. Since Tabitha had been put in isolation because of the possibility of meningitis, all three wore masks and gowns.

"Steve," John said, "do you know anything yet?"

Steve nodded, not bothering to hide his concern with his usual cheery tone. "All the results are in, but I'd like to review all of yesterday's and today's tests to make sure you understand the diagnosis."

John nodded. "Go ahead."

"As you already know, the spinal fluid showed no bacteria, and the antigen test was also negative. The stain was negative for bacteria, although it showed white cells, which was verified by her high white count. Proteins were elevated; glucose was low. All of these point to a nonbacterial infection. That's why we did the CT scan and an MRI to find another source." After that synopsis, Steve took a deep breath before continuing. "I read the film, confirmed the results with the radiologist, and there doesn't seem to be much doubt. The CT indicated meningeal enhancement, and the MRI showed cortical lesions in the basal ganglia portion of the brain. Both indicators are extremely significant."

Melody stroked Tabitha's brow. "And that means?"

Steve tucked the clipboard under his arm. "We're pretty sure she does have encephalitis."

Reaching beneath his gown, John shoved his hands into his pockets but said nothing. Melody burst into tears, and Sarah scooted over to the bed to cry with her mother, holding her as they wept.

Steve pressed his lips together, trying not to cry. Of course tears were appropriate, but he had to show confidence. A lot of hope remained. Still, this was the saddest part of being a doctor, breaking bad news to a precious, loving family. They knew Tabitha had a pain-filled struggle ahead, and everyone in the room, including himself, would have gladly borne it for her.

After taking a halting breath, Steve continued, trying to sound less somber. "I know you're concerned, especially after you've had a close friend die from this disease. Even its name sounds awful. But I think Tabitha's prognosis might be quite good. She's sleeping comfortably now, and her fever is down. Now that she's been here for twenty-four hours and we've virtually ruled out meningitis, she'll probably be taken out of isolation. We're contemplating the treatment based on the test results and should have a schedule very soon."

John raised his eyebrows. "You mean you don't know yet what you're going to do?"

Steve shook his head. "It's not that simple. The traditional treatments have included anticonvulsants or corticosteroids, but the latest studies have shown that they're sometimes ineffective or even detrimental. I'm also a bit concerned about her elevated white count. It will figure into the treatment."

John looked at the floor, his cheeks flushing. "So what are our options?"

"We could still administer the medications I mentioned after we determine the dosage. Some of the people who were not helped by them were already in a stuperous state or even in a coma when they were diagnosed, so they may have been too far gone. In Tabitha's case, we caught this fairly early, so we'll probably go ahead with the meds and watch her progress carefully. We can take her off them at the first sign of a negative reaction."

"Will they hurt?" came a faint voice from across the room.

John turned and walked to the bed. "Tabitha?"

Melody had already taken her daughter's hand and tenderly caressed it.

Tabitha looked up at her father, her eyes just narrow slits. "Will the drugs hurt, Daddy?"

"Well . . ." John looked at Steve, then back at his daughter. "We don't know yet if they're going to give you those drugs."

Tabitha's eyes widened to normal. "Well, if Dr. Van Dorn thinks it's right, then I guess it's okay with me."

Lowering his head, John whispered to Steve. "How many encephalitis cases have you treated?"

"This is my first," he whispered back. He then took Tabitha's hand and kissed her knuckles through his mask. "God knows best, Tabitha, not me. I just have to seek his guidance."

Tabitha's eyes opened wider. "Then we should all pray," she whispered.

Sarah knelt at the bedside, followed by Melody. As they made room around the bed, John patted Steve on the back. "Shall we?" he asked, motioning toward the floor.

"Glad to." Steve reached for the controls and lowered the bed as far as it would go. Everyone laid a hand on Tabitha, and each took turns fervently beseeching God for his healing touch.

* * *

Myrtle pushed the hospital-room door and tiptoed through the opening. Inside, four people knelt at the side of a bed, heads bowed. Tabitha lay in the bed, her eyes closed, while four hands touched her from head to foot. One of the kneelers, probably John, spoke in a praying tone, but the words faded before she could figure out what he was saying.

Creeping closer, Myrtle stayed as quiet as possible. Of course she couldn't interrupt. She would just wait until they were done. Surely they wouldn't mind her presence.

After a few seconds, Tabitha spoke up, her eyes still closed. "Dear God, my head really hurts." She paused and gulped as her brow tightened. After forcing another hard swallow, she continued in a mournful whine. "It hurts really bad. But I know it doesn't hurt nearly as bad as it did for Jesus when he died for me on the cross. So help me to be as brave as he was."

Quiet whispers of "Yes, Lord" rose from each kneeling person. Melody's grip tightened around Tabitha's ankle, and the doctor reached his free arm around John's shoulder and squeezed him tightly.

After another brief pause, Tabitha went on. "Jesus, I don't want to die yet, so please heal me and help Dr. Van Dorn know what to do."

Myrtle stifled a sob, tightly clenching her fist against her mouth.

With a breathy gasp, Tabitha continued. "But what I want most of all is for you to somehow let Dr. and Mrs. Grayson know how much you love them." Her pain apparently easing, she let out a deep, satisfied sigh. "I know Rose is with you, but I don't think they believe it yet. I drew that picture you showed me, and I think Mrs. Grayson liked it, but I don't think she really believes what it means. Maybe you can convince both of them somehow. Anyway, that's all I have to say right now. As always, I love you. In Jesus' name, amen."

With her hand still on her lips, Myrtle wept as she stepped toward the bed. "Oh, you dear, precious girl," she cried. But when she drew close, she stopped, finally noticing the masks and gowns as the four kneelers stared at her.

Tabitha looked at her with loving, innocent eyes. "It's all right, Mrs. Grayson. They all love you, just like I do."

Tabitha seemed to glow. Her smile in the midst of pain was unearthly, a peaceful tranquility beyond comprehension. Her pale face was framed by her golden locks as they lay delicately spread about on her pillow.

Myrtle found a gap in the otherwise perfect thick strands, evidence of a missing lock, so lovingly given to her departed daughter. She again burst into tears, this time crying harder than ever.

"I'm sorry," she said, her words punctuated by spasms. "I just . . . I just . . ."

She turned and dashed out of the room.

* * *

"Myrtle!" Phil called as he walked through the house. He stopped at the kitchen and glanced around on the countertops. Since the car was gone, not finding the keys was no surprise, but no note? That wasn't like her. After another scan of the room, he headed for the telephone and looked at the answering machine's display.

He punched a button and waited. A mechanical voice announced, "You have no new messages. You have one old message. Message one." A female voice followed, sounding through the tiny speaker. "Myrtle? It's Mom. I know you're not answering the phone, but I need to talk to you. I was at the doctor's just now, and I saw that little girl who was at the funeral, you know, the one who cut her hair and gave it to Rose. I didn't recognize her at first, my eyesight being what it is, but when the nurse called her name, I remembered. Tabitha Hanson. She looked really sick, poor dear. Maybe you could call and check on her, and I'd like to send something if you could get her address for me. Let's see. It's Tuesday, and it's about four fifteen. Please call me. Bye." The machine finished with, "Four fourteen p.m. End of messages."

At the sound of Tabitha's name, Phil stared into space, barely comprehending the rest of the message. Again, his mind locked on the heavenly image, his beloved daughter happily creating a loving gift for someone special. His hand trembling, he punched the erase button.

"Message deleted."

Tabitha's sick? Phil clutched his stomach. Dizziness fogged his vision. Rapid-fire images flashed by—his own sick little girl, lying helplessly in a hospital bed, tubes protruding from her body. Then another scene emerged, the church altar—Rose enveloped in his bloodstained and rain-soaked coat. Finally, the funeral appeared, Tabitha pushing a lock of hair into Rose's stiff hand.

Phil wagged his head, as if slinging off the tenacious shadows. He took a deep breath and let it out slowly. "I . . . I'm sure it's nothing serious," he mumbled. Yet why would Myrtle rush out without leaving a note unless Tabitha really was very sick? And the phone message was from yesterday.

Searching the counter again, Phil noticed an address book folded open to the page for the letter *H*. While sliding his finger across the entry for the Hanson family, he picked up the phone. He punched in the first few numbers, then hung up, shaking his head. Calling their house was just too difficult. John might answer, and that would be worse than awkward.

After a moment of thought, he flipped through the pages of the address book again, found the number for the hospital, and punched it into the phone. Waiting through the series of recordings took some time, but after talking to a human being, he grabbed a pencil from a nearby basket and scratched down Tabitha's room number on a pad.

"Thank you very much," he said as he tore off the top sheet. He hung up, slapped the address book closed, and stalked out of the kitchen. With a sudden lurch, he halted, craning his neck and tilting his head, trying to listen to a faint sound. It was that song again. What was it saying?

The ticking of the living room's tall grandfather clock dominated the soundscape. He tried to tune out its methodic click, hoping to key in on the whispering chant in his head. Finally, he marched toward the clock and halted the pendulum, tilting his head once more. It was louder today, the melody as beautiful as ever. But what were those words?

He pressed his hands against his ears. The sounds had to be coming from inside his head. They just had to be.

For several seconds, he stood motionless.

What's that? The children? What about the children?

He closed his eyes and stooped. Maybe a lower plane would be a better place to hear the scant sound. After dropping to his knees and listening for nearly a minute, he opened his eyes wide.

"I know what they're saying!" he said out loud.

He jumped to his feet and looked around the room, but no one was there, no one who could have chanted the haunting rhyme. He had to tell someone, write it down, record it on tape, or he might forget the words, those mysterious lyrics that finally revealed what Rose was making in his dream. Almost tripping over an ottoman, he ran back into the hallway.

Trying to regain his balance, he placed a hand on the wall and took a deep breath. It all made sense now! But how could it? It didn't make sense for it all to make sense! It was just a coincident experience, just a mirage, nothing more than that. A mirage doesn't need explanation.

Phil straightened his body and stared straight ahead. After a few moments, he swiveled his head slowly from one side to the other. The drawing. Where was it?

He trotted to the dining table and scanned the surface; then he searched underneath, throwing the tablecloth to one side and dropping to his knees. Not there.

Slapping his hand on the table, he stood again, taking a deep breath. Of course it wasn't there. He told Myrtle to get it out of his sight. But where could she have put it?

After scanning the room a final time, he ran toward the front door, snatched his jacket from the foyer closet, and burst out of the house, slamming the door behind him.

Chapter 13

MELODY RUSHED out of Tabitha's room, pulled her surgical mask over her head, and looked both ways down the hall. There she was—Myrtle turning a corner to start down another corridor.

After stripping off her gown and throwing it into a laundry bin, Melody hurried to the adjacent hall. When she turned, Myrtle was nowhere in sight. Where could she have gone? The new hall was so long, she couldn't have reached the other end that fast.

Melody spotted another hallway to the left, as well as many rooms along the length of the corridor—too many to search.

Taking her time now, she walked across the expanse, swiveling her head back and forth and glancing into the rooms on each side. Most were patients' rooms. Myrtle wouldn't have barged into one of those. A maintenance room? Not likely. Elevator? Maybe, if the door had already been open. Otherwise, not enough time.

As she walked, fluorescent lights passed overhead in a rhythm of glaring flashes. Finally, she reached a set of double doors on the right and read a sign just above—the hospital chapel.

Melody tapped her chin. Would Myrtle be attracted to a spiritual place of refuge? It was worth a try. She opened the door and looked inside the dimly lit room. A few track lights up front illuminated a series of religious symbols on the wall, a cross and a Star of David, among others. Three short rows of pews faced the icons, divided in the middle to make a center aisle. A crying lady sat in the second row on the left side.

Tiptoeing in, Melody whispered, "Myrtle?"

Myrtle turned, then spun toward the front again. She buried her face in a handkerchief, rocking back and forth as she sobbed.

Melody slid in next to her and draped one arm around her shoulders. Myrtle flinched, stopped rocking, and wept on.

The crying spasms slowly diminished as Melody waited in silence. Although her own worries had been freshly planted, she wanted to play the role of comforter. Her daughter lay in pain in a nearby room, and being away from her ripped her heart, but no one else could do this ministry of mercy. Sarah was too young, and John—well, very few people understood his "bedside manner." Although his heart was filled with love and tenderness, most strangers couldn't see past his academic face.

Melody squeezed Myrtle's shoulder. This was a woman's job . . . a mother's job. No one else could know what it might feel like to lose the fruit of her womb.

As light sneaked through the tiniest cracks to illuminate the darkest recesses, Melody hoped Myrtle would feel her motherly sympathy. Through the loss of her daughter, Myrtle had been brought to despair, her solitary fruit that once held bright promise wrenched from her arms. Her only hope for the future was now buried with her daughter's mortified corpse.

Now there was nothing else. Old age and the promise of physical deterioration would have no garlands of youth to decorate the decay and make tolerable the coming gravesite on the horizon, no grandchildren to scamper through her winter years and warm her heart with shining eyes and loving embraces.

An ache knifed into Melody's heart. She now faced a similar tragedy, not one that would end her genealogy but one that threatened to ravage her soul. Could she stand up to it? Could she endure such a calamity without despairing?

Her lips trembled. Tears welled. As heat began to rise into her face, she shook her head. *Faith! You have to have faith! Don't despair, or you'll lose all hope!*

When Myrtle finally settled down, she turned toward Melody. Her eyes seemed used up, exhausted, having poured forth too many sad stories. After wiping her nose with a tissue, she whispered, "It's encephalitis, isn't it?"

Melody tightened her lips, trying to keep her composure. "Yes. Yes, it is."

"What does the doctor think about her, uh . . . her recovery?"

Melody forced her voice to stay steady. "He's not real sure. He has a fairly positive outlook, because we caught it pretty early. But, as you know, it's a dangerous disease. Tabitha has lesions on her brain and a high white count. She's a very sick girl."

"How can you be so calm? I was a basket case while Rose was in the hospital."

Melody folded her hands in a tight clutch. "I guess I look calm, but my heart feels like it's about to explode. It's just that I've learned how to have peace even in the midst of turmoil."

With that introduction, Melody explained her understanding of life and death, of the future and who held her hopes for eternal blessings. She told Myrtle of Jesus, of his promises of peace during the storms of life and of his power to change hearts of despair into hearts of joy. Most important, Melody spoke of faith in things not seen, of repentance and a transformed way of life.

When Melody finished, Myrtle wiped her tears. "You sound just like my mother." She raised her fingers over her mouth. "Oh, I didn't mean that as an insult. You'd like her very much. She's a Christian, like you. She has a lot of faith."

Melody cocked her head. "And when did you lose yours?"

Tilting her head down, Myrtle smiled. "I didn't know I was that transparent. My brother died in Vietnam . . . well, he was missing in action and never found. I was devastated, but my mother took it in stride, never really admitting he died. 'God will bring him back to us,' she always said. She never lost hope, so I never had anyone to . . ."

"Hold your hand?" Melody asked, reaching over to cover Myrtle's trembling hands.

Myrtle gratefully embraced Melody's offering. "Something like that, I guess. Anyway, I couldn't believe in a God who would let my brother die. I couldn't accept a faith that made my mother look like such a fool."

"And what about your father?"

"He was a lot like Mom, very stoic, but he never had a problem admitting the truth, that my brother was dead. He tried to comfort me, but I didn't want to be comforted. I wanted to cry. I wanted to blame someone, to curse all the heavens, anyone who would dare take my brother away."

"Did your mom ever accept the truth?"

"Not really. I think she knows, but to this day, she wears an MIA bracelet with his name on it."

"Really? An MIA bracelet?" Melody gave way to a little smile. "Does she have a bandaged foot?"

"Yes, she does!" Myrtle exclaimed, but her surprise quickly subsided. "Oh, that's right. She saw you at the doctor's office. She told me. That's how I found out that Tabitha was sick."

"Yes, we saw her there, and I noticed the MIA bracelet, but I was too far away to read it. What's your brother's name?"

Myrtle looked toward the floor and answered quietly. "Thomas. We all called him Tommy."

Melody tried to catch Myrtle's eye again. "Did Tommy have the faith of your mother and father?"

"Definitely." She raised her head once more, apparently glad to talk about her brother. "He was the reason I had faith back then. He was so full of life and love! He treated me like a princess. Even though he was quite a bit older, he played games with me, and he never spoke a cross word. He even read the Bible to me whenever Mom and Dad were away. When he was in Nam, he wrote letters, sometimes addressed to me only, and he told me about how God was working through him, even during battles. He said he always thought about me."

"No wonder you missed him so much." Melody stroked Myrtle's knuckles with her thumb. "What a treasure he must have been."

Myrtle turned away, sniffing again. "I still miss him. I was his little Myrtle the Turtle. He used to say . . ." As her voice dwindled, sobs took control once more.

After waiting a moment for Myrtle to compose herself, Melody spoke again. "So what do you think now? Was his faith in vain? Did his life end forever in some jungle far away?"

Myrtle stayed silent for several seconds before shaking her head. "I guess I've never really come to grips with that. Sometimes I imagine him living in a faraway land, unable to get home, and I rescue him on a white stallion, and we ride home to my mother's waiting arms." As she wiped her eye, her frail smile trembled. "But in the waking hours, when my mind is clear, I know he has to be dead."

Melody strengthened her hold on Myrtle's hand. "It's no wonder you're so torn. If God doesn't exist, then nobody's faith in him makes sense, and Tommy is dead and gone forever. You'll never, never see him again."

"Now that sounds familiar," Myrtle said, allowing herself to laugh. "Phil's said something like it many times, but for a different reason."

Melody bit her bottom lip. Now that Phil had been drawn into the conversation, she had to be careful. Casting doubt on her husband might backfire. "Myrtle," she said gently, "did Phil draw you away from faith?"

"No!" Myrtle set her fingers over her lips. "I'm sorry. I mean, I had already renounced my faith when I met Phil in college in a philosophy class. We studied together and had a lot of long talks. I guess you could say he solidified my doubts and unbelief, but I had already decided on my own."

"Would he object if you turned back to God?"

"Are you kidding me?" Myrtle said, laughing again. "He would think I'm nuts! But I don't think he'd yell or anything, if that's what you mean; he'd just lecture me to death."

"And try to dissuade you?"

Myrtle tilted her head downward again. "Something like that."

Melody looked up at the cross on the wall. Time to redirect the conversation. "When was the last time you talked to your mom about all this?"

Myrtle shook her head. "It's been quite a while. Nothing much has changed. I don't see what good it would do."

Melody rubbed Myrtle's shoulder. "You've been through a lot. I'll bet she could help." Melody eyed the cross again, remembering the tiny golden one Myrtle's mom wore. "Have you tried asking her what the bracelet means to her?"

"What do you mean? It's just like any other MIA bracelet."

Melody pictured in her mind once again the silver band and imagined the Christian soldier it symbolized, a beloved son and brother, gone but not forgotten. Why would Myrtle's mother continue to cherish Tommy's memory in this way, even at the risk of alienating her daughter?

After a few quiet moments, Melody enveloped Myrtle's hands again. "Do this for me. Talk to your mother. Bring up the subject and ask her what *missing in action* means to her."

"What? Why?"

"Trust me. I think her reasons might surprise you."

* * *

"Visiting hours are now over." John looked up at the speaker on the ceiling and then at Sarah. Both had pulled their masks down below their chins, allowing them to see each other better.

"Mom's been gone quite a while," Sarah said. "Should I go look for her again?"

"Where would you look?"

"I don't know. I guess I'm just antsy."

"Don't worry. She heard the announcement. She'll be back soon."

Sarah paced a three-foot-long path, glancing every few seconds at her watch. "So do we have to leave now?"

"Do you *want* to leave?"

She looked back at Tabitha, both hands trembling. After a hefty sigh, she resumed her pacing, slower now. "I'm torn. It hurts like crazy to see Tabitha like this, but I don't want to leave her. She needs me."

"She'll probably sleep for quite a while, so she won't even know you're gone." John slumped down in his chair and closed his eyes. "You and your mother get some rest at home. I'm staying here for the night, and you can come back in the morning."

"In the morning?" Sarah asked. "May I skip my classes?"

Peeking at her with one eye, John laughed. "Let me rephrase that. You can come back when you finish your classes."

Sarah looked around the room. "There's no bed for you."

He tapped the arm of his chair. "This folds out into a bed. It won't be too bad."

The door creaked open, and Melody walked in. John jumped up and gave her a gentle peck. After bending her lips into a tired smile, she stepped to Tabitha's bedside. "How's she doing?"

John joined her. "Resting comfortably. They can't give her any pain medications, because they have to do neuro-checks, but she managed to go to sleep anyway. She moaned and groaned for a while, but she's been pretty still for the last ten or fifteen minutes."

"Did Steve say anything about her treatment?"

John nodded toward the IV bag. "The last I heard, he's going to try something new in the morning and just treat the symptoms until then with some kind of steroid." He looked at his watch and yawned. "I think you and Sarah had better head for home soon."

Melody grimaced. "I've been delaying that as long as possible."

"That was our agreement. We've already been over it."

Melody reached around his waist and drew him closer. "I know. But first I want to tell you about my conversation with Myrtle. I think you'll find it very interesting."

* * *

The gravesite looked different in the fading light of dusk. The tombstone's letters seemed harder to read, and with no other visitors moving about, loneliness settled upon the cemetery in an eerie vigil of lurking shadows. Fear and desolation would be the sentries for the night, as they were every night, with reminders of death scattered throughout the grounds.

Phil usually visited during his long meditative drives in midday, but this evening, as if beckoned by the voices that sang in his mind, something mysterious drew him back to his daughter's resting place.

He knelt at the foot of the grave and read the tombstone's inscription.

Rose Grayson 1978–1990
Beloved of her Parents
We Will Miss You

He scowled. Was that all he and Myrtle could come up with? The other markers held such beautiful sentiments—wishes for heaven's glory, hopes for future reunions, messages of peace and comfort. By comparison, their choice to avoid religious verbiage made them look like hard-hearted infidels, and with the mysterious choir in his head chanting poetic sentiments over and over again, their pitiful inscription seemed like a hasty afterthought.

He touched one of the votive gifts on the burial plot, a bouquet of daisies, one of several he had placed during his visits. The oldest bouquets had wilted, their fading glory an apt symbol of Rose's physical corruption. The newest, laid just hours before, displayed fresh carnations, their white blossoms still radiant in the failing daylight.

Phil picked up the carnations and held them close to his nose. As the gentle aroma washed over his senses, tears welled and dripped for the thousandth time. Words poured forth in his mind, a soliloquy from his broken heart.

If flowers could sing, these would be singing the angels' song. They bear the white robes of that host of heaven, the company that frequents my night visions. Why does the fear of death bring out such spiritual longing? Is it the pride of existence, thinking ourselves so important as to manufacture an imagined eternal soul? Is the loss of a loved one so draining as to make us lose our sense of reality? I feel it myself. It would be so easy to accept the religious view, to have hope for something more than this life, to believe Rose really does dwell in happiness.

But I can't throw my brain away. I have to live by what's reasonable. I admit that Tabitha's picture made me doubt for a moment . . . well, maybe for more than a moment. It had the ring of truth, like the school bell at college. Such a wonderful sound. It summoned me to lectures that held me entranced for hours, aged men orating while I copied their wisdom into notebooks I would later study for days on end. But how could two clarion bells ring such conflicting notes? It still makes me wonder, but Tabitha's drawing can be explained in terms of the here and now, and her bell has to be the song of overwrought emotions.

And what about Tabitha herself? She has a gift, to be sure. She's bright and perceptive, able to see and remember images that most people bury in dark places. But now she's sick. I really should go and see her, but somehow I'm afraid. Afraid of what? I really don't know. Maybe I think she'll say something else that will strike another blow on my wall of rationality. Maybe it's the sight of a sick girl that I fear, and I'll see Rose all over again and suffer more pain, pain I could hardly bear the first time, pain that comes back to seize me by the throat when I least expect it.

His internal debate now at an end, Phil picked up another gift he had laid next to a basket of daisies, a laminated photo of three-year-old Rose sitting in a playground swing. In his mind's eye, the image animated. Little Rose swung back and forth, her smile bright as he propelled her high into the air.

"Higher, Daddy! Higher!" She giggled in perfect delight, and a younger Phil joined in the laughter, the purity of innocent joy radiating from both father and daughter. Then, with one final push, Rose swung high into the air, and she squealed with pleasure. But this time only an empty swing returned. Phil, now graying and gaunt, bent over the vacant space, then fell to his knees, weeping. Still on the ground, he looked up and scanned the skies, searching in anguish for his little lost angel who must have flown away somewhere into the brightly lit heavens.

As soon as the imagined scene faded away, Phil wept bitterly. Seconds became minutes, and minutes became hours. Darkness covered the cemetery, and the closing rattle of the entrance gates finally prodded him out of his meditative trance.

After hurrying to his car, he drove past the watchman with an apologetic wave, and the gate closed once again behind him. At the first stop sign, he paused. Should he go to the hospital? Would Myrtle be there? Did he really want to talk to John yet? As he thought, a new image entered his mind, Rose and Tabitha blowing bubbles on his front porch, giggling and prancing around as they pretended to be a train, puffing soapy steam spheres into the air behind them. Tabitha always made sure Rose had longer turns with the blower and insisted that Rose's bubbles were bigger and lasted longer. Whenever Tabitha was around, Rose seemed happier, full of life and energy, glowing.

Phil pushed the gas pedal. He would swallow his fears and his pride and challenge the darkness in his soul. He would visit the little angel of light.

* * *

Tabitha fluttered her eyelids and looked around. Where was she? What was this place? Her head pounded. The pain wasn't new. But everything around her seemed veiled by mist, including the strange creature looming at the side of her bed. She blinked again. The creature was a blue box attached to a tall metal pole. The bag at the top of the pole seemed to dangle from a hundred feet above, precarious in its perch from the end of the creature's long arm. The face on the box blinked its eyes in a precise rhythm, not a threatening stare, but still scary as she lay helpless beneath its scrutiny.

A tube descended from the bag to her left hand, the end hidden by criss-crossed strips of tape. Tensing her muscles, she looked all around. The rest of the hospital room came into view, snapping her out of her daze. The creature became the IV apparatus, and its eyes transformed into rhythmic counters.

Grinning, she mumbled, "No wonder I feel so awful. A strange alien is sucking out my blood."

She glanced to her right and found her father, sound asleep, his breathing heavy. Even asleep, his presence felt good. Just a call would bring him to her side in a heartbeat. Her guardian was on duty.

Tabitha yawned and turned away from the light coming from the hall, but the light suddenly brightened. She turned back, but, just as quickly, the room grew darker. Someone had come in, opening and closing the door in silence.

Glancing at her father, she searched the dimness. She didn't want to wake him, not if it was just the nurse.

A few seconds later, a familiar face emerged from the shadows. Dr. Grayson.

"Hello, Tabitha," he whispered.

"Hi, Dr. Grayson," she whispered back. She raised a finger to her lips. "*Shhhh!* My daddy's asleep."

Dr. Grayson winked. "Then let's be sure not to wake him." He straightened the covers on Tabitha's bed, smoothing some wrinkles and missing others. "So how are you feeling?"

"I have a terrible headache, but it's not as bad as it was when we came in." She pointed at the IV bag. "I think they're giving me something for the swelling."

"Did the doctor tell you what you have?"

She nodded. "I have encephalitis, just like Rose did."

He thrust his hands into his pockets, his face turning grim. "That's what I heard the nurse in the hall say. You certainly are a brave one. When Rose went into the hospital, she was scared."

"But she was a lot sicker than I am, and besides, she came into the hospital without the Lord in her heart. She left it holding his hand, though."

Dr. Grayson raised his eyebrows. "That's very eloquent for a girl your age."

"I'm not trying to be eloquent." Widening her eyes, Tabitha gazed up at the ceiling. "I saw it. She walked with him through a valley and then into heaven."

"Oh, yes." He withdrew his hands from his pockets and clutched the bed rail. "Your dreams."

"And yours, too," she added.

He cocked his head. "How do you know about my dreams?"

"Mrs. Grayson told my mother, and she told my daddy. They thought I was sleeping, but I was listening." She covered her lips with her fingers. "Oops. I guess I was eavesdropping, wasn't I?"

A tear formed in Dr. Grayson's eye, and he quickly wiped it away. "Don't worry about that. It wasn't really a secret."

Trying to ignore the pain, Tabitha grinned. "But it's exciting, isn't it—"

Her father coughed. She watched him for a moment as he turned to his side and pulled a blanket high over his shoulders. She then turned back to Dr. Grayson, lowering her whisper further. "But it's exciting that God showed you the same things he showed me."

"Exciting?" He lifted an eyebrow. "I suppose you would think so." He leaned closer, so close she could smell his peppermint breath. "Was your dream a still picture, like what you drew?"

"Oh, no! It moved. While Rose kept working on whatever she was doing, the angels danced and sang."

"So you don't know what Rose was working on?"

"No. I looked and looked, but I couldn't tell. I could see yellow, but that was about it." Tabitha tried to read his eyes, still sad, but filled with curiosity. "Could *you* tell what it was?"

He shook his head. "I couldn't see it in my dreams either. But I think I imagined an answer."

Tabitha furrowed her brow. "Imagined?"

"Yes. I've been seeing the same things you have. We've added our sorrow to some image we've both seen and blended in our hopeful imaginings of what would make us happy."

Tabitha tried not to frown. "I don't mean to be disrespectful, Dr. Grayson, but I haven't imagined anything. My dreams come true."

He shook his head. "No offense taken, young lady. But it's me I'm worried about. I think my imagination has run a bit wild, and it added a few things that your dream didn't have. Now if our dreams matched in extras like those, then that would be more than a coincidence."

"What extras did you imagine, then?"

"Well, I think I imagined what Rose was making, but it was the song that started me thinking about it."

"A song? What song is that?"

"The song the angels were singing while they danced. It haunted me for a long time, because I couldn't catch the lyrics. My mind was certainly playing some strange tricks on me, but I finally figured it out, and it gave me a clue to the mystery of Rose's craft."

Tabitha let her smile grow in spite of the pain. "Oh, I know that song, Dr. Grayson. I've heard it so many times, I've got it memorized."

He swallowed hard. "Memorized?"

"Yes, it goes like this." After clearing her throat, Tabitha sang in a whisper:

Now let the children come to see the blessings of the king,
For only those who hear his word may with the angels sing.
The gate is narrow, straight the path, and few come by this way,
So welcome children pure in heart who step in here today.
Now come and sing a song of praise, uniting in one voice,
Of narrow gates and welcome mats, we gratefully rejoice!

She paused, then added, "That's what the angels sing, but I still don't know why they dance."

Dr. Grayson stared with wide eyes. His face grew pale, and with shaking hands he patted Tabitha's shoulder. "I . . . I have to go now."

Turning clumsily and nearly falling over his own feet, he hurried out the door.

Chapter 14

PHIL PULLED into his driveway, unlatched his door, and jumped out. Although the cool, breezy night air offered a refreshing nip, there was no time to enjoy it.

He hustled to the house, swung the door open wide, and hurried to the kitchen. Glaring at the answering machine, he read the text on the screen. One message.

He pounded his finger on the Play button. *I hope it's Myrtle. It'd better not be some solicitor.*

"You have one new message. Message one."

"Phil, it's Myrtle. I've been at the hospital visiting Tabitha. She has encephalitis, poor girl! But she's doing pretty well, considering. Right now I'm at Mom's. I know I didn't tell you where I was going, but I didn't get a chance with you being gone. If you didn't get any supper, there's some of that stew left in the refrigerator. Don't wait up for me."

Phil blew a long sigh. She was okay. That was good.

As his heart settled down, he stared at the kitchen counter—clean and tidy, nothing out of place. He swung around to the table. A vase of fresh flowers decorated the center of a clean tablecloth. The floor, too, seemed spotless.

Phil picked up a frame from the counter, their family trio posing for a professional photo shoot. It was all so wonderful back then, and now . . . now one was missing and his heart had a hole, a deep chasm that would forever ache.

He touched Rose's face, then Myrtle's. She was such a good wife, putting up with all his nonsense, giving up her career to be a stay-at-home mom for Rose, making sure meals were ready and the house was always in order. She was so . . . so perfect.

And now? Now she had walked out, at least for a while. And why not? He had left her so many times to search for answers to his grief, while she stayed home alone, buried in her own sorrows with no one to talk to. It made sense that she would seek out comfort from her mother. He certainly hadn't been around to offer any.

Yet when she came back, what would happen? She would want to talk, to ask a thousand questions about how he was feeling, to try to get him to explain his emotions.

He shook his head. That would be too much. It hurt badly enough just to live. How much worse would it be if he had to rehash the tragedy and its consequences on an hourly basis?

Still, just to have her there meant so much. Her presence, her loyalty, her love gave him something to live for, far more than his patients ever could. They were paying customers. She was a giving heart.

He needed someone to talk to, someone who cared to hear him out. And who but she would understand? If he tried to talk to anyone else about Tabitha's revelations, they would think he was going crazy. Even talking to Myrtle would be embarrassing, because he'd have to raise the spiritual possibilities, even after so many years of lectures to the contrary. Of course, John Hanson would gladly talk to him, especially about the spiritual issues.

Phil shook his head. No. He wasn't ready to swallow that much pride yet. He just had to think—just sit quietly and calmly and think; let his logic and reasoning capabilities take over.

A shivering tingle crawled up his skin, raising tiny goose bumps from his toes to the nape of his neck. He turned toward the front of the house. What was it? Was he really that close to the edge, imagining a presence he couldn't see or hear?

He walked to the kitchen entrance and peeked around the corner. The front door was open, letting in a stiff draft.

Shaking his head at his own paranoia, he stalked to the door in a huff, but just before he slammed it, he noticed a brown package resting on the front porch, obviously a wrapped book.

He stepped out, picked it up, and read his name on the address label. *Hmm, UPS must have dropped it off right after I left.*

As he walked inside, touching the neatly wrapped edges, he closed the door gently. Then, still standing in the foyer, he ripped away the paper, dislodging a small yellow note that fell out and wafted to the floor in spinning circlets. He snatched it up and read the handwritten message, speaking out loud in a mock announcer's voice.

"This book is for highly intellectual minds, like yours. Sincerely, John Hanson."

He grinned at his impersonation, then felt ashamed, mocking someone who wasn't even there. How childish! Sure, he and John didn't see eye to eye, but he was just trying to do him a favor the best he knew how, and the poor guy was suffering. No need to mentally tear him down.

With one more rip, he revealed the book's cover.

"*Scaling the Secular City* by J. P. Moreland," he murmured. "Now that's an intriguing title." As he wadded up the paper, he strolled down the hall and into his den. He tossed the wad toward a trash can in the corner, missing. No matter. He'd get it later.

With a grunt, he plopped himself down in his well-used, over-stuffed easy chair and began flipping through the pages of the book. After a minute or two, he looked up. *An apologetics book? What am I going to do with a Christian apologetics book?*

He slapped it closed and looked around his den. Was there anything else to do? With the cemetery closed for the night, that option was out. He could drive there and park, but looking at the shadowy tombstones from afar would drive him nuts. Besides, Myrtle might come home, and he'd miss her return.

Scanning the room, he took in the memories. Maybe that would be enough of a distraction, anything to get out from under the ten-ton boulder, this horrible weight of lonely feelings.

Although fat books filled the shelves, and papers lay strewn about his desk, the room never felt so empty—yes, empty, even with his usual inanimate companions still in their usual places. His valedictorian trophy stood proud and tall on its shelf of honor along with his other awards, and the same haunting pictures hung in their assigned locations on the wall.

In one, an eleven-by-fourteen-inch framed photo, Phil, Myrtle, and Rose stood in silly positions in front of Cinderella's castle at Disney World. Rose was seven and wearing mouse ears, her facial expression shouting the pleasures of fun family times. All three had their hands on their knees in mock football stances, as if they were about to charge toward the cameraman, Phil losing his balance and about to fall down.

He chuckled. *I fell flat on my rear.*

Scanning the room again, he stopped. Next to a pile of old magazines sat a stuffed animal—a scraggly old lion. One ear was missing, the victim of an incident with their neighbor's dog. His mind flashed back to a Christmas morning eight years ago when four-year-old Rose gave him this special gift. "My daddy is like a lion," she said, adding a little roar. "He's the king of the jungle and protects me from the crocodiles."

From all across the office, memories begged to be replayed, but each one pounded like a hammer on his heart. They once brought warmth and life, but now they were empty shells, cold and wasted, like a pregnancy miscarried, a womb that had its promised treasure torn away. Yes, the room was truly empty, empty and silent.

Burying his face in his hands, Phil listened to the silence. This had been his mode of grieving during these lonely days, sitting in tense solitude and quiet meditation, and the hardening emotional calluses had grown to protect him. There would be no new tears this time.

He looked up at the ceiling. If there was a God up there, would he listen to someone who didn't believe in him? Would it hurt if he said a prayer, just a short one? If God didn't exist, who would know?

He cleared his throat and spoke softly but clearly. "God, if you really are there . . ." He paused, feeling those hated tears pushing through. He pressed his eyelids closed to shove them back, but his voice gave away his emotions, shaking, pitching high. "If you really are there, I guess Rose is with you. I'd appreciate it if somehow you could let me know. This pain is more than I can take."

When he finished, the new silence seemed more ghostly than ever. It was too quiet, unsettling even. *Maybe I should go back to work. The hustle and bustle of busy staff workers, patients' questions, the yakking and joking around with the other doctors would take my mind off all this stuff. When it's quiet, all I can do is sit and think about Rose, and then that infernal singing starts again.*

He tilted his head and sat as still as he could.

No, not a sound.

He sighed and settled back in his chair, propping his new book in front of him. Well, it promised an escape, and besides, this would be an easy way to hear what John had to say without actually having to talk to him.

"Okay," he said out loud. "I'll read it. It's a good place to bury my mind for a while." Once again, he flipped open the book. "At least till Myrtle gets back."

The next few minutes melted into hours as Phil engulfed himself in arguments about cosmology, epistemology, and absolutes. Even though it pulled him in ways in which he was unaccustomed, he thoroughly enjoyed it, feeling as though he was back in college, stretching his mind toward horizons unknown. When the sound of the front door opening reached his ears, it seemed foreign. Who would be coming in so late at night?

He jerked himself back to reality and jumped to his feet. "Myrtle, is that you?"

"Yes, Phil," she called from the foyer. "Did I wake you?"

Phil grabbed a piece of scrap paper from his desk, marked his place in the book, and hurried from the office. He met her in the hall, almost colliding with her, and kissed her warmly.

"Well, I guess you're not mad at me," she said, laughing.

He tucked the book under his arm and helped her take off her coat. "No, just concerned. I haven't seen you since I left this afternoon."

Myrtle pressed close to his side. "I left in a hurry, too. I just had to see Tabitha; then I went to see Mom. Did you hear that Tabitha's sick?"

"Yes. I listened to your message." Phil took her by the hand and led her toward his office. "But why were you out so late?"

"Seeing Tabitha and talking to her mother brought back a lot of memories. I felt like I really needed to talk some things out with Mom."

Phil stopped at the doorway and turned toward her. "I understand." He moved the book to his hand and rubbed his fingers across the cover. "She's a remarkable little girl."

"Yes, she certainly is." She touched the book's spine. "What's this?"

He laid it in her hand. "John sent it to me. It's an intellectual defense of Christianity. It's pretty good, actually."

"Are you persuaded by it?" she asked as she flipped through the pages.

Shaking his head, he let out a chuckle. "It's going to take more than vigorous, logical argument to get me to change my mind."

"Oh, really? I thought logic was everything to you."

Phil held up a pair of wiggling fingers. "Two positions may both seem logical, but I can't choose the one that's incomprehensible."

"And I assume you're saying that God is incomprehensible?"

"Certainly the Christian concept of God is." Phil lifted both hands high into the air and waved them around. "Can you imagine an eternally existing, all-powerful, infinite, uncreated being?"

"No," she replied, handing the book back to him, making him drop his hands to receive it, "but I'm not sure I can imagine there not being a God either." As she released the book, something shiny gleamed on her wrist.

Phil pointed at it. "What's that?"

She stroked a smooth metal band that peeked out from under the end of her long sleeve. "It's an MIA bracelet. Mom got it for me right after Tommy was reported missing, but I refused to wear it. She saved it for me all these years."

He set the book on the floor and pulled her closer. "It's a nice sentiment, I suppose, but why now? You've always been upset at your mother for carrying that torch so long."

Myrtle smiled and again rubbed the bracelet. "I never really listened to her with an open mind before. When the last of the prisoners were released years ago, she refused to take it off. I hated her for it. She just wouldn't let go, so I couldn't put it behind me either, I thought. Tonight she explained to me that even though Tommy's dead, he's really just missing in action."

She hooked her arm through his and rested her head on his shoulder. "She read me a letter from one of his buddies, a guy named Sam. He didn't see what happened to Tommy, so we didn't get any clues about that. But he told a great story. Sam had been shot in the leg, and Tommy dragged him out of a swamp and saved his life. Before he hurried back to the battle, Tommy gave Sam a pocket New Testament and told him to read it while he waited for the medic. Tommy was in action spiritually as well as physically, and now he's just missing from us. Mom knows we'll be reunited someday."

Phil gave Myrtle a long stare. "I guess you're the one who's been persuaded," he finally said, turning away.

She touched him on the back. "Are you mad at me?"

He whirled around again, his cheeks warming. "Mad? Why should I be mad? After eighteen years of intellectual sharing and communicating on common ground, you decide to throw it all away because of a string of coincidences and emotional upheavals. I don't see why I should be mad about that."

Myrtle set her hands on her hips. "Sharing and communicating? You've got a lot to say about sharing! Our daughter dies, and you're the one who runs off every day for hours on end, not telling me where you're going, and leaving me here to cry alone. And here I am worrying about you getting mad!"

"I told you, I'm not mad!" He lifted his hands and began pulling his hair in mock insanity. "I'm frustrated, confused, and disturbed, but I'm not mad!" He then clasped his hands to the side of his head and rubbed them down his face, mentally counting to ten as he tried to calm himself.

"You're right, though," he said, quieting down. "I have left you alone too much."

As her hands dropped from her hips, her face took on a pleading look. "I couldn't stay alone, Phil. I had to talk to someone. What did you want me to do?"

He waved a hand. "Just do what you want. I can't blame you for turning to religion after all that's happened. I don't blame you for anything."

"You don't blame me?" she asked, rubbing his arm. "Do you mean that?"

He shoved his hands into his pockets and tried to make his voice as soothing as possible. "Myrtle, I've felt the longing, too, the need for something more than this life. I've been thinking about this for a long time. You know, we've both felt guilt and pain, more than we ever imagined we would. We've blamed ourselves and each other even if we never said so. We need comfort. We need to be filled. We need joy again, to somehow think that Rose's life isn't really over. But I can't believe in something just because I want it to be true."

She combed her fingers through his hair. "That's something I've always loved about you, Phil."

"What's that?" he asked, trying for a playful tone. "My hair?"

"No, silly! That you're always honest with your feelings, even when you don't like them."

Reaching up, he grasped her hand and pushed her palm against his chest. "Myrtle," he said, his voice trembling. "I think I've been running away from my feelings lately." In slow pulses, he repeatedly pressed her hand closer and then released the pressure again, simulating his heartbeat. "I've felt so . . . so dead in here since Rose died."

"Phil, I know." She leaned her head against his chest. "But if only you could have heard Melody tonight. She is so full of life and faith! And Tabitha! Oh, what a little angel!" She pulled back and looked him in the eye. "She has a gift, and every gift must have a giver. You can't deny that, can you?"

He studied the MIA bracelet on her wrist. "No. I can't. There's something very different about that girl." He then looked at Myrtle again. "I saw her tonight, too."

"You did? Was she asleep, or did you get to talk to her? Did you talk to John?"

"John was the sleeping one," he said, laughing, "and I talked to Tabitha all right. She always seems to knock me for a loop."

"She knocked you for a loop? What do you mean?"

"Well, the first time was when she drew a picture of my dreams. Tonight she sang the song that's been going through my head, the one the angels sing while they dance."

Myrtle stared at him, her mouth agape. "That's incredible!"

"Incredible?" Phil repeated. "*Incredible* can't possibly describe it. I was so shocked, I had to leave. All the way home I theorized and calculated, trying to think of a rational explanation. Maybe we both heard that song sometime in the past, an old TV program, a radio show. Then, after a while, I felt like such a fool. I've heard Christians trying to explain away my intellectual challenges to their faith, and here I was, ready to blindly hold to my faith in nothing at all, trying to find some idiotic argument against a more reasonable conclusion."

"God giving Tabitha a vision of heaven seems more reasonable to you?"

Phil crossed his arms. "I'm just saying I felt foolish arguing against the Christian interpretation. It doesn't mean I'm ready to embrace it yet."

For a few seconds, they just stared at each other. Phil drank in her lovely gaze. It was so trusting, so accepting, far more than he deserved. Finally, she took both of his hands into hers. "Would it upset you . . ." She paused, biting her lip for a moment. "Would it upset you if *I* embraced it?"

He raised his brow and took a deep breath before answering. "I can't say that I'd like it, but I wouldn't object."

Myrtle rubbed his arm again. "Then I'll call Melody and ask her what I need to do."

"To become a Christian?" he asked with a snort. "Don't you know? Haven't you heard the mantra? 'Repent of your sins! Believe in Jesus! He'll save you from hell and give you eternal life!' Didn't your mother or Tommy ever tell you?"

Her gaze dropped to the floor, her trembling lips parting as she shifted her weight from side to side. "I'm sure they did, but I think I was too young to understand. Obviously it didn't take."

"Whatever." He waved toward the telephone. "Go ahead and call Melody. I'm sure she'll be glad to tell you how to get saved."

"Is that sarcasm?" she asked, looking up at him with fiery eyes. "You really don't want me to call her, do you?"

Phil raised his right hand as if making an oath. "I don't have a problem with Melody. She seems to be a fine lady."

"But you still have a problem with John."

Sliding his hands into his pockets, he brushed his foot against the carpet. "I do, but I really can't say I know why anymore. I was annoyed when he saw something positive in Rose's death. I mean, that was about as ignorant and unfeeling as you can get. But his speech at the funeral was beautiful, truly beautiful and upbeat, and I did like what he said about Rose. I can't deny his sincerity."

"What do you want from him? You're the head doctor. What would heal the rift between you?"

"Head doctor, huh?" He smiled. "You haven't pulled that one on me in a while."

"Only when I have to."

"Okay. Time for my psychoanalysis." Pacing slowly, he took on a scholarly tone. "Actually, the rift, as you call it, is probably just on my side. I'm the one holding a grudge. During the funeral, I wanted a mournful speech and for everyone to cry with me, and he didn't deliver. But at the same time, I understood. From his point of view, everything he said was a loving gift."

She pointed at him. "There you go again."

He broke out of his doctor mode. "Go again? What did I do now?"

"You're being honest with your feelings. Keep going, Doc. What's making you hold on to that grudge?"

"Well," he said, stroking his chin. "I suppose I was offended because he wouldn't think the way I wanted him to think. He couldn't feel my pain, and all he could talk about was Rose in heaven, and I couldn't deal with that."

"Then you should talk to him. Tell him why you were upset. I mean, he's really a nice guy. He'd probably want to know that he isn't exactly Mr. Sensitive all the time. I think he'll listen."

"You're right. He probably would." He reached down and picked up the book. "I'll get in touch with him tomorrow. Maybe I'll have this finished by then."

* * *

A laugh shook John awake. He opened his eyes and stared at the dim room. Yes, it was the hospital room. Tabitha's illness wasn't just a bad dream. He had awakened to a continuing nightmare. The laugh must have come from a nurse outside, or maybe a visitor.

Still lying on the makeshift bed, he yawned quietly. So tired. During the night the door had opened and closed several times, the usual bustle of hospital personnel—checking vitals, giving medications, and changing shifts. Yet, his body had enjoyed a few hours of sleep. It would have to be enough.

He sat up, rubbed his eyes, then stretched them wide open to adjust to the room's odd blend of light and darkness—a ray from the partially open door cut through the room, illuminating part of Tabitha's bed, while diodes, red and white, emitted both steady and blinking lights that shot through the pattern.

Sniffing, he took in the distinctive hospital smells. The aroma of rubbing alcohol, mixed with a hint of bandage gauze, served as a pleasant mask against the pungent cleaning ammonia that seeped in from the hall. But when the door opened once again, a new wave of the bitter odor swept in, stinging his nostrils.

"Oh, good morning, John," Steve said, marching in. "I trust you enjoyed our deluxe accommodations."

"Perfect." John stood up and began folding his bed back into a chair. "By the way, when does the maid come in? I didn't get a mint on my pillow last night."

Steve fished through his pockets. "I'll see that you get one. They're on special today for a hospital bargain-basement price of only twelve dollars."

John replaced the chair's cushion, shoving it firmly into place. "Think insurance will cover it?"

"Not a chance. Your sweet tooth is definitely a preexisting condition."

Both men laughed. "I'm afraid it's a congenital defect," John said. "Maybe we should discuss it over a doughnut."

Steve's bright smile withered a bit as he held up his clipboard. "I'm glad you're awake. We can discuss Tabitha's treatment. Depending on her test results, we may be starting something new this morning."

John stretched into a wide yawn. "Good. I was kind of uncomfortable with doing nothing."

"Oh, we weren't doing nothing. The medication we gave her last night is supposed to reduce swelling in her brain, but we started with a relatively small dose to see how she would respond."

John lifted his eyebrows. "And?"

Pursing his lips, Steve nodded. "She tolerated it well. Her vital signs are in order. No bad reactions."

"Then is she getting better?"

Steve paused, his smile now forced. "It's a bit premature to say that. We'll do more tests this morning and schedule another CT. It'll be interesting to see how she feels when she wakes up."

"So it's kind of a guessing game right now."

"In a way. Our job is to keep the virus from endangering her body until she can fight it off herself. We can keep the swelling down and help prevent seizures, but there are no real cures."

"Fair enough." John shoved his hands into his pockets. "Not much else we can do."

Steve leaned over Tabitha's bedside. "Let's see if she's ready to talk to us."

"I'm already awake," Tabitha announced.

"Good morning, sweetheart," John said as cheerily as he could manage. "Why are you lying there with your eyes closed?"

"When I open my eyes," she replied softly, "my head hurts more."

"And how much does it hurt now?" Steve asked.

As if on cue, Tabitha grimaced and shifted her body under the covers. "It's pretty bad."

"Can you give it to me on a scale of one to ten? One is perfectly fine, and ten is the worst pain you've ever felt."

"My head is about an eight or a nine. When I came in, that was a ten."

"Okay. That helps." After readying his stethoscope, Steve pulled her covers down, exposing her sky-blue hospital gown from her shoulders to her waist. "Does anything else hurt?"

Tabitha squinted at her body, as if taking a mental inventory. "My neck hurts. About a six, I guess. It felt better during the night, but it hurts this morning."

John stroked her wrist. "Is that a bad sign, Steve?"

Listening to Tabitha's heart, Steve tilted his head and tightened his lips into a thin line. "I expected her head and neck to hurt, so that doesn't sound an alarm, and she hasn't convulsed." He patted

Tabitha's covered thigh. "And she's alert. That's important. Some encephalitis patients are stuporous or comatose. That would be a very bad sign."

John looked down at his precious daughter. That wasn't enough. Being alert and not comatose might be good signs, but until she was laughing, singing, and dancing again, there would be no rest. "So should we be optimistic?"

Steve turned and grasped John's shoulder, lowering his voice. "As you well know, Christians should always be optimistic, but medically we won't treat her optimistically until we see her brain lesions and white count shrink."

"And you'll know more about that later today, right?"

"Right. But don't expect a clean report. It takes time."

Steve flipped through the pages on a clipboard—Tabitha's vital statistics. John walked up behind him and read the figures over his shoulder. He understood some of the tiny, muddled numbers, blood pressure readings and heart rates, but he had no idea what Tabitha's white count should be, and some of the other categories were completely foreign.

He glanced at the doctor, catching the back side of his profile—so dutiful, so attentive, so loving—but was he the right man for the job? Of course he was a superb family practice doctor, but could he handle this illness? Should they ask for a specialist? But would it hurt Steve's feelings to question his abilities? Maybe. But this was too important. He had to risk the question.

"Uh . . . Steve?"

Steve turned. "Question about the data?"

"Not really." John cleared his throat. "I was just wondering . . . are you making all the decisions in Tabitha's treatment?"

Steve tucked the clipboard under his arm. "No. I've been consulting with specialists. I'm not experienced with this particular disease, but I'm your doctor and your friend, so I've been hustling over here from my office whenever I can. I'm acting as sort of a go-between for you and the specialists." Steve touched Tabitha's blanket. "Dr. Smithers examined her this morning while you were sleeping. He treated several encephalitis patients during the last outbreak a few years ago."

"And he woke me up," Tabitha said, her eyes still closed. "He has cold hands."

Steve laughed. "She still has her sense of humor. That's good."

Tabitha's eyebrows lifted, but she kept her head still. "Daddy, Dr. Grayson also came to see me last night while you were sleeping."

"Really?" John raised his arms into another yawning stretch. "I must have been out cold. I didn't hear a thing."

"Dr. Grayson?" Steve asked. "Rose's father?"

"Right." John set his hands on the bed rail. "What did he say?"

Tabitha strained to open her eyes, but she quickly shut them again. "Well, first he asked how I was feeling, but he really seemed to want to talk about what my picture meant."

"The drawing from your dream?" John asked while glancing toward Steve. "The one with the angels dancing?"

"Right. He said he imagined what Rose was making."

John looked at Steve again. "Rose was sitting on a rock, working on a craft," he explained. "Tabitha drew the picture and showed it to Rose's father."

He turned back to Tabitha. "What was she making?"

Tabitha heaved a sigh. "He never got around to telling me. After I sang the angels' song, he just left all of a sudden."

"The angels' song?" both men asked.

Tabitha smiled at the chorused question. "Yes, it's the one they sing when they dance, at least it's the one I hear. They might sing other songs, too."

John pressed his body against the rail and leaned over her. "You sang a song to Dr. Grayson?"

"Yes. He mentioned it first, because he said that's how he figured out what Rose was making. But when I sang it, he got kind of upset and left right away."

John and Steve glanced at each other before turning back to Tabitha.

She opened her eyes again, a tight grimace furrowing her brow. "Why do you think he did that, Daddy?"

John caressed Tabitha's head, combing her now-oily hair with his fingers. "I'm guessing you both heard the same song in your dreams. He just couldn't handle the shock that you could know the words."

"Because he doesn't believe in God," Tabitha concluded with a nod.

"Right, sweetheart. Do you think maybe you could sing it for—"

Tabitha's nod seemed to cue a growing, racking pain. She stiffened her body and cried out. "Ohhh!" Crossing her arms over her chest, she tried to squeeze out the contorting, twisting spring that threatened to bend her bones like rubber.

"Aaaar!" she wailed. Her eyes rolled up into her head, and her body wrenched backward, her torso rising from the mattress and her head bending back.

"Tabitha!" John yelled. "What's wrong?"

Steve reached for a bite protector with one hand and restrained John with the other. "Don't touch her, John! She's convulsing. I'll take care of her. Just run and get the nurse."

Chapter 15

JOHN AND MELODY stood together at Tabitha's bedside, hand in hand. Their daughter lay still—alive, but motionless. Her convulsion had been short-lived, mercifully so, to say the least, but the effects of its exhausting strain on her body lingered. She had lost bladder control for the duration of the seizure, but, being unconscious, she didn't have to suffer through the embarrassment. The nurse cleaned her up without Tabitha realizing what had happened.

The doctors warned of possible lasting effects, but since her vital signs recovered so quickly, they tried to spread optimism around like a healing salve on broken hearts. "A long period of sleep is normal after a seizure," Steve had explained. "Her heart rate is back to normal, and her blood pressure is fine. Don't worry."

"Loss of muscle control is expected," Dr. Smithers had added. "It's not necessarily a bad sign. We just change the sheets and go on."

Melody had rushed to the hospital as soon as John called. Fortunately, she had already packed her car with dozens of gifts from well-wishers, lovingly provided the night before. Tabitha's siblings had crafted several colorful delights, from baskets of papier-mâché flowers to finger-painted landscapes. Several brightly colored balloons, a plastic globe filled with gumballs, a teddy bear hugging a candy cane, and at least ten handmade get-well cards now decorated Tabitha's room, carefully placed in strategic locations so she would be able to see one of them no matter where she looked, if only she would awaken to savor this bounty of love.

Now John and Melody waited for new test results, watching each slow minute pass by on the pink-lined sheet that rolled out of the heart monitor.

Melody slid her hand up John's arm and around his elbow, leaning her head on his shoulder as they looked down on their precious daughter. "I'm glad the other kids aren't seeing Tabitha looking like this," she said. "Andrew begged and begged to come with me, and Joshua very nearly had to hold him back. They don't understand that she can't have visitors. They miss her so much!"

John set a hand on the bed rail. "I'm standing here looking at her, and I still miss her. I miss her beautiful smile, her happy voice . . ." He paused to escape a choking sob.

Melody patted him on the shoulder. "This could have been a happy time," she said, trying to get her husband's mind off his sorrows. "It's not often I get to answer a question like I got this morning."

John kept his eyes on Tabitha. "How did she say it, exactly?"

Melody raised a pretend phone to her ear to act out the conversation. "Melody, what do I have to do to become a Christian? I want what you have." She put away the invisible phone. "That was pretty much it."

"Incredible. And you led her to the Lord right there on the phone?"

Melody shrugged. "She was ready. It wasn't anything I said. It was really her mother . . . well, her mother and Tabitha who primed the pump."

John turned back toward Tabitha. "I wonder what Phil's going to think about it."

"Oh, he already knows. He's not crazy about it, but he didn't give her a hard time. He's pretty impressed with the book you sent him and embarrassed about trying to explain the dream . . ." Melody drew quotation marks in the air. "Coincidences."

Steve strode into the room. He didn't bother to exchange pleasantries, and his grim face warned of bad news even before he spoke. "John, Melody, I'm afraid the tests show new lesions, and the older ones have grown surprisingly fast. Her white count is extremely high, higher than what we would expect while she's on the meds. I'm afraid it's time to become even more aggressive."

Melody covered her face with her hands. "Steve," she began, but as a tremor in her hands spread to her arms, she pressed her fingers over her lips and just stared.

John wrapped her up from behind with two strong arms and whispered into her ear. "It's going to be all right."

"I think Tabitha's doing all she can to hide her discomfort," Steve said. "Her seizure seemed to come on suddenly, but since she's such a trooper, she didn't show any signs before it happened."

John pulled away from Melody and paced back and forth in front of Tabitha's bed, the first lap with his hands in his pockets, the next with his hands on his hips. His voice shook, almost quaking. "Well, you know her history. Either she's never been sick or she's never let on."

Crossing his arms, Steve nodded. "Like I said, she's quite a trooper. We're not giving her anything for her pain. It's obvious she has a very high tolerance."

"No doubt," John said, his eyes trained on the floor as he continued to pace.

Melody grasped his arm, stopping his nervous walk. She turned back to Steve. "But why has she been out for so long?"

"It's not unusual after a convulsion." Steve bent over the bed and pushed Tabitha's eyelids up. "She's just asleep. It's hard to say how long it will last."

"She won't like that," Melody said, lifting a hand to stifle a new sob.

"What do you mean?" John asked.

"She always wants to know what's going on. She notices everything, drinks in everything, and remembers everything. And I know she would want to know about Myrtle. She's done all she could to show her love, and she's been praying for her every morning and night."

Steve ran his finger up the IV tube and read the bag at the top. "Well, she might wake up soon, so you can tell her all about it. We're not giving her anything to help her sleep." Pushing a hand into his lab coat pocket, he looked down at her. "Frankly, I'd like to see her wake up. It's easier to evaluate her that way."

John joined him at Tabitha's bedside. "So, what's the bottom line, Steve? What do you and the other doctors think?"

Steve firmed his lips, apparently buying time to decide on the best way to answer. "She's got a bad case," he finally said. "We're in for a long haul, I think. It's time to put our prayers into high gear."

"I've *been* praying," John shot back. "My knees are sore from kneeling at her bedside, and I'm not about to quit begging God for help. I just need to know where we stand. Tell me straight out. What do you think Tabitha's chances are?"

Melody laid a hand on his shoulder. "Now, John . . ."

He reached up and patted her hand. "I'm not mad at Steve. I'm just frustrated with not knowing enough."

Steve joined them and clasped John's other shoulder. "It's an unpredictable disease. I'll be frank with you. It's pretty bad, but we also have reason to be optimistic. She's strong and a good fighter, and she's in good hands. It's not time to despair."

Shaking his head, John softened his tone. "I'm not despairing. I just want to be realistic. I don't want to be taken by surprise. Give me all the possibilities."

Steve drew back a step and folded his arms across his chest. "John, the possibilities are pretty gruesome, but she may not suffer through any of them."

"I need to be ready, just in case."

"Okay, you asked for it. No surprises." Steve leaned against the bed and began speaking in monotone. "There may be more convulsions, she may become stuporous, she may hallucinate. She could have a seizure so terrible, it will contort her body unmercifully, make her lose bladder control again, choke the breath out of her. She may have grueling pain so bad that she'll scream for mercy."

He returned his hand to John's shoulder. "She could die tonight."

John lowered his head. Melody did the same. There just wasn't anything to say.

Steve turned back to Tabitha and ran a finger up and down her arm. "But I'm convinced of better things for you, little child. God is our provider, and he will carry you through this, no matter what happens. And he will be there when you awaken, whenever and wherever that may be."

* * *

After Melody went home to be with the other children, John settled down to spend his third night in the hospital. Of course, Steve's dire warnings had rattled Melody. She wanted to stay, but new troubles at home persuaded her otherwise. Jonathan had come down with an intestinal virus, and his cries for Mommy had become inconsolable. There was no headache or fever, no sign that he, too, would suffer from the dreaded mosquito-borne illness. So Melody settled on being the one who would comfort their youngest. Besides, she needed the rest, rest that the hospital environment could never hope to offer.

John pulled out his bed and set the pillow in place. His wife's company would surely have been welcome, but her presence at home was far more practical. "Just gather all the kids and pray for us there," he had said. "We need all the prayers we can get."

After making his bed, he took the single step over to Tabitha's bed to tuck her in. She lay motionless now, only her steady breathing revealing the presence of her soul. With trembling hands, John smoothed over covers, though they didn't need it, and pushed Deborah under her arm. Then, leaning over her body and reaching across to the opposite side of her face, he slid his hand under her head and lifted, cradling it as her shining locks sifted through his fingers. With his other hand he fluffed her pillow, punching it lightly with an open palm. When its surface bent and folded, he paused, staring at his daughter.

How easy it is to push and shape a pillow to match my will! And look how effortlessly I hold her precious head in space, protecting her with ease. I have power, yet, when it really counts, I have nothing. I would face a roaring lion for her, but I can't do anything to fight a microscopic virus.

He laid her head back down and tenderly rubbed a finger across her cheek. "Tabitha," he whispered, "if I could take your pain I would gladly do it. I would sell all my possessions, submit myself to torture, and beg to die in your place if it would bring relief to your suffering."

With his back now aching, he rose and pulled a chair to the bedside. After lowering the bed as far as it would go, he took Tabitha's hand with both of his and sat down to continue his verbal love letter.

"You slept all day, sweet darling. I hope it was peaceful. Even Mama couldn't wake you, and Sarah came later, and she couldn't wake you either. Dr. Van Dorn says it's not a coma, but he seems uneasy about how you're doing." He squeezed her hand ever so gently, and the poetry of love swept through his heart. "I know I don't have to tell you to be brave, for you have the courage of a lioness. I don't have to tell you to trust the Lord, for your heart beats in time with his. Yours is the faith that has moved mountains, the mountains of stony hearts and unbelief. You have cast fear and selfishness into the deepest sea. You are more precious than gold."

With tears finding their way down his cheeks, John closed his eyes and bowed his head. "My God and Father," he prayed out loud with as little trembling as he could manage, "You have heard my many requests over the past couple of days . . . well, just one request really, over and over again, and it gets harder and harder to wait while she suffers. You know my daughter loves you with all her heart. Her faith is pure and undefiled; her love and compassion are unquestioned." Now, no longer able to control his voice, he fell into a weeping lament. "Dear Father, please touch her body . . . make her whole . . . ease her pain. She's so young and has so much ahead of her. If someone must suffer, let it be me."

He drew in a big sniff and then remained silent for a minute or two before continuing with a steadier voice. "I have been frustrated with not knowing the answers, with not knowing what to do. I know even Jesus became frustrated from time to time and handled it with righteousness. Help me to do the same. Help me to prevent my frustration from spilling over into offense against others. I know Steve and the other doctors are doing their best; help me to show them grace even as we suffer."

After several minutes of silence, John raised his head and looked at Tabitha again. He stood and caressed her lovely face once more. "My little dreamer, you are so beautiful. I have always seen the face of an angel in your countenance; little did I know that God has been dressing your mind with visions from above. And even when I found out, I didn't understand why. Now I see you were sent to bless both the lost and the found, to shine the light of day in dark places. You have touched the heart of the most stony atheist, and you have taught this crusty old academic that he has to learn to speak to the needs of the soul." After biting his lip to quell a sob, he continued. "But do I really understand fully your special gift?"

He gently stroked the top of her head. "Tabitha, are you dreaming now? What new truths has God taught you during these hours of slumber?"

Suddenly, Tabitha's eyes shot wide open. They rocked from one side to the other before finally focusing on her father. She began breathing heavily and rapidly, and she latched onto his hand with a vise grip.

"Tabitha, what is it? What's wrong?"

"I know!" Tabitha gasped. "I know!"

"You know what?" John's body shook so hard, he could barely speak. "Did you have a nightmare?"

"No," she replied, heaving rapid breaths. "N-n-not a nightmare. It was another dream, and I know the answer now."

"The answer to what?"

Tabitha grasped her father's shirt collar, twisting it as she wrenched him closer. Her lips and eyes locked tightly in pain for a moment, and John steeled himself once more, desperately fighting the tears.

As she looked into his eyes, the tender gaze seemed to bring back her peaceful glow. Her own eyes sparkled as she pulled him ever closer. "I know why the angels dance!"

John shook his head. As mental chaos clung to his brain, he silently begged God for an interpretation. "The angels? Do you mean the angels in your drawing?"

Tabitha grinned through pained lips, her eyes now wide. "It's a celebration!" she sang out. "When someone repents and is saved, the angels dance for joy!"

Caught up in her excitement, he let her contagious delight whisk away his worries. "You mean like when a lost sheep is found?"

"Right! And Rose was dancing with them this time."

"Because of her mother? She danced because her mother is saved now? So you know about Mrs. Grayson?"

"Yes, she . . ." Tabitha's brow suddenly furrowed. Her mouth gaped, catching in place for several seconds. A large droplet formed in her eye, and during the terrible pause the tear found its way past the lid and caressed her cheek with a glistening ribbon. In this new spasm of pain, her eyes grew wild, then closed tightly. For a moment, she couldn't breathe, her attempts caught in the clutches of the wrenching contractions that twisted her abdomen. Finally, drawing in a long gasp, she released her grip on her father's shirt, and her hand dropped limply to the bed.

"Tabitha?" John said weakly, swallowing a large lump in his throat. Transfixed in terror, he stared at her deathly still body for several terrifying seconds.

Slowly, two small slits appeared through Tabitha's relaxed eyelids, and she breathed a deep sigh. Her eyes opened in loving circular pools, gazing upon him as if she were now the comforter. "Don't worry, Daddy," she whispered. "I'm okay, but I felt real strange. What happened?"

John exhaled, seemingly for the first time in several minutes. "You had me worried, little angel. It looks like you might have had a seizure. You had one yesterday, but I don't think this one was as bad."

Tabitha grinned. "I'm not an angel, Daddy. I know. I've seen them."

"Is there anything I can do for you? Water? Fluff your pillow?"

She nodded. "There is something you can do for me, and it has something to do with the angels."

"What's that?"

With a weak wave of her hand, Tabitha beckoned him closer. He leaned over, placing his ear within a whisper's distance. Her lips barely moving, she spoke in a hush, and her words floated from mind to mind.

"Make them dance again."

Tabitha closed her eyes and fell asleep once more. Obviously, even the slightest excitement exhausted her. John caressed her cheek and tucked her in with loving, practiced hands, feeling some security in the rhythmic, even expansions in his daughter's chest and the comfortable little smile on her face.

John pushed the "nurse call" button and waited for a response.

"May I help you?" a friendly voice asked.

"Yes. Tabitha woke up for a minute and went right back to sleep. She was in a lot of pain. Should she be checked out?"

"I'll be right there."

Leaving the bedside, John slumped back into his chair, aware now of what he must do. "Make them dance again," he murmured. This time there was no need for an explanation.

Chapter 16

A PITIFUL MOAN shook John awake. He jumped up and checked on Tabitha. She lay still, breathing normally, her face smooth and calm. As he tucked her doll back under Tabitha's arm, he kept an eye on her angelic face. Had another dream filled her mind with terror? Did another convulsion threaten to twist her body into a knot?

He studied the monitors. Her heart rate seemed normal. Same with her blood pressure. After nearly a minute, he nodded, satisfied. She would be okay for a while.

Looking back at his bed, he noted the mess he had made—his single sheet wound into a rope and his pillow teetering on the side of the folded-out chair. He shook his head. It seemed that sleep wasn't in tonight's forecast.

Tiptoeing through the dimly lit room, he walked to the door and pulled it just far enough to slide through. As he closed it again, he scanned the corridor. It was more peaceful than it had been during daytime hours—no visitors milling about or darting from elevator to room and back again, no rumbling mealtime carts rolling from station to station with clattering trays being stacked one by one as the meal crew made their rounds.

Over near the stairway door, a man with a mop barely made a sound, just the *plosh* of wet strings plastering the tiles with sudsy water. His low, whistled tune contributed to the tranquility of the moment as he stepped through his cleaning routine in a lumbering waltz.

As John passed by the nurses' station, a sorrowful moan emanated from somewhere nearby. He perked his ears, searching for the source. It had come from down the hall, not Tabitha's room.

A nurse at the desk spoke up. "That's the lady in seven fifteen. She does that four or five times a night."

John turned toward her, a petite black woman, perhaps in her fifties. He had seen her several times before. She usually just nodded a quick greeting as he passed by. He assumed she was the head nurse for the shift; she clearly held the respect of the others, despite her size. The younger nurses jumped to a quick march whenever they passed by her, even if they were on break, just walking from the coffee pot to the restroom. She had a ship captain's demeanor, but she was civil. Even now she sat stern faced, busily jotting numbers down on a report.

John took a step closer to the desk. "Good evening," he said, squinting at the nurse's name tag. "Thelma, is it?"

"Yes." Thelma looked up from her work and offered a smile, though it seemed more of a professional courtesy than a truly warm greeting. "How are you tonight, Mr. Hanson?"

"Please call me John," he said. "I'm okay. Just having trouble sleeping."

Thelma put her pencil down and rested her chin on her hand, keeping her somber expression intact. "Are you trying to tell me that you're having trouble sleeping in a hospital?" Her serious countenance finally broke as she gave him a genuine smile. "My nurses are efficient, but they're not always the quietest people around. I hope we're not disturbing you."

"Oh, no. It's not the nurses. I slept pretty soundly last night, but not tonight. It's just that my subconscious is listening to Tabitha's every breath. I wake up with the slightest grunt or shifting of her body."

Thelma turned back to her report, again scratching figures onto the paper. "I can understand that. We'll try to stay out of your room as much as possible."

John stood on tiptoes to try to get a look at her work. "I was wondering about that. What if she has a seizure, and for some reason I don't wake up? You won't even know she's in trouble."

Thelma breathed a sigh, and, with a dramatic drop of her pencil, stood up and walked around the end of her station. Then, taking him by the arm, she led him around to her side of the desk. With a schoolteacher's deportment, she began explaining her workstation, pointing with her finger as she spoke. "See this monitor? Here's Tabitha's heart rate, here's her blood pressure, and this number here is her respiration. As you might expect, we can't sit in every patient's room all night, but from here the nurses can keep an eye on everyone. If something changes suddenly, an alarm will go off. You don't have to worry."

John crossed his arms over his chest. "What about last night? I had to call you."

"I saw her heart rate and respiration go up," Thelma explained, a hint of defensiveness coloring her tone. "It wasn't enough to worry about, but I was getting ready to check on her anyway. It might not have been a seizure at all, just a bad dream that got her real excited."

John winced. Had he insulted Thelma's professional pride? Switching to an apologetic tone, he gave her a nod. "I should have known you had it under control. You obviously run a tight ship. The night shift is the most efficient crew of nurses I've seen here. And you were right about Tabitha having a dream. I wish I had time to tell you all that's been going on."

"You are a charmer, aren't you?" Thelma set her hands on her hips, a twinkle in her eye. "But why can't you tell me what's going on? Are you going somewhere?"

"No, I . . ."

"Well, neither am I, and it's a quiet night." She sat down, folded her arms, and pushed back in her swivel chair. "I love a good story. Let 'er rip."

John gave Thelma a "why not?" kind of look and leaned back against the desk. He told her about Tabitha's friendship with Rose, Rose's death from encephalitis, Tabitha's dreams and her drawing, how the Graysons each visited her by surprise, and every relevant detail he could recall. The very retelling of the saga helped him relax and once again see God's guiding hand in the midst of all the trouble.

Thelma's smile had vanished early on in his tale, and now she displayed her serious side once again, but this time with a sympathetic air. "That's some story, John."

They both paused in silence for a moment until Thelma added, "I'm not very religious, but I can tell you one thing. God's got a reason for this suffering, and right now your daughter is in very good hands. Dr. Smithers really knows what he's doing, and Dr. Van Dorn is a gem. They're good doctors. You can take that to the bank."

John grasped Thelma's hand and shook it warmly. "I'm thankful for devoted professionals like you. I appreciate all that everyone's doing."

Thelma almost smiled again, but her all-business face quickly took over. "Don't try to flatter me, John. You've already gotten on my good side. I'm just doing my job, and right now it's to take care of that angel daughter of yours."

* * *

Sometimes insomnia comes to souls troubled by the ills of others. The night of true slumber never seems to fall, for the worries of the daytime are not allowed to fly away into the darkening wind. With others, their dawn comes before the sun is ready to rise. The excitement of a new resolution squeezes extra adrenaline into their bloodstream, even during the supposedly restful hours.

Phil Grayson stepped gingerly through the dark until he arrived at the side of the bed where his wife slept. He laid a palm on her shoulder and shook her ever so gently. "Myrtle, where's that picture Tabitha drew?"

"Huh?" Myrtle grunted. "What?" She opened her eyes and stared. "Phil? Why are you up so early?"

"I couldn't sleep."

She reached for her lamp and flicked it on. "And you're all dressed. What are you doing?"

"It's not that early," he said, pulling up his arm to get a look at his watch. "It's almost six o'clock."

"But you're still on leave. You don't have to—"

"Where is Tabitha's picture?"

Myrtle sat up in bed. "In my dresser," she said, pointing across the room. "Why?"

"I'd like to see it again." Phil looked toward the dresser. "Which drawer?"

"Top left." She pulled on his sleeve. "Has something changed?"

He sat down on the bed, his feet still touching the floor. "I decided I've been acting like a child about it," he explained, taking her hand in his. "I'm going to face my fears and try to figure this thing out."

Myrtle pinched Phil's sleeve and gave it another tug. "Why are you wearing your coat?"

"It's pretty cool this morning, and I'm going for a drive. I'm taking the picture with me."

She scrunched up her eyebrows. "You're taking the picture to the cemetery?"

Standing up slowly, he released her hand. "So you figured out where I've been going," he said, shoving his hands into his coat pockets.

She gave him a disarming smile. "It wasn't too hard. I saw a couple of florist receipts on your dresser. I know daisies were Rose's favorite."

"I realize she can't see them," he said. "I guess they're really for me. Besides, the cemetery's a good place to be alone and think."

"I'm sure it is, but I was hoping you were going to see John."

Phil waved a hand, laughing under his breath. "I don't think I'm ready for that."

"But you said you wanted to face your fears, and it looks to me like he's one of your biggest."

He dug into his pocket and jingled his keys. With a slow, plodding pace, he strolled to the other side of the bed, his head angled upwards. "As I mentioned before," he began, "I mentally turned against John because of his attitude about Rose's death. But that's not what started it. It was really my fault. At his grandmother's funeral, I suggested that I could evaluate Tabitha's hallucinations, but I don't understand his family's beliefs any more than he understands mine. It was rather arrogant of me to suggest that I could help."

"Arrogant? Not really. Presumptuous, maybe, but not arrogant."

"Okay. I'll give you that. But I think that was the first crack, a . . . a tremor before the earthquake, if that works."

"I understand. Go on."

"So, he never called to ask for my help. No surprise, of course, but I'll admit it took a while for me to convince myself that they'd be better off with a Christian counselor. Then, when he started pushing Jesus on me, I couldn't take it anymore. Now he was the presumptuous one. How dare he? She was dying, Myrtle! He was preaching to me while our daughter lay there dying!"

"I know." Myrtle brushed a tear with her knuckle, her voice fading. "I know."

"Anyway, I don't think I'm afraid of him. We just don't see eye to eye. We offended each other, and I don't see any way to resolve it." Phil spread out his hands. "We're just so . . . so different."

"Come here." She patted the space on the bed next to her. "Sit with me."

He kicked off his shoes and sat next to her, Indian style, smiling. "Is it time for another psychoanalysis, Doc?"

"I think you could use another one." She put both of her hands behind his neck and pulled his head toward hers. "Deep down, Phil, aren't you afraid he'll convince you of his faith, and you don't want to be convinced?"

He replied in a soft voice. "I told you that I can't believe in something that can't be comprehended. How can anyone make me understand the incomprehensible?"

She pulled him a little closer. "There are lots of things you don't understand, and you still believe in them."

"It's not that I *don't* understand the Christian concept of God; it's that it's *impossible* to understand. Can you name one thing I believe in that's truly impossible to understand?"

She released him, allowing their faces to drift apart. "Just because I can't think of one doesn't mean there aren't any."

"True enough," he said with a smile, "but until you do think of one, my point stands."

"Oh?" She flashed an impish grin. "Is this a debate now? How many points do I have so far?"

He tapped her on the nose. "Enough to make me think, but not enough to convince me."

"If you want a debate, why don't you ask John about it?"

"Ask him about what?"

"If he can think of something that you believe in that can't be understood."

Phil shook his head. "It's a nonsense question. He won't be able to do it."

"Don't be too sure," Myrtle said, wagging her finger. "I thought that my mom wearing an MIA bracelet didn't make any sense. Melody suggested that I ask what missing in action meant to her, and she answered in a way I didn't expect."

"Okay. More points for your side."

"I don't want brownie points." She spread her arms, her palms open. "Phil, I was an atheist for so long, I could only think that way. I didn't have the ability to ponder the spiritual side of things. Their explanations didn't even occur to me. It's like having a debate with a wall. It never answers your arguments, so you always win, but you don't learn anything. You're just arguing with yourself."

"I see your point."

She patted him on the knee. "I'll bet John would surprise you. Didn't that book surprise you?"

He nodded. "I admit that it has a more intelligent approach than I expected. It definitely has good arguments."

"Then talk to him. Face all your fears. It doesn't make sense not to. Besides, you know the bad time he's going through. It would probably help him to focus on something besides Tabitha's sickness." She gazed at him lovingly, then pulled him into a long, tender embrace.

"I don't know," he whispered. "I just don't know."

She released him again, her eyes now pleading. "Will you do it for me, Phil?"

Warmth surged into his cheeks. "Well, when you put it that way, it's kind of hard to say no."

* * *

"Ooooh! Where did all the balloons come from?"

John dropped the book he was reading, jumped up from his chair, and leaned over Tabitha's bed. "Good morning, sweetheart."

Her smooth eyelids, underlined in a flaming red hue, fluttered. Her glazed pupils appeared smoky gray rather than their usual obsidian black, and they shrank to squeeze out the onslaught of the shiny spotlights hovering up above. "Good morning, Daddy."

He pushed one of the Mylar balloons next to her bed, making it sway. "They're from your brothers and sister. Your mother brought them to you yesterday."

"Yesterday?" She squinted, moving her lips as if counting. "What day is it?"

"It's Friday."

"Friday?" Her brow wrinkled. I thought I came to the hospital on Tuesday."

"You did. You slept through most of Thursday, and now it's Friday morning."

"Oh. I guess I did sleep a lot. I had a bunch of dreams." She looked down at her side where a little rag doll protruded from the crook of her arm. Moving slowly, she pulled Deborah higher and hugged her close. "Someone brought Debbie, too!"

John covered her hand with his. "Do you remember your dream from last night?"

Tabitha rolled her eyes upward. Suddenly, they brightened again. "Yes, I do! The angels danced again! And I told you about it. . . . Or did I? Was that part a dream, too?"

"No. You really did tell me."

"Is it true, then?" Tabitha asked excitedly. "Is Mrs. Grayson a Christian now?"

John could hardly hold back. He wanted to jump and shout the news like a child at Christmas, but he swallowed his glee and spoke calmly as though the happenings of the previous days were the most normal events in the world. "Yes, she is. Your mother led her to the Lord, and she'll be here in a few minutes. I'm sure she'll be glad to tell you all about it."

Tabitha beamed. Her broad smile seemed to brighten the whole room. "Oh, I'm so happy! And so is Rose! You should have seen her, smiling and spinning around. It was like she was floating on a cloud of joy!"

John tried to choke back his emotions, but a single tear managed to find its way into his eye. "That's a beautiful way to say it, sweetheart."

She cocked her head, puzzled for a moment. "I think I heard someone else say it."

"Someone else? Who?"

"I'm not sure," she replied, now frowning. "This time it was like I had a narrator explaining things to me."

"A narrator? That *is* different." John looked at her pained expression. No use wearing her out. Remembering her dreams seemed to put a strain on her. "How are you feeling this morning?" he asked in a near whisper.

"Pretty bad," she said, mimicking his low tone. "My head's worse than ever, and I feel hot."

John felt Tabitha's forehead, then pressed the call button.

"May I help you?" came the quick response.

"Tabitha's awake, and I think her temperature's up. Can you check her out?"

"I'll be right there."

Within seconds, the nurse appeared at the door, a nurse with whom John had just become acquainted that morning. Thelma was gone for the day, but she had come into the room several times after their meeting to "check on the equipment; just routine" and once to help with a minor convulsing episode.

The new nurse placed the thermometer under Tabitha's tongue. "She does look a bit glazed over."

"That's what I thought," John said.

When the timer beeped, she pulled the thermometer out and read the digits. "It's 104.2. I'll check with the doctor right away." She hurried out of the room.

As the door swung closed, John let his stare linger. The nurse's words repeated in his mind, each number sounding like the toll of a bell. *104.2!*

A slight tug made him turn. Tabitha had pinched the back of his shirt. With her eyes wide and her brow arched high, she seemed to plead for mercy as she whispered, "Daddy, am I going to die?"

Trying to keep his hands from shaking, John pulled Tabitha's covers down to her waist. "Why do you ask that?"

Tabitha kept her gaze trained on her father. "I was just wondering," she replied softly. "If I die, I hope you won't grieve for me. I'll be in heaven, and I hope you'll be happy for me just like I am for Rose."

He kept fussing with the covers, though he didn't really do more than fold back the edge. "You know I believe in being happy for Christians who die. It's like I've told you before; Jesus just wakes them up in the morning." He cleared his throat and placed a hand on Tabitha's cheek. "But who says you're going to die? Did you have a dream that made you think you might?"

"You mean in the misty dim place like with Nanna and Rose?" she asked.

"Yes, something like that."

Tabitha turned her head toward the window, saying nothing. For several tortured seconds, John chewed his lip, waiting, wondering if he should ask again. When she finally turned back, tears streamed to her cheeks and chin, though her face carried a heavenly aspect.

John trembled. What could it mean? Was this a sign of her impending departure? He looked again, studying her visage for another clue. Her eyes were sad but somehow enlightened, forlorn but peaceful. They appeared as iced jewels dripping in holy melt. In her haunting stare, she radiated joy and heartache, the warm splendor of her Master's growing presence stripping away her temporal mask. For John, it was terrifying.

"I heard voices," she replied, her glow quickly fading. "I heard one voice a lot of times."

John, still shaking, drew closer, trying to hear Tabitha's trailing whispers. "What did the voice say?"

"Well, one time, I woke up," she began, now with a very weak whisper. "At least I think I woke up." She turned her head and rested on her cheek. "Maybe it was all a dream. I could see you sleeping over there. My head was hurting so bad, it felt like it was about to explode. I started shivering, and it was really scary. I was about to call you, but then I heard the voice." Without moving her head, she looked at her father, excitement growing in her eyes. "It said, 'Do not fear, Tabitha. I am the first and the last.'"

John analyzed Tabitha's words, silently trying to place them in context. She must have had that dream right before her seizure early that morning. But two seizures in one night? Was that a lot? Are the dreams tied somehow to the ebb and flow of this disease?

"The first and the last," he repeated. "That would have to be Jesus."

"That's what I guessed, too. I know I heard the voice other times, but I don't remember what it said. I just remember I always felt better after I heard it."

John laid a hand on her shoulder, clasping it tenderly. "Well, I remember what you said to me last night."

Tabitha tried to nod her head but only managed a slight jiggle. "I remember, too. 'Make them dance again.' I didn't mean to give you an order or anything. I couldn't help saying it for some reason."

John let out a short laugh. "Don't worry, sweetheart. I know you weren't being disrespectful. I understood completely, and I intend to do it."

"How?"

"As soon as your mother gets here, I'm going to pay Dr. Grayson a little visit. I assume you won't mind if I leave you for a little while to do that."

"No. But can Joshua and Sarah and the others come, too?"

John rubbed his hand up and down Tabitha's arm. "So far, the doctors have said no, but I can ask again. If today's tests look better, then maybe they'll say it's okay."

Tabitha's lip protruded. "I don't think the tests will be better."

John put a finger under her chin. "Now where's my little Miss Positive?"

As Tabitha tried to smile, her whispers carried a slight whimper. "It's just that every time I wake up, I feel worse and worse. I feel so weak, I don't think I can even lift my head."

He made a shushing sound. "It's going to be all right."

"If I don't get better, will you make a promise?"

"A promise? Sure. What?"

"Like we just talked about. Don't grieve. If you really believe I'm in heaven, don't cry for me. I don't want anyone thinking you're selfish. You're the least selfish person I know . . . and, Mama, of course."

He could barely breathe out his words. "Of course."

She looked up at him, her eyes again sparkling. "Then, promise me. I won't be able to dance in heaven if you're crying."

Closing his eyes, John took in a deep breath. "Okay. I promise. I'll just—"

A new voice interrupted, loud compared to the whispers he had grown accustomed to hearing. "Good morning, Mr. Hanson."

John greeted Dr. Smithers with a strong handshake. "It's good to see you."

The doctor looked over John's shoulder. "So how's our patient? Running a fever, I hear?"

"Yes, it's up to—" John began.

"104.2," the doctor said. "The nurse will be back momentarily with something for that, and she'll give her a sponge bath to cool her down."

"Oh, good. That should help."

"How about the pain? Is it any worse?"

"Yes, and she says she feels real weak, too."

Dr. Smithers scanned Tabitha's body. "We'll do more tests this morning, but considering her seizures, I think we'll be moving her to the ICU."

John lifted his eyebrows. "ICU? That means no visitors, right?"

"We typically allow visitors during the first fifteen minutes of the hour, but in pediatrics, a parent can stay as long as he or she wants."

"No siblings?"

Dr. Smithers shook his head. "Although Tabitha doesn't have a communicable disease, children tend to carry germs around. In her weakened state, we can't risk the exposure."

Tabitha tugged her father's shirt again. "But I want to see Joshua and Sarah, and Andrew, and . . ." Grimacing, she closed her eyes, disappointment coloring her downturned face.

Dr. Smithers leaned over and felt Tabitha's forehead, pulling up her eyelids at the same time. As he released them again, he sighed deeply. "How many brothers and sisters does she have?"

"Three brothers. One sister."

"And how soon can they get here?"

"I'm sure Melody has them out of bed," John replied, hesitating for a moment. "Even if she's already on her way here by herself, one of my older two can bring them. But I thought you said—"

Dr. Smithers laid a hand on John's back and guided him away from Tabitha's bed. With both men facing the door, Dr. Smithers rested his chin on his fist, while John waited. Finally, the doctor spoke in a hushed tone. "See what you can do to get them here right away before we move her. We can take the proper sanitary precautions. I think they should all see her again." He then paused and added, "Just in case."

Without another word, Dr. Smithers walked quickly out of the room, leaving John staring as the breeze from the door swept across his face.

Chapter 17

J UST IN CASE? The words pounded John's brain. *Just in case*
what?

Still picturing the doctor's troubled expression, John tried to
probe him from afar. Did Dr. Smithers know more than he was
telling? Why would he risk exposing Tabitha if he were optimistic
about her recovery? Why is she going to the ICU?

He turned back toward the bed, trying to hide his turmoil. "I'm
going out to the nurses' station to call your mother. I'll be right back."
He stepped quickly away, but as he reached for the door, it swung
open, making him step back as Phil Grayson walked in.

"Phil!" John said. "I'm sur— I mean . . ."

"You're surprised to see me?" Phil gave him an uneasy smile.
"Don't worry, I'm pretty surprised to be here."

John extended his hand. "I'm glad you could come," he said with
as much warmth as he could muster.

"No problem." Phil stared at John's hand as he shook it.

John tried to steel himself. Could Phil detect the trembling? *Better for both of us if he didn't.*

Phil regained eye contact. "I wanted to see Tabitha, if it's all right."

"Well, certainly, but I thought they were letting only family members in."

Phil chuckled. "The nurses outside don't ask any questions if you just walk by like you know where you're going." Fidgeting, he looked at Tabitha, then back at John. "Is it all right? I can leave if you want me to."

John waved a hand. "It's quite all right. I'm really glad you're here. I was just going out to call Melody and ask her to bring all the kids for a visit."

Phil pointed at a white telephone next to the bed. "Your room phone isn't working?"

"Oh . . . it works. I just . . . uh . . . didn't want to disturb Tabitha. She's feeling very weak."

"I'm sorry to hear that." Phil turned to leave. "Maybe I'd better go."

John grasped Phil's forearm. "No, it's okay." This time he couldn't stop the trembling. "All the kids will be coming soon anyway."

Phil turned back. "But you said she's not allowed to have visitors, and if she's so weak . . ."

"They're moving her to the ICU," John explained, glancing at Tabitha to see if she was listening.

Phil offered an understanding nod and whispered. "Go make your phone call, John. I'll stay with Tabitha."

"Thanks." John patted Phil on the shoulder and hustled out of the room.

* * *

Phil waited for the door to close, then walked straight to Tabitha's bed and stared at the ghostly white little girl. "Tabitha," he whispered, "are you awake?"

Tabitha's eyes fluttered open, but they had none of their usual radiant sparkle. "Hi, Dr. Grayson," she said with a faltering whisper. "Thank you for coming to see me again."

"My pleasure, but please, save your strength. You don't have to say anything." He grasped the bed rail. "We talked about your picture, and I didn't get a chance to tell you how much it means to me." He unbuttoned his jacket and pulled the drawing from underneath. "It was very kind of you to think of Myrtle and me during our grieving time."

Tabitha shifted her body, apparently trying to get a look. She grimaced before finally settling down. "I was hoping it would make you feel better," she whispered, now with a little more strength. Her eyes brightened as she continued. "Rose is as happy as she can be. Last night she danced with the angels."

Phil's throat caught. "She . . . she danced?"

"Yes. And now I know why. The angels dance whenever someone repents of their sin and starts following the Lord. Their loved ones in heaven join in to celebrate. So Rose was dancing for her mom."

Tears welled in Phil's eyes, one spilling over the lid. "For her—" He couldn't finish.

Tabitha reached out a hand. "It's really all very exciting, isn't it?"

He took her hand in his. "I . . . I don't know what to say."

Tears trickled down her cheeks. "You would rejoice if only you understood."

Phil pulled a tissue from a nearby box and dried Tabitha's eyes, dabbing them with shaking hands. "Please don't cry, honey," he begged, now nearly sobbing. "I didn't mean to make you sad."

Tabitha's voice rose above a whisper. "My daddy says that we should weep with those who weep. I'm not sad for myself. I'm sad for you."

"Sad for me?" He wiped his own eyes, desperately trying to compose himself. "Why? You're the one who's sick."

"Lots of reasons." She fingered the yarn on her doll's head. "Because you miss Rose so much, for one. But you'll never feel better, because you don't believe she's still alive." Tabitha closed her eyes and let out a long sigh, grimacing again as she exhaled.

"What's wrong?" He glanced all around the bed. "Should I call the nurse? Can I get you something? Water?"

"I'm sorry," she said, coughing and clearing her throat. "I get so tired when I try to talk, and I get so sad when I see what you're doing."

"What I'm doing?" He gripped Tabitha's bed rails again, steadying himself. "Can you tell me? Can you whisper? I'll lean close."

As Tabitha nodded ever so slightly, Phil bent over her bed. Her whisper broke into stuttering gasps, tired and trembling. "God listened to your prayers. He tried to make you feel better. He showed you a picture of Rose in heaven, and you're just ignoring it."

"Ignoring it?" He stayed close, not daring to budge an inch. "What do you mean?"

"You still don't believe, even though God showed you something he didn't show me."

"Showed me something? What was that?"

As Tabitha's voice weakened further, Phil stood on tiptoes to set his ear next to her lips. "The thing Rose was making," she said with nothing more than a wispy breath. "You said you knew what it was. Could you tell me now?"

Phil rewound his mind to his last visit. He had an idea about what Rose was making from the clues in the angels' song, but now, for some reason, he knew without a doubt. Shaking violently, he raised up, stuttering. "I . . . ah . . . I'd better . . . what I mean is . . ." Finally he exclaimed, "Dear God!" and covered his mouth.

* * *

John hung up the phone and hurried back to the room. That took way too long. With Tabitha in such a fragile condition, getting her back in sight seemed more important than anything.

He opened the door, spilling the corridor's light into the room. Phil stood next to Tabitha's bed, a hand covering his mouth. His cheeks had paled to an ashen gray, and his ears glowed cherry red. As he pulled his hand down, his mouth, open at first, quivered, opening and closing in turn.

"Phil? Are you all right?"

He stalked toward John, his hands trembling as he reached out and grasped John's arm. "I have to talk to you." Phil swiveled his head toward Tabitha, then back to John. "Alone."

John glanced at Tabitha. Her chest rose and fell in a normal rhythm, and her heart monitor pulsed at a comforting rate. "Sure, but I don't really want to leave—"

The door opened again. A nurse walked in, pushing a cart loaded with bathing supplies. "Time to get that girl's fever down." She pointed a sponge at John. "I think you male members of the species should scoot for a while."

"Will do," John said, nodding. He set a hand on Phil's back. "Let's go to the waiting room."

After walking down the hall, they entered the waiting room. Although the television perched near a corner of the ceiling blared, no one sat in the sofa or two cushioned chairs to watch it.

John reached up and turned off the TV. Setting his hands on his hips, he surveyed the seating area. Apparently someone had recently spilled something dark on the sofa, leaving them the two side-by-side chairs. He pushed one around, changing the angle to one more suited for conversation.

As soon as they sat down, Phil raised a hand as if he were about to speak, then closed it into a fist and pounded the arm of his chair.

"What's the matter?" John asked.

"It's Tabitha . . . she's . . ."

"Isn't she all right?" John pushed against the chair to get up. "I'd better . . ."

Phil waved for John to sit back down. "Don't worry. She's fine. She was strong enough to talk to me for a while." Phil leaned back in his chair and sighed. "It's what she said that has me all shaken up."

"I know how you feel," John said with a nervous laugh. "She's always coming up with something to make me wonder." Raising an eyebrow, he peered at Phil. "What did she say to you?"

Phil stretched his back; then, after taking in a deep breath, he replied. "I guess you know about her dreams and how they seem to come true?"

"Seem to?" John said. "I would call it a certainty."

"Yes, yes, I suppose you would." After pausing for several seconds, he gestured with his head, as if indicating something outside of the room. "That book you sent me . . . very good. Thought provoking. But there are two things missing for me."

John set his forearms on his knees. "Well, let's start with the first one."

Phil leaned away from him. "I guess you could say that I can't believe in something that's incomprehensible." He pointed at John, not lifting his hand from his lap. "Historically Christians have risked and even lost their lives for the sake of something they can't possibly understand."

"You're right. We do give our lives for a God we don't understand. I certainly don't claim to understand him."

"Then how can you dedicate your life to something so absurd?"

John leaned back and crossed his legs. "I didn't say it was absurd; I said I don't understand him. To me, the absence of God is the absurdity. I'm sure you read the arguments in the book."

"Yes, I read them. But they don't address the comprehension issue to my satisfaction. At least I can comprehend the absence of God. That there is no all-powerful, eternally existing, all-knowing, perfect, heavenly Father is something I can grasp."

John smiled. "Can you really?"

The simple question seemed to rattle Phil. He clasped his hands together, his arms trembling again.

After a few seconds, John raised a finger. "Tell me, is the universe infinite or finite?"

Narrowing his eyes, Phil drew his head back. "What does that have to do with anything?"

"Just follow along. It'll make sense soon."

"I, uh, I really don't know . . . I would guess infinite."

"Infinite?" John dropped his foot back to the floor and leaned forward in his chair. "Phil, can you possibly comprehend an infinite expanse of space, billions and trillions upon trillions of light-years not even beginning to cover its scope? Can the universe even be described in the largest units of volume imaginable? If you could live so long as to travel at a billion times the speed of light for a billion years, you would not even come closer to the edge than when you started, because there is no edge. It goes on forever and ever and ever. It has no beginning and no end. Is your mind such that you can wrap your thoughts around such a concept?"

Phil stroked his chin for a second before giving John a sheepish grin. "No, I suppose I can't. I guess I should say it must be finite, then."

John grabbed an imaginary steering wheel. "Okay, that means if you could get in a spaceship and travel far enough, you would eventually get to the end of the universe, some sort of wall. Maybe a sign would be there that says Dead End or something like that." John smiled at his own joke, but Phil's eyes had rolled upward in thought. "If you could do a space walk right next to the sign, you could pound your fist on that impenetrable wall at the end of the universe. Guess what? There's nothing on the other side. Nothing, period! Not even empty space. Can you comprehend that?"

Phil shook his head. "That seems even worse than the other."

"Yes, it does, doesn't it?" John settled back in his chair again, waiting a few seconds for the thoughts to sink in. Finally, he raised a pair of fingers. "We have two opposite ideas, an infinite universe and a finite universe. We can't comprehend either concept. We don't have to decide right now which one is true, but would you agree that, logically, one of them must be true?"

Phil folded his hands tightly before answering. "Yes, I suppose logic would force me to admit that. One of them has to be true."

"Therefore," John continued, now displaying only one finger, "no matter which one is true, finite or infinite, logic demands that something incomprehensible is most certainly true."

Phil shook his head. "You've definitely cornered me."

"So your contention that belief in God is an absurdity, simply because you can't comprehend him, is not valid."

Phil stayed quiet for most of a minute, his shoulders sagging. "Touché, John. Without a doubt, your logic has beaten me. At least I can't use that argument anymore."

John licked his lips, forcing himself not to smile. Phil had given in, taking one step closer to the truth, but to show any hint of triumph would be way out of line. The victory was God's, not his own. Yet, something about Phil's tone bothered him. He seemed resigned, but not convinced. John raised his fingers again. "You said there were two things missing for you."

"Well, now I see that the two are related." Phil pointed at John, his shoulders now squaring. "You're good with your words, with your apologetics, with your persuasion tactics, but they still fail."

John swallowed. "Why is that?"

"You want me to put my heart and soul into this religion, but you've only convinced me with your mind." Phil tapped his finger against his temple. "The only comfort you offered was that Rose is in heaven. And now you probably wouldn't even shed one tear for your own daughter if she were to die. If that's the way Christians think, then I can't be one." He placed his hand over his heart. "I can't live with a heart of stone in my chest."

Drawing back, John sank in his chair. The comment stung, really stung. He had often thought of Phil as the "stony atheist," but now Phil had turned the tables. How could he show him otherwise, that love poured from his heart? He was messing everything up again, and this might be the worst time ever.

Reaching deep within, John tried to transform his tone, to somehow change from a dry academic into a compassionate, loving friend. "When Rose died," he began with a trembling voice, "I tried to comfort you with the truth as I saw it. To me, announcing her entrance into heaven was the most joyous news I could share to ease your pain." His voice trailed off, and he buried his face in his hands for a few seconds. When he raised up again, a tear tracked down his cheek. "And I have cried many tears for Tabitha. She's sick and hurting, so I'm hurting with her. But if she dies, her suffering will be over, and any pain I might allow for myself after that would be selfish." He stopped and took a deep breath, trying to compose himself as he searched for what to say next. Should he tell Phil about his promise to Tabitha, that he couldn't grieve for her now even if he wanted to? That probably wouldn't help. That would shift the blame, if there was any, to a sick little girl. Finally, he asked, "Are you familiar at all with the Bible?"

"Uh . . . sure . . . from my religion classes in college." Phil eyed John, apparently taken aback by his sudden change. "I'm familiar with quite a bit of it, but probably not as much as you are."

John rubbed his eyes before continuing. "King David once sinned in a horrible way, so God made his baby boy very sick. David fasted and prayed with many tears, but when the baby finally died, he got up, washed his face, and grieved no more. David said, 'He has died; why should I fast? Can I bring him back again? I shall go to him, but he will not return to me.'"

"I read about David and Bathsheba," Phil said, "but I don't remember the part about the baby."

"Well, I'm approaching this in the same way. I believe God will restore Tabitha to good health, and I'm fasting and praying to ask God to bring that about. But if he doesn't, I'll know where Tabitha is and that I'll go and see her again someday. I won't grieve."

His face reddening, Phil stood up and pointed at John with an outstretched arm. "You have all the logical answers," he growled, "and I can't use the Bible to contradict you, so we're not on a level playing field right now."

"But, Phil, I—"

"No buts!" Phil paced around the room. "I might be an atheist, but this much I know." He pounded a fist against his chest. "Worshipping God has to be from the heart."

"It *is* from the heart. I—"

"Oh, don't give me that song. I see your tears, but they came at your bidding, not from your heart. Your actions speak louder than your words." Phil raised his arms, his voice growing in fervor. "Maybe there is a God who gives dreams to people. Maybe foolish men like me and innocent children like Tabitha want so much to believe, we imagine a glorious paradise where everyone is happy and dancing, singing songs and just having a grand old time. It's all heart and no mind for fools like us. That's the kind of brainless faith I usually see in Christians."

He stopped and pointed at John again. "You're different, John. You really understand what you believe, but it's all mind and no heart. The things I've seen in my dreams are so real I couldn't tell if I was awake or asleep. Even after I wake up, I'm never sure if I've been sleeping. But the visions I saw were dazzling, so dazzling they were frightening, and so frightening they shook apart everything I've ever believed in."

John sat quietly. It was no use. Phil wasn't going to listen, and who could blame him?

Phil threw his hands up in the air again, nearly shouting as he resumed his pacing. "But our dreams aren't true. They can't be true. If there is a God, he wouldn't let them be true. He wouldn't take a man's daughter away and then tease him, give him tidbits of delight and then thrash him to the ground in doubt and despair when heartless evangelists come knocking at the door."

He stopped once more, this time right in front of John. The two men stared at one another with sad eyes. Finally, Phil shook his head despondently. "No doubt, I'm the fool," he said quietly, turning his gaze away, "or maybe even a madman."

With another shake of his head he walked to the door and turned back. "I don't know what I believe anymore," he said, trembling in both body and voice, "but until I see a heart and mind as one in true faith, I refuse to believe in your God or anyone else's."

Chapter 18

JONATHAN TOUCHED the door. "Is Tabitha in that room, Mommy?"

"Yes, dear." Melody held the two-year-old in her arms. "But I have to check to make sure it's all right for us all to go in."

She transferred her burden to Joshua, a lanky twenty-year-old who looked more like his father every day. Four sets of eyes watched as she tapped on the door with her knuckles.

While they waited, an orderly rolled a bed through the hall, carrying a gaunt, elderly man. His eyes were closed and his mouth hung wide open with a stream of drool dripping over the edge. Out of a patient's room three doors down, a middle-aged lady emerged, wailing pitifully. She ran to an open elevator and disappeared behind the closing doors.

As another orderly pushed by them with a loaded bin, Jonathan wrinkled his nose. "What stinks?"

"It's laundry," Sarah said. "There are a lot of sick people here. Sometimes they throw up or can't control their bowel movements, and these orderlies help them stay clean."

"Oh." Jonathan looked at the door. "Does Tabitha stink?"

Sarah pushed the tip of his nose. "We'll find out, won't we?"

John opened the door, slid out, and closed it behind him. Leaning close to Melody, he whispered, "She's . . . uh . . . getting her sheets changed."

"Another episode?"

Pressing his lips together as he glanced at the others, he nodded. "Not the worst, but bad enough. It'll be a few minutes." He fished his wallet from his back pocket and handed it to Joshua. "Son, please take everyone to the cafeteria for a drink, and try to be back in about ten minutes."

"Sure, Dad. I understand." Joshua took the wallet and led the way down the hall. Sarah trailed, looking back at her parents, grief obvious in her eyes.

After the kids disappeared around a corner, John led Melody into the room. Inside, a nurse was tucking a lower sheet under the mattress, while Tabitha lay with a blanket over her from knees to chest, still and quiet.

When they drew near her bedside, just out of the way of the nurse, Melody laid her head on John's chest. "I don't know how much longer I can take this."

"I know what you mean." He rubbed her back tenderly. "I don't know which is worse, watching her suffer or staying at home and wondering."

"I wouldn't know. I've done all the staying at home."

"Is Jonathan well enough for you to take a turn here?"

"I think so. He's keeping everything down now. No sign of fever."

"Are you getting much sleep at home?" he asked.

"No, but probably more than you're getting here."

John heaved a deep sigh. "I don't know. I just can't imagine being away from her. It's like I wouldn't be able to breathe if I couldn't watch her breathing." He looked Melody in the eye. "Do you know what I mean?"

She nodded. "Sometimes I wake up in the middle of the night, and it feels like something's sucking my breath away, and I wonder if Tabitha's suffering. But I can't call you at two in the morning to find out, so I just lie awake and pray until I fall asleep again."

"I think I would just pace the floor. I wouldn't be able to stand it."

"Well, Jonathan cried for you last night. Joshua was able to comfort him a little, but it's not the same. He needs you."

"Tell you what," he said. "I'll stay one more night and then come home for the day. We'll trade places in the morning. I don't want you to have to spend the night in a chair."

"I don't mind—"

A loud gurgle sounded from John's stomach.

Melody laid a hand on his belly. "Have you had lunch yet?"

"No. I'm fasting. You?"

"I fasted all day yesterday, and I had a banana before I left. That's all."

"Then you'd better eat." Smiling, he pressed a finger against her nose. "That's an order."

The nurse spoke up from the bedside. "The cafeteria closes for lunch in a few minutes. Better hurry if you're going there."

"How about if I get you some lunch?" John asked. "We'll pray over Tabitha again and then I'll run home, get cleaned up a bit, and reacquaint myself with the kids for a while." He looked at his watch. "I'll be back, say, in two hours."

Melody pushed away but kept hold of his hand. "Why don't you take a nap and make it four hours. I'll be here. Don't worry."

"Okay. I'll be back by five. Steve will probably be visiting around that time."

"And maybe her test results will be in by then." Melody turned to the nurse. "Do you know when her tests are scheduled?"

The nurse spread the blanket over Tabitha's feet and smoothed it out. "It's not on her orders." Carrying a clipboard, she breezed past them as she headed for the door. "I think the doctor will be in here in a few minutes."

John led Melody to the bedside. Tabitha lay with her face toward the door, her eyes open. For some reason, she seemed a million miles away, but when she caught sight of them, she blinked, and a hint of her cheerful smile returned. "Hi, Mama," she whispered.

She stroked Tabitha's hair. "Hello, sweetheart. How are you feeling today?"

For a few seconds, Tabitha just stared. Then she cleared her throat and said in a wispy voice, "Not too good."

"Do you want more company? Your sister and brothers are here."

A thin line dug into her forehead. "In the room?"

"No, but they're here in the hospital. If you're too sick to see them, they'll understand."

"It's okay." Her arm lifted sluggishly, her finger pointing at the bed controls. "Can you raise my head a little?"

"Sure." Melody read the instructions, then pushed the button. "Say when."

The motor hummed, tilting up one side of Tabitha's bed. With each inch, her face tightened more until she grunted, "When."

Melody released the button. "Are you okay?"

With her eyes closed, she nodded.

"I'll see if the kids are back," John said as he headed for the door.

Melody took Tabitha's hand. "I've been praying for you."

Her reply seemed to come from somewhere far away. "I know."

Biting her lip, Melody looked around the room. What could she talk about that would change the subject from the gloom of this place to something . . . something less gloomy. "Did you see the flowers and balloons?"

"Uh-huh." She grimaced again.

Melody sighed. Asking questions wouldn't do. They just made Tabitha work. But the kids would be loaded with questions, so she had to be sure to deflect as many as she could.

Soon, the door opened again, ushering in John and Tabitha's four siblings. As expected, Andrew and Jonathan buzzed with questions. For the most part, Tabitha just looked at them while her mother and father answered, though she added a nod or a shake of the head a few times.

"She feels pretty bad right now, Andrew," Melody said, "but the doctors are going to move her to a special room in just a few minutes so they can keep a closer watch on her. Did she lose bowel control? Well, that's kind of a private matter. Yes, Jonathan, we'll move a balloon to her new room if they'll let us. No, I'm sorry, you can't give her a kiss."

When the questions ebbed, Tabitha tugged on her father's shirt. He leaned over, lowering his ear close to her lips. "What is it, sweetheart?"

John listened to the soft whisper. He stared into her eyes for several seconds and then turned back to the children, his whole body trembling as he clutched the bed rail. "Tabitha says that she loves you all and she expects to be perfectly well and going home in the morning."

"Yay!" Jonathan clapped his hands.

"That's Tabitha for you," Andrew said. "Full of faith and confidence."

"It's time for Tabitha to go to another room," a man in a white lab coat announced as he entered. "We don't want to tire her out too much."

"Dr. Smithers," John said, gesturing toward Melody. "This is my wife, Melody."

As an orderly entered behind him, the doctor nodded. "Glad to meet you."

She returned his nod and spread out her arms to round up the kids. "Say good-bye, everyone."

After they all said their good-byes, Joshua herded them the rest of the way to the door, but Sarah stayed behind. She stepped up to the bed and kissed Tabitha on the forehead, large tears streaming as she spoke. "I'll see you in the morning, dear sister."

Tabitha stared at her, her eyes wide and longing. She mouthed, "Bye," her own tears making their way down her cheeks.

Sarah turned and hurried away, but as she walked out the door with Joshua, Melody caught her arm. "Sarah, are you all right?"

She sniffed and nodded, rubbing her finger under her nose. "I'll be okay."

"You'll drive?" Melody asked Joshua.

Holding Jonathan in one arm, Joshua laid the other around Sarah. "Yes, ma'am. And don't worry about Jonathan. We'll take care of him. If he gets real cranky again, we'll give you a call."

As the group walked down the hall to the elevator, Melody watched from the door, her arms crossed as she shifted from side to side. Jonathan squirmed in Joshua's grip, begging to push the button. Could they handle it? Under normal circumstances, sure. But they had never faced something like this before, a situation that could change their lives forever.

When she turned back toward the room, the door opened. The orderly rolled Tabitha's bed out into the hall, John marching alongside, holding Tabitha's hand.

Melody joined them. She wanted so much to ask John about Tabitha's cryptic message, but now was not the time. She walked on Tabitha's left, trying to think of encouraging words, but the same gloom filled her mind. Nothing seemed to pierce the dark curtain of sorrows.

Finally, she managed, "We're right here with you, Tabitha, and one of us will stay with you all the time."

Except for blinking her eyes, Tabitha remained motionless as she passed under the lights in the hall. With expert precision, the orderly turned the bed through a doorway.

John and Melody stayed back a few paces while the bed went through, then followed hand in hand until the bed stopped at a care station inside. A nurse in green scrubs walked up to the bed and began attaching monitors to Tabitha's body. "Are you two staying?" she asked without looking up from her work.

"Just me, for now," Melody said. "My husband will come back later."

As they watched the nurse work, Melody pressed close to her husband. "What do you think Tabitha meant?"

"You mean about being better in the morning?"

"Right."

"It was so strange," he said, "like she was talking from a dream."

"Another prophecy?"

"That's what I was thinking, but . . ." His voice faded.

"But what does *home* mean, right?"

"Exactly." John kept his gaze fixed on the activity at Tabitha's bed. "Maybe home is heaven."

She tightened her clasp with his hand. "Should we ask her?"

"Maybe, but I'm not sure she even knows. I'm not even sure where she wants to be, home here or home there."

She turned him face-to-face. "What do *you* think?"

He let out a long sigh. "I was thinking that Tabitha's prophecies have been amazing, but sometimes she doesn't understand them herself. Maybe she really believes she'll be miraculously healed during the night."

"Let's hope she believes that." Melody hooked her arm through John's and laid her head on his shoulder. "Otherwise, she might not have the will to fight anymore."

* * *

Melody sat in a low-backed chair, shifting for the hundredth time to try to get comfortable. On the table next to her, a partially eaten sandwich lay on an otherwise empty plate, and a bent straw dangled over the side of a root beer can. Since John had arrived too late at the cafeteria to get a hot lunch for her, the vending machine offerings had to do.

Something clattered in the distance, making her jerk her head up. The ICU had been crowded all afternoon, forcing the staff to place patients on either side of Tabitha's area, making it a lousy place to catch some sleep. The humming monitors helped. They sang a boring but effective lullaby.

Ceiling-to-floor curtains separated Melody from the unit behind her, dull yellow fabric suspended from runners in the ceiling where sliding pins allowed them to be drawn all around the bed. Several of the pins had tangled in one corner, preventing the curtain from making it all the way around, leaving a two-foot gap in the makeshift wall. Earlier in the afternoon, the gap had allowed Melody to catch a glimpse of the patient in the next unit, another little girl, perhaps a year or two younger than Tabitha.

After a round of tests, Tabitha had gone back to sleep. Her fever had fallen below 102, but struggling to stay awake during the tests had exhausted her. Melody tried to take this opportunity to nap in the chair, but to no avail.

A low moan sounded from the other girl's bed. Melody peeked through the opening. Another worried mother doted over the struggling child, stroking her head and trying to help her into a comfortable position. The two women caught each other's glances. As silent sympathy passed between them, both moms began to cry.

Melody rose from her chair to see if she could help but stopped when a soft whisper reached her ears.

"Mama?"

Melody whirled around. "Yes, Tabitha?"

"Can you talk to me? I want to hear your voice."

"Of course I can. Let's see . . . Do you want me to tell you what's going on at home?"

"Yes," she replied weakly.

"Well . . ." Melody began, changing to an upbeat tone. "Sarah finally finished that dress she was making. Remember the navy blue one with the sash?"

"Yes, she—"

"Oh, don't answer. It'll tire you out." Melody walked around the bed, trying to stay active to keep her voice chipper. "Anyway, I declared a vacation from school this week, so she had more time to work on it. Would you believe she had to rip out half of the hem and do it over?"

As her mother went on and on, Tabitha kept her eyes closed, but her eyebrows moved and the corners of her mouth turned up during the funny parts, especially during the descriptions of Jonathan's adventures and the new things he was learning.

"Excuse me, ma'am?" The voice came from the other bed.

"Yes?" Melody replied, turning.

A woman's face appeared through the gap in the curtain. "My daughter wants to know how old Jonathan is."

Melody laughed. "He's two and a half, and don't forget the half or he'll be sure to remind you."

"Okay. Thank you."

Melody pulled the curtain to one side. "Do you mind if I leave them open?"

"Not at all." The woman smiled, though it seemed a sad sort of smile. "I'm Barbara."

"And I'm Melody." She walked to the bed Barbara was guarding and gazed at the girl lying in it. "And this is . . . ?"

"Kaitlyn."

"Kaitlyn," Melody said, "I'll be sure to speak up and include the details."

The girl managed a fragile smile, but it soon evaporated. Her face was pale, in stark contrast to her dark hair, but her cheeks were full, testifying to her normally good health.

Melody gave her a smile in return. It was probably best not to ask what was wrong with her, at least not yet. Since she lay in ICU, it couldn't be good.

As she walked back to Tabitha's bed, Melody raised her voice. "Now, Tabitha, where was I? Oh, yes. Jonathan's frog. Well, the frog jumped across the kitchen floor . . ."

After about fifteen more minutes of listening to Melody's stories from the home front, Kaitlyn fell asleep, peacefully this time. When Melody noticed, she lowered her voice and finished telling Tabitha about how Sarah and Joshua had whipped up tacos for supper the night before.

Finally, she sat down and wiped a hand across her brow. "Tabitha, that made me a little tired, and I'm not sure what else to tell you. You've only been gone a few days." After taking a deep breath, she added, "But I'll keep talking if you want me to."

"If you don't mind," Tabitha whispered.

Melody picked up her purse and pulled out a book. "I brought *Caddie Woodlawn*. Do you want me to read to you?"

Tabitha smiled. "Sure."

"Okay, then. We'll read." Melody slid her chair closer to the bed and opened the book to page one. "Caddie Woodlawn, by Carol Ryrie Brink. Chapter one. Three Adventures. In 1864 Caddie Wood-lawn was eleven, and as wild a little tomboy as ever ran the woods of western Wisconsin."

Melody read on and on, stopping every once in a while to take a sip of water. At times it seemed that Tabitha had fallen asleep, but no matter. The sound of her mother's voice would be soothing regardless of what stage of wakefulness Tabitha was in.

The unit nurse stopped by the bed several times, taking longer than necessary to read Tabitha's vitals, obviously listening to Melody's vivid rendering of the more exciting parts.

Finally, Melody closed the book. Her throat now tired, she read a clock on the wall—4:35. John would be back soon. He usually arrived early for everything.

She rose and looked at Tabitha. Yes, she was definitely asleep now. Darting her eyes, Melody tried to read the many confusing monitors, then zeroed in on the heart rate, one of the few numbers she understood—a hundred and ten beats per minute.

She kept her stare on the number. It was so fast. Wasn't that an indicator of an elevated temperature? She laid a palm on Tabitha's forehead. No cooler than before, but no warmer either.

Once again, she walked the few steps over to the other girl's area. Barbara stood up to greet her.

"Do you mind if I ask what's wrong with Kaitlyn?" Melody asked.

Barbara looked down at her daughter and combed the bangs from her face. "She has food poisoning. It might be botulism."

Melody stepped toward the bed. "Do you mind if I pray over her?"

"Oh, please do." Barbara moved back to allow room.

Leaning over, Melody laid a palm on Kaitlyn's head. The little girl, now asleep, didn't budge. Although her throat still ached, Melody summoned the strongest voice she could muster. "As your word says, Father, 'The righteous cry, and the Lord hears and delivers them out of all their troubles.' Lord, I have come to you many times over the past few days for my own daughter, and now I lift up to you Barbara's daughter, your precious child."

At this point, Melody took in a deep breath. Her words were too staid, too filled with religious formality. Digging deep down again, she let her emotions speak. "Oh, dear God, our hearts are aching. Our children—our babies—are sick. Through pangs of labor we push them out, but the joy of new life brings our mourning to cries of praise and unspeakable delight, the anguish of delivery soon forgotten. My precious Lord, we anguish again, and we ask for healing for our babies, our little girls, so that you will turn our mourning into dancing and their sorrows into smiles."

As tears dripped from her cheeks to the bed, she continued with a shaking voice. "For Kaitlyn, I pray that you will purge the poison from her body. For Tabitha, I ask you to expel the virus. Please make them both well. And once again we will cry out in praise to you when you cause the troubles of this day to melt away from our minds and all that will remain is memories of your mighty deeds."

She paused. Should she go on? There were so many needs, so many things to pray about. But John would be there soon, and she still needed to tend to her own daughter. As she took in a breath to finish, the sound of curtains sliding made her turn back toward Tabitha.

"Melody?"

It was Dr. Van Dorn.

She raised up, kissed Barbara on her teary cheek, and hurried to Tabitha's area, closing the curtain behind her. "Steve," she said, glancing at the clock. "I didn't expect you so early."

"I called and heard that Tabitha was in the ICU. My last appointment canceled, so I came right over."

"I expect John to be here any minute."

Steve scanned Tabitha's environment, reading the monitors and recording tapes. "I looked over Tabitha's records," he said, nodding at a clipboard in his hands. "We're being as aggressive with this bug as we can be."

"That's comforting, I guess. From where I sit, except for one nurse who stops by, it seems like everyone's ignoring her. I can't tell what the doctors and nurses are doing behind the scenes."

"I know, but trust me. She's top priority around here right now."

"Did they tell you her fever keeps hanging on?"

Steve dropped his gaze. "I saw that in the report."

"Are the test results in?" she asked, peering over the top of the clipboard.

He looked toward the hall, obviously avoiding eye contact. "They were ready a while ago. They're already treating her based on the results, but with a virus like this, our options are limited."

Melody set her fists on her hips. "Why didn't they tell me about the results sooner?"

"Well . . ." Steve flapped the clipboard against his chest. "I think Dr. Smithers wanted *me* to tell you."

His words seemed distant, surreal. What could he have meant? It had to be terrible news. "Is it . . . is it bad?"

Steve placed a hand on Melody's shoulder. "Nothing God can't handle. If you think John's going to be here soon, why don't I wait for him and tell you both all about it? There's another doctor I need to talk to for a few minutes, and then I'll come right back."

Melody nodded. As Steve left, the breeze in his wake seemed to suck out her spirit. Every ounce of energy drained away. Her legs now wobbly, she sat in the chair, picked up the book, and fanned her face with it. Why was it so hot all of a sudden?

The curtain slid back again. Barbara peered in, her face still half hidden. "May I come in?" she whispered.

Melody nodded again, unable to speak. If she tried, she'd lose control for sure.

"I'll just stand here with you," Barbara said, rubbing Melody's shoulders. "You can be quiet if you want to. I'm not much at praying, but at least I can soothe your muscles while you wait for your husband."

As Barbara dug her strong fingers into Melody's stiff back and neck, Melody let out a soft groan. This woman had the strongest fingers! Might she be a pianist? A masseuse? In any case, this wasn't the time to ask. Just sit and allow this kind lady to administer a blessing in her own way.

After a few minutes, John walked in, stepping more lightly than he had earlier. With freshly washed hair and a clean-shaven face, he seemed rejuvenated. "Hi, Angel Face," he sang out. "Who's your new friend?"

After the proper introductions and chit-chat about Tabitha's condition and Kaitlyn's illness, Barbara returned to her daughter, closing the curtain behind her.

John and Melody, now alone, stood together and watched their precious, sleeping girl. Melody squeezed her husband's hand. The sight of Tabitha attached to all those lifeless machines had already brought his mood crashing down.

"Are you okay?" she asked.

"If you mean, 'Are you going to manage to take another breath?' then I guess I'm okay. Just barely."

"That's about how I feel. It hurts just to think, just to exist."

"I know. I'm definitely getting a better picture."

"Of the Graysons?"

He nodded. "Their shoes hurt. Know what I mean?"

She leaned her head against his shoulder. "I know exactly what you mean."

The curtain pulled to the side. Steve had returned, his face gaunt and gray.

John gave him a nod. "Melody says you have the test results."

"I do." Steve opened a file folder and scanned the first page. "I was told the results over the phone; I just wanted to get the report myself so we could go over it together."

"And?" John prompted.

Steve shook his head. "Medically, it's not good. From all we can tell, the infection hasn't slowed down. The lesions keep growing and multiplying." He hesitated, looking down at the floor, then back at John. "You want me to be completely straightforward, right?"

John swallowed, glanced at Melody, and nodded. "Yes, go ahead."

"Well, with the severity of her condition, we should be prepared for the possibility of moderate to severe brain damage. It's not a hundred percent, but the chances are pretty high. If she survives, she may need long-term therapy. Right now, that doesn't appear to be the case. In her waking moments, she's still lucid. But the statistics don't bode well for full recovery."

Melody wept. She hooked her arm around John's and leaned her forehead against him, spasms shaking her body.

As he took her hand in his, John shifted his weight. "Is there any good news at all?"

"She is a very strong little girl," Steve continued. "She hasn't had any seizures in the last several hours, while many patients with her lesions would be in a coma by now. I told you it wasn't good medically, but that's not the only battlefront. We should count our blessings and keep praying. God has done greater miracles than what we're asking for."

John took Melody into his arms, laid her head against his chest, and looked back at Steve. "You're right," John said. "God *can* heal Tabitha. He could touch her tonight and destroy the virus and the lesions with less than a blink, if he's willing, but . . ." His voice trailed off in a weak tremble. "Do you think he's willing?"

Steve tossed the folder on the chair and wrapped his arms around both parents. He, too, wept. As they huddled, he whispered a prayer. "God of our fathers, Great Physician, Lover of souls, we beg you to visit this daughter and touch her with your healing hand. She is your child, so precious, so full of faith, never doubting your love for one moment. She has heeded the dreams you have sent her way, obeyed your call to tell of your love to others, even to those who deny your existence. She is a brave warrior, but now she is a crippled lamb. Merciful Father, take her in your arms and bind her wounds. Let her once again sing and dance as she did before, carefree and overflowing with love."

As the minutes ticked by, John and Steve took turns adding to the prayers, while Melody added "Yes, Lord" between stifled sobs. As their cries drifted heavenward, a wave of comfort washed over them in a cool rinse of mercy.

After a moment or two of silence, Steve whispered in John's ear. "I really don't know if God's willing, John, but I think we'll know one way or the other very soon."

Chapter 19

JOHN SAT in the chair next to Tabitha's bed, half awake and half asleep. At times, he jerked his head up and read the clock, finding that he had dozed for twenty minutes. Then, watching the seconds slide by as the monitors continued their haunting hums and beeps, he tried to keep his heavy eyelids open. Why? Who could tell? Maybe because sleep took him away from his vigil, making him unable to fulfill his guardian duties. Maybe yet another prayer would show his love and determination, unlike the apostles who couldn't stay awake to pray with Jesus because their flesh was too weak.

The unit nurse helped him stay awake during her frequent visits, recording instrument readings, monitoring fluid intake and output, and even swabbing Tabitha's brow and arms to help cool her down. She always offered a kind smile and whispered words of comfort, but they seemed empty somehow, promises she had no power to keep.

Of course, Melody wanted to stay. Although home pressures mounted, the image of her deathly ill daughter tugged at her heart. The cramped ICU room had only one chair, a miserable place to sleep, so she opted for a more comfortable bed, a cushioned bench out in the waiting room down the hall.

When John checked on her an hour ago, she had reported little sleep, and a call home had revealed a new problem: Jonathan had taken a turn for the worse.

She had given Joshua and Sarah specific instructions on how to care for their sick brother, Tylenol for fever with lukewarm sponge baths if the temperature exceeded 102 degrees. Just to be safe, she had given orders to take him straight to the emergency room if his fever went over 103 and have her paged when he arrived. Still, even with two older teens taking care of their younger brother and John watching over Tabitha, Melody couldn't sleep well, torn between two crises, neither of which she had the power to ease.

Earlier in the evening, Barbara and Kaitlyn had left the ICU, Kaitlyn having improved greatly. Barbara's thankfulness had cheered Melody, but even that proved little comfort as she passed between fitful dozes and shivering wakefulness.

A soft moan sounded from Tabitha's bed. John jerked his eyelids up. Tabitha had shifted slightly, just enough to bring a new pang. All through the night, her erratic facial expressions had moved from peaceful bliss to wrenching agony and then back again. He had to stay awake—keep watching, keep praying.

A woman's whisper shook him from his meditations. "John?"

"Yes?" Rising from his chair, he focused on the new arrival—Thelma, the nurse from down the hall.

She stepped past the curtain, her profile now easily visible in the unit's dim light as she extended a sheet of paper. "I brought you something." Her voice stayed at whisper level.

"Thank you." John took the page. "What is it?"

"A summary of a doctor's report." She tapped a finger near the top. "Check out the date, the age of the patient, her condition. It's all there."

"I will." He blinked at the dim letters. "Can you give me a summary of the summary?"

"A girl, eleven years old, encephalitis. She was comatose, worse lesions than Tabitha has, and the doctor gave her almost no chance of survival."

He tried to keep his hands from shaking, but they wouldn't obey. "And?"

Thelma grasped his arm. "She lived, John. She's alive and well with no complications. The doctor called her healing miraculous."

John's throat clamped shut. He couldn't say a word.

Thelma's voice rose above a whisper. "I looked into it. Her parents are a lot like you, very religious. They prayed for her constantly. Do you know what that means?"

Swallowing, he managed to squeak out, "I think so."

"You think so? Isn't it obvious? This proves there's still hope."

"I haven't given up hope, Thelma. I'll never give up hope."

Smiling, she gave him a gentle shove. "Of course you won't. You have a father's love. That child is a part of you, part of your very body. You'd better not give up hope!"

"Thank you." He waved the page. "I'll hang on to this."

"I blacked out the name," she said, pointing at the text again. "Confidentiality, you understand."

He nodded. "Of course."

"I'll be watching her progress." Thelma turned to the bed, stroked Tabitha's arm, then hustled out.

John sat again in the chair, staring at the report, unable to read the tiny letters in the dim light. Still, just holding it brought comfort, a message that God, indeed, still heals encephalitis-stricken little girls.

Soon, his eyelids grew heavy again. He dozed on and off, again checking the clock at every waking moment. At about two in the morning, a hand rested on his shoulder. "John?"

He jerked around. "Melody?"

"Yes."

He shot to his feet. "Is everything okay?"

"No. Joshua brought Jonathan into the emergency room. I've already been there to check on him. He's okay, but he's crying a lot, so I think I'd better stay down there with him. I just came back to let you know where I'll be."

"What did the doctor say?"

She kissed him on the forehead. "Don't worry. It's not at all like encephalitis. But they want to watch him anyway."

"Okay. That's good . . . I guess."

As she pivoted toward Tabitha, her face moved into brighter light, showing the glistening tears in her eyes.

John squeezed her hand. "Go be with Jonathan. I'll take care of Tabitha. Just keep praying."

She ran a finger along Tabitha's hand. "As if I could stop." Without another word, she hurried out of the ICU.

With Melody gone, the remaining hours of the night belonged to Tabitha and John alone, alone with their thoughts, their dreams, and their hopes. Yet what hopes remained? Sure, God healed Miss Confidentiality, but how many other little girls had died? The current outbreak had proved that this bug was an indiscriminate killer, taking young and old alike. God seemed to pick and choose whom he would snatch from the brink of death. How could anyone be sure who would fall over the edge?

John sat down heavily. Every moment seemed a battle. On one side lay a view of a black void—the future, unknown, impossible to predict, terrifying. On the other, the light of faith—faith that God, who so far seemed unwilling to prove himself, would crush the marching enemy, a teeming horde of mindless misery.

He straightened, peering at Tabitha again. She slept peacefully, on and on and on, the dreamer, the one who seemed able to pierce the black void with her prophetic eyes. Who could tell what God might be revealing to her now? She gave no signs, save for the twitching muscles in her brow and lips. What could those mean? New struggles looming on the horizon?

The early morning hours brought one new seizure, stronger and longer than any previous, apparently corroborating the slowly failing vital signs the monitors so cruelly announced moment by moment. John could interpret these now, and he asked the nurse time and again if critical points had been reached. Should he call his wife back from the emergency room? No, there was no need yet, she had assured him. Tabitha was going through normal peaks and valleys, and they were doing all they could do. Her medications were at a maximum. She was in God's hands.

At about six in the morning, Tabitha let out a moan.

John leaped to his feet. "Tabitha? Do you need anything?"

Her eyes wide, she moved her lips, though nothing intelligible came out in the midst of her whimpering sounds.

Bending over the rail, he leaned closer. "What are you trying to say, sweetheart? Please try again. I'll get whatever you need."

Her shallow, pain-racked breaths ripped at his heart. "What?" he asked, now in tears. "What did you say, Tabitha?"

"Life has conquered death," came the panting whisper. "Life has . . ."

As her rapid breathing continued, John fussed with her sheets, forcing himself to talk to keep from breaking down. "You are a warrior, my little angel. This is your greatest battle, a war against the final enemy. But . . . but you're prepared, aren't you?"

"Armor . . . ," she whispered.

"Armor! Yes, the armor of a champion. The . . . the helmet of salvation, the shield of faith, remember?" With his voice squeaking, he cleared his throat to bring it down. "The Devil's flaming missiles won't touch you. No, sir! Not my daughter!"

Her eyelids fluttered. "My sword?"

He searched the room. Wouldn't a Bible be around somewhere? Yet no Bible lay in sight. No matter. He had taught her well. She already had her sword, but was he ready to see his little one wield it so soon in a battle for her right to wear the spotless robes?

Finally, he laid a hand on her chest. "Your sword is within you, dearest one, implanted right here."

She grimaced, the tightest facial twist yet. Panting, her whisper grew louder, sobs punctuating her words. "Death . . . death is swallowed up in victory."

Tabitha's sword stabbed his heart. "Tabitha," he cried. "Sweet daughter, how can I help you?"

She opened her eyes and stared at her father. She spoke through the crushing agony, tears rolling down her pain-creased cheeks. "No . . . need . . . Daddy. . . . I'm not . . . afraid."

Her words did little to ease his tortured mind. Instead, his passion erupted, along with hot, flowing tears, dripping heavily on her sheet. She kept her eyes open, resting her gaze on him as she managed to squeeze his hand.

At that moment, the light of dawn began to brighten their part of the ICU. She turned her head toward the light, then back to her father. For the first time in hours, the pain seemed to leave her face, melting away, like vermin fleeing when light floods the room. She smiled a glorious smile, finally showing again her lovely spirit through a countenance as bright as the sun. "I am the new dawning," she said happily. "That's what he said in the dream."

"Who said it? What's happening?"

With a mighty strain, Tabitha rose to a sitting position, her glow as bright as ever. As John caught her, she flung her arms around his neck. Somehow, her grip was strong, and their close embrace shot an image through his mind, an image of his little girl folded up in his lap in that old rocking chair.

He begged for the serenity of that night to return, replacing this terrible nightmare. But reality dashed the imagined comfort. The phantom smell of clean hair and fresh breath was spoiled by the odor of death, and he saw once again the desperately sick child in his arms.

The monitors next to her played a death knell, her blood pressure tumbling, her heart and respiration failing. Their faces only inches apart, Tabitha sang out with joy. "Morning has broken, Daddy, and I can see the light! It's just like you always taught us; there's nothing to fear."

With these words, Tabitha's eyes rolled up into her head, the beautiful orbs closing in a pain-locked nightmare.

John allowed her stiffening body to fall safely back to the bed. "Nurse!" he shouted frantically. "She's having another seizure!"

Screeee! A sawtooth line on the heart monitor spelled out the danger in wild, cacophonous jumps, an emergency call wailed from the bedside, and the nurse rushed in.

"She's in V. fib!" she yelled. With a mighty reach, she slammed her hand on the code button. "Stand back, Mr. Hanson!"

As John took several steps back, a doctor burst into the room, running at full speed. Then, before the doors could close, a second doctor rushed through.

The scene looked like a frenzy of arms and equipment flying from place to place. Breathless, John could only watch as hands and electric paddles were thrust onto Tabitha's delicate chest, causing her arms and legs to bounce around the bed. During the rush, one of the doctors threw a little rag doll to the floor.

John scooped up the doll and clenched her tightly to his chest. "Oh, dear God!" he finally cried out, falling to his knees. "Dear God, have mercy!"

In his daze, time passed in strange pauses and leaps. Was it minutes or hours? How long could this torture go on? Finally, still on his knees, a blurred image passed by—a doctor shuffling out of the room, slowly, with drooping head and shoulders. If he said anything to him as they passed, he never heard his comment. When the second one walked out, the bed and the monitors came into view. Most had been turned off, but for some reason the heart monitor remained on.

A flat line on its CRT monitor pronounced Tabitha's untimely death.

John rose slowly from the floor, his mouth wide open, the doll hanging limply from one hand. He tramped toward the bed with anchored feet. In his weakness, he could only manage to lean over Tabitha's bed and cover his face with his hands. The doll dropped to Tabitha's side.

"I'm so sorry." The nurse laid a trembling hand on John's shoulder and tried to squeeze comfort into his nearly limp body. "We did all we could. I hope you know that."

John nodded without lifting his head. "I understand."

The nurse flipped the switch on the heart monitor. "I'll leave you alone for a minute."

As she turned to leave, John held out his hand. "No . . . no, it's all right. I'm fine." He sniffed and wiped his eyes on his shirtsleeve. "I said my good-byes."

"Oh, I thought you might want to stay with her and cry for a few minutes."

John managed a weak smile. "Thank you. You're very kind. But the time for crying is over. I have to call my wife now." He cast his eyes toward the floor, a fog invading his thoughts. "No, I'll just walk down to the ER."

"Are you sure you can make it? I can get an orderly to—"

"No. I'm okay." He looked up again. "Please let Dr. Van Dorn know as soon as you can."

The nurse just nodded, obviously fighting to keep back her own tears.

John took his time gathering the few items he had brought with him, an empty snack bag, a book on Justin Martyr, and his jacket. With listless stretches, he managed to pull the jacket on, leaving a crumpled collar and twisted sleeves.

Out of the corner of his eye, Tabitha's lifeless body came into view. As he clenched his eyelids shut, her weak voice floated through his mind. *Don't grieve. If you really believe I'm in heaven, don't cry for me. . . . I won't be able to dance in heaven if you're crying.*

He leaned over and felt for Deborah. After snatching her up, he lowered his head, opened his eyes, and shuffled heavily out the door. As he walked down the hall toward the elevator, his head still down, he passed by Thelma.

She jumped up and stood behind her desk. "Mind if I join you for a minute?"

"Not at all." While waiting for Thelma to catch up, he shoved his hands into his pockets, Deborah in one of them.

Thelma took several jogging steps and hooked her arm around his elbow. "The whole staff already heard," she said. "We just want you to know that your daughter was . . . I mean, is, the sweetest, most wonderful little girl, a beautiful young lady, really."

John pushed the elevator call button. "Thank you, but I didn't realize you had a chance to get to know her."

They walked into the empty elevator together. "Oh, yes! The first night I had a nice little chat with her while you were sleeping."

"Really? I guess I slept a little more heavily than I thought."

"Well, the only person she wanted to talk about was you. She said, 'My daddy loves Jesus, so if I die, he won't grieve for me, because he knows I'll be happy in heaven.'"

She looked up into John's face, apparently trying to read his emotions. "Are you grieving, John?"

"No." He gave her a little shrug, barely able to lift his shoulders at all. "I'm just going to look forward to seeing her again in heaven."

Shaking her head, Thelma shifted her gaze to the lighted numbers above the elevator door. "I told you I'm not a very religious person." The doors opened, and they walked into another hall. "But that doesn't seem right to me."

John stopped, and the two turned to look at each other. John reached up to wipe his eyes, but they were dry. The tears were gone.

"Let me get this for you." Thelma straightened his collar, giving his shoulders a friendly pat when she finished. "There you go."

He stretched out his arms, allowing his sleeves to line up properly. "Thank you." Taking in her sympathetic expression, he added, "Please come to Tabitha's funeral. We hope to show you the faith we're trying to live." He pulled away and marched down the hall.

"I'll be there," Thelma called after him.

* * *

As if floating above a twilight scene, Tabitha looked down at her lifeless body. It lay in a bed of dull cloth, surrounded by gray dimness. The box that held her seemed ancient and rotten, more like an antique treasure chest than a coffin. Everything around her sagged like an old garment, fit to be cast off and thrown away. Mist covered her eyelids, painting them with shining dew, but as the light grew stronger, it chased away the gray surroundings, and the mist evaporated in the burning radiance.

A large, strong hand grasped the frail, limp one in the box, and a voice echoed like distant thunder in the night.

"Little girl, I say to you, arise."

The moment the tremors from the command passed into the distance, the color in the grim face blossomed like a fresh flower. As if part of the mist, Tabitha felt herself being drawn into the body, sweeping everything from her view.

Now in darkness, she forced her eyes open. A man stood over her, a tall man holding her hand in his.

"Are you Jesus?" she asked as she rose to a sitting position.

"Yes, dear child." His voice seemed gentle, yet strong. "I am."

"I thought so. My daddy said you'd wake me up."

"Yes, your father is wise about many things. Come with me now. This is a valley of death and oldness. I want to show you newness and life, a place that I have prepared for you."

Tabitha giggled. "Just for me?"

"For all who love me." He raised Tabitha to her feet, and the two walked together through hazy darkness. There seemed to be no ground or sky, and the box in which Tabitha had lain vanished behind them, leaving no discernible surroundings at all.

She listened, but no sound reached her ears except for the sweeping of robes. She looked down at her clothes. A long white robe dressed her from neck to ankles. It felt wonderful—soft, warm, and tingly.

Tabitha's holy Guide walked swiftly and effortlessly, yet she had no difficulty keeping up. As they passed through what seemed like curtains of mist, damp and cool, she tried to see something, anything, but all was darkness. How much time had passed? How far had they come? What kind of ground supported them? It felt almost nonexistent.

Eventually, light began to filter in. When they reached what seemed to be a garden, the haze and darkness scattered away, revealing a narrow path beneath her bare feet. Suddenly they stopped, and her Master pointed at a gate in the distance.

"Do you know what that is?" he asked with a majestic resonance.

"It's the narrow gate!" she cried out. "Am I to go through it?"

"Yes, but we must go together."

The two strode toward the gate, but Tabitha stopped in front of it. At the foot of the gate lay a simple, pretty yellow mat with "Welcome, Tabitha" spelled out on top. "Jesus," she said, pointing at the path. "It's a welcome mat, and it has my name on it!"

"A dear friend made that for you," Jesus explained, "and she is looking forward to seeing you."

Tabitha leaned closer. "So that's what Rose was making! And it shines like gold! What's it made of?"

"It was woven with a gift you gave with love not so long ago."

Tabitha twirled the ends of her long tresses. "My hair?"

Jesus smiled and touched the back of her head. "Yes, and your friend awaits you on the other side."

Tabitha bounced on her toes. "Then can we go now?"

"Yes, but when we pass through the gate, all will be changed. You still see yourself as a child, and you continue to think as a child. On the other side, everything will be different."

"Different? How?"

"You would not be able to understand the other side even if I explained it to you."

Squinting, Tabitha looked into his eyes. "But how did I see it in my dreams?"

"You saw through a mirror, dear child. I showed you heavenly bliss in a way you could understand. It was real, but it was a riddle, a prophecy that you will soon understand. Then you could see only in part. Let us go now together, and you will see the perfect."

"When will I see Mama and Daddy again?" she asked. "How about Joshua and Sarah and the others?"

"Some of your family await within. Your great-grandmother entered my Father's rest not long ago. Others will follow in due time, and you will greet them when they arrive." He set a hand on her back. "For now, come with me, and you will gain the wisdom you will soon need to help your loved ones."

Her questions vanishing, Tabitha took his hand. The Lord pushed the gate open, and the two passed through into eternity.

* * *

John stepped up to the ER desk and asked the nurse where to find his wife and son. After following her directions, he paused next to a curtain-cordoned room, again reciting his promise to Tabitha. This would be the true test. Could he really show the truth—that God's promise of heaven must mean that Tabitha is happy now, that he should rejoice that she was in a better place and her suffering was over?

Pushing the floor-length drape to the side, he walked in. Melody sat in a chair, her head drooped forward, her chin resting on her chest. Jonathan lay sleeping on the hospital bed, his face to one side with a hint of drool seeping from his mouth.

John leaned over and felt his son's forehead. It was cool. He then stepped toward Melody's chair and cleared his tightening throat. What could he say? What words could possibly be right at a time like this?

Melody's eyes flickered open. As she gazed at him, her mouth dropped open and her soft wet lips quivered.

Looking back at her, John shuffled his feet, his hands buried in his pockets. He felt the rag doll and pulled it out, letting it flop faceup over his open palm. He stared at it, his mind again in a fog.

Melody jumped to her feet, her trembling hands covering her mouth. Her knees buckled. John grabbed her and took her into his arms.

"Oh, John!" She buried her face in his chest. "It's not true! Tell me it's not true!"

John dropped the doll onto the chair and rubbed Melody's back. He could barely manage a hoarse whisper. "Just a little while ago, maybe half an hour."

Shaking, Melody wailed, "Oh, my dear sweet girl. My darling little angel!"

John made a few shushing sounds, but even these seemed inappropriate. He just ran his fingers through her hair and let her cry.

After a few minutes she tried to speak, her words interrupted by heaving breaths. "What . . . what do we . . . do now?"

"All we *can* do. Get Jonathan ready and go home." John grimaced at his words. They sounded so callous, so practical. Of course

Melody should see Tabitha's body first and make sure it was properly cared for.

He tried again, whispering his words gently. "We need to pray. Let's pray right now, and then you can go to the ICU."

John cleared his throat and began praying in a tired monotone, beginning with Scripture, as was his habit. "But we do not want you to be uninformed, brethren, about those who are asleep, so that you will not grieve as do the rest who have no hope. For if we believe that Jesus died and rose again, even so God will bring with him those who have fallen asleep in Jesus."

After swallowing hard, a growing passion strengthened his voice. "Father, I thank you that Tabitha was in Jesus when she fell asleep. If anyone ever died in the comfort of Christ's arms, it was she. Thank you for allowing me to see the light of your glory in her eyes before she passed into your kingdom and to know that she faced the last enemy without fear. Thank you for the few years we could have that sweet angel among us."

As Melody's sobs grew louder, he paused again until she settled down. Pulling her closer, he went on. "Now help us to face life without her, to be happy for her as she rests in peaceful bliss, forever with you. Strengthen us in the coming days as we prepare to formally say good-bye with all of our family and friends, especially in the next few hours as Melody and I must break the news of this tragedy to our remaining children. Help us glorify you with every word, every hug, and every breath that we take. In Jesus' name, amen."

* * *

It is said that many hands make for light work. In a similar way, many friends help carry a weighty load of emotional burdens. On this first day of grief, while John and his family struggled to carry their burden, the church family pitched in mightily. Pastor Jenkins set up the basic funeral and burial arrangements, saving the details about content, music, and order of service for later. The women's ministry handled the meals and housecleaning chores that day, a Saturday that found the house teeming with women, some young and some elderly. One, an eighty-year-old saint, read stories to Jonathan and played blocks on the floor, acting like an overgrown playmate.

Joshua, Sarah, and Andrew went for a walk together, finding a long, power company easement to follow as it cut a swath through a dense forest. The sagging cables cast dark stripes on the varied-length grass and painted long frowns across the expanse.

Andrew tromped between the shadows, playing games with the lines as they swayed with the breeze. Hand in hand, Joshua and Sarah walked several yards behind. Although watching his frolic provided sweet diversion, the graceful little imp couldn't chase away the darkness, a darkness that had never been so deep.

Reminders cropped up so many times, whether a cloud obscuring the sun or a tree bending in a mournful pose; thoughts of their sister always managed to return to the forefront, and new tears followed.

One awful task lay ahead for John and Melody as they drove to the funeral home. Although they had spent most of the day in their bedroom—talking to each other, answering the phone when their helpers were unable to handle a call, and trying to sleep when they could—this late afternoon chore threatened to drain their last drop of energy. It was time to see how the mortician had prepared Tabitha's body. Her siblings begged not to come. Seeing her at the funeral would be enough torture, they explained, so John allowed them to stay home.

After parking, John helped Melody into the funeral home, keeping an arm around her at all times. As they walked down the chapel aisle, escorted by a friendly counselor, John stared straight ahead. What would Tabitha's body look like now? They had asked for her to look as natural as possible. But since she never wore makeup, would they be able to do that without making her look too . . . too dead?

When they neared the casket, Melody stopped, apparently unwilling to draw close enough to see Tabitha's body, at least until she calmed herself.

The counselor stood in front of a huge arrangement of red carnations at one end of the casket. "Would you like to be alone?" she asked.

John nodded. "For a few minutes. Thank you."

After she left, Melody stayed at the same spot, trembling. John lifted her higher and bore most of her weight. She took several deep breaths before clenching his hand. "Okay," she said. "Let's look."

John drew Melody to the side of the casket. With her hand over her mouth, she stared at Tabitha's body. Her physical features hadn't changed—the same blonde hair, cute nose, and narrow cheeks—but the glory was gone. Tabitha's spirit had departed. She simply wasn't there.

The staff had done a fabulous job with Tabitha's lovely face. Her skin bore normal tones, and her lips were a healthy shade of red, and only the closest scrutiny could detect the delicate makeup they used to achieve the result.

Biting his lip hard, John drank in her features one more time, not to remember this image as a lasting portrait, but to remind himself that they weren't leaving a person behind, only a used shell. The beauty had flown away to a new life above. Somehow, this final look brought refreshment, confirmation.

Melody said nothing. Even her sobs had ebbed. She touched Tabitha's cheek, then her chin. Finally, with a sigh, she combed her fingers through the blonde locks, now clean and soft instead of the stiff and oily feel it had when she died. After a few more seconds, she said, "I think I'm ready."

After a final glance, John turned Melody toward the rear of the chapel. Now guiding her with only a hand on her back, he thought she seemed to walk with a stronger gait—quick, straight, and sure.

They stepped out into bright sunshine, forcing them to shield their eyes. Melody stopped on the sidewalk. Her body trembled again.

"It's only a short walk to the parking lot," John whispered. "But I'll bring the car up if you'd like."

Pressing her lips together, Melody shook her head. Her voice began in a whisper but quickly grew to a lament. "They're going to bury her in the ground! I know it's just her body, but I can't stand the thought of it!"

John wrapped his arms around her, watching a pair of sympathetic onlookers as they passed by. One woman stopped as if ready to offer help, but she just nodded and hurried on.

Rubbing Melody's back again, John let his voice rise above a whisper. "That body is just an empty shell, Melody. She's not there anymore. Our angel has gone to a better place."

"I know," she wailed. "I know."

Competing thoughts raced through John's mind. Melody needed him to cry with her, to grieve with the same passion—to weep with those who weep. Yes, he could do that, dive into her anguish and offer the solace that only another weeper can provide. But what would that mean? A broken promise? Lack of faith that Tabitha had now taken up residence in heaven, ready to dance with the angels?

He shook his head. He couldn't grieve. Breaking a vow to grant Tabitha's last wish would be beyond sinful. But wasn't allowing his dear wife to suffer such pain alone just as bad? What could he do?

Looking up at the bright blue sky, John lifted up a desperate prayer. *I need your help, and I need it now.*

Chapter 20

HOW FRIGHTENING is the terror of the night, the kind that makes dreamers beg for the break of dawn. As morning seeps into their eyes, they find sweet relief in the answer to their first words of the day, "It didn't really happen, did it?" But how tragic it is when the nightmare is found to be true, and the gripping pain of the night once again strangles its victim, this time in the light of day.

"Oh, dear God, no!" Melody called out.

"Melody!" Throwing the covers back, John sat up. "What's wrong?"

"Oh, no, it can't be true, it just can't be true!" Melody rocked back and forth, her hands covering her face. "She's dead. I can't believe she's dead!"

John rubbed her back, but she pushed his hand away. "Please leave me alone," she cried. "You don't understand." She covered her face again, her fitful sobs continuing.

John held his rejected hand in the air as though it had been suspended there. What could he do? He couldn't force comfort, certainly not by laying an unwelcome hand on her body. He scooted a few inches closer and whispered, "Because I'm not crying, too?"

Melody nodded, her face still buried in her hands.

Drawing his knees up, John wrapped his arms around his legs. What could he do? Lecture her about being selfish? Of course not. The promise not to grieve was his alone, regardless of the logic behind it. Heaping more sorrow onto her exhausting burden would be the worst thing he could do.

If only he could break down and cry with her! The emotions he had swallowed down again and again were even now ready to erupt and flow, but what of his promise? Wasn't it sacred? Shouldn't he be a self-denying soldier for Christ and fulfill his vow, even at such a great cost? Yet did Christ demand this sacrifice, or was it a foolish decision prompted by the fever-induced emotions of a dying girl?

He shook his head. Where were the answers? Where were the brilliant, academic syllogisms that would solve this logical puzzle? But what good were they, anyway? Sure, he could win debate upon debate, but logic's triumphs won only cold trophies that swelled the mind. They brought nothing for home's gentle fires, no fuel for setting hearts ablaze, nothing that could melt the frigid blasts of death's cruel stroke.

He looked over at his wife, still weeping, still rocking. Logic definitely offered nothing warm to soothe her heartaches, and he, too, felt the emptiness of futility. His own warmth lay suppressed deep within, bound by the chain and lock of a sacred vow.

"I'll be getting dressed if you need me." With a quick roll, he slid out of bed and shuffled to the bathroom.

* * *

Melody wiped her eyes and sniffled away her last few sobs, listening to the sounds coming from the bathroom. The usual series of short bursts of water from the sink had just ended, signifying that John had finished shaving. In a few more seconds . . . *Yes, there's the shower.*

Still sitting in bed, Melody looked around the room. What day was it? Sunday? Yes, it was Sunday. Was John planning on going to church this morning? What would it be like there? Wouldn't they be bombarded with questions?

The image of caring faces floated through her mind, her lady friends asking one question after another.

"How are you getting along without Tabitha around the house?"

"Are you going to have another baby now?"

"You realize she's in a better place now, right?"

She sighed deeply. Of course they would mean well, but it would make her cry every time someone mentioned Tabitha's name. And not only that, how could she find the energy to get all the children out of bed and then push them to get ready for church when they probably didn't want to go?

She looked around at the walls and ceiling. She felt safe here, as though the house, with its closed doors and strong roof, shielded her from pain. She clutched her pillow close to her chest. She needed that shelter, at least for now.

After a few minutes, John emerged from the bathroom, buttoning a white dress shirt. Melody rose from the bed and brushed a stray thread from his shoulder. "You're planning on going to church, aren't you?"

John stopped fastening the buttons. "Well, yes. It's Sunday."

Melody bit her lip hard. How could he think this was just any other Sunday? Wasn't it enough that he couldn't relate to her crushing grief? Now he had to carry on as if nothing had happened?

John unbuttoned his shirt and pulled the tail out as he turned toward the bathroom. "It's okay. I don't have to go."

Melody sat back on the bed. "Go ahead and go." She pulled the edge of the bedsheet and covered her mouth.

John stopped and turned, his hands still clutching his shirt. "I'll do whatever you say. I don't need to go."

She bit the sheet, unable to talk. Tears flowed. One word would bring the sobs crashing back.

Taking tentative steps, John walked up and stroked her back. This time she allowed his hand to stay as he spoke in a soft, soothing voice. "My dear Melody, you're so conflicted, so torn by options that seem good and bad at the same time. You want our lives to go on, but at the same time, you still want to pause and take notice. You don't want us to act like nothing's happened."

Melody looked up, her flowing tears unabated. "Yes, that *is* how I'm feeling. Did you practice that speech in the bathroom?"

A hurt expression sagged his features. "Only because I'm desperate to find the right words. I really meant them."

"I know you did. I didn't mean that as a slap."

"I'm trying to understand," he said, continuing the back rub. "I do feel some of the same things you do. I just can't let them push through. I can't really explain why right now. I'm sorting through it myself."

Melody pulled his arm around her body. It felt like a lifeline to his heart. "Thank you for caring how I feel."

* * *

The Sunday morning ritual, normally well-rehearsed, with even bathroom usage scheduled to the minute and departure times set in stone, went by the wayside. The younger children rose later than usual, wondering why they had not been awakened earlier. Although it didn't take long for them to adjust to the strange schedule, they felt the heaviness, an emotional darkness that weighed everyone down.

With Jonathan shadowing her every step, Melody had to maintain a smile and keep her voice cheerful, a huge strain on her sagging energy reserves. Just before noon, when she and John sat down in the living room to discuss funeral details, Jonathan crawled up into her lap and leaned his head against her chest.

She stroked his soft locks. "Can we talk later?" she asked John.

Before he could reply, Joshua walked into the room and extended a hand. "C'mon, Jonathan. Let's find Sarah, and we'll read a book or something."

As the little boy jumped down and grabbed his brother's hand, Joshua turned back and winked. "We'll find a long book. Take as much time as you need."

John, wearing a clean polo shirt and cargo pants, settled back on the sofa. "I asked Pastor Jenkins to make the announcement this morning. At least everyone will know the whens and wheres of the funeral on Tuesday. We won't have to make so many calls."

Dressed in baggy sweats, matching the dreary emptiness of her mood, Melody took his arm and draped it around her, then snuggled close. "Do you think anyone will have a problem with the burial being private?"

"I doubt it. Since we're having the service at the church, everyone will be able to view her body and say their good-byes then. I don't think anyone really likes those long motorcades anyway. I know I don't."

Melody searched John's eyes, as if trying to read his mind. "Still no tears?" she asked.

"No. No tears."

Melody laid her palms on his chest and massaged him gently. "After all these years, this is the first time we haven't shared something."

"Do you mean torture or grief?"

"Both, I guess."

"Trust me." He laughed under his breath. "I feel the battle."

"It's not that I want you to suffer, John. It's just that I feel so alone."

Taking one of her hands, he stroked her skin. "You're not alone. I'm here with you." He pulled her hand closer and wrapped her up in his arms. "I'll be strong for both of us, and if you feel like you're sinking, just hang on to me. The Lord will use me to keep us afloat."

Melody luxuriated in the warmth of her husband's embrace, feeling a surge of strength that seemed to pass through their touch. "I guess I can live with that."

The two remained in their cuddle, intertwining their fingers and exchanging sighs. After a few minutes, John spoke up, a back-to-business tone in his voice. "Are the Graysons coming to the funeral?"

She kept her head on his chest. "Yes," she replied, her voice muffled in his shirt. "I talked to Myrtle this morning."

"And the hospital people?"

She counted on her fingers. "Steve is going to tell everyone at the hospital tomorrow. Pastor Jenkins arranged for the funeral notice in the paper, and the news is even on the front page this morning, because of the encephalitis alert, I suppose."

"On the front page? I should have known our sensationalist media would pick up on this." He rolled his hand into a loose fist. "So what does it say? Mosquito kills girl?"

"No, it's very well done." She pushed herself up, walked to the dining room table, and picked up the newspaper. "See," she said, pointing, "one of Pastor's friends was the reporter, so he got all his facts straight, and it was very sensitive." She handed the paper to him. "I think it's good, in a way. With all the publicity, we should get quite a crowd at church. I suppose that's what we hope for, isn't it, if we want the gospel to be presented at the funeral?"

"I suppose so." He scanned the whole page. "Good. No pictures."

"Actually, there's a message on the answering machine from a TV station. They'd like a picture for tonight's newscast, but it sounds like you'd probably be against that."

"Not really. I didn't want to see her picture, because . . ." He paused, his face turning red. "Well, I guess I'm not sure why."

"It's okay. You don't have to explain. I know it would tear *me* apart right now."

His eyes moved from side to side as he read. "Did the story mention Tabitha's prophecies at all?"

"No. I guess Pastor kept that to himself."

John folded the paper and tossed it back toward the table. "Good. I think those pearls were meant for the faithful, and it's best that it stays that way."

Melody watched the newspaper land on the table and slide off the other side. "Pearls? You mean as in, 'Don't cast your pearls before swine'?"

"Right."

Smiling, Melody poked him in the side. "That's pretty harsh, Mister. Are you sure you're handling all this okay?"

"I'm sure." He looked around the room, then leaned back to peek down the hall. "Where are all the kids?"

Melody drew her head back and gave him a worried look. "Joshua took Jonathan out to read a book, remember?"

"Oh, yeah, right."

"Andrew said he was going to look for grasshoppers to feed to the gerbils."

"And what are you going to do?"

"I just feel so tired. I didn't sleep much last night, so I think I'll take a nap. How about you?"

"I'll just sit for a while, maybe read or think about things."

Melody yawned, kissed him, and padded down the hall. "Wake me if you need me."

When she entered the bedroom, she kicked off her slippers and sat on the bed, alone again. As she looked around the room, framed photos stared at her, at least two of each child at various ages. Her gaze stopped at one of Tabitha, a recent photo, taken maybe six months earlier. With her eyes as bright as ever and a beautiful smile gracing her lovely face, it seemed that she had to be around somewhere—sewing in the next room with Sarah, catching grasshoppers with Andrew, reading with Joshua and Jonathan. All Melody had to do was call her name, and she would run in with her sweet little voice.

Melody let the words form on her lips. "Yes, Mama? Did you call me?"

But it would never be. Call as Melody might, Tabitha would never answer. She was gone . . . gone.

Crying again, Melody wrung her hands. Oh, if only John would share this toil! Bearing it alone would surely grind her heart into dust.

As she blinked away her tears, she whispered into the air, "Lord, please speak to him. Tell him it's okay to cry. He loved her so much, and he wants so badly to do what's right. Show him how to break through the prison he's constructed, the iron bars of logic that won't allow him to see his heart. And show me how to serve him. At this point, it's really all I know how to do."

* * *

Stretching his arms, John walked into the family room. As he sat in the rocking chair, the old wooden friend creaked a grumbling hello. He pushed his shoes off, and they tumbled noiselessly to the carpet. Several deep sighs later, he leaned back in the chair, his eyes closed.

In his repose, the guardians of his brain seemed to waver in and out of slumber. Was this the first time he had allowed his mind to truly rest since Tabitha died? Dozens of unfiltered and disorganized thoughts began to seep in unbidden—scenes of death, images of grieving mourners, even the face of Nanna, his departed grandmother.

Many ghosts of the past paid him a visit, memories that had not found their way to the surface in a very long time—playing on the swing sets in elementary school, his days in seminary in Dr. Wilkins' class, and the moment of birth for each of his children. The babies' faces contorted with their first cries, reacting to the initial breath of life and the coldness of the new world they had been forced to discover.

John even saw himself at the present moment, sitting in the rocker, somehow surrounded by apparitions, the buried memories coming to life in floating, misty phantasms. Finally, he saw himself as an old man standing next to Melody. Both of them seemed tired, bent, and wrinkled. Their faces reflected the deep sadness of heart-wrenching anguish, their emotions trapped in cruel, self-created prisons. Chains suddenly appeared on their wrists and ankles, just before a dark door slammed shut, blocking them from his sight.

What was this? Was he creating guilt-bearing images, a way of punishing himself for refusing selfish pain, or was this his personal *Christmas Carol* with the ghosts of past, present, and future haunting his first unguarded thoughts? The Dickens's ghosts brought with them an eerie sensation, almost as if he were being watched.

He opened his eyes wide to shoo away the specters, then gasped. Someone *was* watching him, a girl standing across the room.

"Sarah," he called with a sigh of relief. "Can I do something for you?"

Sarah folded her hands in front of her waist. "I was hoping I could do something for *you*."

"For me? I don't need anything. I'm fine."

"Really?" She took a step closer. "I can see from here that you need something."

He glanced down at his body. "Did I spill my juice this morning?"

"No, silly." She marched across the room and climbed into his lap, wrapping both arms tightly around his neck. "Tabitha told me about your poem," she said, curling her legs up. "I thought I'd fill up the empty space for a while."

"I see." He enveloped her in his arms, letting her body conform to his. She was right. He really needed her there. It felt so good.

"Well?" she said.

"Well, what?"

"Aren't you going to rock me?"

"Oh . . . sure." He pushed his feet against the floor and rocked the chair. It responded with its familiar creaking complaint. "Is that better?"

"Perfect," she said, snuggling close.

He caught a glimpse of her tear-stained face. "You've been crying?"

"Um-hmm." She picked at a button on his shirt. "Don't you miss Tabitha, Daddy?"

"Well, sure. Why would you ask?"

"Because I miss her, and I've cried my eyes out. You haven't shed a tear."

"Have you been talking to your mother?"

"Not lately." She looked up at him. "Why?"

"Just wondering." He let out a heavy sigh. "I'm sorry. I shouldn't have asked that question."

"It's okay." She pressed her cheek against his chest. "I already figured out what's going on."

"I should have guessed. You're as smart as a whip."

After a few seconds of silence, save the creaking of the chair, Sarah looked up at him again. "I know what you can do for me now."

"Anything. Name it."

"Would you say the poem? The one you and Tabitha wrote together?"

"I can do that." He winced. The words sounded far too confident. Could he really say it without breaking into sobs?

As Sarah curled tighter, the sound of the chair, accompanied by the presence of a precious daughter in his arms, brought more memories flooding back into his mind. How few days had passed since

Tabitha sat in the very same position, her sweet-smelling head near his face and her legs cocked just so! The words of their silly poem pushed forward to his lips in a whispered singsong.

> My Daddy's lap is warm and snug,
> My favorite place to sit.
> His arms abound with tender love.
> It's there I truly fit.
> I'll never get too old or big.
> To take my special place.

His voice began shaking, but he pressed on.

So Daddy, dear, when I grow up—

As he tried to take a breath to speak the final words, he gasped, the spasms in his chest breaking his rhythm. Finally, he forced out the last words in a breathy lament. "Reserve my parking space!"

Wrapping Sarah ever tighter, he whispered a feeble cry. "Oh, dear God! For one more chance to hold her again!"

Sarah kissed his cheek. "It's okay, Daddy. Go ahead and cry. I'll cry with you."

"But I can't!" He took a deep breath, inhaling and exhaling slowly. He had to control himself. He had to keep his promise, concentrate on the truth. Tabitha was happy, so he had to rejoice with her.

Soon, his emotions settled. As he continued rocking, he stroked Sarah's head tenderly. "I'm okay now," he said.

She pushed back. "Are you?"

"Yes." He breathed another sigh. "Yes, I am. Thank you."

She climbed out of his lap and smoothed out her clothes, new tears making their way toward her chin. "I think I'd better leave that space open for a while."

He looked down at his lap. "Why? You fit just fine."

Pressing her lips together, she shook her head. "I think . . ." She paused, then looked away. "I can't say it. It wouldn't be respectful."

"Go ahead. I give you permission."

After taking a deep breath, she pointed at his lap. "I think you need to feel the emptiness for a while longer." She brushed a tear away, turned, and hurried from the room.

* * *

"No." John squeezed a pencil as he spoke on the telephone. "No on-camera interviews. I don't want my family's privacy violated. If you come to my house, you'll have to leave the cameras behind."

"I understand," the female reporter said, "but without something visual for our viewers, we won't be able to run the story. It is television, you know."

"Look, I already sent my daughter's photo to the station. Don't you have that?"

"We do, and she's a beautiful girl, but we'll generate a lot more sympathy if we can show your family. A few tears generate a lot more tears, if you know what I mean."

Under the glow of his desk lamp, John tapped his pencil on a notepad. The thought of thousands of people gawking at his crying wife and children made him boil inside. "Listen, we're not looking for sympathy. We just want the story told so people will know about the funeral. If you come, I'll be glad to talk to you all you want, but no cameras. If you can't do that, then we'll have to call it off."

"I understand, Mr. Hanson. I'll let you know if we decide to come."

"Thank you for talking to me so late at night. Good-bye." John hung up the phone and held his pencil above his notepad. The newspaper ran the story this morning. He drew a check mark next to that entry. The Christian radio station announced the funeral throughout the day. He made another check. The Christian TV station would be at the funeral tomorrow to videotape the proceedings. Another check.

Tapping his pencil on that entry, he imagined the producer, Vincent, a friend from church. Surely he would be sensitive to the spiritual nature of the event and would give his viewers a full account of the miracles surrounding Tabitha's story. He had already promised not to close in on the family—no grief shots to invade their privacy. The whole point was to help other believers aspire to the tremendous faith and boldness of his precious daughter, not to dwell on the suffering of those left behind.

After a long yawn, John dropped the pencil, flicked off the desk lamp, and half staggered from his office. Glancing at his watch as he shuffled down the hall, he listened to the sounds of midnight's approach. A fan in Joshua's and Andrew's room, a slight buzz from a monitor in Jonathan's, and a soft radio playing in Sarah's.

He paused in front of Sarah's room. It hurt even to think in such terms—Sarah's room instead of Sarah's and Tabitha's room. He touched a poster on the door, a montage of photos Sarah had gathered showing her and Tabitha in dozens of poses—jumping rope, sewing doll clothes, making a mess in the kitchen while baking cookies, and giving a reluctant cat a bath.

As his finger came to a photo of Sarah and Tabitha dancing together, he stopped. Was Tabitha dancing in heaven now? Had his attempts to be happy helped? Did they really make any difference at all?

He trudged the rest of the way to the bedroom, kicked off his slippers, and sat on the bed. Melody was already asleep, curled up and facing away from his side of the bed. A small lump raised the covers near her neck. He pulled the spread back, revealing Deborah lying facedown, her little calico dress wrinkled and faded. Had Melody brought her to bed, something to cuddle in his absence?

John slid into his place and picked up the doll, cradling her in his hand, making her arms and legs flop over his outstretched fingers. With his other hand he smoothed out the wrinkles and placed her against his chest, gently at first, then tighter and tighter until he wrapped her in both arms and rocked her slowly back and forth. He squeezed his eyes closed, clenching them with all his might as he tried to catch back his gasping breaths.

No tears. Mustn't cry.

He lowered himself to his pillow and turned toward Melody, still clutching Tabitha's doll. With the battle raging, would he be able to sleep? Would that photo of Tabitha dancing plague his mind as he wondered about his daughter's joy?

Soon, wakefulness fled from his weary mind. At first, he slept peacefully, a merciful, dreamless slumber that refilled the stores of energy that had gone wanting for days. Sometime during the night, however, a voice interrupted the serenity, calling in his mind as if from far away.

"Daddy!"

"What?" he answered instinctively, without moving from his pillow.

"Daddy, come dance with me!"

He lifted his head. As streams of radiance flowed through the bedroom, an angelic being floated at his bedside, dressed in luminous robes of alabaster white with tassels of shining gold.

"Tabitha?" he murmured.

"Yes, Daddy. Come. It's time to dance."

"Dance? What do you mean?"

John looked down at Melody. She remained sound asleep.

Tabitha took John by the hand. He floated above the bed, becoming absorbed in the radiant light. Blinded for a few seconds, he rubbed his eyes, but as he adjusted, he began to see something in front of him, something familiar. Could it be? Yes, it was Tabitha's picture of heaven, but life-size. At first, it stood flat and unanimated, just the simple sketch of a child, but as he drew nearer, the lines melted and reformed into a three-dimensional reality.

Yet, it seemed more than reality. It had depth and detail that transcended the senses. He drank in luscious colors of richness beyond royal splendor, gold in Tabitha's robe that Midas could only imagine and red in Rose's lips that carried the crimson blush of flaming apples. The brightest sapphire in Tut's treasure could never match the blue sparkle in the brook's prancing waters. And the sounds! The simple splashes over little stones played the clearest chimes ever heard.

And could the singing even be described? Was it the sound of a newborn's first cooing? The morning songbirds after the night's storm? The rhythmic rise and fall of gentle waves on an ocean shore? None of these blissful sounds could possibly compare to the pulsating joy, the swirling, thick reality of waves of ecstasy that plunge into the heart, making breathless its willing victim, capturing his innermost desires and raising them to the height of passionate emotional climax, bringing along the hands in elevated praise. How long could he bear the ecstatic symphony that poured into his senses?

As Tabitha pulled him toward the whirlpool of radiant dancers, he felt his entire essence being absorbed into a mass of jubilant celebration, his heart threatening to split open from the overwhelming joy. He sang with the everlasting throng, not the song Tabitha had heard in her dreams, but a new song, one he understood but would never be able to utter again in the temporal plane.

Then, just when his mortal mind was reaching its limit, overcome and bursting in ecstasy, the colors, the sounds, and even the radiance disappeared, swept away in an evaporating whirlwind. He and Tabitha stood alone, not in a room, but in an empty expanse with no apparent light source and nothing else to see. They stood face-to-face, John slowly lowering his arms from their praise position, and Tabitha standing erect, her hands folded in front of her.

She looked at him solemnly, no longer as an adoring daughter. She seemed now to be a devoted sister. "Do you remember why the angels dance?" she asked, her lips straight across in composed sincerity, but her eyes continuing to dance to the holy music.

"Yes," he replied, trying to match Tabitha's sober manner. "Who were we dancing for?"

"You will find out very soon. The heart has been prepared—planted, watered, and ready to harvest."

John looked all around, turning his body completely about and back again. "Am I dreaming?" he asked, spreading out his arms. "Or is this real?"

Tabitha laid her hands on his shoulders. Resplendent warmth spread from the locus of touch throughout his body, filling him with peace and the assurance of reality. "When God sends a vision," she said, "even though you sleep on, it is real. You see images in a spiritual mirror, but let's just say it's a dream. It's my last dream, Daddy, and it's for you."

John stared at his daughter. He must never, never forget her glorified visage. Somehow she still looked twelve years old, innocent and fair, her hair more golden than ever, but at the same time an eternal aspect enveloped her form, radiant and ageless.

"A dream for me?"

Tabitha held her hands in place, her thoughts now streaming into John's mind.

"You asked God for help, and he has sent me."

The light in the expanse dimmed, leaving only Tabitha's glow. All he could see was her face, her shining eyes and ruby lips, pursing to deliver her message.

"You are being needlessly torn. In your desire to be holy, in your commitment to keep your vow, you deny the flesh, making your body your slave, and the Lord is very pleased with you. But if someone cuts you deeply, do you not bleed? If someone takes your eyes, are you not blind?"

"I . . . I think I understand what you're saying. . . . But how does a grieving man bleed in a holy way?"

Tabitha released him and raised her hands as if giving a benediction. Her sweeping robes sparkled as they moved, leaving a trail of frosty white in their wake.

"I have been here only a short while, but what I have learned I share with you now. Your soul weeps, as does the soul of every bereaved father. It is true that many selfishly grieve for their own sakes, pitying themselves over their own loss. They focus on themselves and their troubles. The spirit of a godly man grants himself no such self-pleasure. His grief is very different; it has its roots in love of others rather than love of self."

She lowered her arms and fully embraced him, sending tremors of rapture throughout his soul. His knees buckled, but something caught his body, molding him into a sitting position, and Tabitha folded into his lap. The shining beauty wrapped her arms around his neck and rested her head against his face. Somehow he could hear the unmistakable creak of his old rocking chair.

"My dear father, you will never see me grow to serve our great Master. That loss is real, it is great, and the grief you hold deep inside is holy. Not only this, but the tearing apart of two who have been bound together brings the unspeakable pain of separation. And truly we were knit together more tightly than any physical bond. Am I not your little angel? But I have been torn out of your soul. Can you deny your bleeding? Is the cut any less a cut because the knife is spiritual? You have true love, the love of a father for the offspring of his flesh. You have been torn, but, in time, Jesus will make you whole. And your promise to me? By the authority of the Most High, I release you from your vow. I asked for it in ignorance, you accepted in love, and now, in wisdom, I break its chains."

As long as he rested in Tabitha's embrace, he felt no pain. Why couldn't this ecstasy just go on forever? No sorrow, no grief, no funerals to signal the never-ending parade of suffering.

Soon, his arms loosened, releasing her. A deep ache throbbed as the pain of separation already stabbed his heart. Gasping for breath, he asked, "So what do I do now?"

Tabitha lifted her head and gazed at him, again shining with heavenly love. "Celebrate my joy while the Lord sews up your wound. Let the tears flow. Only then will your flood of pain be released to water your parched soul. Look to God. Look to others. Serve them as you weep, and the Lord will dry your tears."

"I think I understand. Will—"

"And one more thing," she said, placing her hand on his knee. "Reserve my parking space. I intend to use it again."

With a tender kiss on his cheek, she rose from his lap and stepped back a few paces. "Good-bye, Daddy. It really won't be very long."

"Wait!"

As Tabitha's form grew smaller and smaller, John felt himself being drawn away, not only physically, but like a wind absorbed in the draft of a passing world. Something pushed into his heart, an invisible hand, drawing, tugging, dragging the emotional pain from its hidden recesses.

"Tabitha, don't go!" he cried. "Don't go!" In an instant, he felt the weight of his body again resting on the bed, the covers still in place. Finally, he shouted, "Dear God, don't take her away again!"

Melody shot up to a sitting position. "John, what's wrong?"

John cried, weeping, sobbing. "Oh, Tabitha, my sweet daughter, my little angel! Oh, she's gone, she's gone!" He continued bawling as he rolled off the bed and onto his knees.

Melody crawled out on her side, hurried around the bed, and knelt next to him. Rubbing his shoulders, she laid her head on his back. "It's all right, John, I'm here. Just go ahead and cry."

"Oh, Melody, Tabitha's gone! What am I going to do without her?" He raised his head and looked at his precious wife, her hands so tenderly draped around his neck. "She was my baby girl, my precious baby girl! Oh, dear God, my baby's gone!"

John wept through the early morning hours, and Melody never left his side, crying with him, drawing from a fresh supply of tears as she comforted her husband, weeping with the brokenhearted.

Chapter 21

I N MANY WAYS, Tabitha's funeral carried the celebratory atmosphere of her great-grandmother's festive good-bye party. Bright flowers helped to brush away most of the gloomy feelings, and the stereo speakers blared tunes from an upbeat Christian string ensemble. The setting, however, differed greatly. The crowd gathered in a church auditorium instead of a funeral home, and the shuffling and talking of members and newcomers alike filled the sanctuary with a lively buzz. The television crew added to the aura of excitement. Everyone knew that another child dying of encephalitis was news, headline news, in fact, as the epidemic plagued the area.

At the head of the center aisle, directly in front of the stage, an open coffin sat on a table. Two ushers guided the mourners into a viewing line. As John had requested, the viewing would take place before the service with the family lining up last after everyone else had been seated.

The large numbers made for a long procession as many stopped and stared at the lifeless body that still captivated them with its lovely features. Many children carrying gifts—small Teddy bears, colorful bouquets of flowers, handmade cards—left their treasures near and around the casket. Many tears flowed, even from large, burly men, unable to bear the sight of the lifeless child of gold before them. Strangers, too, seemed mesmerized. If she could so dazzle in death, what must she have been like in life?

John sat next to Melody at one end of the front pew, his eyes finally dry but his heart still aching. Their four surviving children sat next to Melody, each one quiet, Jonathan with his head leaning against his mother.

A voice came from the pew behind them. "Melody?"

She and John turned. Myrtle sat on the pew and whispered, "I have something for you." She reached for Melody's arm and slid a silver band over her fingers and onto her wrist. "It's an MIA bracelet with Tabitha's name on it. I had it made yesterday."

"It's lovely," Melody said as she fingered the bracelet. "Thank you so much!"

Myrtle held up her arms. "I have two now. One for Tommy and one for Rose." She hugged Melody. "God bless you. If it weren't for you and Tabitha, I never would have found my faith."

As Myrtle walked toward the back of the church, Melody showed the silver band to John, tears welling. "It says, 'Make them dance again!'"

He touched the engraved letters. "I think we both know what that means."

After everyone took their seats, the extended family lined up— Grandpa Hanson and all the aunts, uncles, and cousins. Few paused more than a second or two as they passed by. Aunt Betty stayed longer, crying bitterly for nearly a minute before Grandpa Hanson escorted her away.

Finally, Tabitha's siblings lined up from oldest to youngest, with Melody and John following at the back. Joshua looked at her body, then pivoted and left in a hurry. Sarah lingered, her legs trembling.

John hurried to her side and wrapped an arm around her shoulders, propping her up. "Are you okay?" he whispered.

Sarah shook her head. "I shared a bedroom with her for twelve years, Daddy. I can't just look and leave."

"Stay as long as you want. I won't let you fall."

Weeping, she reached into the coffin and touched Tabitha's hair, feeling the still obvious gap. "Isn't it like a war wound, Daddy?"

He looked away from the body. "I'm not sure what you mean."

"Her hair. It's a war wound. She's just missing in action, like a soldier who left the battlefield to receive her reward. And the bracelet will remind us of that forever."

With tears welling in his own eyes, John held her closer. "No doubt, sweet princess. No doubt."

Sarah leaned over and kissed Tabitha's forehead. "I'll see you in the morning, dear sister."

When Sarah returned to her seat, John guided Andrew and Jonathan as they took their turns, still averting his eyes from Tabitha. It was just too painful. His glance while with Sarah proved that this good-bye would be the hardest thing he had ever done in his life. He tried to steel himself while he waited, praying for strength.

After Jonathan toddled away toward Sarah, Melody slid her arm around John and looked into the coffin. He forced himself to look with her. Leaning over, she fussed with Tabitha's clothing, straightening a wrinkle on a sleeve and tightening the bow in her hair.

John focused on the rag doll, lying face up on Tabitha's chest. Her hands covered little Debbie, placed there in honor of Tabitha's love for Nanna. Now the grand matriarch and the golden child would be together for eternity. Soon Melody would remove the doll and ceremonially give it to Sarah, the only remaining daughter in John's family line.

After tenderly lifting Tabitha's hands and taking Debbie, Melody cried again, this time so pitifully she had to grasp the coffin to keep from toppling over. John pulled her upright and helped her to her seat. As sounds of weeping rose from the other pews, John whispered, "Pray for me," then returned to the coffin.

As a hush descended upon the sanctuary, he set his shaking hands on the coffin's dark wood. In front of him lay the body of his beloved daughter, nestled in soft linings of silk and velvet. Her delicate face and soft hair rested in perfect stillness in this unnatural bed. He reached down to caress the motionless, pale cheek, then withdrew his hand, jerking it up to his mouth to prevent an emerging sob.

Yet, the tears would not be thwarted. Starting with a trickle, they soon cascaded in rivulets down his cheeks, one after another dripping into the silk-laden box.

Finally, he summoned the strength to touch her face. "Why am I crying so, dear sweet daughter?" he asked out loud as he gently ran his thumb across her lifeless lips. "You are in the arms of the Savior. There is no more sorrow, no more evil, no more suffering. Why is sadness overwhelming my joy?"

As if on cue, his quiet weeping transformed into sobbing. His body shook. The lights dimmed. The entire sanctuary swayed back and forth. He looked up at the light fixtures, hanging globes that orbited a central point in a dizzying spin, a dance of lights.

Something clamped onto his arm, supporting, lifting. "Dad, are you okay?"

John gave his head a shake, clearing the fog. Joshua stood at his side, his brow furrowed deeply. "Yes, son. Thank you."

A second hand grasped his other arm. "John, it's me, Phil. We'll help you back to your seat."

His strength returning, John pushed against the floor with his feet. "I think I'll be all right. Just overwhelmed by the moment, I think."

"Trust me," Phil said. "I know what it feels like."

John patted him on the back, then climbed the stairs to the stage and sat in a chair several feet behind the pulpit. Pastor Jenkins followed. He stood behind the pulpit and surveyed the crowd, waiting for the murmuring to die down. Then, speaking in a somber tone, he began.

"Ladies and gentlemen, we gather together today to celebrate a life and to mourn a loss. All of you who knew Tabitha Hanson surely understand the magnitude of this loss to the family. When Tabitha walked into a room, she filled it with light and love, because she carried with her the love of Jesus Christ." He reached into the pulpit and pulled out a hymnbook. "This service will be short, with only two songs, one before and one following the eulogy, which will be delivered by Tabitha's father, John Hanson. Afterward, there will be a private burial for family members only. The family has given me a list of Tabitha's favorite songs, and I chose one that I'm sure reflects what Tabitha feels now. Its chorus begins, 'Hallelujah! I have found him!' and I have no doubt that Tabitha will be singing along. So turn with me to page three-seventy-five and we will sing, 'Satisfied.'"

As the congregation sang, John stood and joined in, letting his gaze drift across the sea of faces. Soon, he found the Graysons, Myrtle singing along while Phil seemed to hum the tune, his lips moving now and then. What could that mean? Did Phil recognize the song as the one Rose whispered to him in this very room while huddled on the floor, shivering under a wet, bloodstained coat?

John shifted his eyes to that spot. He could almost see her, gazing upward with a peaceful countenance, these same words flowing sweetly from her lips. Could Phil hear the song? Would the words be a soul-cutting knife, the spiritual blade of a heavenly surgeon?

When they reached the chorus, John shifted his eyes again to Phil. Now he sang, every word clearly evident in his lips. "Hallelujah! I have found him, whom my soul so long has craved!" Myrtle slid her arm around his waist and pulled him closer, her smile more radiant than ever.

As the last chord of the piano died away, Pastor Jenkins gave way to John. He stepped up to the podium, his legs much steadier than before. After taking a deep breath, he surveyed the congregation again, taking in the sanctity of the moment and reading the passion in each face. Tabitha's casket lay in front of him, but he tried to resist the urge to catch another glimpse of her body.

Yet, as if ordained from above, he dropped his gaze and stared at her once again. The composure he had worked so hard to regain melted into streaming tears. He averted his stare and tried to sniff away the new onslaught.

Sarah jumped up and reached a tissue toward him. He took it thankfully, and after wiping his face and nose, he began speaking with a quivering voice. "Many of you know that—" His voice squeaked. He paused and tried to relax his throat muscles, but they tightened even more. "Many of you know that I have never believed in grieving for a Christian who has gone to be with the Lord. I spoke up for the notion at my grandmother's funeral, and I caused my family to suffer while I maintained that idea after Tabitha died. . . . I apologize if I have misled you. I hope you'll indulge me for a moment while I explain, beginning with this poem."

He withdrew a piece of paper from his pants pocket and unfolded it, his hands shaking so much that the paper's crinkling echoed throughout the sanctuary. He tried to clear his throat before reading, but his voice continued to falter, rasping and trembling.

> I taught in faith that death is naught;
> We dwell in God's abode.
> Grieve not the child that lies in state
> 'Neath earth's dread-heavy load!

> But now my child lies cold and still,
> And torn from arms of care,
> The pain that crushes hearts to pulp
> Now mine to bleed and bear.

Shall I perform the words I teach
And celebrate her death?
How can a man sing songs of joy
With lungs so starved for breath?

But through a child's small humble hand
I learn the reason why—
That anguish, grief's cruel, lonesome march
Breaks men who dare not cry.

After taking another deep breath, he tapped the open pulpit Bible with his finger and kept his eyes on it as he spoke. "I defended my position by quoting King David when he said of his son, 'He has died; why should I fast?' But I neglected the following verse, 'Then David comforted his wife Bathsheba.'"

John looked up from his Bible and continued. "She was the one who carried the child for nine months and bore him in travail. She was the one who felt the greater pain. David understood and provided the comfort she needed."

After closing the book, he paused, scanning the audience yet again. With slumping shoulders, he pushed his hands into his pockets. "Christian grief seems paradoxical; we are in tremendous pain yet celebrating at the same time. A marathon runner burns in the agony of spent muscles while trying to gasp for breath. At the same moment he exults in finishing the course and taking the prize for winning the race."

John pressed his palms against his chest. "I hurt in my body, in my temporal existence, for although I did not bear this child, I held her in my heart for twelve wonderful years. But at the same time, I rejoice that my daughter no longer has to endure the throes and sufferings of this world. She completed the course early in life, sprinting to her finish line with all her might, and there are many here whom she encouraged to run with her, to run for the goal and gain the crown."

John motioned toward the casket with his hand. "I have received comfort. Even as I stood at the casket, I felt the Lord teaching me. I still don't know all the whys of life and death. But this I do know; Tabitha's passing is for the glory of God. Today I grieve, but I can look on her face with joy. Those eyes will once again laugh when they see me enter the narrow gate through which she so recently passed. Her legs will move again, running to embrace me in the midst of the Holy City. My mourning will be turned into laughter as I share eternity in the place God has prepared for us. I have learned to grieve, understanding that my precious daughter has been torn from my soul and that she will never know the joy of a long life of service for the Master. But at the same time, I will not forget to celebrate my daughter's peace and happiness in heaven."

John stepped down the stage's stairs, walked up to the casket, and placed his hand on the lid. "Now we close the casket of our minds to this shell that served Tabitha's spirit during her short stay with us. Those of us who love and serve Christ will not be very far behind." He lowered the coffin lid solemnly; then, after it shut with a muffled *clump*, he rested his hands and cheek on its cool, smooth surface, whispering an echo to Sarah's farewell, "I'll see you in the morning, my sweet one."

Lifting his head, he turned toward the crowd, standing upright and staring. It was time to speak again, but no words would come. Looking around, he found the Graysons again. Across the aisle sat Thelma, the nurse, tears streaming down her lovely dark face. Steve sat two rows behind her. He made eye contact and gave John a nod of encouragement.

Unfamiliar faces spanned the congregation. With all the publicity, surely some came as sympathetic, yet unchurched mourners, hoping to pay their respects. Did they understand the song they had just sung? Had they learned what it meant to be satisfied?

John repeated his own words to himself. *Tabitha's passing is for the glory of God.* The harvest was before him, a field that his daughter had planted and watered. It was time to reap the harvest.

With passion boiling within, his jaw tightened and his face grew hot. Then with the fire of a prophet, he raised his fists and shouted, "I know why the angels dance!"

He stopped. Hundreds of bewildered faces returned his passionate stare. As tears flowed, he laughed and shouted again, "I know why the angels dance!" Gesturing with his hands, he addressed his transfixed onlookers, passion still spiking his voice. "In the glory of heaven, the angels celebrate the finding of the lost sheep. When someone turns from the foolishness of this world and surrenders to Christ, the angels dance! Do you hear me? They dance! And the sheep who are already in the fold dance with the angels in joy, because they know their loved ones will someday walk down the path that leads to the narrow gate, and that beautiful gate will swing open for them."

Along with the spellbound crowd, Phil Grayson listened intently, measuring John's words with a spiritual rod for the first time, but John's last sentence caused a deep stirring within.

"Mine was closed," he said, loud enough for Myrtle to hear.

"What?" she asked, trying to listen to him and to John at the same time.

"Tabitha's picture. The gate was open. In my dream, the gate was closed."

John remounted the stage and took his place again behind the pulpit. "The angels dance because of love, the love that comes from God, who gave his only Son, that through his death we might have life. So, as we end this time of grief and celebration, let's sing of that love. Turn with me to page two-forty-seven, a special request from Myrtle Grayson, 'Love Lifted Me.'"

John spotted Phil again. He was smiling at Myrtle as he flipped through his hymnbook.

"As we sing," John added, "feel free to come to the front and kneel at the altar if you are ready to give your life to God, if you are ready to make Tabitha's dreams come true."

He looked again at Phil and waited for him to make eye contact. It was time. He had to go for broke. "Phil Grayson," he asked, his hand outstretched, "will you allow Rose the opportunity to dance with the angels today?"

Not waiting for an answer, he spread out his arms and led the congregation in song. "I was sinking deep in sin, far from the peaceful shore . . ."

At least two dozen people made their way to the front. Thelma, still the assertive one, led the way. Barbara and Kaitlyn came forward as well. Finally, as if compelled by Christ in the flesh, Phil shuffled to the center aisle and marched toward the front, his head high and his eyes straight ahead.

John signaled for Pastor Jenkins to finish leading the song and hurried down to the altar. Again extending his hand, he welcomed Phil with a warm grasp.

Phil looked around at the others. "I guess I'm supposed to kneel, right?"

John knelt and touched the empty spot next to him. "It's a sign of humility. You helped me learn that lesson."

As Phil settled into place, John glanced at Melody. She had joined Barbara and Kaitlyn as they prayed. Steve knelt beside Thelma, his arm over her back.

Tabitha's harvest, indeed, was great.

Phil turned toward John, his voice quivering with passion. "I know what Rose was making."

John stared at him for a moment. "Oh, yes, her craft. I've been wondering about that." He patted Phil on the back. "Why don't you tell me all about it after we pray together?"

"Okay. What do I say first?"

As the song continued, John put his arm around his newly found brother. "Just say whatever is on your heart. God is listening."

* * *

"Love lifted me." The song of love was lifting, indeed, and it filled the sanctuary with symphonic majesty. Humble prayers of repentance rose to blend in perfect fusion, an audible fragrance ascending from the contrite of heart. Such a sweet harmony travels far and without corruption, sailing through walls, sweeping through souls, and soaring into the heavens. A message of love always finds willing ears, reaching even to those in another realm, the domain of angels where the saints dwell in peaceful bliss. Flowing back to earth on the enlightening streams of visions, they return the message in kind.

"Oh, so many tears!" they cry out in wonder. "Ours have been wiped away! Laugh with us! Our mourning has been turned into dancing, and we step to the beat of holy song on streets of gold. While you dwell on earth, bear the wounds of Christ in honor, and we will sing your name throughout the beautiful city, spreading the good news, knowing that your journey of suffering will soon be over. The faithful ones you have lost are not lost at all; they are embraced forever in the arms of the Great Shepherd, and you will see them again when the sun finally sets on your days. Weep now, dear friends, but not for their sakes, for their joy has just begun."

As time goes on, those left behind will continue singing their songs of encouragement. The gaping wounds of daughters lost will heal, ever so slowly, but just as surely as the Lord of comfort lives. Mothers and fathers who mourn in the sackcloth and ashes of empty sorrow will again find joy, for the love of God still beats vigorously in their hearts. As the days melt into weeks and then into years, the mourning becomes more memory than manner, with only brief bouts of tears when a simple melody drifting on the breeze catches the ear and then the imagination, flooding the mind with golden recollections. Even then, the tears transform into smiles as warm anticipation builds, anticipation of that coming day when hopes are made reality and broken hearts are finally made whole.

The song goes on. The dance never ends. A softhearted mother is called to her knees. A reluctant father is made willing. The sounds of glorious celebration go forth, rising into the eager ears of the heavenly host. The spiritual lineage of a faithful girl's great-grandmother reaches out to capture another family, and they are bound as one forever.

And somewhere up above, where the finite perception of man meets the infinite mind of God, two hearts of love listen and laugh with joy. Tabitha and Rose join hands with the angels. And they dance again.

Other Books
by **Bryan Davis**:

RAISING DRAGONS
ISBN-13: 978-089957170-6

The journey begins! Two teens learn of their dragon heritage and flee a deadly slayer who has stalked their ancestors.

THE CANDLESTONE
ISBN-13: 978-089957171-3

Time is running out for Billy as he tries to rescue Bonnie from the Candlestone, a prison that saps their energy.

CIRCLES OF SEVEN
ISBN-13: 978-089957172-0

Billy's final test lies in the heart of Hades, seven circles where he and Bonnie must rescue prisoners and face great dangers.

TEARS OF A DRAGON
ISBN-13: 978-089957173-7

The sorceress Morgan springs a trap designed to enslave the world, and only Billy, Bonnie, and the dragons can stop her.

EYE OF THE ORACLE
ISBN-13: 978-089957870-5

The prequel to *Raising Dragons*. Beginning just before the great flood, this action-packed story relates the tales of the dragons.

ENOCH'S GHOST
ISBN-13: 978-089957871-2

Walter and Ashley travel to worlds where only the power of love and sacrifice can stop the greatest of catastrophes.

LAST OF THE NEPHILIM
ISBN-13: 978-089957872-9

Giants come to Second Eden to prepare for battle against the villagers. Only Dragons and a great sacrifice can stop them.

THE BONES OF MAKAIDOS
ISBN-13: 978-089957874-3

Billy and Bonnie return to help the dragons fight the forces that threaten Heaven itself.

Published by Living Ink Books, an imprint of AMG Publishers
www.livinginkbooks.com ✦ www.amgpublishers.com ✦ 800-266-4977